D0645555

ON LINE

ALSO BY RICHARD COX

Rift

THE GOD PARTICLE

BALLANTINE BOOKS • NEW YORK

THE
GOD
PARTICLE

A NOVEL

RICHARD COX

A Del Rey Books Trade Paperback Original

Copyright © 2005 by Richard Cox

All rights reserved.

Published in the United States by Del Rey Books, an imprint of The Random House Publishing Group, a division of Random House, Inc., New York.

Del Rey is a registered trademark and the Del Rey colophon is a trademark of Random House, Inc.

Library of Congress Cataloging-in-Publication Data
Cox, Richard, 1970–
The God particle / Richard Cox.
   p. cm.
"A Del Rey Books trade paperback original"—T.p. verso.
ISBN 0-345-46285-8
1. Scientists—Fiction. 2. Higgs bosons—Fiction. I. Title.
PS3603.O925G63 2005
813'.6—dc22   2005041337

Printed in the United States of America

www.delreybooks.com

9 8 7 6 5 4 3 2 1

For Chera

Any sufficiently advanced technology

is indistinguishable from magic.

—ARTHUR C. CLARKE

ACKNOWLEDGMENTS

The God Particle was an interesting story to research and write, and at the end of this book I acknowledge the sources that guided me along the way. I'd also like to thank those close to me who shared their ideas and support, who each helped shape this novel.

Mark Tavani, my editor, whose brilliant suggestions and edits uncovered the story I wanted to write but wasn't quite sure how. Matt Bialer, fantastic agent, good friend. Ed Stackler, whose enthusiasm and insight helped shape the early drafts.

L. Scott Rubin, who loved the book more than anyone, who suggested the Universal Relational Database.

Matt Reiten, who tried to keep the physics (and my storytelling) in order. Blame me for any problems with the science, not him.

Chera Kimiko, whom I met while scratching out the first draft, and whose influence can be found throughout this book. Thanks for your love and support, Peb.

To my family: Chanda and Brandon, Mom and Dad, thanks as always.

And of course the early readers, friends, and loved ones whose feedback I couldn't do without: Jeff and Laurie Keeley, Elaine La Fontaine, Chris "J-Hole" Logan, Eric "Johnnie" Romero, Adam "The Man" Aichele, Tony Frazier, Shonda Johnson, Natalie Matheson, Joel McDonald, Mischa Gorrell, Abbie Peraza, Blake Mathews, Lisa Rubin, and Charla Pearcy.

THE GOD PARTICLE

1

Steve isn't stupid.

He can tell by the way she keeps stealing glances at him, by the way she follows everything he says with squeaky titters, by the gradually shrinking perimeter of his personal space this afternoon, that Serena wants him.

He's known about her crush for months. Frequent visits to his office with no real purpose. Hemlines and necklines drifting inexorably toward each other. Projects stretching into evenings, into weekends, into fuzzy, indeterminate hours that find the two of them alone with the soft rumble of the air conditioner and the laboring hip-hop bass signature of her portable CD player. Serena is familiar with her product offering, after all, and she markets it well.

But Steve isn't stupid. He's withstood her voluptuous body and subtle signals because sleeping with his administrative assistant would be more trouble than it's worth, because he's never cheated on a girlfriend in his life. And if Serena has figured this out by now—tomorrow they'll be flying back to L.A. after a full week in Switzerland—it hasn't stopped her from making a last-ditch effort this afternoon.

Which is remarkable, considering that he spent his entire morning searching for an engagement ring. Up and down the sidewalks of the Bahnhofstrasse, beneath the overcast Zurich sky, weaving between men and women dressed in outfits that cost more than Serena makes in a month. Around lunchtime he found a winner, a stunning three-carat solitaire set on a thousand-year-old band forged somewhere in the Alps to the east, a uniquely European item he purchased for just under thirty thousand Swiss francs.

The ring is for his girlfriend, Janine. She'll be waiting for him at LAX in less than twenty-four hours, one expectant face in a field of them beyond the post–9/11 security checkpoint. A smile and a kiss and a seventy-five-minute drive to Valencia. A dip into the Jacuzzi tub with a *Sports Illustrated*. And a few minutes later she'll bring him a lime-garnished Corona, join him in the tub, and he'll be waiting with the ring.

Serena knows he plans to propose tomorrow evening. She knows because it's all they've been talking about since he met her at the train station and showed her the ring. He even told her about Lucerne, a beautiful lakeside city here in Switzerland, where he plans to take Janine for their honeymoon next summer.

And still Serena casts smoldering glances at him, brushes against his arm a little too often as they walk along the shadowy Limmat River. She takes his hand as they hurry across the rail tracks, just beating an oncoming commuter train.

During a life spent pursuing women, predicting their behavior well enough to have scored more often than most men, Steve still doesn't understand *why* women do what they do. Why is Serena so attracted to a man eight years her senior, a man with a serious girlfriend? Why is she *more* attracted as she listens to him talk about that girlfriend? Perhaps the exotic setting has something to do with it, their visit to this ornate and historic European city. The odd warble of police sirens, the constant rush of intercity trains, the ancient texture of cobblestone streets under their feet. But it's more likely that Serena's aggression is driven by the overpowering attraction a woman feels for something denied to her. This isn't the first time he's met one who suffers from a fixation on unavailable men.

The two of them pass the train station again and make their way toward the Niederdorf, a touristy sliver of Zurich where claustrophobic streets have been closed to all but foot traffic, and multilevel buildings advertise all manner of food and drink and sex. Serena keeps going on about her obsession with Italian food, so Steve is directing them toward Santa Lucia, a busy restaurant with a chef who is a master of masonry-oven pizzas.

Rain begins to splatter the cobblestone street as they push through the Niederdorf crowds. Serena spots Santa Lucia and takes Steve's hand, compelling him to run. With his other hand he pats the side of his overcoat, reassuring himself with the slight and squarish bulk of the ring box, and groans as he notices a clot of wet and hungry folks in the restaurant's entryway. He could locate a cab in sixty seconds, after all, and find shelter in the warm, dry bed of his hotel room thirty minutes after that. Instead, he watches as Serena wriggles her way inside, leaving Steve and an elderly Germanic man to brave the rain.

Fifteen minutes later they're seated in a dark corner of the restaurant. Steve is thoroughly soaked.

"I hope this food is as good as you say," Serena says. "I'm starving."

She chatters on while they wait to order, and Steve struggles to guide her away from the deeper waters of intimate conversation. He reveals the imminent acquisition of a new product database. He asks her opinion about moving the U.S. Web servers to Zurich. Serena responds by asking whether he prefers Merlot or Chianti, but before he can answer she grabs a passing waiter and orders something that doesn't sound like either one.

"Janine is going to be so *surprised*," she says, turning back to him. "I mean *really*. Three *carats*. She is *so* lucky."

"Well, it wasn't the size of the stone I was after so much. I was just looking for something unique."

"I know, silly. But you have to understand girls. Rings are very important to us. Engagement rings, I mean."

Steve smiles politely. He's not sure what else to say.

"Let me see it," Serena says.

"Now?"

"Come on. Just a peek."

Steve retrieves the box and places it on the table. He tries not to notice how dark it is in this corner of the restaurant, how candlelight twinkles in Serena's face as she opens the box and removes the ring. He wishes Janine were here. He wishes she were sitting across the table from him, twirling the ring between her fingers, smiling. He wants to reach out and snatch the ring back. He wants to wipe that dreamy smile right off Serena's fleshy face.

Instead she presses the ring against her left hand. "Do you mind?"

The waiter arrives with their wine, and Serena proceeds to order her entrée, absently fingering the ring. Steve orders a pizza and glares at her.

"It probably won't fit," Serena says when the waiter is gone. "But I just want to see what it feels like. May I?"

He looks again at the ring. The stone is nearly pure in its color and clarity, a supernova in the candlelight.

"Actually," he says, "I'd like to put it back now."

Serena's smile withers. "Right. Don't want to tarnish the precious ring with my cooties."

"Serena, it makes me nervous to have it out. I paid a lot of money for that thing."

"Money, money, money. Is that all you ever think about, Steve?"

Predictable as they are, Serena's mood swings constantly amaze him—from sunny skies to tornado warning in an instant—but such volatility has its place, and he'd guess (were he interested in such a thing) that she probably makes love like a monster, probably screams and moans and shouts obscenities that curl paint. But he can't be interested in such a thing, because tomorrow he'll be in L.A. with his soon-to-be fiancée, and any guilt Steve incurs here will undoubtedly follow him all the way home. It will taint the first sight of Janine's smiling face and forever color his memory of the proposal. Serena might even tumble off her precarious ledge of good judgment and fall into the *Fatal Attraction* abyss.

"Are you going to answer me?" she asks him. Her eyebrows are arched perfectly above heavy liner and green irises. Red lipstick over straight white teeth. Her pink tongue dancing—

"I'm sorry, what did you say?"

"Jesus, Steve, are you so lovesick that you can't even listen when I ask you a question?"

"I'm sorry. I'm really tired. What did you say?"

She slides the ring box across the table. "It doesn't matter."

The waiter arrives with their entrées, and Serena plows immediately into her spaghetti, washing down every other mouthful with a swallow of wine. Steve's Pizza Dante blisters the roof of his mouth before he finishes the first bite. Their entire bottle vanishes in minutes, and Serena orders another as she uses her fork to chase the last orphaned bits of spaghetti around her plate.

"What's the matter?" he asks when the waiter takes away their empty plates.

"Nothing."

"Come on, Serena. You haven't said a word in ten minutes."

"I stopped talking because you weren't listening."

"I said I was sorry," Steve says.

"Answer my question, then. Is money the only thing you ever think about?"

"Of course not. Money is just a means to an end."

"What end?"

The waiter appears again, and Steve requests the bill.

"Why are you asking for the check?"

"So we can pay. Did you want to stay here all night?"

"Jesus, Steve. Do you *ever* have any fun?"

"What kind of question is that?"

"I paid *this* much. Bring the check *now*. It's inefficient to remain in the restaurant any longer than necessary. They don't bring the check, Steve, because they *expect* you to sit here and have a *conversation*. That's what people do over here. They don't rush home from the restaurant to watch *American Idol*."

"We can have a conversation in the cab ride back to the Hilton."

"Cab ride? I thought we were having a drink after dinner."

"We have a ten o'clock flight tomorrow morning. We have to be at the airport three hours early."

Serena stands. "Fine. We better get plenty of sleep now. Wouldn't want to doze off during the thirteen-hour plane ride to L.A."

Steve tries to say something, apologize, but she's already heading for the door. He drops two hundred francs on the table and takes off after her. In the entryway he is confronted with an array of black overcoats, all seemingly identical to his own, and by the time he finds the right one, Serena is long gone. It's dark now, and the crowds have dwindled to a few umbrella-toting stragglers. Steve has no umbrella. He turns right and walks in the direction of the nearest road, hoping to find a cab quickly. Wet cobblestones glisten beneath his feet. Rain pours from his hair in tickling streams.

Someone grabs him.

He turns quickly, ready to strike, but it's Serena. She has stepped out from a narrow opening between two buildings, and mascara streaks her face like black ink. She pulls him into the alleyway. Her brown hair is now jet black and draped over her shoulder like thick rope.

"Are you *happy*, Steve?" she asks, breath humid with garlic and red wine.

"What are you talking about?"

"It's a simple question, honey. Are you happy? Because you don't seem like it."

She's holding him by his upper arms. Her face floats mere inches from his.

"I'm fine. But I think you need some rest."

"I don't want you to be *fine*. I want you to be *happy*. Ever since I met you—it's been two years now, do you realize that?—you've been so serious, so driven. You think you've got this *plan*, that you've got life all *figured out*, but life is flying right past you and you don't even realize it. I've waited for you to open your eyes, for you to see this for yourself, but you won't. You can't. Life isn't about staying on schedule or making money or retiring by a certain age. It isn't about marrying some girl just because you think it's time."

"What are you—"

"Life is like *this*," she says, kissing him with her mouth wide open. Steve is ready to push her away, immediately, but the combination of her lipstick and the wine and the garlic is so human, so organic, that for a split second he enjoys the moment, finally enjoys it. Then he pushes her away.

"Steve—"

"No. Stay away from me."

A percussion of rain envelops them. The nearby buildings seem to shrink even closer. Footsteps of passersby grow louder, then fainter. She stands there, chest heaving, her overcoat wet and clinging. He can't help but notice the swell of her generous breasts.

"You wanted me," she whispers. "I could feel it."

Steve steps out of the alley and she follows him.

"No, I didn't."

"Why can't you just *live*, Steve? Live! Enjoy yourself. All I want is to see you happy."

"Then leave me alone. That would make me happy."

She blinks once.

"You're an asshole," she says.

"I'm going to be engaged tomorrow. What kind of person would I be if I betrayed Janine *tonight*, right before I propose to her?"

"But she's not the *one* for you, Steve. Can't you see that? She only thinks about *herself.* You need someone who will put *your* needs first, who knows how special you are and will love you for that."

"You're drunk. I'll get you a cab. Come with me so I can put you in a cab."

"No."

"Come on. Let's get back to the hotel. I don't want you to miss the flight tomorrow."

"I can't sit next to you on a plane for thirteen hours now! I poured out my heart to you and you crushed me. You hate me."

"I don't hate you."

"Yes, you do." She's crying hard now, shivering, and though Steve's instinct is to reach for her, comfort her, he holds his ground.

"Serena—"

She runs.

"Serena!"

The street bends a few feet ahead, and she quickly disappears. Steve knows he should run after her, but Jesus Christ, this isn't high school. Even drunk, Serena had to know the odds of seducing her boss were against her.

He stands in the rain. He knows he should take his own advice and head back to the hotel, but he can't stop thinking about Serena's kiss. About what she said.

Are you happy?

You're always so serious.

You live life like you have a plan.

As a matter of fact, he does have a plan. A *written* plan. Because he knows that people who don't have plans don't succeed.

He's sure Serena will find a cab and go back to the hotel. She's afraid of Europe and doesn't know the city well enough to do anything else. And her kiss, her hands on him—the desire for more sings unexpectedly inside him, electrifies him. Right now, he wants her. Right now, he would have no problem at all accepting her offer.

Which means he can't go back to the hotel. Not yet. There's a decent bar about a half block away, a small place with tropical décor. Maybe he'll have a couple of drinks, wait out the itch, and then return to the hotel. For the sake of his engagement.

He leans into the rain and starts walking.

2

Inside the bar, an eclectic assembly of patrons sits at tall, round tables, exhorting each other in German and French and English. Isolated molecules of fresh air choke their way through rivers of cigarette smoke. He approaches the bar and orders in German a Red Bull and vodka from a dark brunette with brown eyes and silver earrings.

In his limited European experience, the women of Zurich are the most like the women of America, in both appearance and personality. Like Iris, for example, a blonde he once met here at the end of two weeks of budget meetings. He remembers her sparkling eyes, her penchant for sarcasm, her perfect breasts shaped by a Jewish plastic surgeon in Miami. In her black BMW, she assaulted his ears with Limp Bizkit and Kid Rock; back in her apartment, she very nearly wore him out.

The interlude with Iris came just over a year ago, back when Janine was still the cute blonde who sometimes wore glittery eye shadow and always showed up at Bobby's Tap with the six-foot-four behemoth that Steve and his friends named Cro-Mag. Janine had seemed so different to him, so mercifully different—her infectious laugh, her obvious confidence, the way Cro-Mag followed her around like a puppy. Steve wanted to date a woman like that, a woman who could perhaps pry his fingers loose, interrupt his fierce grip on life. A few weeks later, he got his chance. Janine showed up without Cro-Mag and Steve left with her phone number. She was a real estate agent, she told him, the top closer in her office three years running, with designs on opening her own firm. Never married and few relationships because most men couldn't match her thirst for success.

Steve said he understood what she meant.

The date ended with sex, sex that quickly became a habit. She liked to talk and made squeaking sounds when it was particularly good. But over time the animality gave way to something more human, and he watched, fascinated, as Janine changed and enriched his life. When he decided to refurnish his living and dining rooms, he enlisted her help—not because he couldn't decide for himself, but because he realized her opinion was important to him. One morning, he awoke from a dream of her in a hospital room, legs in stirrups, giving birth to their first child. A boy, to be sure. Steve Jr. He had nearly laughed out loud with joy.

And though the last few months had been hectic as they gathered the assets and information required to launch her real estate firm, his mind had grown calm the way it always did when a watershed event was imminent. One of the major goals of his life—#4, actually—was in his grasp: Marry a grounded woman with whom he could forge a new and fruitful life. And achieving #4 meant that #5—fathering four wonderful and well-adjusted children—would become a real possibility.

So he decided to propose. And since his visit to Switzerland was only a few weeks away, he figured he could wait to find a spectacular and unique ring that would properly dazzle her. But tonight, when Serena asked to try it on, something snapped in him. Something powerful and alien made him want to slap her when she fingered the ring and smiled that faraway smile. How dare she, even for a moment, assume the identity of the woman he planned to spend the rest of his life with? How dare she suggest that he loved her?

He loves Janine.

Steve loves Janine.

For a moment he is overcome with an impulse to grab the stinking fellow next to him and reveal what is obviously life's elusive and essential truth. Or perhaps the female bartender would be interested to know. To know that it isn't the ring that matters, it isn't that Janine can help him fulfill goal #4 (and #5), but that he is in love with her. That he wants to spend the rest of his life with her because he cannot imagine continuing otherwise. In this moment he realizes that Serena is right, that life isn't about making two hundred thousand dollars a year before his thirty-fifth birthday (goal #3), it isn't about the VP position that will be his by the end of the month, it isn't about any of those things. He realizes that his numerous disposable sexual relationships have amounted to nothing, have in fact pushed him away from this fundamental truth, the search for someone to love, someone for whom he would sacrifice his life, someone with whom he could set about the quest for—

His cell phone rattles against his chest, jerking his attention back to the smoky Zurich bar. When he pulls it from his pocket, the phone glows phosphorescent in the dark and announces: CALLER ID UNAVAILABLE. For some reason, telephone numbers from the States never display properly. He answers and then presses the phone hard against his ear.

"This is Steve."

No one seems to speak on the other end.

"Hello?"

He thinks he hears something this time, but can't be sure, not with electronic music obliterating his ears. His options: Disconnect and wait for the caller to try again later or head outside and get wet all over again. Steve stuffs the ring into his pants pocket and decides to brave the rain. After all, it might be Janine.

The door is twenty or so feet away, and he weaves toward it through a dense crowd of velvety women and serious-looking Swiss men. Steps out into the sprinkling silence.

"Hello?" Steve says.

He can hear something now, a muffled voice perhaps. Mostly what he hears is shuffling sounds. Rustling. As if a cell phone in someone's pocket has inadvertently called him. This sort of thing has happened before—the accidental bump of a friend's cell phone calling him with the one-touch function— and the first time or two he listened closely, for some reason certain he would hear a scandalous tidbit of information unintended for public consumption. But of course he hadn't. Life, after all, isn't a soap opera.

The rain plays with his hair, soaking into his turtleneck, and Steve is about to give up on the call when he hears the voice again. This time it's louder and a little clearer. A woman's voice, perhaps. He pushes the phone harder against his ear and closes off the other one with his index finger. The female voice rises and falls between intermittent bursts of static. Then another sound—another voice—eclipses the first. This one is most certainly male. The guy is cheering . . . cheering or grunting. Now the female joins him, yelping with predictable and hurried regularity. But she isn't cheering.

She's squeaking.

Now Steve maneuvers his finger over the volume control on his phone and turns it up. Three girls exit the bar, laughing and berating each other in French, but Steve barely notices. He doesn't understand the phone call. Who would be stupid enough to have sex so close to a cell phone and not lock the buttons? Not turn it off? Who would—

"That's it, Barry," the female urges. "Fuck me."

Steve drops the phone. It clatters against the wet cobblestones and lands face down. When he picks it up, he is sure the phone will have powered off, jarred by the impact. But no, it's still on. He presses the phone against his ear again.

And, yes: His girlfriend is still having sex with someone who isn't Steve.

His hands begin to shake, badly, and he nearly drops the phone again. His stomach seems to fill with helium—

expanding, defying gravity, rising toward his chest, his throat, where the sour remains of his Pizza Dante make an encore performance. He stumbles in erratic patterns. Nearly falls down. Decides to sit despite the rain.

This must be some kind of mistake. Janine is not having sex with someone else. He's going to propose to her. He's got the fucking ring in his fucking *pocket*.

But still Janine continues to moan. There isn't any question that it's her. He'd recognize that hiccupy desire anywhere.

What the hell is she doing? She's ruining everything.

"Janine!" he yells into the phone. *"Janine!"*

She answers with more squeaking. Then some kind of popping sound. Like a slap. Steve can hear much more clearly now.

"Move your ass, bitch," the man says. With authority he says it, as if perhaps he's forcing himself upon her. But she isn't being raped. You don't invite someone named Barry to fuck you when you're being held against your will.

Steve realizes he should disconnect the call. Obviously he doesn't need to hear any more of this. But is the answer just to let it go? Allow them to rut like animals while he goes back to the hotel room with his twenty-thousand-dollar ring and flushes it down the toilet? Is he really supposed to—

"What *is* that?" asks Janine.

"What is what?" asks Barry.

"What keeps bumping into my head? Stop for a second, will you? I need to . . . I . . . get the *fuck* off me for a second, Barry. What is this . . . what . . . oh . . . oh my God, it's on—"

"*What's* on?"

"The phone! The goddamn phone! It didn't ring! I must have called someone!" Now into the phone directly. "Hello? Is anyone there? Hello?"

Steve says nothing.

"Hello?"

"Just disconnect," Barry says, "and then see who you called. Check the dialed numbers."

"Hello?"

"Good-bye, Janine," Steve says and disconnects.

3

It's unclear to Steve just how long he stands there, phone in hand, staring into the tear-streaked, kaleidoscopic colors of beer signs in the bar window. He's not really crying, not in the traditional, body-shaking sense. It's more like his eyes have developed a slow leak. He cannot return to the hotel. Steve knows himself too well, knows he will just collapse, knows he will imagine Janine in the arms of another man until he drives himself crazy.

Instead he turns left and begins walking with no particular destination in mind. After a minute or two the rain abruptly intensifies, and Steve realizes he left his overcoat back at the bar. His turtleneck lengthens, sucked toward the ground by newly added water weight, and he shoves raw hands into the pants of his slacks.

The universe is trying to force him back to the hotel. Steve can feel the eventuality of it, and this strengthens his resolve not to give in. But what else can he do? One possible option might be to just sit down, anywhere, maybe find a building with an awning so he can try to get out of the rain.

What else isn't clear to him is why Janine hasn't called back. Has she fallen so far out of love with him that she possesses no interest whatsoever in apologizing, in begging him to forgive her, in admitting that she made a terrible mistake but still loves him more than anything in the world? Steve supposes *he* could call *her*, that would probably be the most mature and selfless thing he could do, but somehow he can't. He has nothing to say to her. In his heart there is a place where Janine belongs, where his love for her has slowly and deeply taken hold, but that place is hidden from him now, blotted out like ink.

He walks on, a well-dressed sponge, occasionally raising his head to read the names of businesses on either side of the narrow street. Gift shops, coffee shops, sex shops. Eventually he comes upon one of these shops with darkened windows and a blue door and a sign that says CABARET. There is something inviting about the saturated blue of the door—a surreal, nighttime quality of color that would surely be invisible in sunlight—and Steve wanders inside.

In the darkness he sees a long bar that stretches away from him on the left and a set of circular booths that line up against the wall on his right. At the end of the bar stands a stage; on it, a naked woman is dancing. She is tall and not particularly attractive, and for a moment Steve considers just turning around. But he is tired and wet and instead collapses into one of the booths. A red-haired waitress approaches, and he orders another Red Bull and vodka, this time a double.

The naked woman finishes her dance and disappears behind a curtain. Steve consumes his cocktail in several gulping swallows and then sits there, waiting for the next dancer to appear. Perhaps she'll be a little more pleasing to the eye.

A few minutes go by—two or five or ten, Steve isn't sure—and he's about to signal the waitress for another drink when a dark-haired woman in a red dress materializes in front of him. She mumbles something in German and then slides into the booth, scooting sideways until her legs touch his.

"Hello," he replies, also in German.

She whispers something he doesn't understand.

"I'm sorry?"

Again she says it, a little louder this time, and he thinks she's asking something about his comfort. Probably wondering how he can sit here, soaked to his bones.

"It's better than staying outside in the rain," he offers.

The girl only shakes her head. Her lipstick matches the deep red of her dress. Her heavy eye makeup and nearly visible breasts threaten to tear down his newfound maturity.

"You speak German?" Steve asks.

"Yes," she says. "But only a small amount."

"What country are you from?"

"Russia. I come from Novosibirsk. Where are you from?"

"The United States."

"America! I am speaking some English."

"Okay," he says in his native tongue. "Then we can speak English."

"Yes, we speak English."

They sit there for a moment, not speaking in any language. Steve knows this isn't a singles bar, and that the woman sitting beside him probably wants more than stimulating conversation, but he doesn't want to do this. Doesn't want to need to.

"You are maybe buying some champagne? So we can enjoy some talking?"

Steve could leave, sure, but then he'd have to venture into the rain again. "How much?"

From nowhere she produces a small card with a list of champagnes and prices. They begin at 180 francs and make gradual steps all the way to 500.

"This one is quite good," she says, pointing to something at price point CHF 240. "Not having too much hangover."

"What about that one?" he asks, pointing at the cheapest selection.

"Ooh, not so good. Make stomach hurt."

"You sell champagne that makes my stomach hurt?"

The sparkle in her eyes fades a little with that comment, and the evaporating smile seems to acknowledge the weakness of her calculated sex appeal in the presence of a jaded American. Or perhaps she's wondering how she'll continue to pay the exorbitant rent on her one-room Zurich flat when every single customer only wants to buy the cheapest champagne. Either way, Steve, a little drunk now, decides to give her a reason to smile.

"I guess I'll take this one," he says, and points to the CHF 500 bottle.

"Very much!" she cries. "You are liking that one very much, Mr. American."

She signals the bar, and the waitress brings the champagne almost immediately. It comes in ice with two slender glasses. The label is gold and green, the words on it in French. He doesn't recognize the brand.

"What is your name, Mr. American?"

"Steve," he says. "Steve Keeley."

"Very nice to meet you, Steve. We are making a toast to Steve Keeley."

He watches her lips against the rim of the glass, red and sensual, and catches just the briefest pink glimpse of her tongue.

"And your name?" he asks her.

"I am Anna."

"Like the tennis—"

"No, no," she interrupts with mock offense. "I am much prettier than her."

Steve laughs, and Anna joins him. She puts her arm around his shoulder.

"Don't you think so?"

He can smell her, light perfume on her neck, lipstick and champagne. Her fountain of brown hair tickles his cheek.

"You are much more beautiful than her," he admits.

Generic pop music floats around them, something Steve doesn't recognize. Another dancer takes the stage. He thinks there may be someone watching her from one of the other booths, but he can't be sure, not with such murky interior lighting.

"You like the dancing girl?" Anna asks him. "More than me?"

"No. I just noticed there aren't many customers here."

"Da. Slow night. That is why Steve Keeley gets extra-special attention."

The arm around his shoulder tightens, pulling him closer, and her other arm disappears beneath the table. She takes his hand and guides it between her legs.

"You seem to have forgotten your underwear," he breathes. The alcohol is really working on him now.

"I forget nothing. Should we order more champagne?"

"Perhaps we should."

He doesn't notice any sort of communication between Anna and the waitress, but another bottle seems to instantly arrive.

"You have Visa?" Anna asks him. "The waitress would like to make sure payment is good."

Steve finds his wallet and hands over his platinum card. At 350 dollars a bottle, he's surprised they haven't already asked for it. Anna seems pleased, though, because as the waitress fades into the darkness she opens her legs farther apart, allowing Steve more room for exploration.

Distantly he wonders where all the champagne is going, because the next time he looks, the bottle is nearly empty. He thinks he hears The Doors playing on the sound system. Anna's hand is squeezing his dick, which is only sluggishly responding, and his fingers are slippery with her. She's kissing him on the neck, on the cheek, tickling his ear with her tongue. Steve has no idea what time it is. He has no idea how long he's been in this place. He wonders if he's ever going to make it to the airport in time to catch his plane, in time to find his seat beside Serena and endure thirteen hours of ferocious silence. He wonders what Janine is doing back in L.A. Anna whispers into his ear, sometimes in English, sometimes in Russian, and he can alternate between one and two fingers if he wants, she doesn't seem to mind, she even leans forward when one of his fingers creeps a little farther back. He thinks she invites him upstairs, because the next thing he knows they *are* upstairs, at the third-floor landing, staggering down a narrow hallway, floorboards creaking, passing by closed doors labeled with letter combinations like CA and CB and CC. Someone is arguing in one of the rooms, rapid German accusations he can't understand, and then Anna leads him into CD, a tiny room with a single bed and one beaten chest of drawers. Her dress disappears. Her shapely form is nearly flawless. She undresses him quickly and then pulls him down on top of her.

He finds her mouth with his, absently wondering if she's going to produce a condom. Really he should insist upon it, has always insisted upon it with one-night stands and new girlfriends, but right now he can't be bothered to ask. He just keeps kissing her and reaching between her legs with delicate hands. At some point they must turn over, because now she's straddling his knees, taking him into her mouth, hair playing over his belly. But the plumbing down there won't function properly. The alcohol that has erased his newfound maturity, that has led him into this third-floor room with a Russian prostitute, won't let him cross the finish line. She works valiantly to stimulate him, and Steve tries to relax, because even through the cloud of vodka and champagne he is embarrassed for himself and Anna that neither of them can find success.

Finally she gives up. Collapses next to him, panting and sweating.

"Too much champagne," she says.

"Too much," he agrees.

"Or maybe you don't find me pretty."

She may be paid to do this, but he feels guilty anyway.

"You are beautiful, Anna. Alcohol always gives me this problem."

Steve thinks he dozes for a moment, he must, because a little while later he wakes up to voices. The bed is a sunken mess of old sheets and lumpy, foreign pillows. The wrongness of the moment is overpowering. And those voices, they're in the room with him, and one of them sounds like Anna, except that her previously stilted German is now flawless. Who in the hell is she talking to?

Steve is facing a window. A window that appears to be moving on some kind of curved path. When he turns over, the whole room seems to spin, and nausea blooms in his stomach. There is a man standing beside his bed. Short and muscular and glaring at him.

"No," Anna says in German. "He is a good man. Please do not—"

The short fellow reaches for him. Steve shrinks instinctively away, turning toward the window, looking for his clothes. A hand grabs his shoulder. Jerks him back. Steve reaches again toward the window, straining to get away from this man, finding fistfuls of damp sheet. What the hell is going on?

"Please," Anna says. "Let him get dressed. He is not a bad man. He should not—"

The man must be a bouncer, some kind of strong arm who throws out fellows who have stayed past their welcome. He grabs Steve by both shoulders now and pulls him back. Throws arms around his torso, wrenching him off the bed. The room spins faster. This is too much. He doesn't deserve this.

"Let me go," he breathes. "I'll pay her and go. Just tell me how much."

But the man doesn't let go. Doesn't respond at all, in fact.

"Let me go!" Steve yells. He struggles to slide out of the man's grip, and the two of them stumble backward, into the wall.

Something falls to the ground. Something that causes the man to relax his grip. Steve drives him into the wall harder, thrusts elbows at him, and manages to finally wriggle free.

Now he spins around, looking for the door. But the man is blocking his way. The room spins, whips around him.

"Please," Steve says. "Just let me pay and go."

The muscular man responds by rushing him again. Steve puts up his hands, but it's no use, he can barely tell up from down at this point. The man holds him with one hand and punches him in the face with the other. Pain flowers in his cheek and nose, flaring agony tempered by the haze of alcohol. Steve wonders when the man will realize his opponent is bested and stop punching him. He wonders how he got himself into this mess. And then, as the man grabs him yet again, as they stumble into some kind of breakaway wall, he wonders what that shattering sound is, wonders what that slashing pain in his neck is, wonders why he seems to be falling, why rain again patters his face, and then, just as everything becomes obvious to him—not just that he has fallen out the window, but everything—just when *everything* becomes obvious, one last, powerful impact administers a knockout blow and sends him into an endless, swelling world of thrumming darkness.

CHAPTER TWO

1

If you were to ask Mike McNair, chief physicist and director of the North Texas Superconducting Super Collider, to discuss something as profoundly important as Einstein's special theory of relativity, he could charm you with a witty and informative discourse about the far-reaching consequences of relatively simple but grandly beautiful concepts of physics. No problem.

But if you were to ask him about the best way to approach a woman in an Atlanta airline terminal, specifically about the blonde in the white blazer and black skirt seated at the end of his row here in American Airlines gate T11, Mike would have nothing intelligent to say. No insightful nuggets of wisdom to share with a curious observer. Nothing.

Until a few moments ago, he'd been suffering over the GEM printouts in his lap, looking for something, anything, any kind of idea that might help him find Higgs before Donovan decides to replace him.

Now he can't stop looking at the woman in the white blazer. She's hunched over a laptop computer, and while he can't see her face from here, Mike is fascinated by her well-proportioned thighs and sculpted calves. By her golden hair. Her butterscotch skin.

A couple of televisions in the area are tuned to American's corporate news network. Hidden speakers bark stories about politics and terrorism and NFL preseason highlights. A few seats to Mike's left sits a breathy, overweight man in a cheap gray suit, and to his right, a smarmy salesman in a striped polo branded with an AT&T logo seems to be talking to himself. Gate attendants mingle around the information desk. The digital monitor tells anyone who cares to look that Flight 1479, non-stop service to Dallas/Ft. Worth, will depart on time at 4:45 PM. He wonders what the blonde is working on, intent as she is on the laptop's display. Mike knows he should get up and move closer to her, close enough to inquire politely about her work. But he can also guess how a move like that will appear from her point of view— the typical airport predator hunting for a woman trapped by her gate assignment—and even if he could push aside his self-respect, if he could somehow summon the nerve to go over there and speak to her, what would he say? Ask questions about her, sure, but when it came time to hold up his end of the conversation, what would he talk about? Physics? The illusory nature of human reality? Yeah, she'd really dig a chat like that.

Special relativity can be expressed mathematically by $E=mc^2$, an elegant equation with profound implications.

Mike's theory of courting, on the other hand, is burdened by a chaotic maze of incompatible equations that produce nonsensical answers.

And still he keeps looking over at her, unable to concentrate on the data in his lap. He doesn't want to think about Donovan. He doesn't want to worry about the rumors that have been flying for weeks now, stories of Mike's impending demise, stories that he hopes are nothing more than entertaining gossip.

The super collider has only been operational for nine months, after all. Nine months, which isn't a long time when you're a high-energy physicist, when the visionaries in your field have spent the last century observing and cataloging the particles that have emerged from accelerators in the United States and Europe. It's not a trivial matter, trying to pick apart the stuff of the universe, but Donovan isn't a patient man. And it's not like Mike didn't explain this to him before he took this job, that it could take years to identify Higgs. Somehow, though, Donovan's selective memory has chosen to delete those particular conversations.

It doesn't help that every time Mike encounters an attractive woman, his mind eventually turns to Carrie. Because just as the equations of relativity break down under extreme conditions, so does the nature of relationships. What did they think was going to happen when he left her in Chicago, when he was awarded the job in Texas just as she was about to secure tenure at UIC? A couple of smart people like themselves shouldn't have tried so hard to avoid the obvious, the inevitable, but try they did. For three years. So here he is, reduced to this business again, walking through life with that one open eye, checking out women in airports and grocery stores and gas stations. And not talking to them.

The gate attendant opens the intercom and invites first-class passengers to board the aircraft. Mike looks toward the gate entrance as he reaches for his briefcase. A small group of passengers has already converged on the ticket agent, and the blonde—her back to him now—is one of them.

2

At the plane entrance a traffic jam forms as a fat executive tries to squeeze his carry-on into the closet meant for suit jackets and winter coats. The blonde is still up ahead, maybe five six and standing perfectly upright except for the slight tug of a laptop bag on her right shoulder. He wonders what she looks like. He wonders if other men do the same thing, imagine a beautiful face on every woman they can't quite see. He wonders if this un-

founded optimism is genetic predisposition or a learned behavior.

The executive finishes with his luggage and steps onto the
plane. Behind him the rest of first class climb aboard, stowing
briefcases and laptop bags and small suitcases. Mike glances
again at his ticket: seat 4A. He likes to sit by the window so he
can rest his face on the glass and pick out landmarks and geo-
logical formations on the earth's crust below. Ahead of him,
near the back of first class, the blonde pushes her laptop bag beneath the aisle seat in front of her own. Then she sits, notices
him looking at her, and smiles.

Mike's love of the scientific method, of logic and proofs and
truth, induces resentment for humankind's general lack of pre-
cision. Grandiose announcements of the strongest and fastest
and most beautiful often irritate him, because people generally
have short memories and tend to assign superlatives to individuals and situations with a frequency that is statistically invalid.
There can be only one strongest, after all, only one fastest, and
only one (per beholder, anyway) most beautiful.

And yet this woman, this blonde with whom he has just
accidentally made eye contact, is, by a wide margin, the most
attractive person Mike can remember seeing in all of his thirty-
two years.

He shuffles forward, wondering if his hair is presentable,
and fights off an urge to smooth his shirt for visible wrinkles.
The passenger walking in front of him, an elderly woman
dressed in a severe blue business suit, veers to the left and slips
into the last open aisle seat. There is, in fact, only one remaining
seat in first class—against the window, next to the dazzling
blonde. He looks at his ticket, just to make sure. 4A. The blonde
is seated in 4B.

"This must be yours," she says, nodding toward the window.

"That's me," he replies.

She stands, allowing him to enter the row. Mike thanks her
with a polite smile and slides into his seat. Ahead, a flight atten-

dant is already taking beverage requests. None of the passengers are talking to each other, not that Mike can hear, and besides, the blonde is already reaching again for her bag. He takes this cue and retrieves the GEM data from his briefcase. Not that he's actually going to read the data, not that he could possibly concentrate on tables and diagrams while this stunning woman sits twelve inches away from him.

My God, he thinks. *What the hell can I possibly say to her?*

A woman like this, he is certain, must be used to such behavior—men either frightened away by her beauty or induced by it to worship her. But the smart guy recognizes the dazzling woman's dilemma and handles her with measured indifference. Speaks to her without awe. Smiles when pleased and laughs when amused. The smart guy employs standard cues of human communication that so often go out the window when a man encounters a beautiful woman.

A moment later the flight attendant appears at their row. The blonde orders a Diet Sprite, and Mike asks for a Coke. From the corner of his eye he thinks he sees her looking at him, maybe ready for small talk, quick comments about their beverage choices that might act as lift, air passing beneath wings, enough to get the lumbering fuselage of real conversation off the ground. But she doesn't say anything, and neither does he, and soon passengers are filing into the plane clusters at a time.

The GEM data are a blur—luminosity values, collision statistics, error tracking—and Mike absently turns pages. He doesn't realize the plane is full until it begins to back away from the gate. In his peripheral vision he notices the blonde has pulled a paperback book from her laptop bag. He sneaks a peek at the title: *Huckleberry Finn.* Perhaps he could tell her the story of being introduced to Twain by his grandmother, how the story of a boy and a runaway slave helped him understand the world of adults. Or perhaps, instead, he'll just sit here and watch through the window as the plane idles toward the end of the runway. Either way he can't deny the electric charge he feels sitting beside this woman, can't ignore the attraction, the powerful attraction, like the invisible forces that hold together particles he spends his days smashing into pieces.

The plane surges forward, the brute thrust of jet engines pressing him into his seat, and Mike looks out the window. He sees another plane taking off on a parallel runway. It's just behind his own, and the slight difference in speed and acceleration makes him think again of Einstein, his discovery that time slows down as velocity increases. He wonders if the blonde finds him attractive. Does she think it's charming or polite or weird that he hasn't spoken to her yet? Has she wasted even a single moment of conscious thought on him? Logic would suggest that women experience the same sort of anxiety men do upon encountering someone attractive. But is such a thing true with a woman like this? Does she fret over men? Or does she simply tolerate them, fending off their advances until she decides, randomly, to pick one as her husband?

If there is a more frustrating aspect of life than this theory of courting, Mike doesn't know what it is. He's a smart guy. His working life is ruled by logic, by gathering information and drawing reasonable conclusions from it. So why does his cerebral brain refuse to function in the presence of an attractive woman? Actually he knows exactly why: Reproduction of the species is not a cerebral concern. It's a genetic instruction controlled in large part by testosterone, and apparently he doesn't possess enough of it to negotiate romance with flair and abandon. He wants to apply logic to the situation, which is probably just the opposite of what he should do. What he should do is just open his mouth and say something. Anything. Other passengers have begun conversations now that the plane has achieved a constant, quiet acceleration. So Mike turns his head, verifies that *Huckleberry Finn* is still in her hand, and steps into the vacuum.

"Are you a big fan of Twain?"

The blonde promptly fails to respond or acknowledge him in any way.

She is facing away slightly and probably can't see him in her peripheral vision, but Mike is sure she heard him. In fact, across the aisle, the elderly woman in the severe blue suit seems to be watching the situation with interest. In his face Mike feels the familiar rush of blood; the irrepressible, animal response to failure; and turns away. It's obvious that everyone in first class heard his question and the silence that followed. For not only was she not interested, the blonde was *so* not interested that she didn't feel compelled to respond to a direct question. He looks out the window, watching Atlanta fall away behind the plane, thinking of a way he can try again, pondering what he might say this time to—

"Excuse me?"

It's the blonde. The blonde is speaking to him.

"Yes?"

"Did you just say something? I had my earphones in and I wasn't sure if you said something to me."

"Oh," Mike says, pausing as relief surges through him. He glances down and sees the slender black cord snaking through her hair. "I asked if you were a fan of Mark Twain."

She looks down at the book and then back at him with a friendly smile.

"Well," she says. "lately I've been, you know, revisiting the classics. I just read *Lord of the Flies.* But Twain is my favorite. He told the truth."

"You mean how he wrote about controversial topics?"

"Well, yeah, but what I like about him is the unique way he had of looking at the world. The way he described it that was just . . . true."

Mike considers this for a moment and then remembers something. "I'm Mike McNair," he says, and extends his hand.

"Nice to meet you, Mike. I'm Kelly Smith."

Her eyes are remarkable. Hazel and yet somehow not; sparkling, spherical prisms.

"Are you stopping at DFW," he asks, "or just connecting?"

"Stopping. I live in Dallas."

"What do you do?"

"I'm a news anchor for the ABC affiliate there."

"Really. Evening news?"

"Yep. Six and ten."

"So you share the desk with a male anchor? And you guys throw the stories back and forth to each other?"

Kelly smiles. "Like hot potatoes."

"How did you get started in that?"

"Oh, the usual. Entry-level work in a small market. Kept moving around, working my way up."

"Do you enjoy it?"

"It's a tough business. You have to develop thick skin. But you also have to really like it—telling stories, finding the truth."

The conversation stalls as Mike searches for something else to ask, more polite questions that won't stray too quickly into personal territory.

"So you're a physicist?" she asks.

"Is it that obvious? I left the pocket protector at home and everything."

Kelly laughs. "No, I've actually seen you on television before."

"You have?"

"At the station we have feeds, stuff that comes down by video from other ABC affiliates. And CNN affiliates. Anything from war footage in the Middle East to press conferences about super colliders on the Texas prairie."

Mike just stares at her for a moment, her admission wholly unexpected.

"Super colliders *under* the Texas prairie," he finally says. "The ring and detectors are underground."

"Is your office underground?"

"No. I even have a window."

"I would hope so, since you run the thing."

"Well, I'm in charge of our primary project, but Landon Donovan runs the place. You must know about him, too."

"Yeah. He picked up the pieces from the first one, the project the government started in Waxahachie. That one was killed by Congress a while back, right? Because of budget cuts?"

Mike finds it difficult to believe that she already knew who he was. Surprised that she listened closely enough to stories about the super collider to have this conversation with him.

And the dark outline of her mascara. Lips the color of California redwood.

"Landon and his investors," he tells her, "tried to buy the land that had been allotted for the original super collider, because much of the underground tunnel had already been dug. But there were too many owners and not enough cooperation. The reason the project stayed nearby is because of the cheap land, and because one of the largest investors is from Texas. All the biggest things are required to be in Texas, you know."

"Who is this investor?"

"I don't actually know. Landon is our chief executive, but the rest of the ownership has chosen to remain anonymous."

"So what do you do there, exactly?"

"On my project we're looking for a particle that was first theorized by Peter Higgs."

"That's right. The God particle."

Dopamine levels in his brain must be soaring, he is so giddy and confident. "You know about that, too?"

"Well, in my job it pays to actually *comprehend* what comes down on the feeds."

"Rather than just watch our press conferences to check out all the good-looking physicists?"

Kelly grins. "So why do they call it the God particle?"

"A famous physicist, Leon Lederman, he came up with the name. See, we have this theory to describe the particles of matter and energy that make up the universe. It's called the Standard Model. But for it to work the way we think, it's got to have this field—the Higgs field—and our machine is supposed to be able to find it. The Higgs field is special because we think it played a role in the universe forming the way it did. I guess Lederman was trying to be melodramatic."

"What made you want to study physics?"

"Curiosity, I guess. I've always been interested in understanding how things work. As a kid it was mechanical things, like my bicycle or an automobile engine. Now my job is to figure out how a much, much bigger machine works—the whole universe."

Kelly, who has been holding her place in *Huckleberry Finn* since they began talking, replaces her hand with a bookmark. She sets the volume aside and turns further toward Mike. Opening herself to him. A small confirmation of the larger-scale theory.

"So I take it you're not a particularly religious person?"

"Why do you ask?"

"Because you called the universe a machine. I tend to think of it more as a miracle."

"Oh, it's a miracle all right. Just the sheer size of the thing is a concept beyond anything you or I could comprehend. And when you think of the interaction of all those particles and energy, and gravity collapsing matter into stars, and some of those stars exploding, ejecting heavier elements that eventually end up as planets orbiting stars, including at least one that somehow produced an organism complex enough to ask questions of the universe that spawned it—hell, I don't know if 'miracle' is a big enough word to describe something like that."

"That's an interesting point of view," Kelly says. "But all that randomness, all those accidents . . . doesn't that seem a little—I don't know—coincidental to you?"

"It can. But when you think about how long the universe has been around, and how big it is—probability indicates that even the most unlikely events should occur sometime."

"You think?"

"Yep. There's even math to back me up on that."

"But who says the math is right?"

"Well, if you do work like mine, if you want to perform experiments to test theories with observation, it helps to pay attention to what works. Math works. Physics theories work."

"Like?"

"Like anything. Computers, televisions, cell phones. This plane we're flying in."

"Okay, practical inventions are one thing. But take Einstein, for instance. I know he was brilliant, but what was so special about him compared to other scientists?"

"Einstein? He pretty much single-handedly brought us out of the darkness and into the light. He imagined reality in a completely different way, and with beautiful simplicity. He showed how matter—like your skin—and energy—like the light coming through the window—are really the same thing. With that, we were able to harness nuclear power—"

"Oh, that's a compelling argument for the math," Kelly says. "Albert sits in his office and thinks up $E=mc^2$ and now we can blow up the world."

"Okay, but the same general idea explains how the sun works. We all like the sun, right?"

"But do we really need to know how it works? A lot of people are comfortable with 'Let there be light.' "

"Well, okay," Mike says. "I mean, you can't argue with another person's beliefs."

"But you can choose not to respect them. Isn't that right?"

It really is remarkable, this conversation he's having with her. Most of the time, when people unfamiliar with physics ask questions about his work, or about scientific principles in general, they smile and nod at his answers. They say things like "Wow" or "Cool," and certainly don't try to challenge him. But he'd rather not veer into spirituality. Comparing religion and science is an obstacle course he's never cared to navigate.

"If you believe something," he says finally, "how can I not respect it?"

Kelly chuckles. "Nice answer, Senator."

"So why don't we talk about *your* job, then? Like, I've always wondered how folks like you deal with reaction from the public. I imagine a lot of people have strong opinions about the newscasts, since they watch them every day."

"Oh, you can't believe all the calls we get at the station. The stories they don't like, the clothes we wear, my makeup, errant weather forecasts, you name it. E-mails and letters, too. Most people are nice, but a lot aren't."

"Do you mind that part of it?"

"I used to let it bother me, but you have to be tough. Especially in a large market like Dallas."

"Where do you go from there? What's the career path?"

"I'd like to get a network position at some point. Report for a major news magazine. Take Katie Couric's place."

Mike chuckles as the moment floats between them. He notices she's not wearing a wedding ring. He could ask for her phone number now, permission to call her sometime, but those words have no clear idea how to find their way out of his mouth.

"Anyway," Kelly says, "I'm not going to let you change the subject."

"The subject?"

"About how your views are logical and provable while others are subjective and have no facts to support them."

He hopes she's joking. "But isn't that the very definition of faith? To accept without proof?"

"Sure," Kelly says. "But in your line of work, there's nothing holier than verifiable proof, right?"

"Right."

"Does that mean we're at an impasse?"

"No," Mike says, without really thinking about his answer.

"No?" she prods.

"Well, the standard answer, the one spiritual scientists like to use, is that no matter how well we explain the mechanics of the universe, someone had to put it there. Even with new ideas that suggest the Big Bang might not have been 'the beginning,' or the idea of the universe arising out of random quantum fluctuations, we still long to describe a mechanism in which existence moved from a state of nothing to a state of something. For a lot of people, that's where God enters the picture."

"Rather than with the book of Genesis?"

"Look," Mike says. "I don't want to contradict something that you hold—"

"Hey," Kelly interrupts. She reaches forward and touches his arm. "I'm a big girl. I'm asking you because I want to hear your perspective."

At the mercy of chemical response, Mike grins like a fool. "Why?"

"Because you obviously know what you're talking about."

"Well, thanks. But I don't have any idea if what I think is correct. There's always the possibility that God created a universe that appears to work a certain way, but doesn't. Or that he set up the rules and part of the game is for us to discover them."

"But you don't think so."

"Well, many creation stories were written before man had discovered things about the universe that seem self-evident today. To interpret them literally is to believe, for instance, that the Earth is the center of the universe, that the greater and lesser lights are there to create day and night for us. But today we know the Earth orbits the sun, and we know the moon isn't a light at all. It's a big rock that reflects light from the sun."

Kelly doesn't say anything.

"It's just . . . if you knew how vast the universe is, how truly amazing it is that people like Einstein could predict how things would work with the tools of mathematics, that he could compose equations that would take years to verify with experiments, and that those experiments would prove with undeniable accuracy that he was right. . . . Everything we think as scientists, every idea we come up with, we expend enormous effort trying to tear it down. Only the most robust concepts survive. Compare that to ancient texts, stories and fables that contain so

many contradictions, that seem to be influenced by faulty as-
sumptions and observations, stories handed down by word of
mouth for generations before someone finally decided to write
them down. And then they were transcribed however many
times, and translated, and. . . ."

"And what?"

"You know what I think is the most fascinating outcome of
particle physics? The realization that our physical world is so
different from the way we perceive it. You see a tree beside a lake
under a blue sky, and you have a pretty good idea what you're
looking at, right? There is a sense of familiarity as your brain
compares this image to previous, similar images. There could be
an emotional component to that memory. 'I like the lake. The
best times with my family were at Tahoe.' That sort of thing.

"Now, if I were to ask which of those ideas are real and
which are filtered through your perception, what would you
say?"

Kelly thinks for a minute. Her smile has long since disappeared. He's probably gone too far, but there's no turning back
now.

"Well, the lake is there. The sky, the tree. But my memories,
the emotional impact, that's obviously something I'm assigning
to the image that isn't actually there."

"Right," Mike says. "At least that's the traditional way to
look at the world. But there are other ways to look at it. A
philosopher could say there is no verifiable proof the tree is
there. He could say that you're making an assumption about the
tree's existence based on data from your eyes, but who says your
eyes can be trusted? Or your brain? How do you know you
aren't hallucinating the tree? It happens to people every day—
sick people, users of hallucinogenic drugs, once in a while people just like you and me. Until you touch the tree, maybe it really
isn't there."

"Okay, say I touch it. Then what?"

"Then obviously *something* is there, right? Assuming you're a real person, that you believe your sense of touch, then it's obvious something is there. But what, exactly? Think of the reflection on the lake. You see the sky, clouds. If you'd never seen water before, would you think there were clouds in the water?"

"Sure. Until the wind blew and disturbed the illusion."

"So it's an illusion, those clouds. Like your image in the mirror. It looks a lot like you, but it's not."

"So reflections are the fascinating outcome of your job? All that time and effort for reflections?"

"Not exactly," Mike says. "But particle physics helps us understand how strange and amazing the world really is. How it could all be considered an illusion of reflections. Everything you see."

"Now you've lost me."

"Okay, let's get specific, then. When you see something, anything, you're seeing photons. Little packets of light. They bounce off the tree, strike your retina, and your eye sends an electrochemical signal to your brain, which makes a picture for you. The 'seeing' is in your mind, not out in the real world."

"But that picture in my head is accurate. I touch the tree and it's there."

"Sure, but what you're seeing is still just a pattern of reflected photons. Your own little made-up movie. And it's not a very detailed movie, to be honest. Because right now, all around you, there are photons bouncing all over this airplane cabin. They're coming through the windows and bouncing off the atoms in my face, which is how you're able to see me. But you're only seeing a tiny fraction of them. You aren't seeing gamma rays, x-rays, you aren't seeing radio waves. Those are photons, too, with either higher or lower energy. How come you can't see them? Because our earliest ancestors lived in the sea, and eyes evolved to sense photons that weren't filtered out by the water. Imagine if that weren't the case. Imagine what the world would look like if we could detect photons of all energies."

"It might look weird to someone who'd never seen it that

way before," Kelly says. "But if that's how you'd always seen it, it wouldn't look weird, right?"

"That's a very good point," Mike says.

"Okay, but the tree is still there. I still don't see what the big deal is with how my brain chooses to interpret it. I can still touch it."

"I just think it's amazing how much is out there that you don't see. That to see anything at all, you have to sit around and wait for photons to bounce off something and hit your retina. I think it's amazing that evolution created mechanisms powerful enough to extract a coherent reality out of the real world of particles bouncing and jiggling all around us. Right now, billions of really tiny particles called neutrinos are passing through you. They're so tiny they can pass all the way through the Earth without touching another particle. The only way we even know that is because of math, and because of the kind of work done at particle accelerators. Maybe that's the best example I can give you. That particles of matter, real stuff, are passing through you that you can't see. It's reality that you can't see—because you don't need to see it. Somehow our bodies can detect certain photons and create a useful picture of the world. Somehow we have tiny little bones in our ears that detect vibrating air molecules—sound waves. It's amazing."

"Amazing?" Kelly asks, a smile finally crossing her lips. She picks up her book again, apparently signaling the end of their discussion. "Or a miracle?"

3

What an idiot he is. What a moron. Manages to strike up a conversation with a gorgeous woman—who happens to be a captive audience—and he ridicules her religious beliefs. Bores her with particle physics. What a brilliant strategist he is.

Except there shouldn't be a strategy, should there? You shouldn't have a plan to meet someone. And even if you do, you can't shoehorn a mismatch into your life just because she happens to be pretty. Can you? Would you want to?

On his right, Kelly shuts her book again and abandons it in her lap. "Okay. Explain this Higgs field to me, Mike. Why is it so important?"

"Well, we have this theory, the Standard—"

"Right, you told me that. If the Higgs field isn't there, your Standard Model might be wrong. And this field might explain how the universe got started or whatever. But what *is* the Higgs field? What does it do now?"

Now she's exasperated. He can forget about that phone number. "The Higgs field is made up of particles—boson is the technical name for this kind of particle, so really you'd call them Higgs bosons. Just like water molecules make up a swimming pool, these bosons comprise the Higgs field."

"All right."

"All right. And other particles, those with mass like quarks and leptons—particles that compose matter—they exist within this Higgs field. Or you could say the Higgs field sort of permeates everything. It's all around us, everywhere. And the degree to which particles of matter interact with this field determines their mass."

Kelly shakes her head. "But when I think of a swimming pool, I don't imagine densities of water based on who's in the pool."

"Try this analogy then. Imagine a Hollywood party. At this party, your mass is determined by your popularity. So some unknown guy walks into the room and heads for the bar. He'll have no trouble getting there, because no one bothers talking to him on the way. He's a photon, which is appropriate, since you find photons boring. He has no mass at all."

Kelly laughs. Mike pushes on.

"Now imagine a B-movie actor entering the room. He was in one picture about a giant scorpion and maybe something else with deadly asteroids. He gets a little attention, has to stop once or twice on his way to the bar. He's got a tiny bit of mass. He's an electron.

"Finally, Madonna walks into the room. Everyone wants to be next to her, talk to her, see what naughty tricks she can perform with a water bottle. Takes her half an hour to reach the bar. She's the top quark—the particle with the biggest mass.

"All those partygoers following her around, the few who talked to our B-movie actor, the entire room of them that ignored our unknown guy, they're the Higgs field. The more of them you interact with, the more mass you have."

"That's a good analogy. Did you come up with that?"

"Can't take credit for that one, no."

"But can I ask a really dumb question?"

"There aren't any dumb questions in physics," he says automatically.

"Right. So tell me why I care if a quark is heavier than an electron."

"Obviously, not everyone does. But some of us want to understand the underlying structure of the universe."

"The thing is, I still have to get up and go to work every day no matter how the universe is structured. People still kill each other. Little kids on bikes still get hit by cars. I don't know. I guess I'm a little cynical."

"Probably comes with the territory, though," Mike says. "Having to report on stories like that every day."

She shrugs. "It's reality, Mike. As much as those quarks and stuff. Or more so, depending on how you look at it. How much did it cost to build the super collider again?"

"About twelve billion dollars."

"To find this one particle, this Higgs thing."

"There are other projects. We have all kinds of unanswered questions. About the possibility of supersymmetry, the search for dark matter—"

"But the Higgs, are you worried that you haven't found it already?"

Mike sighs. "There are a lot of variables. When we smash particles together, it's the shrapnel from these collisions that we examine. And there are billions of collisions. We have to use software applications to analyze the results, and tuning these tools can be tricky. It could take years to find the damn thing."

"Sounds like you need a better set of eyes," Kelly says.

4

He's thirty-two years old, and he's only been in love once, and just like any single man his eyes are always open. His radar is always on. But the shots he fires, they never seem to hit their intended target. He fires too soon, he uses missiles when simple guns would do the trick. She's sitting next to him, and she seemed genuinely interested in speaking with him, and he's made no progress with her whatsoever.

"So how do you like being an anchor?" he asks. "As opposed to reporting?"

"Reporting puts you in contact with a lot of incredible people," Kelly says. "I miss that. But it's stressful chasing lights and sirens. Sitting at the anchor desk is a nice change."

"Instead of being so close to the tough stories?"

"Sometimes I felt like a personal injury lawyer, you know? Chasing down accidents and murders and stuff. Except I couldn't offer the promise of million-dollar legal settlements."

So here they are, descending into the Dallas/Ft. Worth area, and it's time to put up or shut up. It's time to avoid all the trite bullshit he might normally say in this situation and come up with something that will sound natural. That will sound like he hasn't been worrying about this window of opportunity since the moment he saw her. He must force himself to ask for her phone number—but not here, of course, not where the other passengers will hear him. He'll do it after they deplane, during their stroll through the terminal.

A couple of men flash Mike knowing looks as everyone

stands to gather their carry-on luggage. The elderly woman glances at him briefly, her look as severe as the blue suit she's wearing. Mike wonders how much of the conversation she overheard.

Passengers shuffle toward the exit, and Mike finds himself separated from Kelly by the woman in the severe suit. He doesn't think anything of it until the old woman stops to chat with a flight attendant, blocking the aisle and allowing Kelly to continue onto the jet bridge alone. Mike watches her go, blonde hair bouncing behind her as she strides away. The elderly woman seems to know this flight attendant, a tired-looking redhead, and shows no sign of ending her conversation. Passengers back up like floodwater behind him.

Finally the elderly woman moves on, slowly, and Mike waits for an opening so he can dart past her. But he knows Kelly will already be long gone, off the jet bridge and perhaps disappearing into the river of airport patrons and—

And she's standing just around the corner, waiting for him.

"I thought you'd be long gone." He smiles.

"I couldn't spend two hours talking to you and then not say good-bye."

They march off the jet bridge and into the terminal, making small talk as the moment approaches. Mike knows it's coming. He feels himself shying away from it.

She brushes against him once or twice as they walk through the terminal. Maybe she's cueing him with nonverbal communication. Maybe her laptop bag is heavy. And he'd better say something quickly, because here comes the door to baggage claim, the place where she'll bid Mike good-bye and go back to her news anchor job, and he'll probably never see her again.

"You know," he says. "If you like Twain, if you're looking for truth, you should read *Letters from the Earth*. There are some essays in it that are similar to what we talked about on the plane."

"*Letters from the Earth*," she says. "Okay. I'll pick it up."

Mike presses on. "I also wanted to say that I enjoyed talking to you on the plane. It was really nice to meet you."

"It was nice to meet you, too," Kelly replies. "I enjoyed learning about the particles."

The moment is upon him. Say something now or regret it later.

"So anyway," Mike finally says. "I know you must get this all the time, being on television and all, but do you think I could call you sometime? If I had more time, I think I could get you to respect the photons."

Kelly abruptly stops walking. She shoots a glance at the door to baggage claim and then looks back at Mike.

"That's very nice of you, Mike. Really. I enjoyed talking to you, too. But I'm . . . I'm not exactly available right now."

"Oh. Right."

"But it was very nice to meet you. Really. I hope you find the particle, the Higgs boson. I'm sure I'll read about it on the wire if you do."

"Thanks."

Mike extends his hand to her, and they shake.

"You're not going this way?" she asks.

"In a minute. First I'd better head to the bathroom."

"Okay," she says. "Well, see you later."

"Good-bye, Kelly."

He watches her, stunned, as she disappears into a current of harried travelers. Embarrassment momentarily paralyzes him. Finally Mike finds his way to the bathroom, and later the parking garage, where he will climb into his car and make the empty, two-hour drive to Olney.

CHAPTER THREE

1

Death is dreaming.

You go to sleep, darkness envelops you, and then dreams come. Dreams about a wreck you saw during the day, dreams that loop the opening bars to a popular song, dreams of kissing your high school sweetheart. In life, these dreams represent random electrochemical impulses or perhaps a reshuffling and organizing of the brain's file system. Necessary but ignored; vital but invisible.

Pain shimmers all around him, an invisible field that holds his consciousness together. At first the field appears uniform in all directions—constant, homogeneous pain—but that supposition comes before he detects fluctuations and movement. Movement that seems to localize the pain, that turns it spiteful and glassy. And if he can detect these locations, these regions within the field, he should also be able to map them. Identify his location. Identify himself.

Never before has he experienced such intimate sensory input. Pain defines this existence, nothing but pain. No touch or sight or smell. Nothing to hear and certainly nothing to taste.

But then—

Blood. He can taste blood. He can't feel it, can't sense a mouth or tongue from which this taste should originate, and yet there it is. Coppery and organic.

Blood.

If he can taste blood, does that mean he's alive? Alive but suspended in some sensory-deprived limbo?

He is not a religious man. He never really believed in anything he couldn't see, couldn't touch. Afterlife was an attractive but unrealistic concept. But here, now, he may have to reconsider. Maybe life really is just the beginning. Maybe death is not an end. Perhaps falling out of a window onto wet cobblestone is not—

There it is. He was pushed out a window. He was in Zurich. A man attacked him. Janine cheated on him.

He is Steve. Steve Keeley. He can taste blood because certainly he must have bled everywhere, must have damaged numerous internal organs, must have broken bones and split his head wide open on the cobblestone street. No one could have survived such a fall.

And yet movement within the field seems to localize and intensify his pain. Which suggests he is alive but asleep somehow. Unconscious.

Or in a coma.

Steve remembers watching something on television about coma patients, how many of them, after waking, report having been aware of their surroundings, knowing they were alive but unable to communicate this to the outside world. Steve himself can't see because his eyelids are closed, but why can't he hear? Why can't he smell?

He focuses again on the field of pain, trying to determine which areas of his body are injured the worst. There is significant pain to the south. On his east and west the pain is somewhat less intense. But by far the worst pain hovers directly over him, in him, in the center of his tiny, comatose universe. The pain in his head. The pain that signals the presence of death in the area, floating in circles above him, growing closer with each orbit.

And then ahead, on some invisible event horizon, a new field approaches, a field of pure white. He can sense its arrival and cowers before it. Fear like he has never known descends upon him. He does not want to die. He does not possess the faith to meet death with dignity. The various regions of pain begin to radiate with new intensity, torturous agony that ignites new movement, waves of movement, and Steve realizes he is convulsing. That his body is shuddering in the throes of death, attempting one last, pleading defense against impending doom. In this fleeting moment he finds himself yearning, begging, for God. He knows he should accept the spiritual world so that it will, in turn, accept him. But to do this is to release his fear, to have faith that a wonderful, golden experience awaits him on the other side.

It's so difficult to believe this. He wants to live.

He begins to cry.

Hears voices.

Succumbs to the terrifying light.

2

Darkness now, darkness and a kind of fleeting light. Flickering blue and yellow, a live wire in empty space. A curved tunnel. A corridor of some kind. A great presence, a force, somehow like the field of pain, only much more elemental. Extending beyond the boundary of himself, into the space around him, into everything. He marvels at the scope of this experience, the sensation of knowing, of structure, of truth.

And then pure white once more.

3

The darkness is back. And then fluttering light, like the quick strokes of a camera shutter, images of bright, blurry color. Janine's smiling face. The furrowed brow of his father, his mother's artificially brown perm. A roving white coat that steps between his loved ones and nearly blots out the light.

"Mr. Keeley?" a voice says. The accent is clipped, a German speaking English, perhaps.

"Stevie?" This is his mother. "Stevie? Can you hear us?"

More fluttering light, images flickering between beats of darkness, but gradually the shutter begins to stay open long enough for his eyes to focus. Because that's where the images are coming from—his eyes. He can see.

He is alive.

"I think he is coming out of it," the German-sounding voice says.

"Praise Jesus," his mother says.

"I would not read much into this initial alertness," the German voice adds. "We think the procedure was a success, but there is much we do not know."

"But he tried to speak!" Betty Keeley shrieks. "He nearly died and now he speaks. It's a miracle!"

"It's not a miracle," his father, Jack, says. "It's medicine."

"Oh, Stevie! Oh, baby, I can't believe it! Janine, come here, honey. Come see our Stevie."

Steve shifts his head downward, lowering the angle of his eyesight in order to look forward instead of straight up. He sees shadowy cabinets and blurry metal tray tables and indistinct IVs, translucent tubes disappearing into bedsheets. And his visitors: a tall doctor with bushy, black hair and similar mustache; his mother and father; Janine.

The familiar faces move forward, tentatively, while the doctor remains motionless.

"Hi, Mom," Steve says. "Hi, Dad." He pauses, unsure how to

proceed. He remembers the hurt and anger, the shock, but seeing her now somehow blots out those horrible feelings. He is alive, the people he loves are in this room, and he smiles.

"Hi, Janine."

Then a shower of saline, his mother and Janine flooding the room with tears.

4

"You were found on the street by a Russian woman," the doctor says. "She called for an ambulance, and you were brought to this hospital. Apparently you were involved in some kind of struggle and fell out a window three stories high. Do you remember any of this?"

Steve remembers more than he wants to, including the fight, although he's not quite sure how he went out the window. He wonders if anyone in the room knows the nature of the building from which he was thrown. Or if they realize what drove him there.

"I'm not really sure what happened," he says. "The last thing I remember is having dinner with the girl from my office. Serena. Everything after that is kind of dark."

"You were very lucky, Mr. Keeley. If you had not been brought to the hospital immediately, you most surely would have died. I think you owe this Russian woman a great debt."

"It sounds like I do."

"If you owe anyone, Steve, it's Dr. Dobbelfeld," his father says. "Before the surgery, he said your chances of living were one in three."

"Well," Steve sighs. "I really appreciate the work you did to save me, Doctor. It's nice to wake up and see all these smiling faces."

His mother grabs Janine's hand and guides her toward the bed.

"Janine missed you as much as anyone. She got on a plane

straight after we found out about you and was here before your father and me."

"I don't want him to strain himself," Janine says. "He looks tired." Still, she approaches and carefully leans against the bed next to him. "I was so scared, Baby. I thought I was going to lose you."

Steve looks into her eyes, searching for emotion, looking for betrayal or guilt or whatever hides behind her words.

"I'm still here," he says. "I've made it this far at least."

Dr. Dobbelfeld moves closer and politely guides Janine away from the bed.

"Steve has made an important step today, but I do not think we should stress him now. It is time for Steve to rest. The family can rejoin him in a few hours."

After a minute or two of reluctant good-byes, the doctor manages to herd his mother and father and Janine out of the room. Steve reaches for his head and finds, instead of hair, a large, soft bandage.

"What amazes me," Dr. Dobbelfeld says, "is that the only major injury you sustained was the skull fracture and resulting brain trauma. No broken bones, no major internal damage, just a few lacerations from the broken glass. Frankly, this is somewhat difficult to believe."

"But the head injury was bad enough to put me in a coma."

"Yes, but you came out of it quickly. You were only unconscious for four days."

"What? What day is this?"

"The twenty-fourth of August."

"Holy shit," Steve says. His VP interview is in three days. "How soon can I leave here?"

"You do not understand. Four days of coma is a life-threatening matter. You absolutely must remain here for a few more weeks. We will evaluate you for possible brain damage. There will be some physical therapy. If everything seems normal, I will consider releasing you. But even that would be a miracle, to leave so soon."

"A few weeks? I can't stay that long."

"Mr. Keeley, you were virtually dead when you arrived at this hospital. Without immediate brain surgery, you would not have survived another day. Many coma patients do not return home for months. I think you do not comprehend the seriousness of your injuries."

"I'm awake now, aren't I?"

"At the moment, yes, but you could easily slip back into the coma, and maybe next time you will not come out. Sometimes coma patients must learn how to walk again, or relearn any number of routine activities. The brain is a complex and fragile organ."

"Dr. Dobbelfeld—"

"Mr. Keeley," the doctor says sternly. "Please understand me. I insist this only to help you. If I released you from this hospital, there is a significant chance that you would die. How can I be any more clear than that?"

"But why? You said I could slip back into a coma and not wake up. What difference will it make if I fall into the coma here or in the U.S.?"

"I performed the surgery. I am familiar with your injuries. I assure you this is normal procedure."

Steve considers pushing harder, but decides to relent for now. Perhaps the doctor will be more willing to negotiate if he makes swift progress in the next twenty-four hours.

"In a moment a nurse will administer more painkillers and antibiotics," Dr. Dobbelfeld tells him. "Afterward you will go to sleep again for a while. You will be able to see your parents and your girlfriend again after that."

5

A young nurse arrives to record his vitals and hook up a new IV. She is dark-skinned and appears to be of East Indian descent.

"What's in that?" he asks her in German.

"Painkillers and antibiotics."

"Have I been getting this since I arrived?"

She bustles around him, not really making eye contact, and for a moment he wonders if his German was unclear. Or if she is afraid of him for some reason.

"The Russian woman visited you a couple of days after you were brought here," the nurse finally says. "She left something in your clothes."

"Where are they? My clothes?"

The nurse pads across the tile floor and opens a narrow closet door. She reaches into his overcoat. Steve knows what she has before he sees it.

The ring box.

"Is the ring inside?"

"It is," the nurse admits. "This Russian, she must have liked you very much. If I saved six months' pay, I could not afford this ring, and I think the Russian would have to work much longer."

The nurse puts the ring box away and closes the closet door.

"If it were me," she adds, "I would find this woman and thank her."

Steve watches her leave and a moment later tumbles into unconsciousness.

6

He wakes, cold and alone. The hospital room seems brighter than it should, as if someone has deliberately turned up the lights. He looks around for his parents, for Janine, but appears to be alone. Except he is not alone. The unseen presence is here, the field, emerging from nowhere, thrumming as it did during his coma.

Fear gathers in the tips of his fingers, the ends of his toes. Adrenaline-laced blood surges through him. Burns through him.

Something is in the room with him. Something or someone.

She moves out of the shadows, shadows cloudy like the Zurich sky, and she is still wearing the red dress. Her dark hair is full and gorgeous, her eyes more beautiful than he remembers. She climbs onto the bed and straddles him, knees on either side of his hips. Leans forward to kiss him.

"Anna?"

"Hello, Steve Keeley."

"What are you doing here?"

"I came to see you. I am very sorry for what happened. I think I will stay with you for a while."

"But how did you get past the nurses? I don't think I'm supposed to have visitors. And my parents . . . Janine. . . ."

"They wait for you outside."

"Thank you for bringing the ring back, Anna. You could easily have kept it and sold it. You wouldn't have to . . . you could have found a different job."

"I did find a new job," Anna says.

"You did? What is it?"

She places her index finger over her mouth. "He said sometimes it is a crime to break the silence."

"What? Who?"

Steve waits for Anna to answer, but instead she disappears, evaporating before his eyes. In her place the presence returns, gradually, like an electric charge, something sensed but unseen, felt but not heard. The room seems to dissolve around him. To white it dissolves, the pure white field where the presence lives. Where his fear lives. Where death lives. All around him the presence grows stronger, sweeping, thrumming, screaming all around him, inside of him, overpowering stimuli that he cannot hear or see or detect with any of his senses.

Fear consumes him. He wills himself to wake up. This is only a dream. Wills himself to wake up.

7

"Steve."

He opens his eyes. Janine stands before him. Her eyes are bloodshot, teary.

"Janine."

"Oh, Steve, I'm so sorry. So sorry. I know you remember. I know that's why you were at that place, that sex place. This is all my fault. You almost died and it's all my fault."

She puts a hand over her mouth. Her body shakes. Steve considers reaching for her, considers touching her, but he doesn't.

"You hurt me," he says.

"I know."

"Who is he?"

"Nobody. He's nobody, Steve. It was just a stupid thing. I was out with Christina and saw this guy I used to work with. All of us were drinking and I didn't realize how drunk I was and then we just ended up back at his place. It was such a stupid mistake."

He lies there, staring at her, trying to maintain his composure and not feeling very successful.

"I loved you," he whispers. He would wipe the tears from his eyes if his arms weren't so tired and sluggish. "I trusted you."

"I know. I'm so sorry."

"How am I supposed to do that now? Trust you?"

"Because I love you, Steve. I made a mistake, and now I'm asking you to forgive me. Please forgive me."

"How do you expect me to—" He stops and begins again. "I don't know how I'm supposed to do that."

Her breath catches at this. Her chest heaves.

"Steve, please—"

"Do you know what I heard? Do you have any idea how horrible it was?"

"I love you, Baby." She reaches for his hand, wraps her fingers around his. "I love you so much."

He tries to pull his hand away, but Janine's grip is like a vise. "Then why the hell did you do that to me? Is that what you do to someone you love?"

"I messed up! Okay? I made a terrible mistake, and I know it must have really hurt you, and now I'm asking you to forgive me. I don't want to lose you over this. I don't want us to throw away everything over some stupid thing that didn't mean anything."

"You're the one who threw it away," Steve says. "You hurt me and I don't think I want to talk to you anymore."

"Oh, Baby. Please. Please don't do this."

Pain swells in his chest. He can sense reality swimming away from him, the way it does when he drinks too much, time losing linearity, emotions flashing strobelike, on and off, on and off. He hasn't fallen out of love with Janine. At the moment he can't really imagine how he's going to live without her. And yet. . . .

"If you're not home, I'll always wonder where you are. Every time you take on a client, a guy, I'm going to wonder if you're having sex with him."

"Oh, come on. That's ridiculous. I messed up once, Steve. Once."

"You could do it again."

"And you're so perfect, is that what you're telling me? That you've never cheated on anyone before?"

He tries not to shout, but somehow he's having trouble controlling the pitch and volume of his voice. "That's exactly what I'm telling you!"

"Oh, whatever! Such a little angel you are."

"Janine, don't let it turn into this."

"I'm not letting it turn into anything. You're the one who's being unreasonable, who won't give me a second—"

"Look," Steve interjects. "I don't want to make a goddamn . . . I'm . . . shit. My parents are outside. They don't have to know about this now. I'm just saying that when we get back to L.A., I think you should come by and get your stuff."

Janine begins to cry again, softly.

"Baby, I found the ring. In your coat pocket. I didn't mean to. I was just checking to make sure nothing had been stolen. You were going to propose."

Steve doesn't say anything. This embarrasses him, that she knows just how bad it was, how fundamentally his life changed during the short mobile-phone call.

"I would have said 'yes.'"

Steve looks away from her, at the wall, at the empty, white wall.

"And now you're not going to ask me?"

"I'm sorry, Janine."

She leaves him.

He lies there for a moment and breathes steadily, deeply, ignoring the tears filling his eyes.

8

When he decides Janine isn't coming back, Steve pulls the sheet away and surveys his body. He's naked. His left leg is mostly covered with a sprawling, plum-colored bruise. Carefully, turning his torso with a slow, gradual movement, Steve gathers the IV tube so that it won't pull out of his arm. Then he pushes down with his elbows and slides his legs toward the edge of the bed.

The pain is enormous. It shoots from his feet to his groin and from his groin to his feet and beats wildly in his left shoulder and hip. Steve summons every ounce of willpower not to scream. Collapses on to his back. Lies there sweating.

Goddamn Janine. How could she stand there and ask him to forgive her? Did she expect him to get down on his bruised knees and propose like nothing happened? To pretend he didn't hear her fucking another man, that he didn't hear her begging for it? He had been ready to *marry* her, for Christ's sake. He had been twenty-four hours from asking her to spend the rest of her life with him.

Goddamn her.

He draws his elbows close and this time works his hands beneath them, pressing against the bed. Then he pushes upward, ignoring petals of pain in his left shoulder, and scoots his ass backward until he is in a mostly upright position.

This Herculean effort requires a five-minute recess. His skin is slick with sweat. Any minute now the doctor is going to barge into the room, the doctor or a nurse or his overprotective mother, and they're going to secure him to the bed with restraints.

But he can't stay here. He has to figure out if he can walk or not, if he can get around on his own, because there is no way he can remain in this Zurich hospital for a few more weeks. The VP job is virtually his, after all. He was hired for it, groomed to assume the position after Jim Mannheim finished his planned two-year stint. But Steve also knows the finicky advisory board will pass him over in an instant if he can't step in for Mannheim immediately. With the import auto parts business suffering through a devastating slump, the officers of Automotive Excellence see the downturn as a golden opportunity to grab market share from less-robust competitors. They'll cheer Steve on if he comes back gradually, returning to form over a span of months. They'll hold parties in his honor and speak fondly about his dedication and fortitude. But before all that they'll give the VP job to someone else. They'll do it because the health of the company comes before the health of the individual. Were he on the advisory board, Steve would do the same thing to someone else.

Now upright, he pushes with his hands, lifting his legs, and slides them toward the side of the bed. The pain registers in bright bolts. His feet dangle in the abyss between the mattress and the floor. To reach a standing position from here he must succumb to gravity, must allow himself to fall, and somehow this is unimaginable. He might as well step off a cliff. He might as well jump from the third story window of a Zurich apartment building.

And there goes the VP job. His well-charted life drifting off course.

Rather than simply standing, perhaps he could sort of slide off the bed, gradually transfer his weight to his legs and feet, spread the debt of pain over several seconds instead of assuming it all at once.

Or perhaps he could sort of float to the ground. Levitate off the bed and then orient himself into an upright position, standing but really not, because his feet wouldn't actually be touching the floor.

No contact with the floor means no strain on his legs and feet. A lot less pain.

The only real problem would be propelling himself. Initially he could just push away from the bed, of course, but he can't simply hover across the middle of the hospital room. No, he'll need to work his way along the wall in order to gain enough purchase to drive himself forward. And then push against the wall as he opens the door, since he'll have no friction against the ground to hold himself in place.

And yes, it's a crazy idea, trying to move across the room without touching the floor. But in this moment he can somehow imagine it, can visualize the proper set of circumstances to induce such a thing to happen.

Really, it's all a matter of perspective.

So now. His feet. Still dangling over the edge of the bed. He grabs the sheet, the cover of the mattress, and begins to push himself forward.

The levitation effect isn't as strong as he would have hoped. His feet don't seem to be maintaining the proper elevation. Perhaps if he pushes harder, moves faster, he'll gain enough lift to—

He slides right off the bed and tumbles into a heap on the floor.

"Oh my God!" Steve screams. Pain blinds him. Deafens him. Scrambled images as the door flies open and nurses and doctors descend upon him. His mother's quiet, flapping mouth. His father, arms crossed, brow bent.

Of course, now levitation is no problem. Now he manages to make it back to the bed with no physical exertion whatsoever. Well, here are a couple of orderlies with their arms around him, maybe they're doing the levitating, maybe they understand what he does not, how to beat the damning power of gravity.

He tries to push them away, to operate independently; how is he ever supposed to figure this out if they keep treating him like a child?

Then a prick of pain as he shoots into the void at a silent, extraordinary speed.

9

Steve is unable to properly explain himself. His mother is particularly perturbed.

"You thought you were going to *float* off the bed?"

Steve isn't sure anymore what he was thinking.

"Doctor, what's wrong with him? Why would he think he could *float*?"

"Mrs. Keeley, your son's IV contains a strong painkiller derived from codeine. Hallucinations are a common side effect. And because it blocks inhibitory neurotransmitters, it can have a stimulating effect."

"It's one thing if you get out of bed and do jumping jacks. But to think you could *float*? I don't understand."

Dr. Dobbelfeld sighs. "I just told you, Mrs. Keeley, that—"

"Are you sure his brain is fixed?" asks his father.

"The effects of brain injury are unpredictable. Steve may appear well on the outside, but there is no way to tell what sort of impairments he may experience in the future."

"So he could hallucinate like this forever?" Betty shrieks.

"That is difficult to know. But please understand that the first hours after a patient emerges from a coma can be confusing. They can be traumatic. Combine this with possible side effects from his medication, and I do not find his confusion surprising at all."

Steve finally thinks of something to say. "If the painkillers are so strong, Doc, why does it hurt so badly to move?"

"You have been in this bed for several days. Bruising and lack of use have likely tightened your muscles. We will begin your physical therapy soon. I think you will make rapid progress."

"But I'm not going to be back in L.A. in three days, am I?"

"I'm afraid not."

"What?" his mother says. "Why do you want to go back home so soon?"

"I have a job interview, Mom."

"Oh, Stevie. They'll postpone that for you."

"I'm sure they will. But in the meantime they'll be looking for someone else."

"Stevie," she scolds. "You'll be up and around in no time. Just like the doctor said."

"He'll be fine," his father adds, "as long as he doesn't try to fly again."

10

His parents leave the hospital and head back to their hotel, where they think Janine has gone to rest. Steve thinks it's more likely that Janine has already found her way to the airport. He's tried to put her out of his mind, to move forward the way he always has from failed relationships, but she keeps popping back with her bright smile and asthmatic laugh. The most effective way to end these nostalgic interludes, Steve has found, is to picture her fucking another man. It's a matter of perspective, just like with the levitation.

Even now it doesn't seem so farfetched. Steve gets the feeling that if he could just regain the perspective he found earlier, if he could just see the world through those eyes again, everything would become clear. That he is on the verge of some great discovery, that what seems like delusion is actually radical innovation.

And this terrifies him.

11

"I'm so glad to hear you're okay, Steve. Sounds like you've made a lot of progress."

It's Jim Mannheim on the phone. It's the next day.

"It was a freak thing," Steve says. "I'm glad everything turned out okay. I'm eager to get back."

"Get back? Betty made it sound like you'd be out for a few more weeks."

He shoots a look at his mother, who is sitting in a chair across from the bed, and she shoots back a patronizing smile.

"Actually—"

"Look, Steve. You're a vital part of this organization. We need you. I want you to take all the time you need to get well, and that's an order."

"But the interview—"

"The interview can wait, Steve."

He ignores the silky cascade of relief tingling his spine and pushes forward.

"Jim, are you sure? I know the board wants to move quickly on this."

"The board will wait. I'll see to that. Just get yourself back into shape, all right?"

"Okay, Jim. Thanks for understanding."

"No problem, Steve. Give your mother my best. I'll talk to you later."

"I told you," Betty says as he hangs up the phone.

"Mom, you have no idea what it's like at that company. I specifically asked you not to talk to him."

"Stevie, I've been talking to Jim for a week. He's very nice. I wish you could see that I was doing you a favor."

"Thanks, Mom, but this is a political thing. I have to play it very carefully."

"Did he offer to postpone the interview?"

"Yes, but—"

"Did he tell you to take your time?"

"He did."

"Then I rest my case."

Steve gives up.

"Dr. Dobbelfeld says you walked well today," she says.

"It felt pretty good to get out of bed."

"I have to admit, I don't agree with him."

"What? Why not?"

"You were hobbling. I kept thinking you were going to fall down and crack your head open again."

"I was a lot more stable than that."

"I wish they would give you crutches. I asked the doctor to get you some crutches, but he wouldn't."

"He said I don't need them."

"He said he doesn't want you to get dependent on them. It was obvious that you need them. I wish we were home. Dr. Koetter could take care of you much better than these foreign quacks."

"Mom, Dr. Koetter is an immigrant from Germany. He moved to the States when he was sixteen."

"Well, at least we'd be in an American hospital. I don't trust this place."

"Why?"

"I keep seeing men in suits everywhere. They look suspicious to me."

"I wear suits sometimes. Do you think I'm suspicious?"

"These men don't sell auto parts, Steve. They look serious. They whisper. Like they have secrets."

"Mom, you think everyone has secrets."

"And I haven't seen too many other patients. This is a big hospital, and I've been up here and down to the cafeteria, and I just don't see too many sick people. I don't see too many doctors, either. Just men in suits."

"Maybe they're government agents, Mom. Maybe they think I'm an American spy."

"Go ahead and make fun if you want. I just don't like it here, and I want to get you back home."

"Yesterday you didn't want me to go anywhere."

"I've changed my mind."

"Well, maybe I can talk the doctor into letting me go early. Maybe we can leave by the end of the week."

"I hope so," his mother says. "I don't like this place one bit."

12

The days grind by. A ropy, middle-age Swiss woman who bathes with questionable frequency administers his physical therapy, pushing him through rigorous cycles of walking, first with the aid of parallel bars, and then unaided. His muscle coordination returns to form quickly. He scores well on cognitive evaluations. After exactly two weeks, Dr. Dobbelfeld agrees to let him return home, on the condition that Steve calls with frequent progress reports.

His mother is ecstatic, his father proud to return home with his son at his side. The first available flight with three seats together doesn't leave until the next day, so they book a couple of rooms at the Golden Arch (the idea of staying at a hotel owned by McDonald's tantalizes his mother) and decide to spend a relaxing day watching television.

But Steve has other ideas. He calls a cab and heads to the Niederdorf. He can think of a dozen things that can go wrong with another visit to the Cabaret, sure, but he'd also like to know what the hell happened to him there. And thank Anna for returning the ring.

Steve makes his way through the crowds, his feet falling again on cobblestone. His mind whirls, electric, igniting flashes of memory he'd rather not relive. Anna's red dress and stilted English. The sweet smell of champagne. Shards of broken glass. A cold, silent fall through raindrops.

Murmurs of German and French and English float around him, and he wonders if they are about the limping man, the crude American. Bald now, with a white bandage on his head, back to have another run at Anna before he returns to the States.

Will he be waiting, the muscular fellow who jerked Steve off the bed? According to Dobbelfeld there were no charges filed, no clear idea even of who tossed him out the third-story window. But someone here knows. Someone must have seen, and that someone must have told someone else, and now they observe his approach as the street narrows and buildings close in around him. His neck pivots, and he looks toward the third-floor windows above him, imagining his fall in reverse, tumbling silently through the emptiness that isn't really empty at all. Had he understood the nature of the field sooner, he might have saved himself the head injury and ensuing coma. And now here it is, the Cabaret in front of him.

Only it isn't the Cabaret any longer.

No more sexy pictures in the windows. And above the blue door, letters have been pried away, leaving dark patterns of paint unmarred by oxidation. These patterns spell the word *Cabaret*.

He reaches for the door. It doesn't open. His eyes search for a sign, some sort of explanation.

Nothing.

Across the narrow pedestrian street is a newsstand. Steve walks over and addresses the merchant.

"Excuse me," he asks in German. "What happened to Cabaret?"

"Closed," the man says.

"Yes, but do you know why?"

"I don't know. What happened to your head?"

"I fell," Steve says. "Do you have any idea what happened? Did the girls go work somewhere else?"

Now the merchant smiles. "You want a good time, eh? Those were not the only women in town."

"Yes, but there is one I would like to speak with. Anna."

"Why do you want to talk to her?"

"She helped me," Steve says. "I would like to thank her."

"You cannot thank her."

"Why not?"

"Because she is dead."

"What? How do you know that?"

"Because my boss saw the police with her body. He works in the morning, when she was found."

Steve stands there, looking not at the merchant but through him.

"Do you know how she died?"

"Yes," the merchant says, tilting his head upward. "She fell."

Static in Steve's brain now, a fuzzy, soundless noise. He involuntarily steps backward and bumps into an elderly woman. She glares at him and continues walking.

"What did you say happened to your head?" the merchant asks him.

But Steve is still backing away, faster now, and then turns. The merchant calls to him, yelling something, but the sound disappears, absorbed by the white, nebulous static of Steve's consciousness.

CHAPTER FOUR

1

It's been almost nine months, and still Kelly has trouble imagining another man in her life.

She's sitting in her kitchen, scooping peach-flavor yogurt into her mouth. It's 11:35 PM. Home from another long day at the station, decompressing, wondering where her life went off its tracks.

The problem here, the situation she cannot quite resolve, is that the promises she made were for life. She loved James more than anyone or anything on earth, more than herself, and promised she would never betray him, that he could trust her for the rest of his life. And maybe there is more to a relationship than trust, maybe she woke up one day and realized there were a number of ways in which he was not doing his half, but does that excuse her for blindsiding him? For announcing one day that everything she had promised him, every "forever" she'd uttered, had all been nullified? That because James neglected to fulfill certain unspecified deliverables, it was her privilege to throw him out the door and become single again?

Take the guy from the plane, the physicist. A handsome

man whose intelligence had intimidated her, whose easy manner and quiet confidence had been surprising, considering her stereotypical notion of scientists. She'd been a little annoyed at the effortless way he dismissed spirituality, but she also enjoyed listening to his ideas, comparing them to her own rediscovered beliefs.

Most of the men who approach her are star-struck fans, men infatuated with her pancaked face on their thirty-five-inch televisions, with her clear lip gloss and glued-together hair and crisp consonant articulation. *I love your C's,* one guy told her. *My name is Chris Carland. Would you say my name?* Or they're rich or confident men who, because of her high-profile job, consider her a cut above, a woman fortunate enough to stand on a pedestal as high as their own. *You're Kelly Smith, the news anchor. I'm Howard Farris, trial attorney. I'm Fred Haley of Haley's Fine Furnishings. I'm James Delaney; I'm a screenwriter.*

Of course, the last one had worked. James turned out to be creative and in love with language and stories about people, just like Kelly herself. Their chemistry was instant and it didn't matter that he hadn't actually *sold* a screenplay, that he had only finished two so far and they weren't—by his own admission—particularly good. She admired his persistence and determination. She was flattered by the way he was infatuated with her. They dated for a few weeks—he doted on her from the beginning, gentlemanly, perfect—and then found each other's bodies. He was attentive. He tried to please her before he took anything for himself. She loved him for that.

And wouldn't it be easy, wouldn't it solve this heartbreaking dilemma, if she could fall out of love as quickly as she had fallen in? Sometimes she wishes he would call her up on the phone and admit that he hates her, that last night he slept with her sister, and by the way she's never going to get that network job she so desperately craves because she is the worst news anchor in the country. She might get over him if he didn't continue to dote on her. If he stopped e-mailing her with observations about her on-air performance or ideas for her weekly family feature. And while she's being honest with herself, Kelly shouldn't forget that she still does the same kinds of things for him. Because it comes naturally to her. Because she still cares about him.

She could have given her phone number to Mike McNair. She could have met him for dinner, a little red wine, maybe even a kiss. But when Kelly thinks of the conventions of daily life with James—buying groceries, huddling together in a dark movie theater, sleeping safely in his strong, warm arms—and then attempts in these memories to replace James with someone else, it seems utterly alien. James is what she knows. For a time she believed she was going to marry him. How do you erase an idea like that? How do you forget?

Their relationship ended abruptly, a few months after James quit his job to write full time. Kelly had no problem financing this experiment until she realized he was producing even less work than before. He turned inward, away from her, and she realized they could never build a happy marriage if James himself wasn't happy. He refused to seek counseling. He made it clear that he wouldn't look for another job, because to do so was to deny his dream. Could Kelly love him, he admonished, and ask him to deny his dream?

But when the lights go out and she cries into her pillow because his half of the bed is empty, it's easy to forget those reasons. When she pictures him in his shithole studio apartment, selling mobile phones at Best Buy, it makes her want to tear her aching heart out.

At the very least, when James left, she was able to return to church. It had been their most enduring battle, the question of religion—Kelly's strong but somewhat formless faith versus James's clear belief in a universe devoid of metaphysical properties. At the beginning of their relationship she'd strayed away from her mother's denomination, but in the aftermath of the breakup, a friend invited her to a Unitarian church in Arlington, and now she attends every Sunday. The sense of rightness, being a part of something greater than herself, is something she could hardly describe to someone outside the church. And in this collective spirituality she has looked hard for God again, has asked forgiveness for abandoning Him in favor of James. And if He isn't necessarily the God of Genesis and Exodus, if He is a concept of collective love instead of a God of rules and demands, she can learn to live with it.

Kelly dumps the yogurt container into the trash and picks up the telephone. She should have at least given Mike her card. She never walks away from a possible story contact without leaving her card, but nerves had gotten the better of her in the airport terminal. She picks up the phone and dials Information.

"Information. What city?"

"Olney, Texas."

"Listing?"

"Mike McNair, please."

"Please hold for the number."

And on a yellow Post-it note she jots down the ten digits. Writes his first name above them, as if they are old pals already, and sticks the note to the front of her refrigerator. Stares at it a while. Then heads to the bathroom and begins the process of getting ready for bed, changing clothes, scrubbing off her television face.

2

"*You* talked to Kelly Smith?" Larry asks him. "The girl on Channel eight in Dallas?"

Mike nods.

"On the airplane?"

"Right."

"Bullshit."

They're sitting in Mike's office. It's a sparse place, only a few wall decorations (including the plaque he earned for carding a hole in one this summer) and no plants. There is a desk, three separate computer monitors, a couple of cabinets overflowing with computer printouts and diagrams from their plotter. Mike sits in his overstuffed leather chair, and Larry leans toward him from the visitor's chair. He's a small man, Larry is, about five ten and no more than 160 pounds. He insists on wearing a tie even though Landon Donovan has imposed no dress code on their facility, and he wears these ties with shirtsleeves. Mike doesn't understand this uniform but has never felt compelled to ask about it.

"What did you say to her?"

"I asked if she was enjoying her book."

"What was she reading? Romance novel?"

"*Huckleberry Finn.*"

"*Huckleberry Finn.*"

" 'Revisiting the classics,' she said."

"Revisiting the classics."

"Are you channeling in your inner parrot again, Larry?"

"It's just that I'm having a hard time believing you, jackass."

"Why can't you believe I sat next to her on a plane? She has to travel, doesn't she?"

"I just assumed the station flew her around in a private jet. I mean, she *is* the talent, right?"

"She's a local news anchor, Larry."

"Yeah, but she's great. Plenty of intelligence and guts for the tough interviews, but attractive and charming enough to convince everyone she's a sweetie."

"How do you know so much about her? We don't get television from Dallas."

"I saw her on TV once when I was there for a conference."

"You saw her once and you know all this?"

"Okay," Larry admits. "So maybe I reworked my satellite receiver a little."

"So that you could watch her on the news?"

"No, because I can't stand the hick stations out of Wichita Falls."

"You're kidding."

"So you asked her about *Huckleberry Finn*? What else did you guys talk about?"

"Special relativity."

"Special relativity."

"Will you stop that?"

"Why the hell did you talk to her about special relativity?"

"Because she asked me about Einstein," Mike explains.

"Did you even know who she was?"

"No. I don't get Channel Eight. Of course I didn't know who she was."

"He didn't know who she was! Did you hear that, ladies and gentlemen? He didn't—"

Just then Landon Donovan walks in, barrel-chested in his metallic-gray Armani. Behind him stands a Japanese woman dressed in black pants and cream-color blouse, her black hair pulled into a tight, shiny bun.

"Gentlemen," Donovan says with his typical drama. "I'd like you to meet someone."

Mike and Larry stand. Donovan escorts the woman into the room until all four of them are gathered around the desk.

"This is Samantha Aizen. Perhaps you guys have heard of her work over at CERN."

Of course we've heard of her work, Mike thinks. CERN is only the second-largest particle physics facility in the world. Before he can say anything, though, Larry steps forward and takes her hand.

"Yes. Ms. Aizen, I've heard so much about you. I'm Larry Adams, and this is Mike McNair."

Mike leans across his desk and shakes her hand.

"I believe we've met, Ms. Aizen. In Finland, wasn't it?"

"Yes," she smiles. "At EPS. But please, call me Samantha. Or Sam, if you like."

"Samantha has been an important part of the team at CERN for several years now," Donovan explains, as if he missed the previous ten seconds of conversation, as if he didn't just hear Mike and Larry acknowledge her work. "She's been working to optimize luminosity for the Large Hadron Collider."

"That's fantastic," Larry says.

"I think she's the perfect person to help us solve our own luminosity problems," Donovan adds.

Mike could see this coming from ten miles away, considering Donovan's constant intervention in matters best left to actual physicists. He wonders what sort of title Samantha was promised, and how much money Donovan spent to get her. He wonders what Paul Funk, the Beam division head, will say when he hears of this unexpected new hire.

"We're always thankful to have someone else on the team," Mike offers. "Anything to help find Higgs."

Samantha smiles. "I was explaining to Mr. Donovan that even though our ring is much smaller than yours, we plan to compensate for that lower energy with much higher luminosity. But since higher luminosity can create stability problems, we've had to come up with novel ideas to counteract this effect. From what Mr. Donovan has told me, and after reviewing some of the data from your last few runs, I think I might be able to offer some possible solutions."

"Well, like I said, our goal is to identify Higgs. Anything you can do to help us would be welcome."

"Thank you."

"Samantha is going to be our new Beam division head," Donovan announces.

"I'm sorry?" Mike says. "What about Paul?"

"Paul agreed to take on a new assignment. The NTSSC will continue to enjoy his valuable insight and intelligence in another area."

"What area?" Mike asks.

"It's going to be a hectic morning," Donovan says. "I still need to introduce Samantha to our other team leaders. Thanks for your time, gentlemen."

Mike and Larry shake hands again with Samantha, and

then wait in silence until they hear Donovan enter another office, well out of earshot.

"Agreed to take a new assignment?" Larry squeals.

"How can he reassign one of my team leaders and not tell me?"

"Because he's an armchair physicist. If he didn't have so damn much money—"

"If he didn't have so much money we wouldn't be here. But still, you'd think he'd at least come to me before. . . . God, Paul must be devastated. I wonder why he hasn't called."

"I'll go talk to Amy," Larry says. "I bet she knew about this. She always has the inside gossip on Donovan's decisions."

"Don't be gone long," Mike tells him. "I want to talk to you about event selection. I want to hear the latest ideas from your team about our triggers and if it's feasible to loosen them."

"Loosen them? We're already at the limits of our processing power."

"Another argument to beef up the Grid. There's no reason for us to limit the amount of data we generate when Landon can always purchase more processors."

"All right," Larry concedes. "But the first thing I want when I get back is to hear more about your visit with Kelly Smith."

3

Something is wrong.

Steve has been aware of it for a while, the knowledge inside him glowing and hot and nauseating. Since the levitation incident, since he got the idea that he could float off the hospital bed and maneuver around the room with complete disregard for the laws of physics, it's been obvious to Steve that something is wrong with him. With his head. Something Dobbelfeld could not correct, or that he didn't know about, or that he induced with his brain surgery. How could something *not* be wrong? Steve fell three stories onto a cobblestone street. By all rights, such a fall should have killed him. Instead, here he is, alive, sitting in the sterile interior of his Infiniti G35. Sky moves like blue fire through the window in the roof. Modern rock pours from silky, well-placed speakers. He's stuck on the 5 in traffic he would never see on a typical workday, since he usually leaves his house at 5:30 in the morning, but right now it's nearly 8:15. He's at least an hour from work. He wanted to be there earlier but his mother wouldn't let him, adamant as she was that he "take it easy." And he knows something is wrong with him because of a certain concept he is struggling with, a certain silly idea that he can't quite make go away. What he wants is to make the car rise above this frozen line of cars and fly all the way to his office in Westwood.

Or maybe he's being too hard on himself. The levitation incident was, after all, a "traumatic incident," as his mother likes to call it. Maybe all her worrying has gotten the better of him.

Four days ago, as he waited in the business-class line for American's Zurich-to-L.A. flight—waiting as his mother and father badgered each other about who was going to sit next to the window—the impending thirteen hours on a jet with them had seemed like eternity. But he'd been wrong. He'd slept during the flight. And when he hadn't slept, he'd kept the headphones on, eyes closed, pretending to sleep. Steve, after all, isn't stupid. Not stupid, but not that smart either, because when they arrived in L.A. he somehow agreed to let his parents stay with him for a couple of weeks.

They arrived on Thursday. Steve considered going in to work for a little while on Friday, his first full day back, but his mother had drawn a deep line in the sand over that one. *You're jet-lagged*, she said. *Jet-lagged and tired from this experience and you have no business going in to work. Have you lost your mind? Jack, tell him he's lost his mind.*

His father had uncharacteristically agreed with her. And considering Mannheim didn't expect him anyway, Steve allowed his parents this victory in exchange for opportunities to triumph in other arguments. But it didn't work out that way at all. On the issue of breakfast he lost—three days in a row—forgoing his usual bowl of whole-grain cereal for a plateful of eggs and bacon and hash browns that left an oil slick in its wake. When he wanted to drive over to the country club and hit a few balls at the range—something that always relaxed him—his mother complained so bitterly that he gave up without a fight.

Steve loves his parents. And he can handle his mother in Nebraska, in the house where he grew up, because during those visits he doesn't mind being mothered. The badgering, the oft-repeated axioms ("A watched pot never boils, Stevie"), the endless hours of pulling weeds. Somehow the old house allows this sort of regression, as if he isn't really a well-paid executive for an auto parts manufacturer but instead a scrawny teenager. In his own home, though, the aggressive parenting is simply too much, and yesterday he was in the middle of a reprimand for mowing the lawn when his mother finally gave up.

"Well," she told him. "I guess it isn't my place to give you a lecture like this. I guess I'm out of place. I surely *feel* out of place. Did you know this is only the second time I've ever been to this house, Stevie?"

"That's because I only moved in thirteen months ago."

"Thirteen months," she said, shaking her head. "I've been to my son's brand-new house only two times in thirteen months. Do you even want me here now?"

"Of course I do, Mom. You can come any time."

"You never invite us, Stevie. The only other time we visited was when you moved in, and I asked if we could come see the big, fancy house our son had built. You haven't invited us once since then."

"I'm sorry. I get busy. Work is crazy. And then Janine and I were . . . well, you know how it is."

"I hope she's worth it," his mother admonished. "I hope the job and all this is worth it. Living this far away and all."

"Mom."

She stepped away, hands on her hips.

"I know you don't like me babying you. I just . . . I always felt like I was going to lose you. I don't know why. When you were born I thought it was going to be crib death, and when you were older I thought you were going to ride your bike into a busy street and get run over by a car. Don't ask me why. I just always thought I was going to survive you, and there is nothing more awful or terrifying in this world to a mother than to lose a child."

"Jesus, Mom—"

"And then you abandoned the church and moved off to California and every day I worry, and then I get this call from Switzerland, from a *hospital*—"

She began to cry, and Steve went to her. He was surprised at how insubstantial she seemed in his arms. He couldn't remember the last time he had really embraced his mother. Maybe not since elementary school. How could that be?

"Mom," he said. "It's okay. I'm better now. I know it must have been horrible, but I'm fine now, okay?"

"I know you are," she said, releasing him. "And you'd be better off without me bugging you."

"You're not bugging me."

"I am, and I know it. I see it in your eyes. Your dad is telling me all the time. Just a minute ago, before he went on his walk, he said we should go back to Grand Island and leave you to your life. To Janine and your work."

There it was, what he wanted, and Steve hadn't been sure how or if he should take it.

"I'll call the airline. We can fly out tomorrow. We'll get a cab to pick us up so you don't have to drive us to the airport."

"Mom—"

"But you can call me anytime, Stevie." She took his hand in hers and squeezed it. "If you need anything, just call and I'll come back, okay? Maybe you'll be fine. You're a grown man. Just know that I'm always here for you. Just know that you can call me anytime."

He loved her for that. In spite of the nagging and complaining, he loved her. For her unconditional support, yes, but also because he had lied, everything *wasn't* okay, and Steve knew that if he told her the truth she would take him into her arms and make him feel like everything was.

But it isn't.

It isn't okay when you can't shake the overwhelming feeling of being followed—followed or perhaps watched. It's around him, everywhere, something to which he can't quite assign a name. A presence that is at once infinite and infinitesimal, something both ethereal and human. It could be following him south on the 5, or he could be driving through it, this field that lies like fog between hills brown and green, between the hills, within the hills, woven through the fabric of reality, even the uncountable cars and trucks all crawling through numerous, parallel lanes of traffic.

And now the interchange approaches, a curved, multilevel structure of concrete that moves travelers from one road to another. Steve wonders how they are going to manage the flow of traffic when cars are no longer confined by gravity to the surface of the road. And while he ponders this it occurs to him that he's in the wrong lane, that he needs to be farther right if he wants to get on the 405. The 405 is how he'll get to Westwood. But no one will let him in. Well, *there* is a spot, a little gap he could dart into if he times it just right. And then horns blaring and tires screeching as he cuts off a Volkswagen Jetta that he didn't see, that he *completely* missed, and how the hell did he miss it?

Traffic on the 405 isn't quite as bad. Steve nudges the Infiniti up to sixty-five and relaxes his grip on the wheel. The day is perfectly clear, the cloudless sky shiny and antiseptic. He's got to get control of himself. "Traumatic incident" or not, in less than an hour he's going to walk back into the office after a month-long absence, and it's imperative that he bring off this first day back without a hitch. Of course there is still the issue of Serena—he's not exactly sure how he's going to negotiate that minefield—but right now she's the least of his worries. If Jim

Mannheim doesn't think he's back to one hundred percent, after all, whatever chance Steve still has to land the VP job will dissipate into the field like waves fizzling on the pristine beach of some uncharted Pacific island.

And then what will he do?

4

The garage attendant, an aging fellow with bushy white hair, waves to him as he drives by and into amber darkness. His parking spot on the first floor is only steps from the elevators. Soon he stands in front of three sets of doors, each accompanied by a green digital readout, and waits as the middle elevator whines and descends toward him. A motorized lift bears little resemblance to the floating mechanism of the field, brute force instead of energy reallocation, pulling against gravity instead of neutralizing it, and—

And it's frightening the tricks your mind can play on you.

Maybe insanity is reality that no one else can see.

A small lobby separates the elevators from AE's main office, and the wall directly across is a plate-glass window through which he can see the reception desk. Marsha, the fortyish woman who greets all visitors, spots him even before he can make it through the door. She catapults out of her chair and slingshots from behind the desk. A gale of White Diamonds perfume assaults him with comparable velocity.

"Steve!" she cries and hugs him.

"Hi, Marsha."

"Oh, we were so worried for you."

"Thank you. It's good to be back."

She releases him and steps backward, a look on her face almost like awe.

"They said you fell three stories. Is that true?"

Before he can answer, another woman appears from around a cubicle corner. This is Elaine from accounts payable.

She crosses her arms over her chest and remains several feet away.

"Steve," she says. "Why are you back so soon? I thought—"

And then it comes, the crowd, single-file rows of his coworkers pouring forth from various entrances in the cubicle maze. They approach and surround him, a gauzy, welcoming haze, and while a few shake his hand or pat him on the back, most keep a respectable length of industrial carpet between themselves and Steve. He feels like a soldier returning from battle. A soldier who has lived through what they never want to endure, who has glimpsed what they hope never to see. In their eyes he sees respect for his courage, horror at his withered physical appearance, and, perhaps, just a touch of fear.

Somewhere beyond the crowd he can sense Serena, standing there, smiling the biggest, sweetest smile she can manufacture. Waiting for him to acknowledge that he turned down her advances, and that the penalty for such rejection was very nearly his life. Somehow he feels as if they all know what really happened, and it makes him want to run from this place. Now that he's back here, it seems absurd to think that he would return to a normal life. That he would continue this charade. This illusion of reality.

Because now his eyes are open.

Now he knows the truth.

5

"I didn't expect you back so soon, Steve."

Jim Mannheim sits across the desk, fingers laced behind his head as he smiles at Steve, eyebrows arched with inquiry.

"I'm fine," Steve lies. "Really."

"You can have any time you need to recover. You know that."

"I appreciate that, Jim. I do. But I can't just sit at home, not when there's work to be done."

Mannheim absorbs this information by unlacing his fingers and then crossing his arms over his chest. Steve can just make out the real point of conversation, the marketing VP job, hovering in the field between them.

"Your mother is a sweet woman," Mannheim says.

"She and my father were both really worried for me. You can imagine how she might exaggerate the severity of my accident."

"You were in a coma, Steve. For four days."

"I know. But the doctor says I've made remarkable progress."

"And here you are," Mannheim admits. "We're thankful to have you back."

"Thank you."

"What about Janine? How is she taking all this?"

Steve grins stupidly. Though it was easy not to think about Janine in the alien environment of the hospital, ignoring her during this attempted return to familiarity has been something altogether different. But to discuss Janine with Mannheim is to introduce even more instability, something Steve doesn't need before his interview.

"She's fine," he says.

"She must have been really upset," Mannheim adds. "Especially since you guys have been talking about getting married."

"Of course."

"A double-edged sword to love a woman so independent, you know. Earns her own money and develops business contacts. Hell of a one-two punch you guys are. But then again, considering how much AE values mobility . . . the next step after VP will likely be something overseas. You know this, of course."

"I do."

"And that's okay with Janine? Turning her firm over to someone else so she can follow you to Europe?"

A fleeting interruption in his consciousness. A sliver of time. A Zurich-bound Boeing 777 sailing above the clouds, pol-

luting the sky with thousands of gallons of jet fuel exhaust.
What sort of craft, he wonders, could be fashioned to move passengers across oceans and through the field without burning in-
convenient fossil fuels?

"She welcomes the opportunity," Steve says.

Janine's smiling face as she might have accepted his ring.

"Good," says Mannheim. "So what are your plans for the
week?"

Serena's heaving breasts.

"Catch up on e-mail, of course. Evaluate the download rate
from the MX launch and the BMW subsite. Reschedule the
Monday staff meeting for tomorrow so I can actively partici-
pate."

The blinding white presence.

"Maybe you should push the meeting back to Wednesday."

"Why? Do you want be there?"

"No," Mannheim says. "But I was thinking, if you'll be
ready, we could hold your interview tomorrow. At ten. What do
you think?"

"Tomorrow?"

"Wolfgang Rix is in from Zurich this week. The boys back
in Switzerland like to evaluate all officer-level candidates, so it's
a great chance to move this thing forward."

"The sooner the better," Steve says. "I know you guys
wanted someone in place by now."

Mannheim smiles. "But sometimes things change. Don't
they, Steve?"

Regression of the field into periphery. The office emptier
than it was just moments ago.

"Yes, sometimes they do."

He smiles as he rises to shake Mannheim's hand, viscerally
aware of the receding field, of sanity drifting in to fill the void.

Steve leaves Mannheim's office and heads to his own. Any
moment now, he knows, the field could return with reinforce-
ments. Come streaming down out of the HVAC system. Follow

him from its hiding place in Mannheim's office. Or slide, snake-like, out of Serena's cubicle, wrap its body around his leg and jerk him back, toward her, toward the night in Zurich when everything went wrong. He ducks into his office, where he plugs in his laptop and decides the daily routine is maybe welcome after all.

6

Minutes later, a knock on his door.

A figure moving toward him, tiptoeing into his office, the way a mime might imitate the move onstage. Why the hell is she doing that?

"Hi, Serena," he says.

"I didn't want to bother you," she whispers.

"Glad to see one of us made it back from Zurich safely."

Serena shifts her weight from leg to leg. Scratches the back of one calf with the other foot.

"I was *really* shocked to hear what happened. I should never have left you alone, Steve. I am *so* very sorry."

"Hey," he says, "don't be sorry. It's not your fault. *I'm* the one that shouldn't have let you leave. I wasn't much of a gentleman."

"I wouldn't go *that* far, Steve. But anyway, I'm sorry for . . . for what I said to you about Janine. I had no right. I hope we can still be friends."

"Of course we can." Steve turns away from his computer and looks directly at her. "Look, it takes a lot of guts to do what you did in Zurich. To put yourself on the line, tell someone the truth even though they might not feel the same way. I admire you for doing that, even though in our case it maybe wasn't the best timing."

She just stares at him. And if he senses a hint of noise in the room, noise that could be coming from nowhere but his own head, Steve isn't obligated to acknowledge it.

"You can't act the way your heart feels all the time," he adds. "But when it seems right, go for it. What you said that night was right: You've only got one life to live, so live it."

"Obviously you didn't get back here when you expected," she says to him. "How did the proposal with Janine go?"

"I had to postpone it," he tells her and points to his head.

"Oh, of course. Well, I really appreciate what you've said. You were right—I was mortified that night and pretty much have been since. But now I feel better. You're being really cool about this."

Serena steps forward and leans down, gives him a quick kiss on the cheek.

"Thank you," she says. "I don't know how to repay you."

"No need at all. But Serena, can you let everyone know today's staff meeting is postponed?"

"It is? Why?"

"I need to prepare for my interview tomorrow."

"Tomorrow?"

"Yep. Jim just told me this morning."

The noise again, a surge of it, distorting a couple of words spoken from outside his office: Simon Slater.

He thinks.

"Well, good luck then," Serena says. "I'll bet you'll knock 'em dead!"

7

Somehow it seems to rear its ugly head every day, the truth of human duality, the battle between logic and instinct. Mankind struggles to further understand the world but can't escape his need to propagate the species, or to dominate the herd. Here is Larry Adams, a gifted physicist with a deep understanding of the event selection process in large particle detectors, a genius with the software algorithms used to decide which collisions are worth recording for analysis and which are discarded, and he seems more worried about Mike's conversation with a television news anchor than their struggling search for Higgs. Here is Landon Donovan, the arrogant billionaire who arranged the funding for this one-of-a-kind private research facility, and his meddling management keeps getting in the way of their research.

This latest surprise is the most disturbing of all. Mike's trip to Atlanta, after all, was something Donovan scheduled only two weeks ago, a visit to Centauri headquarters to answer questions about their research and development on a quantum microprocessor. But the practical production of such a chip is surely years away, and it's at least possible that Donovan sent him out of town while he removed Paul and installed Samantha.

Until this morning, Mike had believed Samantha a candidate to direct the upcoming Large Hadron Collider at CERN, a particle accelerator on the border of Switzerland and France. Her success there is widely recognized, and Mike doubts she would have left her position just to become Mike's Beam division head.

She's here because she wants his job. Donovan surely knows this, so what the hell does he think he's doing?

And what is Mike going to do about it?

It's not like he can turn up the power on the super collider, it's not like he can *will* Higgs into the detector. The work on this project is meticulous by design, a painstaking effort that requires enormously complex analysis of almost unimaginable amounts of information. The NTSSC as a whole produces enough data in a year to fill 40 million CDs, and even with their linked network of 150,000 Pentium CPUs—what they've taken to calling the "Texas Grid"—sifting through it all is a time-consuming process. The effort required just to maintain their cadre of processors is mind-boggling, and yet somehow he must manage both the teams that produce this kind of data and those who consume it.

If it were simply a matter of organizing the production and flow of information, Mike would be at ease. If it were only a matter of fine-tuning the hierarchy of physicists, of steering the general direction of the Higgs search, Mike would consider himself a perfect fit for the job.

It's the human drama that complicates matters, that prevents the super collider from running like the well-oiled machine he once envisioned. Sure, he's led teams before, but nothing could have prepared him for the sheer scope of the NTSSC. It's as much a city as a scientific facility. Theoretical and experimental physicists, technicians, engineers, maintenance teams, business and clerical staff, political lobbyists, and members of the senior management team—like Landon Donovan and Mike—all working together within the fifty-four-mile oval circumference of the super collider. Nearly nine thousand dipole magnets accelerating protons along a closed path, traveling in opposite directions at velocities that approach the speed of light, colliding inside an underground detector as big as an eight-story building. It's an extraordinary machine designed for an extraordinary task and populated, unavoidably, by humans with ordinary lives.

Humans who often produce remarkable ideas and sometimes make boneheaded mistakes. Who look to him for guidance.

A crazy thought, this.

Most days, Mike eats lunch on campus. He likes to visit the various NTSSC cafeterias and talk with regular physicists, men and women who spend their days with their sleeves rolled up, who are the belts and gears of this massive experimental machine. He wants to be a real person to them, not just a spokesman who makes strategic decisions and issues press releases. He recognizes the need for team structure, for management hierarchy, but he also dreams of a facility without layers of privilege, an organization of scientists whose only goal is the advancement of knowledge.

As much as he enjoys the responsibility for this immense

effort, Mike sometimes longs for the simpler times at Fermilab, where he spent most of his time solving physics problems instead of coaching the efforts of others. This is something he could never admit to anyone, of course, especially not American scientists or (God forbid) Landon Donovan. To confess his lukewarm desire for power in this, his chosen field, would be tantamount to surrendering his male genitalia. To admit that he'd rather not spend his entire afternoon (and probably his evening) guiding a Japanese television crew around the facility would mark him as a man with no passion for success. And yes, sometimes he does enjoy the attention and the privilege, he wouldn't be here if he didn't, and maybe he just needs a little time to himself after that stunt Donovan pulled with Samantha Aizen this morning. Maybe he'll head over to Quizno's and have lunch away from this place.

The heat outside is a rough and tangible thing, the silence somehow unnerving. It's a feeling that has been with Mike since his first visit to north Texas, the sense of rawness, a place where the Old West and present-day America seem to coexist. The whole region is a wasteland, after all, a barbed-wire grid of mesquite thicket and abandoned oil wells, where temperatures range from 120 degrees in the summer to below zero in the winter. Cattle wander flat pastures, watching the locals drive by in their dusty pickup trucks and Chevrolet sedans. Farmers tend desperate crops. This is the life that people from the left and right coasts imagine when they think of Texas—old men gathering before sunrise at the local Dairy Queen, ropy young men racing around town in dually pickups with four rear tires, shotguns mounted to back windows, fist-size belt buckles and epidermal Wranglers, mullets and cowboy hats, country music and tornadoes. Dallas and Houston may be shimmering, gridlocked monuments to Sunbelt suburbia, Austin perhaps a cultural destination for those unwilling to head east or west, but this area south of the Red River and northwest of Fort Worth is truly the hard, forgotten Texas of Larry McMurtry novels.

But Olney, for years on the verge of extinction after empty-
ing its pockets to rogue oil speculators in the mid-eighties, is
now an oasis in this desolate landscape. The arrival of NTSSC
dollars sparked a boom that brought in new industry and housing and increased the population from three thousand to fifteen
thousand in less than five years. Tumbleweeds still occasionally
blow down Main Street, but now they roll past Whataburger
and Tony Roma's and brightly lit Conoco affiliates. There is even
a budding nightlife—one dance club and a few upscale bars—
and the most popular of the latter is Eva's, where a striking business major from Arizona State University mixes spectacular
cocktails and employs the best-looking waitresses this side of
Wichita Falls.

The administrative offices and GEM detector are located
near the southernmost point of the ring—roughly six miles
south of Olney—and it's about a ten-minute drive from the
parking lot of his building to the center of downtown. During
the drive, Mike reviews (in spite of himself) the standard
NTSSC visitor presentation he'll be giving to the Japanese television crew this afternoon. How the machine was funded exclu-
sively by private dollars. How it was born from the ashes of a
similar project abandoned by the United States Department of
Energy and is the most costly civilian scientific experiment in
history. How the original SSC design documentation was first
acquired by Landon Donovan in 1995, two years after funding
for the government project was halted by Congress. Donovan,
famous for transforming Centauri Cystems from a struggling
telecom startup to a global leader in microprocessor development and owner of the biggest fiber network in the world, spent
two years building an international sponsorship consortium
that would eventually raise the twelve billion dollars necessary
to build the NTSSC. It's widely speculated that Donovan di-
verted as much as three billion dollars from Centauri to reach
his monetary goal (okay, he'll leave that part out), and Mike
believes that his boss championed the project in large part to get

a much-needed credibility boost to signal his superiority over that well-known technology giant from the Pacific Northwest.

He'll talk about their special partnership with the Department of Energy, how they cooperate with the government in a way that could be compared to a typical federal contractor. He'll impress them with the manpower of the NTSSC (two thousand physicists, a thousand technicians, and several hundred other non-technical personnel). He won't mention how Donovan discourages his employees from living outside of Olney, or that a variety of draconian rules regarding tardiness and attendance have been in effect since NTSSC construction began, or that many of the physicists commute from Wichita Falls anyway, where shopping malls and television affiliates and some small modicum of culture can be found, if you look hard enough.

"Hey, Mike."

He's standing in line at Quizno's, waiting to order. He turns around and sees Amy Cantrell, who has just stepped inside. She smiles and he smiles back, pretending (as he always does) to ignore her unsophisticated sex appeal, her wide hips and pushed-up breasts.

"Long line," she says. "Can you order a sandwich for me?"

"Sure. What would you like?"

She picks out something and then waits for him at a table. He calculates the personal cost of ordering his food to go, of apologizing to Amy for not having time to stay and eat, then decides it's not the best course of action.

"Don't you usually eat on campus?" Amy asks when he arrives with their lunch.

"I do. But I think it's going to be a late night, so I wanted to get away for a little while."

"Some quiet time?"

"Exactly."

"Well, sorry for bugging you like this," she tells him. "But to be honest I followed you here from the office. I was hoping you'd stop somewhere."

"What's up?"

"I wanted to talk to you about something, but I didn't want to do it at work."

"What is it? Is something wrong?"

"Well, I'm not exactly sure how to bring this up, because I know you guys are friends. But it's . . . well, it's Larry."

"Larry? Adams?"

"Yeah," Amy admits. "I know he's a smart guy. You wouldn't have picked him for his job otherwise. I'm sure he does a great job. But . . . well, he makes me pretty uncomfortable at work."

"Visits your desk a lot?"

"All the time. At least a couple of times every day."

"Has he ever said anything offensive to you?"

"No, but . . . I don't know."

"Amy," Mike says. "If Larry makes you uncomfortable, I'll say something to him. You should never have to deal with that where you work. But I also know you have a fair number of visitors to your desk, and if I single him out—"

"I don't ask for guys to stop by my desk. I'm just there trying to do my job."

Mike is familiar with Amy's reputation as a somewhat well-traveled girl. But he also realizes this information probably came to him by way of Larry.

"I'm not saying you do, Amy. Every person in the office has the same right to come in and do their job and not be harassed. What I'm saying is that if I'm going to talk to Larry—and not anyone else—then it would help if I knew what makes him different than the guys you aren't complaining about."

She nods. "The problem is I can't really put my finger on it. Other guys, they seem harmless to me. Some guys have asked me out. I've gone on a few dates. I guess if Larry would just come out and ask me, that would make it okay. But instead he just stands there and . . . well, he *stares,* Mike. At my chest. Like, 'Hello? My face is up here, Larry!' And his eyes, they just seem *mean* to me. His mouth smiles when he talks to me, but his eyes don't."

Mike isn't sure what to make of this. He has a responsibility to act, to help ensure Amy's work environment is professional and secure, but he owes the same to Larry. And yes, there were complaints like this when they both worked at Fermilab, but Amy probably doesn't know that. What is it about Larry that aggravates women? Mike needs something concrete if he's going to censure the guy, because a horrible truth of corporate America is that for some women, sexual harassment only applies to unappealing men.

"Okay," he finally says. "I'll talk to Larry for you. I'll try to make it seem like I'm the one who noticed, rather than you. But you'll need to help me out, Amy. The first thing Larry's going to do is point out all the other men who visit your desk, so you'll need to be more strict with everyone for your argument to hold water."

She nods.

"What do you think? Is that a fair solution?"

"Sure."

"Great," Mike says. "Now let's eat these sandwiches while they're still fresh."

8

Before the accident Steve would have breezed through the interview. The corporate officers know him well, after all, familiar as they are with his work ethic and proven success in the struggling field of e-business. Before the accident, the interview would have been nothing more than a formality, but now they'll be there to truly evaluate him, searching like jewelers for blemishes and cracks invisible to the casual observer.

Steve spends some time clearing obsolete e-mails out of his in-box. He ignores mental film clips of Janine, the love of his life, squeaking and begging the faceless Barry to defile her. He pushes away the memory of Anna lifting her red dress. Or the stocky fellow who threw him out the window. Or Anna coming to him in the hospital room, an apparition, perhaps already dead—

He's been intentionally avoiding this. He doesn't want to consider the consequences of Anna's mysterious fall. It's not like he could have forgotten what the newsstand proprietor said, that she fell to her death in the exact fashion by which Steve himself nearly died, but how could that have happened? And why? He can't help but wonder if her death is somehow connected to his struggle with the bouncer. That perhaps the man killed her because she witnessed Steve's fall from the window. He doesn't want to believe that, doesn't want to believe her death was in any way connected to him, but how else to explain such a coincidence? And if the bouncer had in fact killed her, why wait so long? Steve knows Anna lived at least a few more days after his own fall, because according to the nurse, that's when she brought the ring to him.

He performs a quick search on the Internet to locate contact information for the Zurich police and then dials the number.

"Zurich Police," a female voice barks in German.

"Hello, I would like to inquire about the recent death of a woman in Zurich."

"Wait, please," the woman says. Unfamiliar pop music replaces her voice, and then a few seconds later a man picks up the line.

"Baltensperger speaking. How may I help you?"

"I would like to inquire about the death of a woman. It would have happened sometime in the last thirty days."

"What is the name of this woman? What information would you like and why?"

"I only know her first name," Steve says. "It was Anna, I believe. I understand she fell to her death from a building in the Niederdorf. Near the business known as Cabaret."

A long, static-filled silence passes as Steve waits. He knows it's only a matter of time before the man berates him for not knowing the woman's full name, for inquiring about someone for which he can offer so little information.

"What is your name, sir?"

Steve, in a reflexive moment of self-preservation, lies to Baltensperger. "Alan Johnson."

"What is your relationship to this woman?"

"I met her in Cabaret a few weeks ago. Later I went back to see her, but the business had closed and I was told she fell to her death."

"I think I would like to speak to you in person about this, Mr. Johnson. Can you come to the station? Now?"

"Now? No."

"May I ask why?"

"Because I am in the United States."

Another considerable pause. And then, "Very well, Mr. Johnson. Perhaps we can do this over the telephone. First, the woman's name is not Anna. It is Svetlana Kiselev. She took the name Anna when she began work at the Cabaret a little more than six months ago."

"I didn't know that."

"Can you tell me the last time you saw Svetlana? What day it was?"

Steve thinks back, indexing the days before and since his fall. "August nineteenth."

"Mr. Johnson," Baltensperger says. "Svetlana was found dead the morning of the twentieth."

From someplace so close he can touch and yet infinitely distant, the field emerges and intensifies as Steve tries to absorb what Baltensperger has just said. His fingers absently find his temples and massage them. This woman, Svetlana, brought the ring to the hospital. He knows this because the nurse told him so, because she pulled it out of his overcoat and showed it to him.

"Mr. Johnson? Does this seem like an odd coincidence to you? Because it looks that way to me."

"Are you sure about the date?" Steve asks. "It was very late when I saw Svetlana. Perhaps as late as four in the morning."

"Which means you may be the last person to have seen her alive. I really must insist, Mr. Johnson, that I obtain an official statement from you, preferably in person."

The presence is all around him now. Silently thrumming. "Do you have any suspects?" Steve asks.

"Of course I cannot officially comment on that," Baltensperger says. "But we could certainly learn more from the owner of Cabaret had he not disappeared. And there is word of an American who died that night, I have his name here somewhere, just a moment while I—"

Unable to listen to Baltensperger any longer, not through the drowning silence of the field, Steve hangs up the phone. At the very least, the call will be traced to AE's switchboard, and the police can eventually obtain internal records if they choose. Not that he has anything to hide. It was probably stupid to lie to Baltensperger about his identity, but that doesn't change the fact that something is obviously, desperately wrong with the timing of Svetlana's death. This is something he cannot deal with right now. This is his office. This is a place of lucidity. His interview is tomorrow. There is no room in his reclaimed life for a Swiss murder investigation.

And yet there is the issue of the nurse. Steve himself had not asked about Svetlana or the ring. He asked about the IV, and the nurse replied, after a pause, how the Russian woman delivered the ring "a couple of days after you were brought here." When certainly she did not. Svetlana could not have brought the ring any time except immediately upon his arrival at the hospital, because she was found dead that morning. But is it plausible to believe that, after his fall, Svetlana had plundered his clothes for valuables, found the ring, let the ambulance take him away, decided against keeping it, taken the train to the hospital, given the ring to a staff member there, commuted back to Cabaret, and then was immediately thrown from the building to her death? Or is it more likely that the ring never left his jacket? That when the ambulance came for him at Cabaret, Svetlana turned over the clothes he'd left in room CD and had never known about the ring in the first place? Or was even dead by then?

If so, it means the nurse fabricated her story. He can think of no other explanation.

But why?

As much as he doesn't want to have to know, Steve is obligated by his place in the middle of this mess to find out. The most straightforward way to accomplish this would be to call the hospital in Zurich, track down the nurse, and ask her. But it occurs to him (for the first time) that he doesn't even know the name of the hospital. In his wallet he finds the business card Dobbelfeld provided, but the hospital information isn't printed on it. And rather than contact the doctor and raise his suspicion (because, come on, if there is some sort of conspiracy, then everyone must be involved, especially his physician), Steve instead places a call to AE's benefits contact, Diana Jackson, and asks her to review the hospital's insurance claim.

"Oh, Mr. Keeley," she says. "I heard you were back. We were all so worried for you."

"Thank you. It's great to be here."

"Did you get a bill from the hospital? Is that why you're calling?"

"To be honest, I'm calling because I don't know the name of the hospital, and I want to give them a call."

"Oh, well that should be easy to find. Let me just . . . well, hold on. Can I ask you to hold for a minute, Mr. Keeley?"

"Sure, Diana. Take your time."

AE's hold music propaganda keeps him company while he waits, as conspiratorial possibilities disturb the field around him. Would the nurse intentionally lie about the ring in order to warn him about something? How could she be sure he would ever learn of Svetlana's death, anyway? Would the bouncer really kill Svetlana? And why had the owner of the Cabaret closed the business and fled?

"Mr. Keeley?"

"Yes?"

"I'm not sure why, but there's no insurance claim for your hospital stay in Zurich, for the medical procedures, for *anything*. Normally such claims are put in immediately, and certainly after a month something should have shown up."

"Could there be some mix-up or delay because it was a foreign hospital?"

"Well, I considered that, so I checked the major Zurich hospitals that come up in my system. With this new SAP software everything is tied together, all the different AE offices share the same information, so I can check it just like I was in Switzerland. Can you believe none of them have a record of you staying there? Isn't that odd?"

"Are you sure our system is complete? Maybe there is a hospital that isn't listed in the computer."

"I'll certainly call headquarters in Zurich and find out. I'm sure they've all gone home for the day, what with the nine-hour time difference. But first thing in the morning I'll call over to HR there and check with those people. Then we'll know for sure."

"That's very nice of you, Diana. I appreciate it. You'll let me know in the morning, then?"

"I'll call you as soon as I find out, Mr. Keeley."

He hangs up and realizes he should summarize it all and form a plan, determine his next steps. He shouldn't sit there and remember Svetlana in her red dress. He shouldn't listen to the noise, or watch the noise, or feel the noise.

The scrambled images.

He must obviously direct his full attention to the field now, to the relationships between it and the physical items in this room. Its individual points are organized somehow into patterns, waves, something, he can feel how their relationships could be altered and perhaps even cancelled altogether, and this, Steve can clearly see, is how he planned to levitate off the bed. Of course it is. He knew if he waited that eventually it would come back to him, the proper perspective. Only now, with this additional information, these patterns of discrete points—though they aren't really necessarily discrete—with this better information he also realizes why his levitation at the hospital was a failure, because seeing the mechanism and being able to manipulate it are completely independent, and he'll have to devote a lot of time and energy and attention to the field, will have to study it closely if he plans to—

"Steve?"

For some reason he can't see. His face is pressed flat against something and his eyes are closed. He opens them and finds his head on the desk. As if he were napping. A pool of saliva sits like mercury just inches from his mouth.

Serena stands before him. Somehow he failed to notice until now that she isn't wearing pantyhose. None of the younger women do, it isn't in fashion right now, but considering the little black miniskirt she has on, there isn't much of anything to cover the aroma drifting from between her legs. An aroma that he is, at this very moment in warped spacetime, enjoying immensely.

"Steve, are you okay?"

"I'm fine," he says, sitting straight up in his chair, presenting himself (he's quite sure) as completely normal.

"You don't look so good," Serena says.

"I was just taking a little nap. I haven't been sleeping . . . well."

"You look a little spaced out."

The noise is more intense than ever. And the voices, hesitant, insecure, whispering.

A name again. Two words.

Before he can stop himself, Steve says, "Tell me what you know about Simon Slater."

"What?"

He can hardly control his own voice. "Isn't that what you came in here to talk about? Simon Slater?"

"No. Have you been reading my e-mail?"

"Of course not," Steve bristles, even though he cannot confirm or deny images of an e-mail to someone named Klaus. "What makes you say that?"

"You know goddamned well what makes me say that."

Klaus. Karsten. Something.

"Serena, I have no idea what you're talking about."

"Let me spell it out for you, then. I thought Simon Slater took your VP job. I heard he was in Switzerland for executive training. So after you and I talked this morning, I sent an e-mail to a friend of mine in Zurich, and it turns out Simon is there for *another* job, something completely unrelated. Which means I was wrong, I made up something in my mind that wasn't true at *all,* and yet you're asking me about it. And the only way you could have known to ask about him was to read my e-mail."

Steve knows he just made a severe tactical error. But how is he supposed to think clearly through all this noise? And now, somehow, he must dig himself out of a fairly deep hole while Serena stands above him, looking down.

"Company e-mail isn't private," he points out, appropriating her accusation for his own purposes, because what other explanation can he offer for blurting out Simon Slater's name? "Your employment agreement clearly states—"

"I know what it says. But I wonder what reason you'll have to give Jim Mannheim when he demands probable cause."

"I don't need probable cause."

"You do when you're thirty-four and I'm twenty-five and everyone in the company thinks we've slept together."

"They do not think that."

"Yes, they do, because of your womanizing past and my . . . reputation."

"Serena, look. You can act tough and puff out your chest, but the fact is that no company policy has been violated here."

"Still—"

"Still," he agrees, "it's obvious that anything you say now could affect my bid for the VP position. So why don't you tell me what I can do to make this right?"

"You can start by staying out of my e-mail."

"Done."

"And," she says softly, glancing briefly at the floor and then back at him. "You can have dinner with me tonight."

"Serena."

"Look," she says, "I'm not mad or anything. And I'm not trying to move in on Janine. But your reading my e-mail is proof that you think about me, even if just a little bit, and I think you owe it to yourself to at least *see* what this could be, what it might be like to be with someone who would completely *devote* herself to you."

The aroma of her, he swears it's getting stronger, but isn't such a thing impossible? To smell her at all? Field or no field, noise or no noise, is this what it feels like to lose one's mind?

"Serena—"

"Or I could always go talk to Mr. Mannheim. Tell him you've been acting weird, falling asleep at your desk, reading my e-mail."

Steve glares at her. Wonders what her neck would feel like between his squeezing fingers.

"Just come over," she says. "I'll e-mail you directions. Just come over and we'll forget everything that happened this morning, okay?"

"Fine," he says at last.

"And you're feeling okay, right? You didn't look so hot when I came in."

"I'm fine. Just tired."

"Maybe you should go home and get some rest."

"I think I will after I get caught up here."

She sashays out of his office. Steve's hands again find his temples, massaging them as the day stretches on toward infinity.

9

Donovan in his office, feet on his desk, door closed. His tinted window looks out over the parking lot and the vast, brown plain upon which the administrative complex sits. Asphalt roads crisscross the fields at regular intervals, roads that were red dirt before he arrived with money to pave and widen them. The road that forms a T at Texas 251 is one he remembers particularly well. Just east of that intersection stood an old graveyard, True Cemetery, and it seemed like a good idea to move it. He couldn't very well have visitors to the administrative complex driving by headstones on the way. But it hadn't been easy finding survivors of the individuals buried there, and securing their approval to have the caskets dug up proved even more difficult.

Then there was Rose Corley's standoff. For emergency egress and tunnel ventilation, there were shafts located every 2.7 miles that descended to the ring, and the old woman's house stood right on top of one of these locations. Her property had been valued at less than ninety thousand dollars, and when Donovan offered twice that, he thought for sure the deal was done. What he didn't anticipate was the house being over one hundred and twenty years old, that it had been in her family for generations. He was forced to go all the way to three hundred and fifty-five thousand dollars before the woman's children stepped in and convinced her to sign the agreement, and still, when the crew arrived to demolish the house, they found Rose Corley standing on her porch with a twelve-gauge shotgun pointed at them. It took the sheriff and nine deputies fourteen hours to get her out of there.

The telephone rings, dragging him back to the present.

"This is Landon."

"Mr. Donovan," Karsten Allgäuer says. "Ms. Aizen is in place, yes?"

Donovan's hand tightens around the handset. Every time he talks to this Swiss fuck it pisses him off. "She is."

"And Mr. McNair is willing to accommodate her?"

"Of course. But I'm still not convinced it's necessary to replace him."

"That is not your decision to make."

"I know that, but I need some latitude here. I'm the one managing these people, and you have to understand that in America our culture is to—"

"Mr. Donovan, I do not give one shit about your American culture," Allgäuer remarks. "You have been instructed to follow my directions."

"And I am," Donovan says. "But the search for Higgs will be delayed if we push Mike out the door. Is that what Lange wants?"

"I do not think it is your business to guess what Mr. Lange wants."

"I could help, you know. If you guys would just tell me what's going on, I could probably make things easier. After all, I'm here at the facility."

"I may be joining you soon enough."

And the line goes dead. Donovan slams down the phone.

"Not my business," he says under his breath. "We'll see about that, you creepy fuck."

10

Steve manages to wade through a couple of hundred e-mails before his jump-cut consciousness finally reaches its limit. Around 2:30 he decides to head home, and hopes he'll be able to successfully navigate the rushing, video-game grid of the 405.

In Nebraska his biggest gripe with traffic was grandmas and grandpas waiting at stop signs on intersecting farm roads. Invariably they saw you approaching on the two-lane blacktop and decided, when you were almost upon them, that indeed there *was* time to go ahead and pull into your lane, which they invaded and then proceeded to accelerate, over a period of minutes, all the way up to the breathtaking speed of fifty miles per hour. As a young man bent on getting the hell out of Nebraska, Steve could not tolerate slow drivers. He honked and yelled and, yes, occasionally brandished his middle finger. He hated the very idea of conservatism and conformism and traditionalism, whether it was affecting him directly or not, and this is why he refuses to be irritated by L.A. drivers treating him the same way right now, on the 405, even though he is all the way over in the farthest right lane.

A used-car commercial ends the song he was enjoying, and Steve browses radio stations until he finds something else more pleasant. Music seems to dispel the field somewhat, or at least distracts him from its abstract and truly infinite population of points. Although as time passes he is more and more convinced that these points are not points at all, that they are conductors of some kind, relaying information or perhaps energy that he can only begin to appreciate. At least this is how it seems when he is observing the field from a certain perspective. Other times it seems as if there is no field at all, but rather the presence as he felt it in the hospital, and for the first time he considers defining the two sensations as separate phenomena, although he lacks sufficient proof to say anything with certainty.

Driving this way, operating his Infiniti with only a fraction of normal focus, is sort of like driving drunk. Steve isn't quite sure if the choices and maneuvers he makes on the way to Valencia are appropriate, but eventually he arrives in front of his house intact. Inside he finds a note from his mother. *Call us if you need anything, Stevie. Your father's knee is acting up again. We'll be calling Dr. Koetter tomorrow morning.* And at the bottom, a message from his father scrawled in slanted strokes instructing Steve to *knock 'em dead in the interview like I know you can. You're always one step ahead of everyone around you.*

Perhaps. Because not everyone can lay claim to this goddamned thrumming in his head, after all. Steve can count on one finger the number of people he knows who have made a reasonable attempt to defy gravity and float around a hospital room. And he's definitely one step ahead of any guy who wants to have dinner tonight with Serena Reed, that's for sure.

Then again, he certainly didn't anticipate Janine fucking another man. Where was his step ahead on that one?

But the field's effect on his splintering mind, that's where his focus is right now. Like what happened with Serena this morning. The voices, the name of Simon Slater, the nervous whispering. Steve has seen the same movies as everyone else. He knows, like anyone would, that hearing voices in your head is a classic symptom of mental illness. It doesn't take a genius to recognize that a head injury and whispering, inner voices indicate some kind of physiological problem. He could call Dobbelfeld about the symptoms. Clearly, he *should* call him. But he doesn't really feel like it.

He doesn't feel like anything.

It's nearly four o'clock now. Three hours to negotiate before he leaves for Serena's apartment in Santa Monica. His growling stomach convinces him to make something to eat, and because he doesn't want to completely spoil his appetite before dinner, Steve decides on soup. Thankfully, the finger-intensive work of chopping vegetables consumes an agreeable stretch of time. Dripping celery, pungent onions, brittle green beans, knobby carrots, florets of broccoli, all this he pours into a boiling pot of beef broth, along with salted bites of seared beef, cans of tomato sauce, and a whole lot of pepper. He doesn't think about Janine, not at all, not her smell still in the house, not the clothes now gone from his closet, not the stray blond hairs he keeps finding on his pillow. And he can't go near her side of the bed. He keeps himself awake at night worrying that he might roll over there and fall into the canyon-size emptiness. So instead of thinking about Janine, instead of obsessing over Serena's phantom whispers, he just watches the roiling universe of the soup, precisely chopped vegetables appearing and disappearing at the uneven surface of hydrogen and oxygen atoms, excited as they are by flames licking at the pot below. He inhales the salty aroma of steam, little wisps of more hydrogen and oxygen atoms, these with enough energy to escape the pot altogether, which once again become liquid on the surface of his skin.

Steve didn't bother much with science in high school or college. He determined the easiest courses that would satisfy his core requirements and ignored the rest. But what he sees and senses now is more than anything he could have ever learned in a classroom. He lacks the training and context to accurately portray the structure of it, to himself or anyone else, but the essential truth of the field and how everything works so efficiently and perfectly within it can only be described as transcendental. He can appreciate—and even enjoy—the field when he can devote sufficient mental capacity to its magnitude. But like a computer whose resources have been marshaled to perform an enormously complex task, when he tries to launch another application, like deciding to stop watching the soup and eat some of it, and later picking which clothes to wear to Serena's, the whole goddamned processor wants to shut down.

11

Serena answers the door in the same clothes she wore to work: black miniskirt, gauzy, metallic-gray top. She isn't wearing shoes. Her perfect toenails are the same shade of red as Svetlana's dress.

"I didn't think you were coming," she says, not quite making eye contact with him.

"I lost track of time," Steve tells her. "Sorry about that."

"No harm done. Good timing, anyway—the garlic bread just came out of the oven."

He steps inside and looks around her apartment. Decorated with androgynous colors—tan sofa, white curtains, gray carpet—and generic paintings of wildlife and famous European landmarks, it's not at all the powder room of femininity he expected.

And here is the noise again, invisible and silent, swimming up from nowhere.

"You can take off your shoes if you like," she tells him. "It's *so* much more comfortable."

In the breakfast nook a bowl of spaghetti towers before a steaming pot of red sauce. Serena pads into her pantry-size kitchen and retrieves a plate of sliced, buttered bread, and Steve waits for her to sit down before he does. Then she grabs a pair of tongs and begins filling her plate with spaghetti.

"So how was your first day back?"

"Weird," he says. The amount of pasta Serena loads onto her plate is staggering. She adds three slices of French bread and begins to eat while Steve is still negotiating spaghetti from the bowl to his plate.

"You looked a little freaked out when I came into your office. I thought for a second you were dead."

"I don't know what happened there. I think I had a headache and wanted to put my head down for a moment. I guess I must have fallen asleep."

Thrumming conductors.

"And then you left early. Did you get some rest?"

A pulsating network of points. Waves of them.

"Not really. Just sort of caught up on bills and other housekeeping stuff."

She takes him through a round of typical questions, almost naïvely, as if she didn't, in fact, coerce him into coming here this evening. Steve listens and nods and occasionally responds, but really what he's thinking of is the drive over, how he pushed back the field by picturing himself with her. Like ripping the clothes from her curvy body. Or pushing his mouth into that shaved and slippery place between her legs, legs that are not toned but shapely with the voluptuous fat of a young girl that will someday become the cottage cheese thighs of an aging woman. It doesn't make any sense, this ridiculous urge he has to ravage her. She is attractive but not exceedingly so. She dresses provocatively but hides her face under layers of cream-color spackle. And still he can barely sit here and listen to her drone on about her overbearing father and her ailing grandmother and how her air conditioner is making some kind of funny noise. All he can see are her heavy breasts in his hands, her torso writhing.

When they are done eating she invites him to turn on the television. He chooses something neutral—a television news magazine, an undercover sting operation—but Serena immediately grabs the remote and finds a show about dating.

"This is my favorite!" she squeals, scooting closer, laughing forcibly as pedantic matchmaking stories unfold on the small screen.

The heat is building in him now, in his legs, in his swollen dick as he considers looting her, as he contemplates grabbing her round ass and bending her over right here on the couch. No amount of Zurich rain could put out this all-consuming fire, no amount of apology could dissipate the pulsing field of his hunger. And after a while Serena finally begins to sense this. Or perhaps she has simply been waiting for him to make a move. Or perhaps she has been—

". . . teasing you, forcing you to suffer the way I suffer every day, as you sit in your office, just steps away from me."

She's whispering into his ear now; he doesn't know when it started because it's all a blur to him now, the entire saturated notion of his vengeance.

"Serena."

"Shh," she says. "Don't say a word. Just enjoy yourself. Just relax. I can see it in your eyes, the tension. Just relax and let me make you feel good."

Her hand is on his pants, playfully squeezing. The field and its conductors fervently respond. She kisses his neck, his ear, her lips full and soft and warm, and then she's on top of him, tasting his lips, tongue darting against his own, playing with his teeth, licking the textured roof of his mouth.

And the noise. The voices. No longer bothering to whisper, but speaking directly to him now. Chanting. His name. The name of her father.

Do you like me am I pretty do you think I'm pretty Steve?

And murky, misshapen noise. Disorder.

Do you love me?

Blinding joy. Ecstasy.

I love you love you love you Steve.

Confusion.

Her skirt hikes itself as she straddles his legs, and his hands go to her thighs.

Love me hold me touch me Steve.

She moves against him, rubbing dryly against his fire as he unfastens the silvery buttons of her blouse. And here are her breasts, pale and soft and held in place by a black, vinyl bra. His hands find her back, the clasp, and he buries himself in the warm fat of her.

"Eat them, Steve," she says.

Love me hold me touch me Steve.

Lust flows over him like warm water. He releases his attention, trying to let go of the delusion. It must be a delusion. He is not hearing Serena's thoughts. It's just guilt. It's Janine. It's his injured mind. Delusions of revenge.

Serena slides off his lap. Pushes the cocktail table out of the way. Kneels before him. Unzips him. Pulls him free. Into her mouth.

Give me love me nurse me Steve.

Nurse me.

He leans back, relaxing further, and it's working somehow, the noise seems to be fading as she bobs, as she takes him in further and further, working him. Needing him. Milking him. And then shaking, and moisture dripping into his pubic hair, onto his thighs. The wet sound of her sniffles. Shallow breaths that he doesn't realize are sobs until she is running away, her sounds muted suddenly by the slam of a door.

Steve looks down at himself, wet and shrinking, and the absurdity of it all overwhelms him with resentment. He puts everything back where it belongs and goes to find her. The noise is back already, like the hiss a cassette makes when you play it in a sound system, like the snowy screen of a mistuned television set. Except that he can't hear it or see it. It's just there. She's just there.

"Serena?"

"I'm sorry," she calls between sobs. "I'm so sorry."

He finds her door around a corner and knocks lightly. "Are you okay? Can I come in?"

"I just want you to like me."

Love me love me please *please*—

"Serena, I do—"

"I don't mean like that," she cries. "I mean *like* me."

It would be wrong to lie, even to console her.

"And all you do is look at my body. That's all you want."

Nothing. He can say nothing.

I am so stupid I am so stupid I am such a stupid fucking stupid!

"You were going to fuck me, and you don't even *know* me. Why don't you want to *know* me?"

"Serena, what am I supposed to say?"

Stupid little girl such a stupid fucking stupid—

The door flies open, and her unsexy, naked breasts sway as if blown by a strong wind.

"I want you to tell me the truth. Why don't you want to know me?"

From a distance he senses the field's amplification, rushing and unwelcome in his head. He's helpless to stop it. He doesn't know how to tell Serena the truth without unleashing its wrath upon her.

"I *do* know you, Serena. I know you and . . . I'm sorry . . . I just don't feel that way."

Her tears spill through the field, conductors surrounding and influencing their saline journey toward the Earth's gravitational center.

Oh my God oh my God what's *wrong* with me what's the *matter* with me no one likes me no one *loves* me—

"But *why*? I invited you here, I *cooked* for you, I would do *anything* for you, Steve."

"Serena," he says. "You started eating before I even had spaghetti on my plate. You changed the channel without bothering to ask. You pretend to be selfless, but every single nice thing you ever do is to get something in return. That's not how love works."

"And you think you're so good at it? You think you and Janine have the perfect relationship?"

"No, we don't. She cheated on me. I left her."

What? She *cheated* on him? He *left* her he's *free*!

And the field, ringing in his ears, obscuring his vision. His hands go to his temples. He falls to his knees.

Serena leans down and puts her hands on his shoulders. "Steve! Are you okay?"

Through watery eyes he sees her breasts, big and blurry, inches from his face. Perhaps he could induce the field to retreat again by rekindling his lust. But no, he—

"I think I should leave," he says.

Stay here Steve stay with me.

"But what's wrong with you? Is it your head? Is it because of the fall?"

He stumbles to the door and pulls on his shoes.

"Are you sure you should drive?"

Don't go Steve don't go—

"I'll be fine."

"Are you—"

He leaves the noisy apartment and shuts the door behind him.

12

Crawling again down the far right lane of the 405, wary of a bored CHP officer who might decide to pull him over, Steve somehow finds his way out of L.A. proper, miraculously negotiates the interchange at the 5, and makes it back to Valencia. He creeps through neighborhoods and finally stops in front of his house, unwilling to direct his car into the garage lest he rip a side mirror off the Infiniti or crush his mountain bike.

Once inside he heads straight for his room and collapses into bed. Now, finally, he can succumb to it again, the field, the presence, whatever delusion keeps trying to claw its way into his brain. He closes his eyes and welcomes it. Absolves himself of responsibility. Accepts fate.

The blinds are shut and no lights are on, but the room seems to brighten somehow, gradually, until it appears completely saturated with white light. He must have fallen immediately asleep, his taxed mind succumbing at once to REM, because here is the presence again, manipulating the field to take on physical form, assuming the identity of Svetlana.

"Hello, Steve."

She hovers over him as if propped up by her arms, but he doesn't feel her mass pressing against the bed.

"Go away, Svetlana."

"It's okay."

"It's *not*. It's *not* okay. You are a figment of my imagination. This whole fucking hallucination, this obsession with fields and conductors, I'm making it all up because . . . because I don't know why. And I want out. I want it to go away. So *you* have to go away."

"I am sorry for what happened, Steve. If you need me, I am here."

How can he turn away from those luminous eyes, how can he reject the kindness in her angelic face? But he must. The interview. He needs sleep. Dreamless sleep. Not infinite, white-field nightmares. Not his imagination, not this betrayal.

Not this pain.

13

At 4:30 in the morning Steve calls an executive cab for pickup an hour later. Then he steps into the shower and stands beneath a searing waterfall, wondering how he ever fell asleep last night. He can't remember anything after the Svetlana hallucination, so obviously it happened then, and somehow he made it all the way to the siren of his alarm clock at 4:15. And now here he is, somewhat recharged, thinking about the interview.

He did virtually nothing yesterday to prepare. Luckily interviews at this level—especially when you know the men who will be evaluating you—aren't the same as those for entry-level positions. Mostly they'll discuss Steve's ideas for the position, for specific and new initiatives to increase sales for lagging product lines and to further AE's brand-awareness campaign. They'll talk about mobility, his desire for an international position, about his general philosophy regarding leadership and teamwork. So all he really needs to do is put together a few hours of undisturbed reflection, organize his thoughts, and then calm himself enough to appear coherent in the presence of Mannheim, Rix, and Fairchild. Because that's what they'll really be evaluating, after all—his continued status as a sane, rational member of the corporate team.

The cab is a tactical precaution. It's become obvious to him over the past couple of days that the stress of concentration (like navigating L.A. traffic) increases his susceptibility to the delusion (field). And once the fucking thing gets into his head, getting it out again is not so easy.

The cab arrives on time, a navy blue Lincoln Town Car, and Steve climbs into the back seat. The Town Car rides like a yacht on ten-foot seas as it devours freeway at ninety miles an hour, but he arrives in front of AE's building at ten minutes after six bothered by only the faintest hint of the field.

At this early hour Steve is alone in the office, and he makes use of the time by imagining the interview and how it will transpire. A warm, artificial welcome from the three men, words masking their attempt to determine how sturdy and dependable he still is by just looking, which is certainly an innate but impossible exercise. And then polite questions about his mother and father. About Janine. AE prefers stable relationships for their truly strategic team members, especially those who might eventually relocate permanently to Zurich. And of course he isn't what they want, he isn't stable, he's just as single as he's always been. Except that when solitude was a chosen condition, he reveled in its noncommittal freedom, and now, instead, he is quietly and desperately lonely. Lonely but not alone. With the relentless company of the field, with the flickering and mystical presence, with the hallucinogenic effects of it all, he is never alone.

And it waxes and wanes as the interview draws closer, as the gradual arrival of AE's staff is signaled by elevator chimes and footsteps and fingers clicking on keyboards. And Janine's squeaking voice. And Svetlana's red dress. And Serena's tearful fellatio. The field binds it all together, unbroken and boundless, real time counted by nothing more than the dispersal of systems, by chaos, and Steve decides that it's pointless, that his desire for the VP job and the Janine vacuum and his set of goals, it's all pointless in the infinite and doomed evolution of the field. When ten o'clock rolls around he finds Mannheim standing outside his door, inquiring politely if Steve wants to join him in the staff meeting room, and Steve says, no, he'd rather not, and proceeds to stand up and walk past Mannheim's open face and Serena's empty cubicle and finally onto the bustling Westwood sidewalk, with no method of transportation and no destination. He navigates the field by observing its tendencies and density around areas of moving and stationary matter (and in doing so recognizes the men following him, the men who have been following him since Zurich) and goes on, navigating blindly until he is lost.

CHAPTER FIVE

1

"Get out of the left lane, fuckface," Larry growls.

Tuesday evening. Cruising down Kell Boulevard, one of the few controlled-access freeways in Wichita Falls, watching some old fart pilot his Crown Victoria all alone in the motherfucking *left lane,* for Christ's sake.

He approaches the old fart from behind, about to pass on the right. Some human zeroes, he thinks, don't bother watching for other drivers. They just toodle along and clog up the freeway like human cholesterol.

Watching it happen pours adrenaline into his bloodstream.

Accelerates his heart rate.

Fingers of pressure pushing on his temples.

"You're not supposed to drive in the left lane, asshole," he says as he drives by. "You leave it *open* for *passing.*"

There is plenty of room in Larry's own lane. The freeway isn't crowded at this time of night. But who gives a shit? The left lane is for passing, and the other lanes are for—

"Driving like a fucking slack-jawed yokel you fat gray-haired sack of donkey shit!"

Right. So he shouldn't yell at the top of his lungs when the guy isn't watching him and certainly can't hear him. Unless Larry is going to follow the guy to his destination and then beat the holy shit out of him, there is no point in getting angry. He's just raising his own blood pressure. Inflicting the damage to himself.

He takes a drink from the glass of Crown and Coke sitting between his legs. Switches on the radio. Dr. Laura is on again. Fucking bitch with her stupid advice. Why in the hell do these pitiful losers call her in the first place? Just to be berated on *national radio*? And right now she's ranting again about homosexuality, trying to convince her listeners that gay marriage is going to tear the very fabric of our great country apart, and he just *hates* her, he doesn't know why he listens to her because it just drives him insane, and yet he can't turn it off. Somehow he enjoys the fury, enjoys it the way he enjoys the pain of digging wax out of his ears with a pen cap. The way he enjoys scratching the flared patch of ringworm on his thigh until it bleeds. The way he likes to scrape layers of dried snot out of his nose like mica shavings and savor their buttery taste.

So Mike thinks he spends too much time talking to Amy? That's a fucking crock of shit if he's ever heard one. Mike has said a thousand times that he doesn't care how his team members spend their days, so long as the work gets done. He knows Amy is the one who complained. He knows she laughs at him when he isn't around. He knows that she knows that he likes her, and she knows that he knows, and she obviously went crying to Mike, who conveyed the message to Larry in his condescending, offhand way.

It's just another example of how the Jillians of the world conspire to keep him out of their pretty club. If it were Mike visiting her desk all the time, Amy surely wouldn't care. Larry has seen how she looks at him. How she longs for him. How they all long for him, even the news chick, Kelly Smith. Even she probably turned moist for the great Mike McNair. He's in the club, and Larry is not. Good ol' Larry, who just keeps plugging along, doing his job. Good ol' Larry, who doesn't want a girlfriend because the girls he likes don't seem to like him. Good ol' Larry, who shouldn't spend so much time at Amy's desk because she's having trouble getting her work done—

"*Even though half the guys in the administrative office do the exact same thing!*"

No, he shouldn't yell at the top of his lungs when no one is there to hear him. And yes, it's time to throw Mike another wild goose. He takes another drink.

And up ahead, someone else is crawling down the highway in the left lane.

2

"People admire you," Samantha Aizen shouts.

She and Mike are standing together at the bar, sipping on experimental cocktails that Eva offered free in exchange for their honest evaluation. The drink is sweet and interesting, but not as interesting as Eva standing behind the bar in her low-rise jeans. Mike tries to keep his attention on the woman in front of him, but it isn't easy, not when she insists on talking shop instead of relaxing after a tough first week.

It's been four days since Landon introduced Samantha to the team. This morning was Mike's first official meeting with her. To his surprise (and dismay, if he wants to be honest with himself) her suggestions to improve beam luminosity were novel and seem likely to provide significant benefit with very little time and cost.

"Admire me?" he says. "I don't know about that."

"No, really. Of course people talk about how young you are, how you haven't published enough, that there are dozens of physicists more qualified for the job—but what you won't hear is that most of the older guys are surprised that you've lasted as long as you have. That you've been able to hold up under Donovan's pressure and his profit-driven science."

Smoke floats in the air, wispy like cirrus clouds, and the bar resonates with jukebox-driven, hundred-decibel sound waves taking the form of "Sweet Home Alabama." It's not quite four o'clock on Friday afternoon, and aside from his administrative staff, the bar is mostly empty.

"I know there are plenty of physicists out there with more experience than me, who have paid more dues than me," Mike says. "Sometimes I wonder how I ever got the job. Landon keeps telling me that he refuses to observe the hierarchical structure of the physics community. He says he got a 'feeling' about me. Whatever that's supposed to mean."

Samantha takes another sip, and in the intervening nano-seconds Mike's eyes shift to Eva again. This time it's her T-shirt, skin-tight and way too short.

"I think he made a good decision," Samantha says. "Despite what other jealous physicists might think."

"That's nice of you to say."

"I call 'em like I see 'em."

"So how did Landon approach you? When he recruited me, he went through this whole theatrical bit about how we were going to use the NTSSC to make discoveries that would change the world."

"Sure, he did that with me, too. But I cut him off pretty quickly. My work at CERN speaks for itself, and when he called I knew exactly what he wanted. So I told him what *I* wanted if I was going to come work for him."

"Went straight to remuneration," Mike observes. "Very nice."

"No, salary negotiations came later. That's not what I cared about the most."

"What was it then?"

"I told him that if I improved beam luminosity enough to resolve Higgs, I wanted to share the Nobel with you."

Mike is startled silent for a moment. And then, "But he doesn't decide who—"

"He decides how the announcement is made. He decides

how to position the work and the scientists here doing it. You're the spokesperson for the research, but he still gets more camera time."

With no answer for this, Mike elects not to speak.

"You would have found Higgs already if it was possible at present luminosity," Samantha prods. "If you find it after my adjustments, is it not fair that I share the spotlight?"

"My goal is to find Higgs. For the sake of science. I welcome any assistance you can provide."

"Good answer, but not for the question I asked."

He averts his eyes, looks around to see who might be listening. Eva is at the far end of the bar, serving an entry-level physicist whose name he can't remember. Farther away he sees Larry talking to Amy Cantrell, who, judging by her body language, would rather be streaking across the field at Texas Stadium.

"Samantha—"

"Please, call me Sam."

"Look, I'm not. . . . Of course I want to win the Nobel Prize. We all do. But I'm not trying to prove the existence of the Higgs field just to put a trophy on my mantel."

"But that trophy could be a consequence of finding Higgs, right? So I'm asking now if you're willing to share the Nobel."

"I'm sorry. I'm not going to answer that. If Donovan is going to decide, then you should go talk to him."

He turns around and leans against the bar, propping himself on his elbows. Eva sees him and heads over.

"I already did," Samantha admits, "and he agreed."

"Then there you have it," Mike says. And then to Eva, who's waiting for his order, "Can I get another of these?"

Eva beams. "You like it?"

"I do."

"I don't," Samantha says and slides her glass across the bar. "Too sweet for me."

Mike watches Samantha walk away. He supposes he just made a mistake, missed a political opportunity. If Samantha wants his job—if Donovan perhaps even told her the door to it was open—Mike has just given her a reason to pursue it with even more tenacity.

He turns back to the bar, where Eva is waiting, amused.

"I don't think her problem was your drink," he says.

"Still, she was kind of a bitch about it, huh?"

"She really pissed me off."

"But she's the perfect type for you," Eva says.

"What do you mean?"

"Aggressive."

"The woman is trying to get between me and my boss. Is that aggressive or poisonous?"

"What is she doing, exactly?"

"She wants to win the Nobel Prize. She knows that in a large facility like ours, the scientist in charge of the project would get the award. It's something you earn based on what you contribute to physics, to the world, but apparently all she cares about is the prize itself. And she's got it all mapped out exactly how she's going to do it."

"And you don't?"

"I—"

"Because I don't know a whole lot about physics, but I read the articles in the *Enterprise* and the Wichita paper. They're always talking about how the NTSSC was designed to win the Nobel and that it's only a matter of time before it happens. They always say you're the one who's going to win it on account of you being the main physicist on the project, the coordinator or senior team leader or whatever."

"Well, right, that's what I was—"

"So you're saying you haven't thought about it? About what you're going to do and what you're going to say when you find this God particle?"

"Of course I've thought about it."

"Well, from where I sit it sounds like that Japanese chick is just doing the same thing."

"Okay," Mike says. "Sure. But to be so obvious about it . . . it seems tacky."

"Maybe what seems tacky to you is another person's honesty."

"I guess it's a fine line."

"Sometimes it's okay to tell people who you are," Eva says. "Or what you want."

Mike knocks back a couple of swallows of his experimental cocktail. Eva always talks to him when he comes in—nearly every weekend since she opened—but most of the time she simply points out women in the bar that he should approach. And now, when he should be thinking about Samantha and Donovan, preparing a defense for what could ultimately be an assault on his job, he is instead sitting at a bar talking relationships.

"Are you trying to tell me something, Eva?"

"Let me give you an example," she says. "You've been coming in here since I opened, right? That's a little more than six months."

"Okay."

"Okay, so in all this time, did you know you never once told me that you were the head physicist at the super collider?"

"Well, I—"

"I had to find out from Larry," Eva says.

"If you wanted to know, you could have—"

"I *did* ask! Word for word I said, 'So, Mike, what do you do?' And you said, 'I work at the NTSSC. I'm a physicist.' "

"You expect me to say that I'm the chief physicist and director?"

"Yes!"

A customer approaches the bar, a tall fellow with forearms as big around as Mike's calves.

"Hey, Brandon," Eva says. "Bud Light?"

"Two, please."

Eva, in fact, has already reached for them. She opens both and hands them to him.

"Brandon," she says. "What kind of work do you do?"

"You know what kind of work I do."

"Just humor me. What's your job?"

"I'm an HVAC supervisor over at the GEM. I oversee the maintenance team to make sure guys like Mr. McNair don't get too hot or too cold. Didn't we already talk about this?"

"We did. I'm just trying to prove a point to my friend here."

"Hi, Mr. McNair," the fellow says, extending his formidable hand. "I'm Brandon Tate."

Mike shakes with him. "Nice to meet you."

"I heard Donovan hired some new woman to help us find Higgs. What's up with that?"

"Everyone on the project is part of the effort, Brandon. The new woman included."

"Right on," Brandon says. "Well, see you guys later. I'm trying to work my magic on this Wichita girl who came down to see what all the fuss is with the super collider."

"See there," Eva says, as Brandon moseys away. "Not only does he tell me exactly what he does, but he also isn't embarrassed to admit that he's trying to mac with some girl."

Mike grunts agreement.

"You would *never* tell me that," she says.

"I know I'm a little shy with women, but—"

"A *little*?"

"But that's not the main problem. The main problem is that there isn't any reason . . . there isn't any premise for it. Say a girl is just sitting there drinking. She's no different than the other fifty girls except that I think she's attractive. I can't just go up to her and say, 'Hey, you're the best-looking girl here in the bar. Can I sit down?' "

"You could just say 'Hi,' Mike. Did you ever think of that?"

"Hi?"

"Yes. Open with 'Hi.' It's quite accepted, actually."

"And then what?"

"And then whatever. 'What are you drinking?' 'I like your shoes.' If she's interested, she'll say something and then you'll say something, and if you have chemistry it will go on from there. If not, it won't."

Mike has had this discussion before. It always ends the same way: He agrees that he could be more assertive with women, and nothing comes of it.

"No offense to this wonderful establishment, Eva, but I guess maybe I'm not going to meet a girl in a bar."

"Then why do you come here every weekend?"

"Because everyone I know comes here to hang out."

"That's the only reason?"

"I guess."

"You don't hope that maybe one of these days you might hit it off with some girl—maybe she's not Mrs. Right, but maybe she's sexy and fun to talk to—you don't hope that a girl like that might let you—"

Before she can finish, a young woman with a fake tan approaches the bar and orders three beers. Eva is busy just long enough for Mike to wonder the obvious—if perhaps she's really coming on to him this time. But a more likely possibility is that she's just being a friend, like always, and it would be a disaster if he made a pass at her and she rejected him. He could never come back in here.

"What are you thinking about now?" Eva asks him.

"What you were just talking about."

"No, I bet you were wondering if I'm coming on to you right now. If you're reading the signals right and what to do if I say 'no,' and all that shit, right?"

Mike laughs out loud.

"I like you a lot, Mike, but I don't want to lose you as a friend. We'd have fun, sure, but eventually everything would get messed up. Because we'd never make it as a couple."

"For the sake of argument, why not?"

"Because I'm not the one you're looking for."

"Well, since you want me to be more assertive, I'll go ahead and admit that you certainly appear to be what I'm looking for."

"Thank you," she says. "But I'm not. I just run this bar. I smell like smoke all the time and I flirt with a hundred men a night so I can afford my new house."

"So?"

"So, the woman you're looking for is not that. The woman you're looking for is pretty, but she's also really, really smart like you are. And she's above the stereotypical girl shit. Sort of how you aren't all macho, how you don't think the world revolves around beer and college football."

Mike wonders how long Eva has been working on this elaborate hypothesis, but before he can ask her, his mind trundles out a memory to consider, a face he hasn't been able to get out of his mind the past week.

"Do you know someone like that?" Eva asks.

"I don't know."

"Oh, give me a break. You *do* know someone like that. Someone you'd like to date."

Mike looks away from Eva, wondering for a moment where Samantha went, or what Larry might be up to.

"How do you know her?"

"I met her on my flight back to Dallas last week."

"What does she do?"

"She's a television news anchor."

"Not in Wichita, I guess. Not from what I've seen lately."

"No, in Dallas. Her name is Kelly Smith."

"Really? Kelly Smith?"

Mike nods.

"Doe she have dark blonde hair, a little long?"

"That's her," Mike says. "So you've seen her on the news, too? I guess I'm the only one who hasn't. Larry thought I was an idiot for not knowing who she was."

"I don't know her from Dallas. She used to be on Channel three in Phoenix, if it's the same Kelly Smith. Every guy in town was in love with her."

"I can see why."

"So you talked to her?"

Mike spends a few moments relating the story to Eva, from the moment he saw her until their abrupt parting in the airline terminal. He feels stupid as he talks, as if he's assigning too much importance to a fleeting, chance encounter he had on an airplane.

"Well, you have to talk to her again, Mike."

"I just told you she said no to that."

"So what? There isn't anything wrong with trying once, just to let her know you're more than casually interested. The very fact that you initiated an actual conversation with her tells me she must have really done it for you."

"So I just call her up at the station and say, 'Hi, I'm that guy from the airplane. You wanna go out?' "

"Mike, how do you possibly run the super collider when you're this obstinate?"

"But you make everything sound so easy! Just call her up, no big deal. Who cares if she thinks I'm a stalker?"

"One call is not stalking. Besides, she already knows you."

"Right. She already knows me."

"You sound like Larry," she says. "Parroting me like that."

"Are you sure this is a good idea?"

"Did you like her?"

Mike looks away. "Did I like her? Boy, did I ever."

3

Later, he's at home, sitting in the dark, his face bright with the phosphorous light of his computer monitor, eyes droopy with alcohol. From the Channel 8 website Kelly Smith is staring at him, and she's just as beautiful rendered digitally as she was in person.

Her bio doesn't provide much information. Attended the University of Virginia and began her career doing traffic for a small station in Richmond. Then beat reporter in Nashville, morning anchor in Kansas City, and finally her first principal anchor job in Phoenix. She loves Dallas, is a huge Cowboy fan, and so on. Below the bio, two blue, underlined words beckon him. *E-mail Kelly.*

Of course he can't call her. There is no way he could muster the nerve for that. But e-mail? Perhaps, with enough time, he can fashion a reasonably enticing message.

He clicks the link and Microsoft Outlook opens a new mail window.

In the "Subject" line he types

Hey there

The two words sit there looking lonely. He depresses the "shift" key and then the number 1. Now it says

Hey there!

Mike spends five minutes trying to decide if the exclamation point looks too upbeat, too desperate. In the end he decides to leave it.

Finally, after hammering away for twenty minutes, Mike reads the message all at once. The product of his work, he notices, has reached epic levels of nonsense.

Hi Kelly,

My name is Mike McNair. I met you on the plane ride from Atlanta last week, remember?

I wanted to tell you again how much I enjoyed talking to you. It's not that often you meet someone and just hit it off right away, you know? I suppose if you aren't available, that probably means you have a boyfriend. But if you were just worried that I was a stranger, that you didn't know me well enough, then what I'll do here is tell you a little more about myself, and then we won't be strangers anymore!

I was born in New Orleans, but mainly grew up in Williston, North Dakota. My dad was in the oilfield, and his company moved us there when I was three. He thought it would be a short assignment, but I ended up graduating from high school in Williston. I studied at Berkeley and also did a little work with Anton Zeilinger at the University of Innsbruck in Austria.

Finally I got a job at Fermilab, the particle accelerator in Illinois, which is much smaller than the NTSSC. I dated a girl while I worked there, but eventually I   blah blah blah this is such bullshit this e-mail is going nowhere and who in the hell would want to read such boring drivel, it's three-fifteen in the goddamn morning and I'm tired and my job is probably in jeopardy and I ought to just go to bed and

And then the phone rings. ADAMS LARRY, the caller ID says. "Hello?"

"I think we have something."

"It's late, Larry." He glances again at the e-mail and deletes everything but the first line. "What are you talking about?"

"I'm talking about Higgs, you jackass."

"And?"

"And I was talking to Samantha—that woman is a bitch, by the way, she—"

"Larry."

"Right. Anyway, she was going on about luminosity, like she does, and she had this necklace, this stone, it was a diamond but it made me think of silica for some reason, layers, and then I got an idea about the detector, about why our triggers might need to be adjusted."

"Are you sure, Larry?"

"When you see my new models, you'll understand why I called you at three o'clock in the morning. We might have been generating Higgs all this time and. . . ."

Larry trails off, the prospect of success silencing him.

"You think the triggers need to be adjusted?" Mike asks.

"Based on the new models, I'd say we'll need to loosen them. But Landon won't go for it. Don't you remember the last time we upgraded the Grid? He said—"

"I don't give a shit what he said," Mike snaps. "I'm asking for more processors. When we started this project, he told us never to worry about money. If he can hire new people at the drop of a hat, he can buy us some more processing power. I'm telling him Monday morning. And then you—"

"Get my team to work on the new program. I'm there, boss."

And when Larry is gone, when Mike is off the phone and suddenly stone-cold sober, his heart leaps at the sight of Kelly Smith smiling on his monitor. His fingers fly across the keyboard, clicking and clacking, until he fires off the e-mail during a surge of confidence. In this moment, he cannot imagine a negative response from the object of his affection. He cannot imagine Donovan denying his request to upgrade the Grid. Eva was right: Sometimes it's not enough to reason your way through a problem. Sometimes you just have to tell people what you want.

Mike grabs a few bottles of water from the kitchen and returns to his desk. He logs onto the NTSSC network, giddy with the possibility of new and better GEM data, and forgets all about heading to bed.

4

Kelly's normal assignment is to anchor the news desk every weeknight at six and ten, but once a month the second-team anchors do a late Friday newscast to give Ted and her an early start to the weekend. And so Kelly finds herself stuck on Highway 75, enduring rush-hour traffic on the way home, a whole Friday evening in front of her. A whole Friday evening alone.

She remembers a similar Friday months ago, when she and James had been clinging desperately to the years they had built together, years that would be wasted if they broke up. He'd been searching for a pair of shoes, shoes and a tie for an interview with Nortel. He wanted to shine for the recruiter, he told her, because it was time to get a job again. He didn't want to take her money anymore. He made nine orbits around the perimeter of the shoe department and couldn't stop staring at a pair of Johnston and Murphy lace-ups.

"I like them," she said.

"Me, too."

"But James," and she lowered her voice for this, knowing her words would embarrass him. "They're a hundred and sixty-five dollars."

"So?"

"So, do you think it's smart to drop that kind of money for shoes considering your finances right now?"

"I want to look good for the interview," he said. "That's why I asked you to help me shop for these shoes. And the tie. We haven't even looked at the ties yet and already you think I'm spending too much money."

Kelly rolled her eyes. This was exactly the thing he couldn't see, refused to see, that no matter how much she loved him, she couldn't kick in money every time he wanted to spend a little extra. She felt like a bank, not a romantic partner.

"What are you thinking about?" James asked her.

"Nothing. Did you decide on those?"

"I guess."

"Come on, James. If you're going to spend the money on them you might as well enjoy it."

"How can I enjoy it with you trying to make me feel guilty?"

"You're right," she said. "I'm sorry. I like the shoes. If you think they'll help you get the job, then it makes sense."

Finding the tie was easier. A cute red-haired sales clerk named Autumn came around the counter to help him look through the racks. She asked what the occasion was, and James told her about his interview to be a tech writer for Nortel. Autumn seemed impressed by this—"Writing is not my thing," she admitted—so James pushed forward, revealing that he was also a budding screenwriter.

"Interesting to watch you flirt with a girl while I'm standing right there," Kelly said later, on their way out of the mall.

"I wasn't flirting with her."

"Look, James. I know we haven't been intimate all that much lately. You've been going out with your friends, I've had work—"

"What are you talking about?"

"I'm trying to tell you that I understand. I understand how, when that sales girl showed a little interest, how you might have taken the bait. It's nice to feel wanted."

"Kelly," James said.

"Please, Baby. Please hear me out. This—"

"Come on, Kelly. Not here. Not now."

They marched through the mall, and all around them kids were talking and laughing and threatening to buy costume jewelry. To Kelly it seemed as if the two of them were fifteen years older than anyone else around. Older but just as single, and perhaps back to the end of that desperate line where thirty-year-old people stood hoping to meet a spouse.

"All right," James said, after they reached the parking lot. "I see what you're trying to say. But we have to talk about this. We have to think."

"I *have* thought. A lot. This isn't a relationship we're in."

"Then what the hell is it?"

"It's two people going in different directions—and one of them is devoting all his energy to achieving his dream."

"I love you, Kelly."

"I know. But it's not enough anymore."

"You've already made up your mind, haven't you?" he asked.

"Kelly Smith Says What She Means. That's what the commercials say, right? You say what you mean, and you're breaking up with me, and I have no say in it at all. But I guess I never did, since you're the one who makes six hundred thousand dollars a year."

"That is not fair!"

"Yeah?" he said. "Neither is this." He looked at her car and then back at her face. "How in the hell am I supposed to get home? Wait a minute. I don't have a home! You just broke up with me. Where am I supposed to go?"

"James," she said. "You don't have to just up and leave. You can take time to find an apartment. You. . . ."

Kelly steers the Acura into her driveway. She walks inside, and her heels sound like gunshots on the hardwood. It would be nice if James were here now. She'd like to tell someone about the big news at the station, that Jeff Pearson was officially hired today as the new general manager. She'd like to tell him about what her news director, Frank Mitchell, said when he heard the announcement. Just two words: *Big changes.* With three years left on her four-year contract, Kelly doesn't necessarily like the words *big changes* when used in connection with her job. But James isn't here, so she grabs a cup of yogurt from the kitchen, heads to her bedroom, and crawls into bed with her newest book. *Huckleberry Finn* was illuminating, Twain's mastery of language and character so complete that she's decided to read another of his works. *Letters from the Earth,* as it happens.

But it's a battle between her eyelids and gravity almost at once. The next time she opens her eyes the clock radio says 3:16 AM. So she stumbles into the bathroom and squirts saline into her eyes. Wanders around the house in a daze. Probably she should go back to bed, try to sleep for a while longer, but now she's wide awake. Her ears are buzzing. Her head is receiving radio transmissions of some kind. Her mouth tastes like death.

So she brushes her teeth, washes her face, and then stumbles into the kitchen on a search for real food. Screw the yogurt. She makes a peanut butter and jelly sandwich and pours a tall glass of milk. Heads back down the hallway, the empty, echoing hallway. In her office the computer hums, the high-speed Internet connection always on, because Kelly never knows when a story idea might occur to her, when something she read on the wire earlier in the day might inspire the concept for a feature. She sits down and is about to open her browser when she notices the envelope in her system tray.

The e-mail messages from her viewing audience come in all forms, with such predictability and uniformity that she could set her watch by them. Praise, scorn, adulation, contempt, everything in between, repeat.

Take this one from a Mr. Stanley Ferrell (or so he calls himself):

Dear Ms. Smith,

My name is Stanley Ferrell and I just want to tell you what a great job you do on the news. I never watched the local news before you came here from Phoenix, but now I watch every night. You are very talented (and beautiful, too!)

Keep up the good work!

Stanley Ferrell

She taps out her boilerplate reply for male fans:

Dear Stanley,

Thanks so much for your message. It's wonderful to know that our work here at Channel 8 means so much to the viewers. I appreciate your personal comments, and remember—don't touch that dial!

Best,
Kelly Smith

The letters and messages and occasional phone calls, positive or negative, meant a lot to her when she first started as a reporter in Richmond, and her emotions often followed fan reactions to her work, their opinions of her. She cried an ocean of tears during her first several years, until she learned to temper her feelings about it all. She still cares what they have to say—these people are, as a whole, the subject of her stories, and she cares about their lives and how she reports on them—but it's simply impossible to take the feedback too seriously when it differs so wildly from one viewer to the next. Like this one:

Dear Kelly,

You are such a complete bimbo. How could you possibly think the Dallas Desperadoes are an NFL football team? We HAVE an NFL team in Dallas already. Did you ever hear of the Dallas COWBOYS? Winner of FIVE Super Bowls? Helloooo? Earth to Kelly!

Mitch Pellner
Richardson

Kelly knows the Desperadoes aren't an NFL team. The comment the pleasant Mr. Pellner is referring to took place last night, an on-camera joke for which he had likely missed the setup. She won't respond to this message because all it will do is embarrass Mr. Pellner or antagonize him further. Or both. She deletes it and moves on.

A couple of polite messages follow—a woman who thanks her for being a female role model for her daughter, a viewer who appreciated her story on Mexican American children who suffer in school because they can't speak English. Here is a viewer imploring her to wear less eye makeup. Here is one warning her against cutting her hair again (it's finally growing out so please leave it alone this time). And then she clicks on this one from joonoreactor@yahoo.com:

My darling Kelly,

Do you know how truly beautiful you are, how incredibly sexy you are? When you come on the television at six and ten I cannot do anything but watch you and think about you and think how crazy those guys on the set must be to sit right next to you and not be able to kiss you. I want to kiss you and hug you and smell your precious hair. Don't cut your hair anymore okay? It looks so much better long and I can picture it splayed over your naked shoulder blades, thrown there when you look back at me while I fuck you, while I FUCK you and your precious red lips pouty and wet and oh Jesus Christ you are the ONE YOU ? aRE THE ONE I THINK I ANT TO CALL you and please you want to talk to me not hang up on me your beautiful eyes glistening and sparkly

ONE OF ITS HEADS SEEMED TO HAVE A MORTAL WOUND AND THE WHOLE WORLD WORSHIPPED THE BEAST AND IT WAS ALLOWED TO RULE FOR 42 MONTHS AND MAKE WAR ON THE SAINTS. AND THEN I SAW A NEW HEAVEN AND A NEW EARTH AND BEHOLD> BEHOLD>>>BEHOLD? AND THE TIME IS NEAR BEHOLD I AM COMING SOON I AM the ALPHA the OMEGA the FRIST and the LAST the BEGINNING and the END. Amen.

What are you going to do?

GOD IS GOD.

She reads this one again. She wonders what sort of delusion would permit someone to verbally rape her and then quote from Revelations. She saves the message in a folder labeled STALKERS, where she can retrieve it on Monday and print it for Frank.

It's a relatively hidden aspect of her job, this distasteful interaction with disturbed fans. She's received even crazier messages in the past, e-mails with attached image files of men's exposed genitals, men kissing full-page color photos of her, and so on. One guy in Phoenix even managed to get her on the phone and whispered that he loved the way she visited his living room every evening.

The computer chimes. Someone sending her another e-mail. At 3:30 in the morning? She clicks back over to the e-mail list, ready to simply delete the new entry, when she sees the e-mail address: mmcnair@ntssc.com. The subject: HEY THERE!

Hi Kelly,

My name is Mike McNair. I met you on the plane ride from Atlanta last week. Remember the photons?

I know you said you weren't available right now, and I suppose that means you have a boyfriend. But in case you don't, or if it's not serious, I just wanted to let you know that I really enjoyed our conversation. I guess I already told you that. Probably I should just say that I would really like to see you again.

If you don't check these messages yourself then some assistant is surely laughing at me right now. But if you are reading this, and if you would consider getting together sometime, e-mail me or even call if you like. I'm at (972) 555-0409.

Otherwise, it was very nice meeting you.

Mike

Okay, so it's e-mail, not her favorite medium of communication, but he was polite. Unassuming. She turned him down and now he's trying again.

Maybe she doesn't have to turn him down again.

But she can't respond right now. It's 3:30 in the morning. Responding now would make her seem way too accessible. And she should be in bed at this time of night, anyway. And there is the book, *Letters from Earth*. Maybe she can read a little of that and then fall asleep.

Or maybe she can try to read but not comprehend the words, because her mind is elsewhere, because she keeps picturing the airplane and her conversation with Mike McNair.

5

"No," Donovan says.

It's Monday morning, two days after Larry's late-night phone call, and the three of them are standing in Mike's office, discussing the need to buy more hardware. Relaxing the software triggers, after all, will record more events, which means more processing power and more storage. Donovan reserves the approval for such expenditures.

"Landon," Mike says.

"I told you already that I wasn't going to spend any more money on the Grid," Donovan continues. "This is the third time since we broke ground that you guys have asked for more computing power. And I've always given you what you wanted. I've always been a blank check. But no more."

"Landon, you hired me to find Higgs, and that's what I'm trying to do. We've come so far. How can you let a little money get in the way now?"

"It's not a little money!" Donovan thunders. "You make more money than ninety percent of the people in this country, Mike, and still it would take you fifty thousand years to make as much money as I've personally dumped into this fucking super collider. Fifty thousand years! So don't berate *me* for allowing a *little* money to get in the way."

"So what are we supposed to do? I just told you we need to

change the program because we might be producing Higgs and not know it. If you don't want to add hardware, what are we supposed to do? Just give up?"

Donovan glances briefly at Larry—who so far has said nothing—and looks back at Mike. "We're not giving up. You guys have invested a lot of time and energy into your detection process, and I believe it works. You're smart men, and I know you've done a good job so far. What we need is to increase beam luminosity. Produce more collisions."

"What?"

"More collisions means more opportunities to produce a Higgs particle. Luminosity isn't something we've tinkered with lately, so that's what we'll do next."

"Landon," Mike implores. "You know this process is not that simple. You can't just turn up the lights and see better. It's much more complex—"

"Don't talk down to me, Mike."

"But more collisions means more data to sift through. We'll still need additional—"

"If there turns out to be too much data, we can always tighten the software triggers a little."

"*Tighten* them?"

"Mike—"

"Donovan, you've got to listen to me. We can't just—"

"Samantha said—"

"Samantha? Is she the one making decisions around here now?"

"Be careful, Mike. That's dangerous ground you're walking on."

"Landon, these things take time. You don't just fire up a brand-new accelerator and then nine months later take home the trophy. Designing this machine, its software, tweaking everything, it's as much an art as it is science. You have to coax the thing into delivering what you want. It's painstaking sometimes. It could take *years* to find the—"

"You don't have years!" Donovan roars.

"What do you mean? I explained this to you up front. I don't understand what—"

Donovan steps closer to Mike, and Larry all but shrinks out of sight. "I'm going to make it clear for you, sir. I'm the boss here. I built this machine, and with your highly respected input I decide how it is run. Samantha is going to make her luminosity changes, and you're going to help her with whatever she needs. If you don't like it, you know where the door is. Have I made myself clear?"

Mike stands with Donovan, toe to toe, and for a moment considers doing what he has never done in his life—the impulsive decision that makes a good story but mangles a perfectly good career. For a moment he considers walking out the door and away from Donovan, away from his life's work and the NTSSC forever. But in reality he could no more walk away from this multibillion-dollar facility—a project that is as much his legacy as Donovan's—than he could ignore Kelly Smith if she marched into his office and begged him to go out with her. Because while Mike is confident enough to allow that he is something of a gifted scientist, able to understand the most specialized areas of experimental physics and also provide leadership to an army of researchers, he also knows Donovan would simply replace him with Samantha. Who would likely lead the team well enough to eventually find Higgs.

It's a plug-and-play world, after all. Mike himself was plugged into this job when other, more experienced physicists could have been chosen. And it's this humility, this disciplined understanding of his place in the world, that allows him to back down from Donovan. That has in fact allowed him to work so long with such a meddling tyrant in the first place. But it isn't easy. Because as he takes a step backward, as his eyes briefly shift away from Donovan's and toward Larry (who is obviously enjoying his front-row seat in this real-life soap opera) Mike must also admit that his billionaire boss *is* a man who cannot be replaced—it's *his* plug-and-play world, and not only must Mike admit this to himself, he must also survive the smug look on Donovan's face as the jerk waits for Mike to realize it.

"Yes," Mike says finally. "You've made yourself clear."

"Good. Samantha will require your assistance from time to time over the next couple of weeks. You will help her in every way possible. I will see you gentlemen later."

Donovan turns and leaves the office. Mike goes back to his desk without looking at Larry. He clicks over to Outlook and doesn't find a return e-mail from Kelly, but really she probably hasn't even received the message yet. He sent it on Friday night and assumes she is a weeknight anchor. She might not even arrive at the station until three or four o'clock in the afternoon.

Larry gradually makes his way to the visitor's chair and sits. "What do you make of that?"

Mike grunts. He senses (and dreads) Larry's desire to dissect every beat in the previous scene.

"I've seen him get angry before," Larry continues, "but wow. I thought he was going to take a swing at you there for a minute."

"He wasn't going to take a swing at me."

"I know, I know. But he must be under a lot of pressure, because obviously there isn't any other reason why the Higgs search should be on a timetable."

"Why would he be under pressure? Every investor should know it could take years to produce Higgs from the machine, if at all."

"Sure, but why else would he act like that?"

"I don't know. But it definitely seems odd to me. This place has been hemorrhaging money since we broke ground, he's thrown it at anything and everything we've asked for, and now he's watching his pennies? Something's different. I get the idea he doesn't trust me anymore."

"He has to trust someone," Larry points out. "He can't run the show by himself."

"It sounds like he trusts Samantha right now."

Larry looks at him for a moment without saying anything. "What, you think he brought her here to replace you?"

"You heard what he said. 'You'll help her in any way possible.' Sort of undermines my decision-making power a little, doesn't it?"

"Well, I guess we don't have much choice there. But if Sam's luminosity improvements don't help, I'm sure you'll get your money. You always do."

Mike smiles a little. "I hate the stupid games you have to play. I know he helped pay for this thing, I know he's the reason we're here, but come on."

"He's an armchair physicist," Larry adds. "He's the boss."

Mike just shakes his head. "You know, I love it when people come to me, when they've read Greene or Hawking or Lederman, and tell me how much they enjoyed learning about physics. When they admit to spending a few hours trying to understand the fantastic world around them instead of watching a bunch of idiots vote themselves off an island. But with Landon, just because you know more physics than the average person doesn't mean you're qualified to run the goddamn accelerator."

"You don't have to convince me."

"I know."

"So," Larry says. "What's up with Kelly Smith?"

"I don't know. You're the stalker."

"*I'm* the stalker? Didn't I hear Eva tell you to call her?"

"You heard that?"

"Yep."

"And I saw *you* talking to Amy Cantrell."

Larry recoils, and Mike wishes he didn't have to discuss this again.

"I'm not even supposed to talk to her off campus? Is this Nazi Germany?"

"Larry—"

"Anybody else could walk up and talk to her there. I don't see what—"

"Larry, please. We've known each other a long time. I can't command you to leave her alone away from work. I'm just suggesting it as your friend. Remember Rachelle?"

Larry looks away from him. At the floor. At the wall.

"You followed her home, man. You kept driving past her house. If I hadn't—"

"Would you stop reminding me how you saved my ass? Please?"

"I just don't want to see you make the same mistake. Landon is volatile, man. She goes to him, there might not be anything I can do."

"All right. Fine. Can we move on to something else now?"

"Sure. I'm sorry."

Larry relaxes a little. "So what about Kelly Smith? Did you call her?"

"Why would I call her? She said she wasn't available."

"And you told Eva you really liked her."

"Okay, so tell me how those two things are related to each other."

"The woman sat there with an open book in her hand and talked to you for *two hours* on the airplane. Available or not, she wouldn't have done that if she didn't like you."

"She could be engaged. She could be married. She's not going to divorce her husband just because she talked to me on an airplane."

"She's not married. Or engaged."

"How do you know that?"

"I just do. I see the news a lot. They fill in the gaps with those banal segues and sometimes a personal note or two. Over time you kind of get to know the people."

"Get to know them? Larry, it's their job to seem accessible on television. You don't get to know anyone by watching them read the news."

"So Eva thinks you're the man but tells you to go after Kelly. But you don't call her and you don't put the moves on Eva, so you're basically thumbing your nose at both of them. And this weekend you'll be moaning about not having a date."

"I didn't say I didn't call her."

"So you *did* call. And?"

"And nothing. I sent an e-mail. On Friday night. It's Monday. She hasn't even read it yet."

"Oh, boy," Larry says, and stands. "This should be exciting."

"Where are you going? Don't tell anyone, all right?"

"Of course I won't tell anyone. But I've got status reports to run. It's Monday, remember?"

"Right. And Larry?"

"Yeah?"

"Thanks for talking to me. I appreciate having someone to vent to."

"No problem, boss. Glad to be here for you."

He watches Larry go and then turns to his computer, where he begins working on his own status updates. You can't work for Donovan without being a PowerPoint expert, without the ability to summarize the weekly progress of your life's work into terse bullet points and colorful pie charts and—

And it really bugs him, Donovan's apparent shift in allegiance, his new conviction that luminosity is the answer, that Samantha is the key to finding Higgs. Mike isn't stupid. Despite constant praise from his boss, despite the confidence Donovan demonstrated in him by hiring an intelligent but inexperienced physicist to head the super collider, Mike knows that in the end only one thing matters: success. Donovan will do anything to achieve his goals. No amount of money is too much to spend, no friendship is too sacred that it can't be betrayed in order to secure his place in history—the great philanthropist who personally bankrolled a multibillion-dollar project to further the cause of science. Mike understands this. He knows what role he plays in this big-budget film, this special effects–laden project financed and directed by men who control money on the scale of nations. But to be summarily replaced by someone brought in from another facility, to have his work assumed like a qualify-friendly home mortgage, and for Donovan to be so fucking blunt about it . . . it makes Mike sick. He's only spent his entire academic and brief professional life imagining a time when the structure of matter and energy is fully understood, dreamed of a world laid open and bare for man to understand and manipulate at will, a defined and logical universe governed by distinct, organized laws. He tries, really tries, to live a life where the pursuit of truth is paramount. It's his dream to help write a small piece of the universe's instruction manual, and now some asshole businessman wants to replace him. Never mind that it's the same businessman who granted him this opportunity in the first place. The man has no appreciation of the magnificent universe that spawned him, has no concept of the miracle of sentient life, and—

A new idea occurs to him about the triggers. An idea that could make something happen quickly, to convince Donovan that he, Mike, is still a relevant entity, someone to keep around just a little longer. But he needs to see some data on the most recent rejection samples, so he switches over to e-mail and sends Larry the request. Then he goes back to his PowerPoint presentation, drawing text boxes and importing figures from Excel.

In the system tray, right next to the digital clock, an Outlook envelope appears. He clicks on it and finds a reply from Larry that says,

No problem on the rejection samples. I'll get right on it.

I bet when you saw the envelope in your system tray you thought it was Kelly Smith, huh? ☺

L

Mike laughs and calls up his smiling pie chart again.

6

Larry sits there for a minute, staring blankly at his computer. The report. Rejection samples.

Fantastic, then.

Stupid arrogant fuckface. Like it matters if I give you this report or that report. Like you're really going to find Higgs. It's *my* Grid, man. My software applications. And what killer apps they are, let me just tell you. Let's chew on that for a minute, Mr. I'm Just Looking Out for Your Best Interests. Like with Carrie. Always looking out for me, you bet. Keep an eye on Salieri, just in case he goes a little crazy on you. Sure, I'll send you a report. That's what I'm here for. To send you fucking reports.

He hops on the Internet. Googles Kelly Smith. Here she is (in an elegant black dress) accepting an award during her stint in Phoenix. Here she is in Richmond, a little hungrier and less put together, dressed in a blazer and khakis. Here is her bio photo from Channel Eight in Dallas.

Larry doesn't live in Dallas. If he didn't watch so much TV, if he hadn't reprogrammed his satellite dish, he would have never even heard of Kelly Smith. But aside from being a hottie, there must be something special about her if Mike is willing to e-mail her. If there's a pickier man on the planet, Larry hasn't met him. And if Mike is interested, then so is Larry. In fact maybe he's sort of obsessed with her all of a sudden. Sure, he's probably never going to meet her. Obviously he won't. And even if he did somehow meet her, she would never consider him a romantic prospect.

But they never do, do they? Like Jillian with her note. Hey, Larry. I wrote this for you. Jillian was one of the starlets in tenth-grade history, and every day he smiled at her, he tried to dress nice for her. He used all his extra money to buy two expensive wool sweaters just like the rich guys wore. He wore them for Jillian. Sometimes he whispered her name under his breath. *Their* names under his breath. Because sometimes it was Staci

Williams. Sometimes it was Kim Jones. He tried to dress like they wanted. He prayed for one of them to notice him. And one day Jillian handed him a folded-up note, and she told him to wait until after class, but he couldn't, he couldn't wait to read what she'd written him. He unfolded it when the teacher began reading from the textbook, when Jillian wasn't looking, and the note said, *Larry you can't wear a wool sweater with Adidas sneakers. I'm just telling you for your own good. If you don't have penny loafers then you shouldn't wear sweaters at all.* The words he'd memorized long ago. Branded himself with them. *And haven't you noticed that guys wear their hair short now? This is 1987, not 1982. You look like Shaun Cassidy with those wings. And stop staring at me all the time. It creeps me out.* Right there at his desk he'd read it, because of course he'd believed the note to be admittance, not rejection. Even while he was reading it he kept thinking there would be some kind of invitation. Stupidly he kept reading to find an apology or *I'm just kidding* or something. But instead just a final insult. *I told my boyfriend and he said you shouldn't stare at me anymore. He said you were a FUCKFACE. I didn't say it, HE did. So I guess that's all Larry. C-ya! Jillian. P.S. Don't W/B!*

These days his sights are set a little higher. The real starlets of the world are women on television and in the movies. He doesn't bother trying to dress nice for them anymore. That never worked, and besides, these starlets live far away. But distance doesn't stop him from dreaming about them. About Jennifer Love Hewitt. About Jennifer Aniston. Or Britney Spears. Or Shania Twain. So many gorgeous TV starlets. So many letters to write. So many chances to repay the favor. And here is Kelly Smith, she lives so close, she is so much more accessible than the others. He could watch her day in and day out if he wanted. Week after week. And still it wouldn't matter because Mike will end up stepping between them. Just like Carrie.

He can't let it slide anymore. What kind of man is he if he lets such a thing slide?

Samantha's door is open when he approaches, her head hidden behind a massive wide-screen monitor. Larry clears his throat. She peeks around the screen, eyes framed by unusual and attractive glasses, and smiles at him.

"Hi, Larry."

"Hey, Samantha. What're you working on?"

"I'm evaluating your p-bar source. Why?"

"Oh, just curious. I finished my status reports a little early and thought I'd come by to see what you were up to. You're sort of where the action is right now."

"I hope you guys don't think I'm here to take over your project," Samantha says, rolling her chair away from the monitor so Larry can see her better. "I just want to help."

Larry smiles. "I'm glad you're here, actually. It's going to be so exciting when we find it. Higgs, I mean."

"I'm glad, too. But I'm not so sure Mike is happy to have me."

"What makes you say that?"

"A conversation we had at the bar on Friday. He was pretty abrupt."

"Mike's a great guy," Larry tells her. "He's done a lot for me. But he gets kind of stressed sometimes."

"If he doesn't learn to be more of a team player, it's going to cost him."

"Cost him what?"

"Donovan wants this collider to be worth the money he's poured into it, and finding Higgs will go a long way toward ensuring that it *is* a success."

"Are you implying that Donovan might replace Mike?"

Samantha stiffens. "Not at all. But you know as well as I do that—"

"Because I've been kind of worried about him lately," Larry continues. "Donovan's been riding him, even threatened to pull him off the project."

"If Donovan replaced him it could set the collider back six months."

"And Mike would lose his chance for Nobel. Which is all he seems to talk about anymore."

"He told me he didn't care about Nobel," Samantha says.

"Yeah, he tells everyone that. He doesn't want to come across as single-minded. He's afraid people will think he's shallow."

"I guess he doesn't want me here because he's afraid he might have to share the spotlight. Because if my luminosity improvements are the difference. . . ."

"Yeah," Larry says. "I know. But Mike thinks your luminosity review is a waste of time. He's confident it's the software, that loosening the triggers is the key."

"He said that?"

Larry looks away as if suddenly uncomfortable. "I shouldn't have said anything. Mike is my friend."

"Maybe so," Samantha agrees. "But he's also in charge of the Higgs search at a twelve-billion-dollar particle accelerator and shouldn't be playing favorites with the methodology. He should be open to any idea that might help."

"He is. It's just . . . I don't know."

"*I* know. He's threatened by me. Because of Nobel or because I'm a woman or whatever. We'll see what he has to say when I produce Higgs."

"Don't say anything, okay? I don't want him to lose trust in me."

"I won't. Don't worry about that."

He stands there looking at her. Allows himself to smile with her.

"I'm glad we had this talk, Larry. I think we'll work well together."

"Me, too."

"You want to get a drink after work?"

A spike of exhilaration and gooseflesh he hopes isn't obvious.

"Sure."

"Great. But let's go to Wichita Falls. I'm already tired of the bars around here."

"Fantastic, then," Larry says.

7

Mike sits through the Monday morning round of dreadful staff meetings, presentations in dark rooms describing the previous week's lack of progress toward Higgs. He tries to ignore the feeling of things slipping through his fingers. Entertains himself with fantasies of the moment when breakthrough might be achieved, when he might win back Donovan's confidence in him and more importantly prove to jealous physicists around the world that he is, in fact, qualified to be here, that he brings something memorable to the field of experimental physics. And then he's got Larry to worry about; Larry, who always manages to get himself in trouble when he finds an unwilling woman who strikes his fancy. Hell, Mike might as well call himself a stalker now, too, e-mailing Kelly after she specifically told him she wasn't available. Interesting how he can lecture Larry on following Amy around and then sit here, praying that a woman he met on an airplane will write him back. Interesting how he'll sting Larry by bringing up Rachelle, and then walk straight back to his computer after the morning meetings to check his e-mail. How he'll sit here watching the system tray for more envelopes, which occasionally arrive, tantalizing him, only to turn out to be a subordinate's vacation request or a new HR policy or last week's GEM cockpit chart. And this is ridiculous. He can't just sit here and worry about a stupid e-mail message when he should be fighting for his goddamned job. Is he really going to allow Samantha to win Donovan's approval uncontested? Let her take his job?

He picks up the phone and reaches his boss.

"This is Landon."

"You have any plans for lunch?"

Donovan doesn't answer right away. And then, "Nothing specific. I was thinking of taking out Samantha. Is this about her?"

"No, Landon, it's about the Higgs search. And what I'm going to do to make it a success."

Donovan spends a moment considering this. "If that's the case," he says, "I should bring Samantha. So she doesn't get any farther behind than she already is."

"I'd prefer if it were just you and me, actually. There are some personal issues I'd like to discuss as well."

"So this *is* about Samantha."

"Are you free for lunch or not?"

"Sure, Mike. I'll stop by your office around 11:30."

8

Donovan is the world's biggest fan of Tony Roma's Original Baby Back Ribs. Mike can't remember a lunch date with his boss that didn't involve barbecue sauce under his fingernails and pork between his teeth and the lemony smell of Wet Naps (because you can't order anything else on the menu, not when you're with Donovan—he considers such betrayal a personal affront to his culinary tastes). And while they wait for their meaty entrées among a flurry of annoyingly enthusiastic waitstaff, Mike steps immediately into the confrontation he avoided on the way over.

"Did you bring Samantha here to replace me?"

"Right to the point, I see."

"Because if you did, I think it's a mistake. She may be a wizard at luminosity, and maybe it's a good idea to replace Paul Funk if we have her, but she isn't the best person to run this facility."

"Most high-energy physicists think the same thing about you."

Mike nods. "Yes, and we both know that. You knew that when you hired me. I don't understand what's changed."

"Nothing's changed. I didn't bring Samantha here to replace you."

"So am I being paranoid, then? Because I get the feeling if I don't produce something soon, I may not be around to produce anything at all."

Mike expects an immediate answer, hopes for it, something like *Yes, Mike, you're being paranoid.* But Donovan doesn't say anything for a long time. And what he does finally say, he says without the bravado that is normally smeared across his words like grease.

"Mike, you've done a great job here. You've done everything I've asked you, and you've been honest with me, and you've treated me with respect even though it must bug the shit out of you when I try to stick my nose into the physics. But you have to understand that I have investors to answer to. And they may know—as you explained this morning—that it takes time to do this sort of science. They may know this, but it doesn't make them any less demanding. And when they demand from me, I demand from you. That's how the world works."

Just then the ribs arrive, delivered by a glassy-eyed girl wearing a stained striped shirt. Conversation ceases as Donovan dives into the slab of meat.

"You guys need anything else?" the waitress asks.

"More Wet Naps," Donovan mumbles.

Later, as they both push aside caveman plates of clean bones, Mike asks his boss why he chose Samantha in the first place.

"You gotta love Wet Naps," Donovan answers. "I always ask for extras and then put them in my car, in my golf bag, wherever. They're so refreshing."

Mike picks up the plastic wrapper of his Wet Nap and finds a phone number and web address on the reverse side.

"You could probably order a whole case of them from the manufacturer," he says. "Then you could keep them everywhere."

"What a fucking great idea," Donovan says sincerely. "I knew there was a reason I kept you around."

"That's me," Mike mumbles. "I'm the idea guy."

Donovan leans forward a little and lowers his volume. "Look, Mike. Samantha came recommended, all right? I may have poured six billion of my own dollars into this machine, but I still answer to someone, same as you."

And now Donovan looks around, like someone in a movie, as if he's worried about surveillance. "Something's going on. This woman, I was asked to take her on nearly a year ago, and I declined. I have no interest in replacing the people you hire. But over the past few months the pressure has gotten stronger and stronger until I finally didn't have any choice. I don't know what the big deal is, but this guy . . . he wanted her here, and so here she is. All right? And she's going to have her hand in everything. Her title may be Beam division head, but her influence will reach a lot farther than that."

"Landon—"

"And the Grid? I can't just. . . . That thing is the most powerful computer system in the world, Mike. If I ask for more money—"

"Why do you have to ask?"

"Because I'm broke, that's why! I sunk everything I had into this machine and it wasn't enough. I had commitments from hundreds of investors, and then after we broke ground they began pulling out. A few here, a few there, and pretty soon it was looking like the first super collider all over again—dig some of the hole and then run out of money."

"Why did so many investors pull out?"

"I don't know. But I kept pouring in money to keep the project going, hoping for a miracle. And about the time I was ready to throw in the towel, I got one. A big investor. Someone I'd never heard of, believe it or not. And here we are."

Mike leans back in his seat and looks around the restaurant. It's not lost on him that this building, these people, they're all here because of Landon and his secret investor. He wonders what that must feel like, to directly influence so many lives, to change the course of history for an entire town.

"Why are you telling me this now?" he asks.

"Because I'm afraid things might change. I told you before I didn't bring Samantha here to replace you, but that's only part of the truth. Just because I don't want to replace you doesn't mean it can't happen. My suggestion to you is to come up with some results. Anything, even if it's just a tease, to get this guy off my back. But I can't upgrade the Grid for you right now."

"How do you expect me to do the job if I don't have the right tools?"

"You've got the most powerful accelerator in the world," Donovan snaps. "That isn't enough?"

"But if we aren't evaluating the data properly—"

Donovan leans forward, crosses his arms in front of him. "I mentioned this to Samantha, you know."

"You mentioned what?"

"About upgrading the Grid. You know what she said? She said we have more than we need. She said we have a surplus of computing power and storage. Our dedicated network of processors dwarfs what they're planning to use when the new detector at CERN goes live next year."

Mike says nothing. Waits.

"She said if there is any problem with the Grid, it's the software. Either it's not optimized well enough or there are weaknesses in the design."

This is a direct indictment of Larry, who oversees the Grid and the hundreds of developers whose applications run on it.

"She's already looking into the program structure, even the code. Don't tell Larry."

"What do you mean, don't tell him? You're going to let her meddle in his affairs and not even tell him?"

"There's no way to know how he would react. The guy's a little high strung, Mike."

"Landon."

"I know this is a lot to take in. I know it. I wish I had better news. I know you got this fucking collider up and running more quickly than anyone thought possible. I know that. But some people's memories are shorter than mine."

Donovan stands and stuffs a handful of Wet Naps into the pocket of his slacks. A handful of free Wet Naps into a pair of five-hundred-dollar slacks. And before Mike can wriggle his way out of the booth, his boss leans down and adds, "Find me something, Mike. I can't be any more honest with you than that."

9

Donovan, back in his office after lunch. Sitting there, staring at his computer monitor, watching the stock ticker crawl by. Reads a little business news on Bloomberg, checks out the headlines on CNN. Sometimes he wonders what it's all for. What really matters. Since he was a kid it was money, always money. Lemonade stand. Lawn mowing. Bike repair. There seemed to be something alluring and nearly evolutionary about equating success with quantifiable units—I have more bananas than you, I killed more buffalo than you, I control more square miles of Europe than you—so whatever Donovan could do to make money, he did. Worked shit jobs in high school. Alienated his friends by selling Amway in college. His prayers were to the gods of capitalism, his goal to achieve financial immortality. And someone up there must have listened, because one day the market noticed his little, self-funded telecom venture, and the exploding Internet economy turned him into a ten-figure man.

With the money came a kind of power. The ability to direct thousands of employees, the means to purchase companies and land and control a chunk of the Internet backbone. It was heady stuff for a while. But at some point Donovan realized that the most celebrated men weren't simply powerful—they were also benevolent. They championed causes for the greater good of humanity. Abraham Lincoln, Gandhi, Jesus—these men are who Donovan yearned to be compared to, not Bill Gates. He saw Congressional shortsightedness as his ticket to true greatness. The United States of America doesn't have enough money to fund the advancement of particle physics? Landon Donovan does! He would be the answer to short-term politicians and their pork barrels. He would bypass the corruption-saturated lawmaking process and build the super collider on his own. Proving once again the power of human ingenuity. The inherent success of the American dream.

Instead he exposed the illusion, the hidden lie of capitalism. And what hypocrisy that would seem to be, coming from a man of his wealth, but how else to explain the utter lack of interest in his endeavor, the disregard for his grand idea? The stories he told Mike at lunch shame him, because lack of funding wasn't necessarily the problem. The real barrier turned out to be something much more sinister and subversive—the old money power structure.

He couldn't secure building permits from local governments. No cooperation from the state of Texas. Laughter from the U.S. Department of Energy. Wealthy benefactors looked the other way when he tried to arrange financial partnerships. Donovan would have been forced to give up the idea altogether if not for the call from Abraham Lange, if not for the man's six billion dollars and—more important—his magical ability to open doors. A week after their agreement the civil barriers suddenly vanished. Permits were miraculously issued. Land ownership somehow clarified itself. Contractors jockeyed for the chance to bid on the tunnel and the detectors and the hangar-size buildings. It was amazing to Donovan that even in America, even when you built a powerful and relevant company from scratch, even when you were worth almost seven billion dollars, you could still be made to stand outside in the rain, you could be rejected by the old guard simply because you hadn't been born into—

His phone rings. An international number, country code 41. Allgäuer again.

"This is Landon."

"How was your lunch, Mr. Donovan?"

"It was wonderful. Thanks for your concern, Karsten."

"McNair wants to add to the Grid again?"

Donovan doesn't answer this. Doesn't ask Allgäuer how he knows, because the answer is clear. Samantha.

"The Grid will remain unchanged, of course. McNair will make no significant changes to the detection effort during this transition."

"Why don't we just let him go now, then? Why this lame duck phase?"

"Because he is a well-liked spokesman. He is admired among his subordinates. Haste makes waste, after all."

"Yeah, well he's also a human being. He deserves to be treated like one."

"An ironic statement coming from a wealthy American businessman. Corporate leaders in your country are not known for their benevolence when it comes to consideration for the common worker. A certain energy company comes to mind."

"Well, I guess you've caught me. I guess I have a conscience after all."

Allgäuer laughs. "You honestly have no idea what to do with your newfound place in the world, do you?"

"Fuck you, Karsten."

"Either you have no idea, or you choose not to acknowledge it. I read a wonderful passage in an American novel recently. 'Elective ignorance was a great survival skill, perhaps the greatest.' I cannot express to you the enjoyment I felt when I read this—finally an author with the vision to see ultimate truth."

There is nothing to be gained by engaging this man in

conversation, so Donovan just sits there, waiting for Allgäuer to finish amusing himself.

"Can you imagine a world, Landon, in which there is nothing left to ponder? No questions left to solve? The miracle of life is just patterns of matter and energy, after all. The universe is just the sum of its swirling particles. There is no barrier to understanding it, given sufficient time and computational power."

Donovan grunts.

"Did you know," Allgäuer continues, "that if processing power continues to increase at its current exponential rate, if the overall development of technology stays its present course, in the very near future we will have the ability to manipulate matter in any way we choose? Nanotechnology is only the first step. There is no reason why we will not eventually take control of even time and space. Perhaps the most remarkable fact is that this will likely occur much more quickly than most people realize."

"I thought NeuroStor could already manipulate matter at the molecular level," Donovan says.

"Their ideas were novel, yes, but ultimately the technology was crude and produced severe anomalies. Advancements have been rapid, however. Are you familiar with the concept of nano-machines?"

"Machines the size of an atom?"

"Not the size of an atom," Allgäuer explains, "but built from individual atoms. They are essentially man-made molecules. Like carbon dioxide is two oxygen atoms and one carbon atom, these machines are also assembled from individual atoms, but their purpose is to alter or build new molecules. Imagine rearranging a pile of dirt into a potato, or sending nanomachines into the atmosphere to ferret out greenhouse gases and rebuild the ozone layer. There is no end to the benefits of this technology. Nature is a grand system of molecular manipulation, after all. Human beings inhale oxygen and combine it with glucose to produce energy for our cells, and we expel the byproducts of this process, water and carbon dioxide. Plants combine this carbon dioxide and water with energy from sunlight to make food and oxygen. Imagine purposely manipulating matter at this level, or even smaller. We could play God, Landon. We could *be* God.

"People do not seem to realize how quickly our culture has changed with the advent of invention. There was more technological change in the nineteenth century than in the preceding nine hundred years. In just the first twenty years of the *twentieth* century technology advanced more than in the entire *nineteenth* century. At this ever-increasing pace, this century will see a thousand times greater change than in the previous. Can you even imagine what that kind of change in technology could bring, considering the state of the world now?"

"I'd be glad just to have reliable service on my cell phone."

"Immortality will be within our grasp sooner than you think. What do you suppose you would do with all that time, Landon? What would you do with eternity?"

"I don't really see the point," Donovan admits. "In some ways, I've already stopped seeing the point."

"Have patience, Landon. If you help ensure the success of my project, I may have something that will change your mind."

10

Nine thirty PM. Mike still at work, sitting in the dark, watching the color graphs and diagrams describing the newest cycle on his flat-screen monitor. The beam has been at full energy for thirty minutes, and luminosity is up significantly from their last run—surpassing, in fact, the highest reading ever recorded at the NTSSC. He leans back in his chair and grunts. As frustrating as it is for Samantha to be forced on him, it's even more maddening to see her luminosity improvements have such an immediate effect.

It shouldn't matter. They should have found Higgs by now. Mike can preach to Donovan all he wants about how these things take time, that the work is as much art as science, but the real story is that this facility is more than powerful enough to resolve Higgs. Unless the Standard Model predictions are completely incorrect, unless physicists have been barking up the wrong tree for years, this experiment should produce Higgs. Should have already produced it.

If he were Samantha, if he believed, as she does, that there are weaknesses in the software designed to evaluate collision events, he might replace Larry. Find someone else to run the Grid and its team of computer scientists. If he were Samantha, he wouldn't have to worry about destroying a lifelong friendship. If he were Donovan's mysterious investment partner, he'd just fire the whole lot of them and bring in a new team.

He could go home now. There is nothing to be gained by personally monitoring a beam run. The detector records thousands of collisions per second. His brain can evaluate perhaps two or three events a minute. That's why they use computers. Why they built the most powerful network of processors in the world.

He opens Internet Explorer and calls up ESPN. Maybe, with a little luck, the Monday night game will propel his fantasy football team to its first victory of the—

A chime from the speakers and an e-mail envelope in his system tray. Probably someone from the counting house. He clicks on it.

The message is from Kelly Smith.

Mike,

Great to hear from you! I guess you found the online bios? That's where all my crazy stalker friends get my e-mail address. Not to say that you're a stalker. Are you? Ha ha, jk.

How are things going at the super collider? Any leads on the Higgs particle? You're a really smart guy, and driven, and I know you'll have success soon. I can feel it.

So I've been reading that book you recommended. Letters from the Earth. I'm wondering what you meant when you said I might find it interesting. I've heard many of the arguments before, like how did Noah get so many animals on one boat? How did dinosaurs fit on it? And anyway, if the world is only 6,000 years old, how come dinosaurs aren't mentioned in the Bible? You may be surprised to know that I agree with Twain on these points and personally think people who interpret the Bible literally are pretty selective readers.

Because if you sit down and read the actual stories, which Twain did but most have not, it's hard to disagree with his sentiment that God is the most prolific murderer in history. Genesis, Exodus, Leviticus—these are largely bloody stories of lust and adultery. Even incest.

Today it's widely believed by Christians that Satan is the biggest source of misery on Earth, but there is no denying that in the Old Testament, God certainly held His own. Personally, I think the biggest source of misery on Earth is rude, amoral people. But hey, that's just me.

At least Twain made me laugh, as always. I liked how he pointed out that everyone goes to the same Heaven and loves each other, but here on Earth all nations hate each other. Or how everyone's favorite part of a church service is when it's over. Ha ha!

Anyway, I need to finish reading through the newscast, so I better get going. But if you get a chance, I'm curious to know what you think about that book. Why would a non-religious person recommend it to someone like me? To make fun of religion, or to reassure yourself? There is this bumper sticker I saw once that I thought was interesting: "If you're living your life like there is no God, you'd better be right!"

Take care, Mike. Hope to hear from you soon.

Kelly

Mike reads through the message a few more times. He wonders how dumb a person he must be to recommend this Twain book to Kelly. It was only because he had been stalling, making conversation while he gathered the courage to ask for her phone number, but she'd actually gone out and purchased the book. Because she likes him? Respects him? It doesn't matter. Here he is trying to make a good impression, and instead he keeps insulting her beliefs.

Mike opens a reply and begins immediately to type.

Kelly,

It's never a good idea to compare science to faith. One is a universal methodology for acquiring knowledge, the other is a belief system. In the US, many Christians find scientifically acquired knowledge to be a threat to their spirituality. They see evolution or the Big Bang being taught in schools and aren't sure how to reconcile these well-supported theories with their religious beliefs. It's true that, taken literally, Genesis is incompatible with established scientific record. To a person of strong religious faith, this is deeply disturbing. But often I see retaliatory attacks against science that don't make sense. The modern world is thoroughly infused with the discoveries of science. Our culture cannot be divorced from it. So to take a few of the conclusions by evolutionary scientists or cosmologists and choose to refuse just those particular theories is not an intelligent reaction.

The lessons taught by most organized religions have provided our world with an ethical and moral backbone. I was raised in a Western, mostly Christian culture and I can't separate myself from it. I don't find spirituality incompatible

with my work. I would love nothing more than to learn of
some underlying, deeper structure of the universe that we've
yet to uncover. There are fringe physicists who believe that
human consciousness is tied to a kind of collective reality
comprised of all matter and energy. I have never found
evidence of such a thing, but I would love for
it to be true. Because like everyone else, I do not relish the
thought of death.

I keep telling myself not to be so serious with you. I keep
thinking I should tell jokes or something. But we seem to
have stumbled into this profound discussion, and I would
be lying if I said I didn't enjoy it, this thought-provoking
conversation with you. I don't care if the two of us have
different views of the world. It's not often that I meet
someone as intelligent and attractive as you. I'd like to
see you again.

Hope to hear from you again soon.

Take care,
Mike

He reads and rereads the message. Thinks about tweaking
it, about removing big sections of it, deleting the entire composition entirely. The clock reads 9:54. Will he seem too eager if he
sends the message tonight? Should he let it rest and read it again
tomorrow? Should—

He clicks and sends the message. Enough of that shit. Locks
his computer and heads for the door.

11

Near midnight now. Larry lying next to the wrinkled impression in his sheets left by Samantha. He can still smell her perfume, the humid aroma of her, and somehow he doesn't really

care. Somehow the first sex he's had in three months is nothing to him. He does not feel content, he is not basking in the luxurious pleasure of having spent himself inside her. What has your life come to when even sex with someone new is not enough?

They shared drinks at Toby's in Wichita Falls, ostensibly because Samantha wanted to get out of town, but mostly, he knows, because she didn't want to be seen with him. Not that Larry necessarily wanted to be seen with her, either. She's thin, but her nose is too small and flat. Her unprocessed hair just hangs from her head. She doesn't wear enough makeup and her breasts are too small. Even so, drinks at Toby's had pushed their conversation from Grid software architecture (during which he carefully lied) to how big was too big when it came to penis size. And forty-five minutes was a long time to wait as they drove back to Olney from Wichita, especially when her passenger hand found its way to his driver leg. To his zipper, playfully squeezing. Then a mad dash into his house, where the first time was a two-minute sprint. A second event was slower and more rewarding. Then a nap, a little conversation, and a promise to play again another time.

He gets out of bed and pulls on a pair of boxers. Stumbles into the kitchen for some peanuts and Coke. Maybe just a splash of Crown with it. On the counter he sees the magazine, the one he grabbed from the supermarket checkout aisle yesterday, unable to resist the million-watt smile of Britney Spears. She's wearing a revealing sundress and appears to once again be in shape.

Larry loves Britney Spears.

The magazine is *Us Weekly,* and it's his favorite, because printed inside, in addition to the stories about awards shows and benefit dinners and celebrity romances, are pictures with movie and television stars all going about their everyday business. *Stars—They're Just Like* Us! *They Get Pulled Over for Speeding . . . They Buy Groceries . . . They Get Their Prescriptions Filled.* Here is Tom Cruise leaving an unnamed pharmacy with a white paper bag. Here is Shania Twain purchasing vegetables at a Coop in Switzerland. And here is Meg Ryan smiling at a short Beverly Hills police officer. Larry loves this shit. Eats it up even if the manipulation is obvious, even if he hates himself while devouring page after page of celebrities that are *just like him*! And the best part of *Us Weekly* is that most captions are only one or two phrases, that most features are barely one paragraph long. Because that way he is saved the expense of his concentration. His eyes can bounce around the page admiring the likes of Carmen Electra and Lindsay Lohan and Selma Hayek (six times in fourteen pages) without bothering to dwell on the knowledge that Larry himself is not featured in this magazine, that he will never appear in this magazine, because he is forever doomed to anonymity.

Meanwhile, Pamela Anderson goes on dating rock stars, and Paris Hilton is a celebrity for no good reason, and Larry's boss e-mails Kelly Smith. And you just know she's going to answer. You just know she's going to write him back and say how *wonderful* it was to meet him on the plane and he is so *smart* and *handsome* and why don't you drive over here to Dallas and have your way with me, you big stud?

And Larry gets Samantha Aizen, domineering female physicist.

Fucking Jillian. Why does he pin everything on her, anyway? It wasn't she who caught him eating his boogers in fourth grade. She wasn't the one who laughed at him or asked him what they tasted like. Not the one who laughed when he said butter. She's not responsible for the smoldering front lines of puberty, for seventh grade, where other boys walked into the gym showers with hairy billy clubs and Larry held a towel in front of his two-inch pixie stick. Where boys kissed girls and felt their tits, and he jerked off to tattered, coverless copies of *Oui*. She *was* the one who wrote him the letter in high school, but not the one who called him FUCKFACE you didn't say it HE did. C-ya!

He remembers his transformation in college, a change that seemed miraculous at the time. His body finally matured and he found reassuring confidence in alcohol. Somehow an entire cross section of women seemed undeniably approachable, and for the first time he could utter a few lines of bullshit to someone and find himself grabbing her tits in the front seat of his car. And grab Larry did, like a kid in the Willy Wonka Chocolate Factory.

Over time, though, Larry grew bored with his newfound success. The girls he hit on at these keg parties were average looking at best and downright dowdy at worst. He knew the alcohol was betraying him. He was settling for mediocrity when sexy sorority sisters paraded around campus in shorts and white tennis shoes and pink lipstick. There was no shortage of girls with slender arms, with smooth and shapely legs, with bodies toned by a lifetime of good nutrition and regular visits to the gym. And so he redefined his strategy. If alcohol-induced confidence worked on average-looking women, he didn't see any reason why he couldn't apply similar logic to the cream of the college crop. The starlets.

But, predictably, his capacity to approach a dazzling starlet and her willingness to acknowledge his presence were not related in any way. He was told to buzz off, he was laughed at, he was ignored completely. It became clear to him that adults were no different from children. Jillians were everywhere. It would be that way forever. Until Carrie. Carrie with the wavy blond hair, Carrie who genuinely smiled. Who was pouring a beer when the keg ran out and didn't know how to change the tap. So Larry did it and spilled some beer on himself and they had a laugh. When she tried to walk away he asked for her number, and she looked at him with wide, surprised eyes. But she stopped. They talked a little more. He wrote down her number on the palm of his hand.

And then he made the mistake of bringing her to his apartment that night. Made the mistake of introducing her to Mike.

Back to dowdy women for Larry.

One could make the argument that he should be happy. That Carrie is ancient history, that Mike has spent his life since college apologizing. That Larry holds an important position at the top high-energy physics lab in the world and is well known in the Olney community. Occasionally he's even able to cast his spell upon a fallen starlet from Wichita Falls, invariably a divorced or bar-worn former beauty queen looking (finally) for love and financial stability in lieu of muscles and height. But these women—whose untouchable magnificence at the age of twenty-two had been his holy grail—bore him now. They are vacuous and selfish and angry. He hates them as individuals and collectively. And so he is thirty-six and single and lonely, an intelligent man with so much love to give, so much to share, but unrecognized as such by any worthy woman. None since Carrie.

Which means he is left to pine for celebrities, Jillian-perfect women who occupy the culturally elitist and virtually identical social stratum refused to him in high school—pretty, popular girls who date only the richest and most popular men. He visits them on the Internet, reads about them in *People* and *Us Weekly*, watches them in movies and situation comedies and on CNN. And now he watches them on the local news. He imagines himself accidentally bumping into Kelly Smith in the supermarket, has even considered driving all the way to Dallas to shop at the Target Super Center near her house, guessing that Kelly must need paper plates and dish soap and shampoo like everyone else, like *Us*. For such encounters he has memorized a fleet of opening lines, has anticipated an intricate array of her possible responses, and now considers himself ready to prove his worthiness should such an encounter actually transpire.

But really it's all for naught because of Mike McNair, who somehow stepped in front of him again, who has somehow managed to steal from him one more time. Because the more he thinks about it, the more Larry remembers that he has been in love with Kelly for months. Why else would he have reworked his satellite dish? And it's obvious now that he should never have told Mike about that. Admitting to Mike that he watches Kelly every night on the news is the same as bringing her home to meet him. Because Mike could have reworked his own satellite dish. He could have fallen in love with her just as Larry did, could have used the Grid to hack into Travelocity and look up her address and travel arrangements, could have bought himself that seat next to her on the plane. He could have prayed that she would fall in love with him. He could have prayed to her. He could have written her an e-mail message. He did write her an e-mail message.

So did Larry.

He puts down the magazine. Ambles into his study. The monitor winks to life as he grabs the mouse, and soon he is staring at the anonymous Yahoo! e-mail in-box he created for just this purpose. He's going to send her another message. Get down on his knees and pray to her. But he doesn't remember what he wrote last time, so he opens the SENT folder and finds it:

> My darling Kelly,
>
> Do you know how truly beautiful you are, how incredibly sexy you are? When you come on the television at six and ten I cannot do anything but watch you and think about you and think how crazy those guys on the set must be to sit right next to you and not be able to kiss you . . .

He reads all the way to the end, where his eyes widen, and this is why it's a good idea to read again what he wrote last time. Because he doesn't remember what he wrote last time.

> ONE OF ITS HEADS SEEMED TO HAVE A MORTAL WOUND AND THE WHOLE WORLD WORSHIPPED THE BEAST AND IT WAS ALLOWED TO RULE FOR 42 MONTHS AND MAKE WAR ON THE SAINTS. AND THEN I SAW A NEW HEAVEN AND A NEW EARTH

AND BEHOLD> BEHOLD>>>BEHOLD? AND THE TIME IS NEAR
BEHOLD I AM COMING SOON I AM the ALPHA the OMEGA the
FRIST and the LAST the BEGINNING and the END. Amen.

What are you going to do?

GOD IS GOD.

Okay. That sounds crazy. It sounds like a crazy person
wrote that message. Larry isn't crazy.

Loneliness isn't craziness.

He goes into the kitchen and pours himself another Crown
and Coke. Sucks it down and pours another. Double shot.

Back to the computer. Distracts himself from that scary
e-mail by browsing around the Internet and its endless catalog
of images. Its two-dimensional dreams. Sparkling smiles. Shadowy cleavage. Red carpet dresses. Silk and diamonds and shiny
hair. He finds a high-resolution image and opens it in Photo-
shop. Zooms in until the image of her fills his screen.

He needs music for this. With his mouse he calls up something from his trance library, heavy and methodical. Settles into
his chair. Extends his legs to their full length. Relaxes his posture
and slows his breathing. Gazes over her perfect skin, the female
shape of her, the abyss of her eyes.

He reaches for himself. Succumbs to the darkness.

A smile spreads like oil across his face.

CHAPTER SIX

1

Steve fidgets as he waits. The dizziness in his head is connected somehow to the swirling silence of the field, and the best way he's found to maintain his tenuous hold on sanity is to find ideas and situations to occupy his mind. Try to find out what is real and what is not. So he looks around the room, looking for anything, praying for some kind of help before the field swallows him whole.

The walls might be paneled in oak, the floors could be covered with spongy gray carpet. He is definitely the only waiting patient. The receptionist's painted red fingernails click sharply on the keyboard, and occasionally she looks up and smiles at him. Steve smiles back, reassurance that his abnormality will not get the better of him here, that the peaceful environment of this office is dutifully performing its purpose.

It's been a week since his breakdown. Seven days since he walked away from his interview and out of AE's offices forever. Oh, they would probably take him back if he wanted, offer company-paid counseling and less-demanding work while he struggled to regain form. But the VP job is gone, and without a forward-moving career path, Steve has no desire to continue his employment at Automotive Excellence.

He doesn't clearly remember what drove him to walk out or what ground he covered after departing the office on foot. Dreams—hallucinations—have plagued him night and day, especially at night, and he debated for several hundred continuous hours before deciding that he was not being followed after all. Certainly it's ludicrous to believe, even for a moment, that he is somehow part of a conspiracy involving a Russian prostitute, an evil Swiss doctor, and the nurse who let him in on the secret by going out of her way to provide false information.

But to ensure he is applying reasonable logic to the reality of Svetlana's death and the absence of his medical records from Zurich, Steve has made an appointment with this psychiatrist. He remembered her name—Dr. Shelly Taylor—from some long-ago conversation with a golf buddy, and now sits here awaiting his turn to unload problems on her.

Steve would still like to contact Dobbelfeld. He is a little surprised, in fact, that he hasn't heard from the man. But considering the nature of his delusion, the conspiracy and Dobbelfeld's conceivable role within it, it seems reasonable that Steve should first solicit the opinion of a third party. If Dr. Taylor listens to his story and agrees that his fall and Svetlana's are mere coincidence, that the nurse's misdirected assertions are unrelated, then he will hand over Dobbelfeld's card and ask her to contact him.

"Mr. Keeley?"

Steve looks up at the receptionist. He wants to ask about the new man in her life, the one she talked to on the phone for nine hours last night, but this would probably frighten her since she hasn't told anyone about him yet.

"Dr. Taylor will see you now."

"Thank you," he says. The door is on his right, beside the chair. He carefully opens it and steps into a room of similar décor, identical carpet and wall paneling. Also a couple of overstuffed leather chairs, a larger desk, and the obligatory sofa. Dr. Taylor, sitting behind her desk, rises to greet him.

"Hello, Mr. Keeley." She is vaguely attractive, a little severe, and he knows she struggles with her bisexuality. She gestures in the general direction of the sofa and chairs. "Please make yourself comfortable."

"Do I lie down? Or sit?"

"Whichever you like. My chair is the one nearest you. You may sit and face me or use the sofa. Your choice."

The field seems more manageable when he is at rest, so Steve decides on the sofa. Dr. Taylor approaches from the desk and takes her seat beside him.

"I have a little background information," she says. "But why don't you go ahead and explain why you chose to come see me."

"Where would you like me to start?"

"Start from the beginning as you see it. I'll ask if I think I need more information."

The beginning. Does she mean of the observable universe or sentient life or his earliest memory? No, she means the beginning of these delusions. This story.

"I guess the beginning is that I suffered serious brain trauma after surviving a fall from three stories up. I was in Zurich. I was taken to a hospital there, where a doctor performed emergency brain surgery. I was in a coma for four days. And since awakening I have spent an inordinate amount of time fighting off hallucinations."

"Have you contacted the surgeon in Zurich about these hallucinations? Or your local physician?"

"No," Steve says. "That's part of why I'm here. These hallucinations, delusions, whatever, involve Dr. Dobbelfeld. And to be honest I don't think my HMO doctor will be able to help me."

"Why don't you go into more detail about the hallucinations so I can better understand why you desire the opinion of a third party?"

During the next ten minutes, Steve tries to relate his story in a logical and organized manner. He begins with Janine's phone call, his visit to Cabaret, the bouncer, the fall. He explains the initial, potent belief that he could levitate and tries his best to describe the field, the presence, its infinite entirety. He describes how the nurse seemed to go out of her way to lie to him about the ring, reveals the odd nature of Svetlana's death and her visits to him, how he has felt watched and followed since arriving in Los Angeles. That he seemed to read thoughts from Serena's head. That after abandoning his job at AE he was certain he could detect, through some mechanism in the field, pursuit by men from Zurich.

"Now I know," he concludes, "that much of what I have just described to you results from hallucination. I recognize that and accept it. What I find difficult to reconcile are four distinct facts: that Svetlana died the night I met her, that her accident was remarkably similar to mine, that the nurse lied, and that my company could find no record of my stay in a Zurich hospital."

In Dr. Taylor's silence, Steve reads no judgment whatsoever.

"First," she says, "allow me to distill your concerns into two salient points: One, you believe yourself to be experiencing certain hallucinations that have manifested themselves as an ability to sense an invisible field, a force that seems to bind the world—the universe—together."

Steve smiles. "It sounds like *Star Wars* when you describe it like that."

"Yes, it does. And two, because of the odd circumstances surrounding Svetlana's death—that, and the lack of proof that you were ever in a Zurich hospital—you've considered the possibility that you are involved in some kind of foul play."

"That's pretty close," Steve says. "But don't forget the nurse."

"Right. The nurse."

And then silence again. Fleeting, atmospheric sensations of

the doctor's girlfriend, how kissing her is more tender than kissing even the most sensitive man, how they spend hours exploring nothing more than the elemental planes of each other's lips.

"Can you describe to me in more detail how this field manifests itself?"

"Well, I first thought there was the one field, which permeated everything. But now it seems like there are lots of fields. Some are conductors and some are just . . . stuff."

"And you thought, in Zurich, that it might be possible to alter . . . reality, I guess . . . so that you could levitate?"

"That's close enough. But I guess it isn't a purely physical thing, because I also thought I was sensing Serena's thoughts."

"Well, considering her brain generates electrical impulses that are certainly detectable—we do it every day with EEG—your hallucinations are at least consistent. If you can affect these conductors to counteract the force of gravity, why couldn't you also use them to detect electromagnetic waves? Conceivably, you could 'see' in ways not limited to the visible light portion of the electromagnetic spectrum."

Steve searches for traces of irony in her voice and, amazingly, detects none.

"In fact, that you could sense Serena's thoughts and not be able to levitate also makes sense. Sensing waves and energy would be, by many orders of magnitude, easier than manipulating them."

"Why does it matter, though? If I'm just hallucinating everything?"

"Because a good understanding of the delusional architecture might lead us closer to the source of your problem."

"Okay," Steve says.

"Let me ask you something. This might offend you, but we at least need to consider all possibilities."

"Shoot."

"Obviously it appears you have sustained a head injury of some kind. The bandage and shaved head are a dead giveaway.

But can you demonstrate proof that this injury occurred in the way you described? For instance, can you say for sure that you were actually in Zurich?"

"Sure. My parents came to the hospital to see me. They flew back to the States with me a little more than a week ago."

"What about the fall? Have you spoken to someone who actually saw that occur?"

"No," Steve admits. "The man who pushed me was never found. No witnesses were. And Svetlana is dead."

"After all," Dr. Taylor says, "it's remarkable that you survived such a fall, especially with nothing more than head trauma."

"I know. But why would the doctor in Zurich believe it then? Surely he would have been able to tell the difference between an ordinary head injury and one so severe."

"Good point," Dr. Taylor says. "Especially considering your parents were there, and conceivably heard everything the doctor said."

"Right."

"But you must see my point. That since you have experienced a nearly constant hallucination since returning from Zurich, until I speak to your parents or Dr. Dobbelfeld, I, as your doctor, cannot be sure that anything you have experienced during that time is real."

"I see your point, yes."

"For the moment, however, it appears that you are able to distinguish between your hallucinations and reality. Can you give me any good reason why Svetlana's death and your misfortune in Zurich might be part of a conspiracy?"

"Not really," Steve says. "I fell out a window, the ambulance came to pick me up, and a Swiss doctor saved my life, right? Except I wouldn't have gone out the window if it hadn't been for that bouncer. I know they're supposed to be aggressive, not take any shit from customers, but I was just lying there, passed out. And then Svetlana falls to her death, and the business closes down, and the nurse lies to me. No hospital records. Strange hallucinations. What am I supposed to make of all this?"

"I don't know," Dr. Taylor says.

"I'll tell you what *I* know: A woman is dead. You can call this Baltensperger and ask him yourself. He thinks I was the last person to see her alive."

For a long time Dr. Taylor says nothing. So long, in fact, that Steve begins to wonder if she has simply vanished, evaporated into the field the way Svetlana did after her two ethereal appearances.

"Let's talk a little about Svetlana and the way she has appeared to you in dreams," Dr. Taylor says.

"Okay."

"The first time she came to you, she expressed regret and explained that she had found a new job. The second time she again said she was sorry, and also told you she was there if you needed her. Does this make you think of anything?"

"That she's trying to help me? Protect me from something?"

"It makes me think of a guardian angel," Dr. Taylor says. "We haven't talked much yet about the 'presence,' the metaphysical, sentient consciousness that seems to follow you everywhere. To be honest, it sounds to me as if you're looking, subconsciously, for God. And your first, tenuous steps toward finding Him are through Svetlana, who is dead. Who, you could postulate, was partially responsible for your fall from the window, since she may have summoned the bouncer. So perhaps now she has been given the job as your guardian angel."

"I should probably tell you that I'm not religious, Dr. Taylor."

"All the more reason for you to be searching for some sort of guidance. Especially after suffering the emotional trauma of Janine's betrayal and the physical trauma of your head injury."

Steve has to admit that such a thing never occurred to him.

"In fact, the field doesn't have to be separate from the presence. It could just be the medium in which the presence—in this case, God—moves and operates."

"Okay," Steve says. "Let's agree, for the sake of argument, that I'm looking for God. What do I do now? Because to be honest, I don't expect to find Him any time soon."

"That's hard to say. If your problem is purely psychological, then a series of sessions with me could help you. But considering you never experienced anything like this before the injury, I'm inclined to believe that your problem is physiological.

"Some studies of the brain have linked an area of the parietal lobe to intense religious experience and the sense of self. If a neurologist ran tests on you and determined that this area of your brain exhibited irregular blood flow and electrochemical activity, that might explain your problem. Perhaps there are surgical procedures that could help you. I don't know."

Steve allows a moment to pass while he digests this.

"What have you been doing since Tuesday, when you walked out of the office?"

"Nothing," Steve says. "Watching television. Reading. Trying not to go crazy."

"Have you been in contact with anyone? Friends? Family?"

"No. I don't want to alarm my parents yet. They wouldn't understand. Besides, I've kind of felt like being alone."

"I urge you to invite someone to your house. Inject a little human interaction into your life. It's probably not helping to just sit there by yourself."

"Okay," Steve says, although he doubts he will take the doctor's advice.

"In the meantime, with your permission, I'd like to contact this Dr. Dobbelfeld. Perhaps we can clear the air on the issue of your hospital stay and even talk to the nurse. If those two incidents can be explained satisfactorily, then all we're left with is Svetlana's death. And maybe one coincidence is something we can live with."

"I know the likelihood of conspiracy is remote, but if somehow I turn out to be right, contacting Dobbelfeld means he'll know I'm suspicious of him."

"If you're really being followed, Steve, it means they already know you're here with me. All I'm going to do is contact him like any physician in my position would. If anything, it would make him *less* suspicious, since you obviously would have green-lighted the call."

Steve smiles. Whether or not Dr. Taylor believes him, her attitude is reassuring. "Maybe, just to humor me, you could wait a little while before you contact him. Give me a chance to get used to the idea."

"What do you say we meet a week from today?" she says. "Maybe we can call him together, here in my office. Do you think you'll be all right until then?"

"I think so. I feel better already having talked to you."

She walks him to the door and then offers her hand to shake. He notices a wedding ring on her left hand and wonders if she'll ever tell her husband about the girl.

"We'll see you next week, then. If you need anything before that, please don't hesitate to call."

2

Mike McNair is sitting beside her in the car, his right hand (the one not attached to a somehow-invisible steering wheel) tapping musically against his thigh. Kelly is watching him out of the corner of her eye, evaluating his silhouette against a backdrop of impossible colors, when his hand reaches and covers her own. He splays his fingers over hers, working between the gaps until their hands are interlocked. She smiles and turns toward him.

But it's distressing somehow, the music, though she can't quite say why. U2 sometimes does this to her, calls forth images from high school, a time when she hadn't yet learned how to be comfortable with herself, when Bono's tormented voice somehow validated her own angst. For no particular reason she happens to look in the back seat. James is there, mouthing silent words to her. She doesn't really see his lips but she understands him anyway. Warning her. She's late for work. But that's silly because she knows this is a dream, she knows she's asleep, and her workday doesn't start until two-fifteen in the afternoon. Then the U2 song ends and INXS comes on, and the sound must be coming from her alarm clock, and she wonders how long the music has been playing and why she might have set the alarm in the first place, she *never* uses the—

She's got that stupid staff meeting at nine, that's what it is. The meeting to officially welcome Jeff Pearson, the new general manager. She's afraid to open her eyes and look at the alarm clock. Her drive to the station could be fifteen minutes or it could be an hour. The traffic in this city. Maybe it's only eight o'clock. If she's lucky, seven thirty.

It's 8:49.

Kelly grabs across the nightstand for the telephone. Dials Frank's direct line and listens to the unanswered rings, to his voice mail greeting. She leaves a quick message explaining her situation and then tries his cell phone. He doesn't answer that one either. She swears and hangs up and runs to the bathroom with the phone, and naturally it rings just seconds after she steps into the steamy waterfall of her shower.

"Kelly, where the hell are you?"

"I'm in the shower, Frank. I'll be—"

"The *shower*?"

"Didn't you get my message?"

"No, I didn't. You need to get up here, Kelly. Now."

"Frank," she says. "You know I'm never late. Hell, I'm the *only* one who's never late. I must have slept through the—"

"Just get here, Kelly. Okay?"

"Okay, I will. But what the hell is going on? Why are you so—"

"It's Pearson. He was already here when I got in at eight. He's been in a foul mood all morning."

"Jeff Pearson?" Kelly asks. "In a foul mood?"

"Yes. Why?"

She stands there, wet and naked and cold, trying to picture the fist-pumping, wide-eyed Jeff Pearson in a bad mood. "When we met him in August, all he could talk about was how he let the employees run themselves and left decisions to the people doing the work and all that crap."

"Maybe he woke up on the wrong side of the bed."

"There isn't anything I can do now except get there as quickly as I can," Kelly says. "Try to cover for me, okay?"

"Just get here. I don't like this guy's attitude."

Kelly hangs up and steps back into the shower. Frank must be overreacting, she feels sure, because it doesn't make sense that Pearson would come into the station on his first official visit as GM and act like a jerk. For one thing it doesn't fit his personality. For another, the relationship between general managers and on-air talent is usually an agreeable one, because a cast of smiling, familiar faces helps make for a successful evening newscast.

She quickly finishes her shower and then steps back into the bathroom, hopping from carpet to carpet to avoid the cold tile floor. Cringes at her reflection in the mirror, at her smallish breasts and wide hips. Pinches the roll on her stomach. *That's just skin,* James always told her. *If you tried to tell anyone else but me that you were fat, they'd think you had an eating disorder.* He always said things to her like that when she complained about her body. *Your ass is perfect,* when she thought it was too big. *Big boobs age badly,* when she longed to be a C, even a D. *Guys love wide hips. They're childbearing hips.* He was so charmingly innocent. She should have been mortified at the description of her hips as "childbearing," but instead it made her feel special. Like a human being.

Kelly knows she should just put on sweats and go, but she's never been able to leave the house without at least a little makeup. She pulls her hair back and works on her face for a couple of minutes, thinking about all those men who lust after her because she reads the news. All those men who think they know her and don't.

She's never felt like a pretty girl, after all, at least not compared to the standards set forth by royal princesses in her hometown of Augusta, Georgia. Raised among southern aristocrats who regularly rubbed elbows with celebrities and CEOs and golf legends, Kelly's modest upbringing placed her squarely in the high school realm of nobodies. Her mother didn't have money for the proper clothes and on top of that she developed late. All she wanted was out. Out of Augusta and out of Georgia, away from debutantes and garden weddings and the never-ending race struggle. So she worked her ass off in school. Skipped social functions and pretended she didn't want to go on dates. Since no one was asking her anyway. Skipped the prom and even her own graduation ceremony.

In her closet she finds a blouse and a pair of jeans, adds a blazer, and then grabs a pair of shoes. It's already 9:15. Hurries to the garage now and zooms out of her neighborhood, praying she doesn't accidentally speed past a traffic cop.

At UVA she lived at the library and study halls. One day a preapproved Discover card arrived in the mail and she went out and bought some clothes. Good clothes, like the girls in sororities wore. It didn't take long to realize that trivial enhancements to her appearance produced dramatic changes in male interest. Boys smiled for no apparent reason when she passed them between classes. They opened doors for her. They sat with her (sometimes asking, sometimes not) in the library, in study hall, on the lawn in front of her dorm. Sometimes they even asked her to share coffee or a sandwich over lunch.

If she was surprised how much of a difference real clothes made, nothing could have prepared her for a life in television. The love letters and death threats. Marriage proposals, underwear (from both men and women), and, on one occasion, sixteen dozen red roses spread over the floor of her tiny gray cubicle. She couldn't understand why so many people cared about her makeup and hair, why men seemed so interested when all she did was stand in front of a blue screen at 6:30 in the morning and tell people to stay away from I-95.

She still doesn't understand it.

The traffic on Highway 75 isn't so bad after all, and Kelly makes it to downtown in a little less than twenty minutes. She squeals through the parking garage and then sprints to the elevators. By the time she reaches the office it's almost 9:45, and she can tell by the sprinkling of staff in the newsroom that the planned welcome meeting is over. Kelly spots Ted Janzen, her co-anchor, frowning over a printout of some kind, but before she can ask him what's going on, Frank leans out his door and beckons her over. She joins him in his office, still somewhat out of breath, and finds herself standing in front of Jeff Pearson.

"Hi, Kelly," the new GM says, rising to greet her. He's dressed in an expensive navy suit and smells like aftershave. "Nice of you to drop by this morning."

"Hi, Mr. Pearson. Sorry I'm late. I must have slept through my alarm."

"Oh, well. No big deal." He beckons to the second visitor's chair. "Please, have a seat."

Kelly does, her heart beating even faster than during her run through the parking garage. New GM. Big meeting. Frank's terse phone call. She wonders again about the likelihood of re-organization. It doesn't happen often, but it's not unheard of for a new GM to bring radical new ideas to a station. Maybe even a new pair of weeknight anchors.

"Kelly," Frank says, "Jeff has some ideas for the evening newscast."

"Oh," Kelly replies. "What sort of ideas?"

Pearson clears his throat. "To be honest, I hate it when my main anchors come across like talking heads, and after watching the six and ten for a few weeks, that's what I see from you and Ted."

Kelly bristles. The "talking heads" stereotype is something particularly annoying, as if news anchors are simply robots smiling and reading stories written by someone else, as if she hasn't worked ten years for the opportunity to sit in that chair and read that scrolling text.

"I see," she says, glancing at Frank, whose bland expression tells her absolutely nothing.

"Now, I know that isn't true. I know you and Ted put in hard years as reporters. You're here for a reason. You're among the top journalists in your field and paid well for it."

"Thank you."

"So what I want is for you two to spend more time in the field. I want each of you guys—we'll start with one day a week—to do a story on location. Something relevant and lively to showcase the talents that got you here."

Pearson turns to Frank as if to ask him something, but apparently thinks better of it.

"Which means," he says to Kelly, "two nights a week, we'll either have just one anchor on the set, or maybe we'll bring in one of the weekend guys. I haven't decided yet."

Kelly sits there, not quite sure what to say, since what Pearson just announced isn't anything like what she expected.

"I would love to do more hands-on reporting," she tells him finally. "To tell you the truth, I kind of miss the rush of it sometimes, the chance to interact more with the subjects of our news stories."

"Great," Pearson says. "Then we're on the same page here."

"One question, though."

"Sure."

"Well, I guess this is a question for Frank, or both of you, I don't know. Will I get to choose my stories? The features I do now, the softer stuff, are pretty much at my discretion. Within reason, of course. Will this be sort of the same thing?"

"Sometimes," Pearson says. "I mean, if you've got something good, then by all means you should go out and do it. But this is something Frank is going to coordinate, at least at first. In fact, I'll probably have a hand in it myself for a while. You already do 'soft' stories, like you said. What I'm thinking is more the breaking news. Harder stuff. That's where we need our talent, where you can prove to Dallas that you're not just a pretty face."

"I didn't know Dallas thought that."

"Come on, Kelly, that story in *People* turned you into a national celebrity. This morning I searched your name on Yahoo! and came up with eight fan websites."

Kelly offers a diplomatic smile, but there is no smile in her voice. "I know people in this city find me attractive. That's not what I meant. I meant I didn't know our viewers think I'm a talking head."

"Hey," Frank says. "I don't think—"

Pearson's own smile cracks, but doesn't break.

"Let's not get into a semantic argument, Kelly. You said you miss the rush of reporting, and I'm giving you the opportunity to experience a little of that again. There isn't anything wrong with that, is there?"

"No, there isn't. I just wanted to be clear about how you perceive my reputation, that's all."

"Okay, well, let me clear the air. I think you are a great news anchor, and I know our viewers agree. I just want them to see you flex your journalistic muscles a little more. How is that?"

"That's fine."

"Great," he says. "Frank and I have discussed some ideas I'd like to roll out this week. Thursday and Friday. You'll find them on your desk. Thanks for your time."

"Thanks for yours," she says, and finds her way out of Frank's office. As she walks away, Pearson stands and shuts the door behind her.

3

Ted is hunched over his keyboard, right hand maneuvering the mouse as he clicks through stories on the wire. Kelly stops near his chair and grabs the memo, the one he was reading when she first walked in. Her eyes skip past a couple of introductory paragraphs that outline in black and white what Pearson just told her in person, and then she arrives at the details of the next week's field assignments:

Ted Janzen: Thursday. Follow up on the recent bomb scare at DFW and investigate what measures local authorities have taken to ensure efficient response.

Kelly Smith: Friday. Cover the midnight execution of Gary Wilbur Donnell in Huntsville.

Kelly reads the assignment and then reads it again. Ted seems to notice her dismay and looks up from his monitor. His eyes are a fierce blue, and his hair would be graying if he didn't die it ink black.

"Didn't Pearson tell us how he liked to put decisions in the hands of the people doing the work?"

"That's what I thought," Kelly says. "What the hell is this? He wants me to drive to *Huntsville*? On *Friday*? To cover an *execution*?"

"I know. Looks like you drew the shit assignment this time."

"That's putting it mildly."

"It's bad enough," Ted says, "that Frank thinks he's God's fucking gift to news directing. And now we get Pearson in here to order us around even more?"

"Hey, at least you don't have to drive to Huntsville."

"Not this time. I'm sure next week I'll get the shit one."

Kelly drops the memo back on Ted's desk and then heads to her own. She should go back home, or maybe go run a few errands, because she'll have to be back at two fifteen to start her regular work shift. But since she's here, she might as well get a head start on the day's e-mail, and maybe even do voice-over for some footage she shot on Friday, a story about local grocery stores overcharging customers. And of course what she really wants to do is read through Mike's latest message again, and maybe even respond to it.

She powers on her computer and listens for a moment to the vague whirring and beeping sounds, knowing innately that the hard drive must be the source of some of that noise, that maybe her floppy drive does something, and supposes that Mike McNair could explain to her in artful detail each sound and the component from which it originates. He could probably tell her why she must wait nearly three minutes for her computer to stop huffing and puffing and finally be ready to accept a command. He could probably explain a whole library of things she never cared about before, that have always operated beneath her radar. That she suddenly finds intriguing and worthy of consideration.

Kelly realizes Ted just said something she missed. "I'm sorry, Ted. What did you say?"

"I asked how it was going with James. You guys still talk all the time?"

She recently made the mistake of confiding in Ted when a group from the newsroom met for drinks after a late Thursday newscast. She rarely talks about James to anyone, as if revealing details about their relationship amounts to even more betrayal, but after a few martinis her tongue sort of ran away with itself. Ted, in turn, was impressed enough with her candor to reveal doubts about the continued solvency of his twenty-year marriage. Kelly herself has little doubt, especially after his recent automobile purchase (a black convertible Corvette), but tried hard to convince him that twenty years was something worth saving.

He didn't seem particularly willing to accept her argument, and since then has begun to fish for more personal information about her.

"We talk. It's okay, I guess."

"I'm surprised you guys are still friends. When I was dating, I could never maintain a relationship with a girl after we broke up."

She opens her e-mail and is surprised to find only two unread messages from last night. And right below them is Mike's. She clicks on it, savors this line again:

> But we seem to have stumbled into this profound
> discussion, and I would be lying if I said I didn't enjoy it, this
> thought-provoking conversation with you.

"We're too close to cut off communication completely," she says to Ted. "James moved here with me from Phoenix. I can't just turn off my feelings about him."

"But what's your next boyfriend going to think about that?"

> It's not often that I meet someone as intelligent and
> attractive as you. I'd like to see you again.

"I don't know," Kelly says. "I suppose I'll cross that bridge when I come to it."

She wants to reply to Mike, but she can't do it right now, not with Ted asking her about James. And then she notices one of the two new messages is from joonoreactor@yahoo.com, the same guy who sent the last crazy e-mail. The subject line is: Hello again. She can't help but open it.

> Don't be an idiot Kellye open your eyes. This is
> unnacceptable. Cant' you see it isn't FAIR? When is it
> MY turn? Huh. He doesn't love you I DO. I'm not accept-
> ing defeat anymore you FUCKHOLE BITCH . That's right

you are a FUCKHOLE BITCH unless you open your eyes and SEE good and evil. Unless you COME to the lord of LIGHT.

You shall see hail fall from a CLEAR sky. Everything is going extremely well, Hal said.

So I'm just telling you this for your own good Kelly.

C-ya!!

P.S. I shop at Target just like you do!

Kelly reads the message and then reads it again. She's heard the stories, like they all have, of news personalities being stalked by fans. She's familiar with Kathryn Dettman, who was murdered by a disturbed viewer right here in Texas. Of course you never think it will happen to you. You don't expect to open your in-box one Tuesday morning and find someone calling you a FUCKHOLE BITCH.

"Hey, Ted. Take a look at this e-mail."

Ted walks over. Stands behind her and reads.

"Whoa," he says. "Freako alert."

"I know. I got one from the same guy over the weekend. You think I should show Frank?"

"Of course you should."

"But it's not like he can do anything. He can't figure out who it is. Anybody can give false information and sign up on Yahoo!"

"Yeah, but I'd show Frank anyway. Just in case the guy ever shows up here. Better safe than sorry."

"Frank's in there with Pearson right now," Kelly says, and locks her computer. "I guess I'll do it when I come back this afternoon."

"You gonna be all right?" Ted asks her.

"I'll be fine. Just want to get out of here for now. I'm not sure I even want to shop at Target anymore."

This makes Ted chuckle. "I'm sure he doesn't know where you live. You're unlisted, right?"

"Yeah, but you never know these days. The only way to be completely safe from a stalker is to change your lifestyle, but what kind of life is that?"

4

From: Kelly Smith (ksmith@wfaa.com)
To: Mike McNair (mmcnair@ntssc.com)
Subject: RE: Hey there!

Hey Mike,

Thanks for writing back. You are very sweet. I'm not sure I'm smart enough to keep up this conversation with you, but I'll try!

First: full disclosure here. At my church we don't really get into the Genesis debate. I didn't say this before because I was curious how you would respond (quite emphatically, I might add!!) to my comments about Twain, but I'm Unitarian. Our church has roots in Christianity, but we no longer regard the Bible as the ultimate authority in matters of faith (I copied that line off our website!). We think personal integrity comes first and foremost, we don't believe you are born in sin, we believe in the worth and dignity possible in every person. We believe in love and acceptance, in the democratic process, and we believe in an interdependent web of all existence of which humans are only a part.

So you can see how I was pretty interested to hear about those "fringe" physicists who think there could be some kind of collective reality. That sounds a lot like our ideas. See there, my beliefs aren't as far away from physics as you might think!

But I have to be honest with you, Mike. When I said I wasn't available, that wasn't exactly the truth. I'm not dating anyone, but I broke up with someone very special several months ago. I still talk to him quite a bit, and when guys ask me out I tend to say no. But I really enjoyed talking to you on the plane. You are a very nice and intelligent man, and you seem to be very passionate about your work and about life. (And it doesn't hurt that you have a beautiful smile!)

It's sort of ironic that we're even having this e-mail exchange b/c I get a lot of fan mail and some of it is not very nice. I've received a couple of disturbing messages from this one guy just since I met you. But I guess that comes with the job, huh? As long as he doesn't "cross the line" and make contact in person.

Well, I'm going to hit this e-mail ball back into your court. I appreciate you being patient (and persistent) with me. And I'd like to hear more about that collective reality thing if you get a chance.

Best, K

From: Mike McNair (mmcnair@ntssc.com)
To: Kelly Smith (ksmith@wfaa.com)
Subject: RE: Hey there!

Hi again Kelly,

That was interesting what you told me about Unitarians. You're right—we're not as far apart as I thought. I don't know how much more I can tell you about the collective reality thing, though. We certainly haven't found it at the NTSSC! Ha ha. I guess the idea is analogous to what we talked about on the plane, though, how the universe is just a bunch of jiggling particles bathed in force fields. Since there are only a few kinds of particles, and they make up everything from brain tissue to lead to the core of the sun, since they all exist in our same universe and affect each other in some small way, then we're all part of this collective reality (or web of existence, whichever you prefer). The difference between proven physics (like the work I do) and more metaphysical ideas (like the supposition of a collective reality that can be accessed by human consciousness) is evidence. I can prove that two hydrogen atoms and one oxygen atom make up water. But I can't prove that my mind and yours can influence each other at great distances, other than to write you emails or talk to you on the phone. People cite twins with "shared pain" and other examples of telepathic communication as evidence, but no controlled study has ever proven the existence of any kind of real telepathy (at least none that I'm aware of). So even though I would love the idea to be true, I'm not holding my breath to find it any time soon.

As far as your ex-boyfriend, I appreciate your honesty and I understand. When I came to Texas I left someone behind in

Chicago, a girl I had dated, on and off, since college. She is a tenured professor of anthropology at U of I in Chicago and for various reasons we weren't able to maintain our relationship after I moved away. It was a difficult transition back into the "single" world, because I wasn't used to meeting girls and was never very good at it in the first place. But I'm glad I met you.

I understand if you're hesitant to meet new people because of your feelings for your ex, but I don't bite. In fact, I give tours of our facility all the time and would love to give you one. Or maybe you could come do a story on us. Either way, I'd like to see you again. Hopefully sometime soon. ☺

Take care,
Mike

5

Tuesday afternoon and Larry's in his office, absently browsing around the Internet. Happens across a website with a list of the ninety-nine hottest women celebrities, and while he disagrees with the order, he does find a couple of new women he hasn't heard of before. Googles those women and bookmarks a few new sites chock full of hi-res photos. Fields a call from Gerald Miles, who'd like to add a block of code to the trigger, something he thinks might augment Mike's idea for the rejection sample. Lies to Gerald. Hangs up and goes back to the Internet, searching for a good hangover remedy, because water and Advil haven't put a dent in this one. Would rather not have to reach into the desk and take a swig of his emergency Crown.

He was pretty drunk by the time he finally typed the e-mail to Kelly last night, and the result was a nearly incoherent message that even he found somewhat distasteful. Which is stupid, because she could easily forward e-mail threats to her boss or even the police. And maybe he's somewhat safe behind his anonymous e-mail address, but he's not perfectly safe, not if the FBI gets involved and tracks down the IP address from which the e-mail originated.

The knowledge of this, and of Mike's continued interest in Kelly, led to a blackout evening. Because the only way to deal with the cruelty and injustice of this world is to not deal with it at all. Blot the whole thing out with half a bottle of Crown Royal.

There is work to do. New action items from staff meetings, like problems with the middleware (again) and complaints about network speed. There are always problems. The world is full of them. He doesn't understand how it got this way, how *he* got this way, and he doesn't really see any way out of it that's not going to injure someone. Especially since he doesn't care for the idea of injuring himself.

A knock on the door. It's Samantha, smiling. He smiles back, in spite of himself. Decides he shouldn't have been so harsh on her last night, since she was by far the high point of his Monday.

"Hey, Larry," she says. "Can I talk to you a minute?"

"Sure. Have a seat."

He closes his browser and turns to face her.

"I had a good time last night," she says to him.

"Me, too. It was . . ."

"Surprising?"

"Yeah. I mean, when we went for the drink, I certainly didn't think we'd end up back at my place."

"Me, either. It's not usually so fast for me."

"That makes two of us," Larry says.

"But hey, there's something else I need to ask you about."

"Okay."

"Well, I got in early this morning, and I was evaluating the code that builds the rejection sample, and I found something interesting."

Larry just stares at her. He wonders if she can see the hang-over in his eyes, in the pallor of his skin.

"You were thorough, Larry. I have to give you that. Instructing the Grid to ignore Higgs events even in the *rejection* sample? I mean, what's the chance that one of them would make it in there?"

What is this? She comes in here smiling like a little girl, tells him how nice it was last night, and then springs this on him?

"What I don't understand," she continues, "is how you've managed to fool your entire team this long. The super collider has been running for almost a year."

He considers saying something like *I don't know what you're talking about,* but come on. The Crown is really calling to him now. Singing to him.

"I guess no one was looking for a saboteur. I guess that's how."

He wonders what it feels like to dissolve in front of another human being, what it feels like for the human operating system to crash.

"So," she says.

He could strangle her. But then. What?

"I didn't have to look back very far," Samantha tells him. "The detector has been registering possible Higgs events for months. Probably since the whole damn facility went operational. And you've been hiding it from everyone. Why?"

Now. Finally. He. Shrugs.

"You must have it in for Mike. It's the only thing I can come up with. Because I think you lied to me about him. I don't think he said those things about me. I think he would do anything to find Higgs, even if it meant giving me part of the credit."

Fuckhole. Bitch.

"I can tell this is freaking you out. I don't know how you expected to get away with it forever, but in any case you don't have to worry anymore. You unwittingly helped me, Larry. Because now I can have Higgs whenever I like. You show me how to disable all your handiwork—because I'm sure there's plenty of redundancy in the code—and I'll let you keep your little secret. We can even keep playing at night if you like."

"What do you think?" he finally growls. "You'll convince Donovan to get rid of Mike and then announce your 'discovery'?"

Her dark eyes smile. Sparkle. "Sounds like a good plan, don't you think?"

6

Kelly is about to go on set for the ten o'clock show when her phone rings. It's James. He wants her opinion about the climactic scene in his newest screenplay, an apocalyptic story about the destruction of all human technology. He reads her a few lines, and she tells him they're too melodramatic. He says he was afraid of that. Wishes her luck on the newscast. She walks to the set and finds her chair. Presses the IFB into her ear.

People thinks she's weak because she still talks to James.

They tell her to get over him. Get over *it*, as if the relationship was a *thing*, as if it were something you could own for a while, and then toss over your shoulder when you were done with it.

People can think whatever the hell they want. They may be able to say *I'll always love you* and *I don't ever want to be with anyone else* and so on, they may be able to say this to five or ten people in their lifetimes. Say it to boyfriends and girlfriends and second wives and third husbands. Get over him. Move on. Grow up.

Kelly isn't stupid. She knows there isn't just one person for her. But she believes in truth, and truth is not dismissing emotions because of a stretch of bumpy road. A girlfriend told her once that it was okay to renege on promises if you didn't feel the emotion anymore. It might have been true then, she said, but that doesn't mean it's true now.

So what does the word *never* mean, then, in the phrase *I will never leave you*? I will never leave you as long as you don't fuck it up? Is that an understood qualifier? Isn't the whole point of *never* to leave room for the other person to fuck up? Is love contingent on perfection? *I'll never leave you so long as you remain upbeat about not selling screenplays.* Is that what she should have said?

Get over him. Start the whole process over after six years. Courting again. First kiss again (okay, so that one might be fun). First sex, first time to say *I love you,* and then what? More empty promises? The same fucking phrases all over again, the same moving in together and the same settling in phase and then, Whoops! Sorry! I didn't mean *forever.* It just sounded good at the time.

But all those people, they must know something. All those people who have gone through breakups and divorces and found new people to share their lives with, they got over it somehow. Maybe it's just something you have to do. Maybe once you do something that seems hard, maybe it turns out not to be so hard after all.

She'll let Mike simmer for a while. She'll go see him, but she'll let him wait a few days before she agrees to it. Not to torture him, but to let him know it's not a decision she makes lightly.

And also so she can get used to the idea.

She smiles, bright and wide, and once again introduces herself to Dallas/Ft. Worth.

7

A tall, clear glass.

Seven ice cubes.

Snaps and pops as the rich, caramel-color Crown shrinks the ice. Triple shot.

Effervescent carbonation. Top the glass with Coca-Cola.

Ten swallows.

Repeat steps one through five.

Don't even bother to sit down or go into the living room and watch TV. Just stand there in the kitchen and get trashed.

Repeat steps one through five.

'Cause that's just great, the easy-peasy way Samantha came in and ruined his fun. Swooped in and figured out that Larry had built an app to override the triggers. That he had written instructions to toss out any event that looked remotely like the expected decay modes of a Higgs particle. Not toss them out, really, but store them in a place only he knew about.

Let's show Mike who the boss really is, he thought when he first did it. Let's show him who's really in control.

Or maybe Larry is just a jealous fuckface who couldn't stand to see someone else achieve a dream.

His own friend. Fucked over his own friend. And now some undeserving bitch is going to take all the credit. What kind of payback is that? What the hell was he trying to accomplish?

He bought Sominex at the store. Two packs of extra-strength sleeping pills.

Such a chickenshit he is. Not going to fucking kill himself. Hasn't even opened the boxes of pills. Hasn't even taken them out of the goddamned plastic grocery bag.

All his ranting and raving about God is God and all that crappity-ass crap. Stealing lines from electronic music, trying to sound like a freak. A fucking drunk freak, that's what he is. Joonoreactor@yahoo.com. Yeah, so original. Anybody could look up "God is God" on the Internet and figure that shit out.

He picks up the cordless phone. His ears are roaring now; nine ounces of Crown on an empty stomach, that'll do it to you. Speed dial #1.

"Hey there, Mike," he says, concentrating. Confident that he sounds completely sober. "I need you to come over, man."

"Larry? What's—"

"Just come over," he says and hangs up. Repeats steps one through five. Stumbles into the living room.

His doorbell rings.

The light in the entryway is way too bright, as if someone stuck a 400-watt bulb in there. He can hear the screaming photons flying off the filament. The front door. Mike.

"Larry, what's wrong, man? Have you been drinking?"

Sits down on the floor. Starts crying. Blubbers about the triggers.

"Larry, what are you talking about?"

More blubbering.

Some yelling on Mike's part. His mouth is here, the words are over there.

Blubbers about Samantha.

"What? Are you kidding me?"

"Promised I'd give her the Higgs Mike but I can't do that to you man."

"Why, Larry? Why?"

Then darkness.

8

Larry wakes some time later in bed. Mike is sitting on the floor with his back against the wall, a glass beside him, half-melted cubes floating near the bottom. The room in shadows, lit from the hallway.

"How are you feeling?" Mike says to him.

"Like shit," Larry croaks. "What time is it?"

"A little after two."

"Why are you still here?"

"You passed out in the entryway. Your breathing sounded kind of funny. I was afraid you'd stop altogether, so I stayed to watch you."

Larry tries to sit up, but his stomach immediately protests. He smells sour vomit on his shirt.

"I saw the sleeping pills."

Larry doesn't acknowledge this.

"Nothing's that bad, man. I know you didn't take them, but you shouldn't even be thinking about something like that."

For a while neither of them says anything. Mike picks up his glass, takes a drink.

"What are you going to do?" Larry asks.

"I guess I'll review the events you discarded. Then we'll run for a while without your 'enhancements' and see what we get. If it all works out, I suppose we'll have an announcement to make."

"What if Donovan pulls you off the project first? Why don't you just review the events I discarded and then tell him what I did? Why wait?"

"I thought of that. But you'd be ruined."

"Yeah. Well."

"Larry, I need you to help me understand why you deliberately threw the project off track. You sabotaged the main project at a twelve-billion-dollar super collider. I'm embarrassed it happened under my watch, but . . . man, I trusted you. We all did. It never occurred to me someone would *not* want the project to succeed. It's kind of crazy."

Larry doesn't know how to answer that.

"It's kind of crazy what you did."

He wants to tell Mike that loneliness isn't craziness. Instead, he says, "I don't know what to say, Mike. I can't justify what I did."

"Have you ever thought of. . . . Do you think you might need some help?"

"I wouldn't feel like this if it weren't for. . . ." He trails off, afraid of finally confronting Mike, of crystallizing sin into words.

"If it weren't for what?"

"Come on, Mike. Carrie, remember? The only girl I ever really cared about, the one you stole from me. You think I can just forget that?"

Mike climbs to his feet. "What?"

"That's what I figured," Larry says. "It happened so long ago you've let yourself forget it ever happened."

"Forget *what* happened?" Mike asks carefully.

"I brought her to the apartment, remember? I met her at a party, and I brought her home to meet you, and the next thing I know you two guys are in your bedroom having sex."

"Larry, man. Tell me you're kidding."

"Why would I joke about something like that?"

"Larry," Mike says again, and it's becoming annoying, his careful and condescending voice. "That's what *I* did. *I* met her at the party, and *I* brought her back to the apartment. You were watching television, remember? In the living room? I was embarrassed because I was about to have sex with some girl I'd just met at a keg party, and you agreed to leave so we could have some privacy."

"You're a liar," Larry says. "You're trying to make me think I'm crazy. *I* met her at the keg party. I changed the tap for her."

"No, you didn't. That's what I did. I told you the whole story the next day."

Larry just stares at him. Any minute now he's going to throw up again, he's so angry and confused.

"You can't believe that," Mike says. "Please. Please don't tell me you sabotaged my work because you think—"

"There you go again!" Larry says. "*Your* work. *Your* project! You—"

"Enough, Larry. That's enough."

"Don't tell me—"

"Listen to me, man. I'm sorry about your problems. I don't know what to say except you need some help. Serious help. I've known you for a long time, so it hurts me to even say that. But I'll tell you something. You better pull yourself together and come with me to the office—right now—and help me undo your handiwork. Undo it and give me the discarded information. If you don't, I'll shut the place down until we find it on our own, but the whole world is going to know what you did."

"That's right. Threaten me."

"I'm serious. Come with me right now, and I will let this go. If you can figure out a way to hide what you did, help me convince everyone we found a program glitch instead of covering up your sabotage, I'll go along with it. You're never going to see a better deal than that, man. Especially if Landon finds out. I suggest you take it."

Larry stares at Mike so long he almost forgets to speak. He doesn't know what to do, he doesn't know how to reconcile Mike's lies with his own intolerable pain. But finally he agrees to go. It's the only thing he can think to do.

9

Six thirty and still dark by the time Mike returns Larry to his house in Olney. The two of them haven't spoken since leaving the administrative office, and they don't speak now as Larry opens the passenger door and steps out of the car. Mike can't find words to describe how he feels, and wouldn't care to address Larry right now if he could. He drives to his own house a few blocks away and climbs into the shower. Grabs the soap and scrubs. Stands under the hot water for twenty minutes or more, scrubbing. Larry, man. What is he supposed to do? He can't just abandon the guy, can he? It's a colossal fuckup, what he did. Personal and professional betrayal almost beyond words. But it's obvious that his friend is in pain, that something has skewed his interpretation of the world, and what kind of person is Mike if he just walks away from Larry now?

What kind of man is he if he doesn't?

An hour later Mike is standing in Donovan's office. By now he hasn't slept in over twenty-four hours. The story is that a possible Higgs event was found in the rejection sample, and that when they realized the event selection criteria were flawed, it was obvious they could have been producing Higgs particles for months and not realized it.

"The rejection sample," Donovan says. "That's where you look at a small number of discarded events to see if you're throwing away anything interesting?"

"Exactly," Mike says, as if they haven't gone over this a thousand times before.

"What you're saying is that you found money in the trash."

"So to speak."

"And no one around here ever noticed anything like this before?"

"Well, when you told me to make something happen, I—"

"That's just it, Mike. When I said to make something happen, I didn't expect it to be in two days. That seems awfully convenient."

"I know. But like I've told you before, this is a tricky process. No matter how powerful the machine is, for something as elusive and unstable as Higgs, deciding which events to evaluate is difficult. There are a billion collisions per second, Landon. Only certain events trigger the computer to record them for further analysis. We've written millions of interesting events since we began operation, and hardly any of them have been consistent with the expected Higgs decay modes."

"I'm sorry. I've forgotten why the decay modes are important."

Mike wonders what goes through Donovan's mind when he explains these ideas to him. Because it can't be physics.

"We detect many particles based on their charge or energy or both. But some are so short-lived that we can't really 'see' them directly. Instead, we have to infer their presence based on other particles that emerge from their decay. This is how it is with Higgs. We've basically been looking for decay modes that have a certain signature."

"Okay," Donovan says with a gravity that suggests the concept is clearly beyond his grasp.

"And sometimes, when your back is against the wall, you come up with a radical idea. That's what Larry and I did." It's amazing how easily these words come out of his mouth. Misleading Donovan to protect Larry and (if Mike is being honest) his own reputation as the spokesperson for the project. "What interests me the most is that we may have been producing Higgs for several beam runs and not known it."

"*Several?*"

"Landon," Mike says. "This is how it goes. You keep refining the process until it works. It's science. It's meticulous. It creeps forward for a while and every so often a little luck or insight comes along and we leap."

"So when can we announce it?"

"Not for a while," Mike says. "We have to be sure. We have to reproduce our results."

"Why are you coming to me now if you're not ready to announce it?"

"Because you said to produce something. You were very clear. So I thought you should know about this."

"But if you have evidence from the rejection sample, that means you've produced it already."

"Yes, but—"

"I agree that you must be absolutely sure," Donovan says. "So we're not going to announce definite discovery. But I want some press for this. I want the world to know that we're on the verge of a Nobel-worthy discovery. So we'll send out a press release, and then later—after we collect more data—we'll have a press conference to clarify the situation."

"Landon," Mike pleads. This isn't what he expected. He can't go to the media with this fabrication and unverified evidence. "You can't do that."

"I know I can't. But you can."

CHAPTER SEVEN

1

Kelly is sitting at her desk on Friday afternoon, idly clicking through news portals as miniature guests are interviewed on a miniature *Oprah Winfrey Show* floating at the top right corner of her computer screen. In a few minutes she'll be leaving for Huntsville. A three-hour drive will put her there by four o'clock, giving her a full six hours to shoot a story about tonight's execution and set up live shots for the ten o'clock newscast.

She finally tires of reading the same depressing bites of news and clicks over to e-mail. Where she again reads Mike's last message, the one in which he invited her to the super collider. They haven't written each other since then. It's only been three days, and it's not like they're dating, so three days shouldn't seem like that long. But it does.

What's the big deal, anyway? Driving out there isn't the same as falling in love with the guy. If she wants to take it slow, honor her memory of James, then fine. But it's not like she's cheating on him.

So she'll reply to Mike when she gets back from Huntsville. No, she'll call him. Pick up the phone and hear his voice again, talk about something other than science or spirituality, just have a freaking regular conversation. That's what she'll do. There you have it from News 8. Kelly Smith Says What She Means.

A few minutes later she closes out her open programs, spends a few moments synching to her Palm Pilot, and then gathers her briefcase and blazer. Ted walks up just as she's getting ready to leave.

"Hey, Ted. Guess I'm going to take off now."

"Sorry you're having to drive all the way to Huntsville for this new idea of Jeff's."

"Me, too."

"And sorry you have to make the trip with Karl. All he ever does is complain."

"Like any great photog," Kelly jokes. "But I'm not driving with him, anyway. Makes me carsick to ride in that van for so long, so I'll just meet him down there. In fact I better get going if I'm going to be on time."

"Have fun," he tells her. "This could be your Emmy."

"Right," she laughs.

"Hey, you never know where a story might lead."

2

Her Lexus smoothly devours interstate as she drives southward, through suburban Ferris (where some enterprising but not particularly inventive soul has painted *Save* on the city limits sign, so that it now says SAVE FERRIS), and then toward the speed trap community of Ennis. After Corsicana twenty miles later, the rest of her drive will be more than a hundred miles of empty Texas prairie, a stretch of sensory deprivation that should provide her with ample opportunity to imagine a visit to Olney.

She passes tractor trailers and rusted pickups and SUVs. She tries to imagine what the rest of her life might look like. She imagines what would happen if she fell for Mike just in time for her agent to secure her a network job in New York or L.A.

Would she go or stay? It's not like Mike can find a job at another twelve-billion-dollar particle accelerator. And anyway, is there any point in staying together in the first place? Does she plan on getting married? Starting a family? Does some kid really want her as a mother? She can't even keep track of her car keys without an electronic beeper. How is she supposed to balance a crazy career and make time for Mike and be a mother? Her own mom made it look so easy, but she didn't work outside the home, so maybe that was the secret.

Or maybe she, Kelly, needs to grow up and stop being a female automaton. She doesn't have to keep skipping the senior prom forever.

Her cell phone rings when she's less than fifty miles from Huntsville.

"Hello?"

"Kelly. It's Karl." Her photographer, who is likely already in Huntsville, wondering where she is.

"Hi, Karl. What's up?"

"Just wanted to let you know I'm about twenty miles outside of town. You hungry?"

"Not really," she says. "But I should probably eat a little something before we head out to the prison. It's going to be a long evening."

"Yeah, it is. Well, hey, I was going to stop somewhere, maybe Dairy Queen. I didn't know if a skinny girl like yourself would be down for something like that."

"Anything is fine with me. You want to find a place and then call me when you get there?"

"Sure. Okay."

"All right, Karl. I'll talk to you then."

"Hey, Kelly. One more thing."

"Sure. What's up?"

"Didn't I hear you talking about some guy you met on a plane a couple of weeks ago? Some physics guy?"

The only time she remembers discussing Mike at work was

during a staff meeting this week, when she suggested to Frank the idea of doing a story at the NTSSC.

"Did you?" she says.

"Well, maybe Frank or someone mentioned it to me, asking what we might shoot if we ever went out there. From what I understand, there isn't much to see at a super collider. It's a giant underground tunnel."

"Right."

"Right, so I was just talking to Malvin, you know, one of the other photographers?"

"Yes, Karl, I know Malvin."

"Right. So he's getting ready to head out there today. To Olney. I guess they just issued a press release. Some kind of major discovery, apparently. I guess Ted is going to do the story, and he mentioned this guy, Mike somebody—"

"McNair?"

"Yeah, that's him. I thought maybe you'd be interested to know—"

Kelly shivers a little as icy rivers of excitement rush down her spine. "Karl, thanks. I appreciate you telling me this. McNair is the guy from the plane. I should be doing this story."

"Yeah, but you're here in Huntsville tonight, and—"

"And I'm going to call Frank right now. I should be doing this story. I may not come to Huntsville, Karl. I'll call you back in a few minutes."

"But Kelly—"

"I'll call you back."

3

Frank doesn't answer either one of his phones, of course. Considering the generous amount of time he spends in his office, taking into account that his cell phone is mounted to his belt and thus always on his body, Kelly doesn't quite understand why she can never get his bald head on the phone. But finally, after dialing his office number six times in succession, Frank picks up and growls into the phone.

"Mitchell."

"Frank, it's Kelly."

"Hey, you in Huntsville yet? I just talked to Karl a couple of minutes ago."

"Almost there," she says. "As a matter of fact, I just spoke to Karl myself. He told me about the super collider story, that you're sending Ted out there."

"Right. What's up?"

"Frank, this Mike McNair, this is the guy I told you about at the staff meeting. When I brought up the idea of doing a story about the collider?"

"Oh, yeah. Well, looks like you were the visionary on this one. I'll have to tell Pearson so we can get your stock up with him."

"Well, if you want to raise my stock, you should let me ditch this Huntsville story and go to Olney. I know this physicist. I can probably get an exclusive from him."

"Kelly, I can't pull you off a special assignment that Pearson specifically wanted you to do."

"I think he would understand if I get an exclusive from McNair and really nail this thing."

"Or he might fire you for insubordination."

"Not if you give me the okay."

"So you want him to fire me instead?"

"Come on, Frank. You know this execution story is bullshit. The guy murdered his entire extended family. There are barely any protests. The thing in Olney is something different. From what McNair told me, his collider is poised to make the biggest physics discovery in decades. Plus there's the whole angle of it being a private venture, taken over by some shadowy consortium after the government cut funding for it in the early '90s."

"But people don't give a shit about science unless it's health. Or a fucking meteor shower, and then we let weather handle it."

"But this story is in our backyard, Frank. And if McNair is

even half right, the networks are eventually going to pick it up. It sounds that big. And if we get in early . . ."

"Karl is already in Huntsville."

"So am I. I'm just pulling into town. You call off Ted, let Karl and me go up there, and I promise you I'll get this story."

"Are you sure about the exclusive?"

"The guy asked me out, Frank. I'm sure I can think of something."

Frank laughs. "You're a heartbreaker, Kelly."

Kelly decides Frank can think whatever he wants if it will buy her passage to Olney.

"Okay," he says finally. "Get Karl, and you two head up there. As soon as you've made contact with McNair, I want to know about it."

"It'll take me a day or so to script the interview and record it," Kelly says.

"That's fine. We can air it on Sunday, I guess. Assuming Jeff hasn't fired both of us by then."

"It's still a story in the field," Kelly points out. "Just like Jeff wanted. Only this one is actually worth something. I promise you won't be sorry."

"I hope you're right," Frank says.

Kelly tries to imagine Mike's reaction when she arrives in person, and finds herself hoping the same.

4

It's a Friday night party in Olney, Texas.

The press release went out in the afternoon, and shortly afterward physicists and technicians began pouring out of the NTSSC like electrons from an incandescent wire. The various bars and restaurants and honky-tonks filled up quickly, but of course Eva's is always the place to be. And it happens that the owner of this particular establishment, upon hearing the good news, reserved a couple of tables for her favorite customer and his friends. Which is how Mike comes to spend the evening there, apparently drinking away his uncertainty, and also how Larry, who came at Mike's request, stands at his side, wondering what the fuck he's doing here.

Because Mike has been trying to act like it all didn't happen. After managing to convince Donovan with his story, and after (even more miraculously) dodging questions from team leaders surprised by the announcement, Mike has simply ignored the confrontation about Carrie. As if the confrontation didn't happen. As if Carrie herself never happened, as if it was all a big lie fabricated by Larry.

" 'That's what *I* did,' " he mocks, whining, under his breath. " '*I* met her at the party, and *I* brought her back to the apartment. You were watching television, remember?' "

Fuckface liar. As if Larry had nothing better to do than watch television. Implying that Larry wasn't the one who had sex with Carrie, that instead of squirming on the bed with her, he was the one who opened Mike's door and peeked in. Implying that it was he, Larry, who later found their sex tape. Implying that it was he, Larry, who copied the tape, who would get himself off watching Mike thrust himself in and out of her.

After a while he can no longer endure standing there, so he begins to move toward the bar, where maybe he'll talk Eva into handing over the entire bottle of Crown.

Larry loves the sardine-can density of bodies in a nightclub, because it allows him the freedom of seemingly incidental and yet luxurious contact with all manner of gorgeous women. Because if such women are in his path they can't really protest. The bar is there, he is here, and anyone knows the shortest distance between two points is a straight line, even if his definition of straight varies according to the location of that hot blonde and this choice brunette and that woman who from the side looks remarkably like Kelly Sm—

And he is upon her, has already placed his hand on her shoulder to gently move her aside, when Larry realizes the woman, is, in fact, Kelly Smith. She turns and Larry smiles. It seems necessary to add some kind of verbal explanation, to point out that he was just trying to work his way to the bar, but the singularity and enormity of the moment paralyzes him. And still his hand remains on her shoulder. It seems somehow glued there, or perhaps held in place by some as-yet-undiscovered force—not the strong or the weak or the electromagnetic, or even gravity, but some sort of pull exclusive to humans, the nearly supernatural attraction experienced when two members of the opposite sex are perfectly meant for each other, when their personalities lock like atoms joined in a covalent bond. Her prismatic hazel eyes examine him, forensically, and the part of his mind that mediates social encounters screams, *Say something! Anything! My God she is more gorgeous in person than on television!*

"Hello, Kelly."

"Hi," she returns, a prepared smile on her face. "Have we met?"

His hand, finally, pries itself from her shoulder. "No. But I'm in Dallas pretty often, and I've seen you on the air. Are you here to do a story about Higgs?" He waits briefly for Kelly to answer, but before she can open her mouth he adds, inexplicably, "Or to see Mike?"

Her eyes widen at this unexpected turn in the conversation. "Do you know Mike?"

"I report to him directly," Larry says. "We're pretty good friends. He told me he met you on the plane."

"He did?"

"He did."

Kelly appears to digest this information. Her eyes seem lively to him, searching, as if she is looking through him, looking into his mind and finding herself trapped in the colorless abyss.

"Have we met?" she asks him again. "You seem familiar to me somehow."

Larry spends a moment attempting to discern whether or

not Kelly Smith actually spoke those words or whether he imagined them. The interval lengthens into awkwardness.

"I don't think so," he finally says.

"Oh." She breaks eye contact and looks around the smoky barroom. "Well, is Mike around? I dropped by your office and someone said I could find him here."

"Yeah, he's here. I can take you to him, but first I need to get a couple of drinks. Do you want something?"

They're only a few feet from the bar, and he heads toward it so that she doesn't have much choice but to follow him. Eva nods as he approaches—she's at the other end mixing a cocktail—but then her eyes widen, and it's obvious she recognizes Kelly. In less than thirty seconds, she has found her way to this end of the bar.

"Hi, Larry," she says. "Another Crown and Coke?"

"Along with a Captain for Mike. And whatever Kelly would like."

Eva reaches across the bar and the two women shake hands. "I'm Eva. I went to ASU. I used to watch you on Channel Three in Phoenix."

"Nice to meet you," Kelly says, smiling. "Small world."

"Yeah," Eva laughs. "You here to see Mike?"

"I am. That press release today, from what I understand it could turn out to be really big news."

"The press release." Eva smiles. "Of course."

Kelly returns the smile, and it seems to Larry that he just missed some unspoken communication between the two women.

"Well," Eva continues. "Mike is your guy, then. I'm sure Larry will take you to him. Right, Larry?"

"Definitely."

Kelly orders a chocolate martini, and after it comes she and Larry pick their way through the crowd toward Mike's table. Something slick and hot worms its way into his stomach, his stomach and then farther north, into his neck, into his throat.

The table is only a few feet away. Mike is speaking to Gerald Miles now, and Larry considers walking in a different direction. It would be nice if he could lead Kelly somewhere else. Anywhere but here. Maybe all the way to the back of the bar, where there is a somewhat-hidden and rarely used exit that he could push her through and—

Mike looks up as he sees Larry approaching, grinning thanks at the arrival of another freshly poured drink. His boss is obviously in a better mood than when they first showed up here, and Larry smiles back, not to be polite but at the absurdity of this entire situation. Because it's Carrie all over again, Mike once again stepping between Larry and the girl he has fallen in love with. Kelly, Carrie, Jillian—they're all the same. Larry loathes them all. He wants no part of this reunion between the two airplane lovebirds. And still he is forced to watch as Mike's leisurely grin becomes a brilliant, beaming smile, as the man steps down from his bar stool, edges past Larry, and addresses Kelly Smith.

"Kelly!" he cries, and this booming voice is more evidence of consumed alcohol, because Mike never allows himself to be this jovial in public. "What are you doing here?"

"I heard the best team of physicists in the world was celebrating, so I figured I'd stop by to see if you guys know how to party."

The bar patrons at their table and two others nearby explode with approval, determined to demonstrate to this unknown and beautiful woman that they do, in fact, know how to party. Larry stands back and absorbs the scene and somehow finds, drifting on the surface of disappointment and self-loathing, strength to maintain his plastic smile.

"I assume you already met Larry," Mike says.

"I did."

"Well, let me introduce you to everyone else."

Larry turns away then, scanning the bar for a more agreeable place to endure the balance of this evening, but there is no place he can go and nothing he can do to make this pain disappear. So he decides it's impossible for him to remain in this establishment for another minute. Enduring even sixty more seconds of this shame is asking too much of his already-taxed operating system. If he doesn't want to crash, Larry must get the hell out of this bar.

He doesn't say good-bye to Mike or Kelly or anyone else at the table. Instead he simply puts down his drink and disappears into the exultant field of drunken partiers, weaves his way toward the door, and escapes into the oppressive Texas night.

5

Mike pulls a bar stool between his and Gerald's and motions for Kelly to sit. His mind is a swirl of rum and excitement as she climbs into the stool and faces him. He isn't sure exactly why she is here or what he should say. Obviously the timing of her visit means she wants to ask about Higgs, but he's shocked that she would drive all the way to Olney unannounced.

"It's great to see you," he says, aware that everyone at the table is pretending to carry on their previous conversations when in reality they're all curious to find out more about this striking new woman.

"It's great to be here," Kelly returns. "I'm sorry to show up unannounced, but you said you wanted to give me a tour."

"Of course," Mike says, laughing. "Maybe later, though. Right?"

"Right."

She sits just inches away, one hand on her thigh and another around the martini glass. She's wearing a black blazer, cargo jeans, and thong sandals with chunky heels. He remembers the first time he saw her, on the plane, how stunned he was by her exquisite features, her champagne smile. It's probably a good thing he had a few drinks before this unexpected meeting. He leans closer and touches the hand on her leg.

"I'm really glad you came," he tells her.

"Me, too," she says. Squeezes his hand back.

He's forgotten what this feels like. The noise of the bar seems far away, as if it's on television in another room.

"Besides," she adds, "I figured I would come out here and use the opportunity to scoop our competing stations."

"So you're just here to pump me for information, then," Mike says, and takes a drink.

"Yeah, that's it. I just drove straight in, all the way from Huntsville, where I was on another assignment, just to ask you a couple of questions." She looks at her watch. "In fact, could we get started? I've got to get back to Dallas in time to log this story tonight."

Mike laughs.

"I'm not kidding," Kelly says, and brings the martini glass to her lips. But she laughs as she takes a drink and sprays a quick jet of chocolate on Mike's white shirt.

"Hey!" he cries, laughing again.

"Oh, I am so sorry," Kelly says. She stands and steps close to his chair. "I am so sorry. Let's go get that out."

"It's fine. Don't worry about it. I never liked this shirt anyway."

"Come on," Kelly says and takes him by the hand. "We're going to rinse that off. I'm not driving all the way over here and ruining your shirt in the first five minutes."

The improbability of this moment is not lost on Mike. The lottery-winning seat assignment, the long plane conversation, a couple of e-mails—and now Kelly is leading him to the bathroom of Eva's, where she wants to clean off the chocolate martini that she just spit on him. In his wildest dreams he would not have scripted such a silly and intimate moment. The stress of the last few days—the indecision about how to handle Larry's sabotage, the struggle over whether to generate the press release or come clean with Donovan, what to do about Samantha— tonight he'd partially blotted these things out with alcohol, but now they disappear completely as the two of them reach the bathroom. A bathroom that is surprisingly and mercifully empty, where Kelly wets a paper towel and tries to rub out the chocolate stain. Mike stands there watching her for a moment of stretched spacetime, the alcohol barking instructions at him, imploring him to seize the moment, hammering him with the well-known axiom that women love spontaneity, that they admire courage, that they lust for confidence, and finally he takes her face into his hands and pulls her mouth to his and is not surprised at all when she lets him.

6

Larry, sitting in his car outside Eva's. Listening to the *thump-thump-thump* of the jukebox. Thinking he should go back inside and tell everyone what a big fraud Mike is, thinking how stupid that would be, because it wouldn't ruin Mike's life, it would ruin *his* life.

Ha ha ha, what fucking life?

Wondering what the hell happened to Samantha. Mike says she hasn't been to the office since he told Donovan about the Higgs "discovery." She can't be happy, this whole turn of events, but what's she going to do? Tell everyone that she'd planned to hijack Larry's sequestered Higgs events and claim them as her own? What was she thinking, anyway? Who in the hell gave her the fucking balls to think she could come in here and lay waste to everything they had worked for?

Larry's been thinking more about what Mike said. About how it went down with Carrie. About who had sex with her, about who watched the tape. He thought about it all day today, as a matter of fact. Decided there is a chance, albeit small, that Mike is right. Larry would be the first to admit that his memory isn't what it once was. Especially with all the Crown he's been drinking. These days whole evenings are lost in the file system of his mind—orphaned bits and bytes of memory that are floating around in there somewhere, but with no organized way to find them. Yeah, maybe he was wrong about who met Carrie, but that doesn't change the essential truth of the situation—that the Jillians of the world will let someone like Mike into their clique but not Larry. That's what can't be ignored.

And still the *thump-thump-thump* of the jukebox sub-woofer. Mike in there, smiling his cheesy smile at her, and pretty soon they'll go back to his place, because where else are they going to go? And while Larry won't be there to peek through the open door this time, there are other ways to see. Even in a place like north Texas, you can find the supplies you need, if you know where to—

A knock on the glass scares the shit out of him. He looks over and sees Samantha standing outside the passenger side window.

"Larry?" she asks. "Are you okay?"

He considers just driving away, but instead reaches over and unlocks the door. Samantha climbs in beside him.

"Hey there," she says. "What are you doing out here?"

"Hanging out," Larry answers. "Feeling groovy."

"I came to this place looking for you, but I didn't expect to find you sitting in the car. You look awfully lonely out here."

"Right, like you give a shit. I know you're pissed because I went to Mike. What do you want from me?"

"Hey," she says, and touches his arm.

Larry jerks away, as if bitten. "Don't 'hey' me. What did you think, that I was just going to let you steal it from us?"

Samantha smiles. "From *him,* don't you mean?"

"My issues with Mike have nothing to do with you."

"In any case," she says, "it's all right. I would have liked the Nobel, but I suppose it doesn't really matter."

Larry looks at her. The way she's smiling, you'd think she was the crazy one. "What's that supposed to mean?"

"Nothing. Don't worry about it. You want to get out of here?"

"Get out of where?"

"I mean do you want to go back to your place?"

Larry shakes his head. "I don't think so."

"What do you mean, you don't think so?"

"I mean I have better things to do." He nods in the direction of the passenger door. "So if you don't mind, I need to get going."

"Better things, do you?"

"Look," he says. "I—"

But Samantha is already reaching for the door. "That's fine. Suit yourself. But don't forget that I tried. Don't come to me later when you change your mind."

She slams the door and leaves him alone in the car. Implying there is more to her than she let on. The offhand way she dismissed the chance to claim Higgs.

Whatever.

Larry indeed has better things to do.

Starts his car and puts it in gear.

7

To his own house first for supplies. Then over to Mike's neighborhood.

He leaves his car a couple of streets away, in the lot of a recently completed city park, and then strides out into the dark. The night is humid and moonless. The houses here are less than five years old and typical mid-priced suburban Texas fare. Roofs of shallow pitch, facades of uninteresting design, floor plans with small footprints on treeless, quarter-acre lots. Mike's salary would allow him to purchase more luxurious accommodations, but apparently he didn't see the point of opulence in a dusty science town like Olney. Or perhaps he felt his mark on physics would be made in sufficient time to earn the Nobel and subsequent fame, at which point he could move on to a sumptuous job in the computer industry, where real money would finally begin to roll in. But he's not doing that badly now—Larry knows his boss's salary reaches into six figures—and still he lives in this unglamorous neighborhood. It's almost as if Mike is throwing his success in Larry's face, so confident is he with his place in the world that showy possessions just aren't necessary for demonstration. And, sure, Kelly Smith will pretend to be the kind of girl who isn't attracted to money. She will appear to love Mike in this house as passionately as she would love him in a sprawling multilevel spread somewhere north of Dallas. But in reality she is attracted to the potential earnings his scientific notoriety will bring him. Chalk up one more for the preordained stars of the world.

But now, approaching Mike's house under the canopy of stars, Larry's briefcase is the great equalizer. What's inside, you ask? Why, how about a battery-powered color video camera and transmitter housed in a case half the size of a two-way pager? Powered by a nine-volt battery, the apparatus will capture images under light conditions as low as .03 lux at 470 lines of resolution, will detect sound, and will broadcast its signal at a radius of a thousand feet. Of course Larry doesn't need a thousand feet, he barely needs a hundred feet, because he'll be sending the audio/video signal to a tiny recorder in the study.

He marvels at the surging momentum of technology. There's no stopping its intrusion into the shrinking privacy of your life. No way to stop the peepers of the world, like Larry and prying office managers and direct marketers with offers of cheap Viagra.

Video cameras at traffic intersections and retail outlets and airports.

Tiny little chips that monitor the world.

Waiting for someone to connect the dots.

8

"You want to get out of here?" Kelly asks when they are sitting at the table again. For the moment they are alone, the others having left to tap out an impromptu "Cotton-Eye Joe" over by the pool tables. He sits facing her, and little sparks of energy shoot through his body every time their knees touch. Collision events being recorded by his internal detector: 100 percent.

"Sure," Mike answers. "But where to? Olney may be a science boomtown, but there still isn't much to do here."

"What about your place?"

"My place?"

"Why not? I'm sure we can find something to do there."

"All right, then," he says, and extends his hand to her. "Let's get out of here."

They make their way through the crowd, bouncing between a rogue dancer here, a drunken smoker there, weaving through the entire field of triumphant scientists and technicians toward the door. And then outside he pulls Kelly close so that he can walk with his arm around her.

"Did you just abandon your bill?"

"My credit card is behind the bar," Mike says. "I'll get it from Eva tomorrow."

"The cute bartender," Kelly observes. "You know her pretty well, then."

"She's a friend."

"Is that what you call them out here in the sticks? Friends?"

"I haven't slept with her, if that's what you're asking."

His car is only a few rows deep in the lot, and Mike's heart thunders as they approach it. He admires his own situation, which is that he is about to enter his car and drive home with this intelligent, beautiful creature occupying the passenger seat. He finds it amazing, his familiarity with the mellifluous surface of her lips, with the marbled texture of her tongue. And her wicked smile as he opens the door for her. His quickening breath as he finds his way to the driver's side, the crush of her mouth against his as they kiss again in the car.

"Why haven't you slept with her?" Kelly asks, the humidity of her breath condensing against his cheeks. "I saw the way she looked at you in the bar."

"I—"

Her lips against his again, the saline flavor of her mouth. "She's very beautiful, after all."

"She—"

"Or have you been waiting for me?"

"I knew you'd come," he says.

"Oh, really?" she asks playfully. "Pretty confident, were you?"

Mike leans away from her. Searches her eyes. "This is so trite, I can't believe I'm even going to say it. But I've never met anyone like you. When I broke up with Carrie, I was in no hurry to start another relationship. I was still in love with her. I sort of still am. But when I talk to you, I forget all about that."

Kelly covers his hand with hers. "That's very flattering. Thank you."

Mike leans forward and kisses her again, more gently this time. More leisurely.

Later, when he's starting the car, she says, "How far away do you live?"

"About five minutes."

"Can you bring me back here later, then?"

"Sure."

"Good. And I need to call my photographer. We're staying at the Holiday Inn over on Main. Would you have time to do an interview tomorrow morning?"

"That sounds perfect."

"Good." She leans forward and tastes him again. "You're a good kisser, you know."

"So are you."

Kelly smiles and keys a number into her cell phone. Mike drives toward his house, stealing brief glances at her striking profile, admiring her musical and yet decisive enunciation.

During the conversation with her on the plane, Mike never bothered to really picture her as a member of the news media. So overwhelmed was he by Kelly's delightful curiosity, so pleased by her intelligence, that it barely registered how perfectly suited her gifts were to anchoring an evening newscast. But now he sees and hears it clearly, how her sweet, pleasant voice is reinforced with gravity, combining feminine appeal with journalistic respect, and he can imagine hundreds of thousands—if not millions—of Dallas-area residents tuning in night after night to see their local news delivered by this stunning and magnetic woman. He hears the water-cooler conversations of attorneys, of car salesmen, of customer service representatives. Did you see that chick on Channel Eight last night? Dude, she has the most fantastic fill-in-the-blank. Hair. Eyes. Lips. Clothes. Makeup. Hands. Whatever. He guesses that she is recognized wherever she goes in Dallas. He pictures an e-mail in-box filled with scores of messages from mesmerized viewers. And this local celebrity, it isn't the strident, paparazzi fame of Julia Roberts or Jennifer Lopez. It isn't the distant admiration of millions upon millions of fans who will never lay eyes on the object of their fascination. No, the intimacy of this woman appearing in living rooms across the Metroplex likely breeds an apparent (but counterfeit) familiarity with the viewing public that her station most assuredly wields to hammer the other network affiliates into Nielsen ratings submission. A familiarity that generates not only millions of dollars in advertising revenue but also the occasional wayward fan who mistakes her on-camera charm for personal attention. And perhaps this is another reason why she turned down his request for her phone number after the flight—a mistrust of strangers born out of unnerving encounters with overzealous viewers.

But while Mike couldn't care less about Kelly's fame, some part of him is pleased that he currently occupies a position hundreds of thousands of male admirers in Dallas could only hope to achieve: That she is sitting in the passenger seat of his car, arranging with her photographer the particulars of an interview with *him*, with Mike McNair, and all this is occurring as he drives through nighttime Olney toward the hard-to-imagine destination of his very own house.

9

Larry's hands grow increasingly less reliable as he works to install the electronic equipment.

He's having a ridiculous time getting the fucking miniature video recorder to capture the signal from the fucking camera.

He keeps imagining the moment when he first plays the tape, the first glimpse of Kelly Smith's naked starlet body.

But it's affecting his work, this anticipation, and the more excited he gets the more unlikely it becomes that the recorder will capture any footage. If Mike and Kelly even come back here at all.

Yeah, right. Their romantic encounter tonight is a foregone conclusion. And it's not lost on him, this full orbit of fate. The three of them have been headed for this conclusion for years.

Because you'd have to be an idiot not to recognize the regal character of Mike's life. You'd have to be fucking crazy to question his ascension to superstardom, to the gilded stratum of truly fortunate men who have everything, on whose life the sun always shines while, godlike, they trample the balance of humanity. Who can possibly be blind to the way Mike steps upon normal men, men who crane their necks upward to regard him with scorn and envy, men who can't seem to get the fucking video recorder set up because they have to stop to unbutton their pants and grab themselves, so jittery with anticipation are they at the possibility of seeing naked their object of fascination, and so quickly do they bring themselves to orgasm that the ecstasy is fleeting and must be coaxed back for another round?

And a sound not unlike that of a key being fit into a lock.

And the creak of hinges as a door swings open somewhere to Larry's southwest.

And no time now to further tune the recorder, evasive action must be taken at once, and footsteps on the hardwood floor, a flotilla of shoes tapping and shuffling down the hallway, unintelligible human voices between sounds of moisture, of the soft and wet surfaces of individual organisms in constant and luxurious contact, Larry scrambling from his place beneath this desk, moving stealthily across the carpeted floor of the study and into a nearby closet, pulling the door almost shut, almost shut but leaving a crack just wide enough through which to watch the hallway. And there go the two lovers, past the study, their echoing footsteps becoming silent as they enter the carpeted room adjacent to this one, the master bedroom, where he hears the faintest sound of a mattress succumbing beneath the weight of two individual organisms glued together as one. And when sufficient time has somehow passed, when it becomes obvious that the two organisms are hopelessly locked together and not likely to soon disengage, Larry pushes open the closet door, which squeaks but surely not loud enough to be heard by the preoccupied lovers, and he steps across the room and crawls again under the desk. The work goes quickly now, and with his four-inch monitor he is able to finally tune the recorder, the image from the adjacent room now appearing in bright, lucid color, granting Larry visual access to their coupling. Kelly Smith's golden hair is draped over Mike's lower torso, her head moving gently up and down and then up again, and because no speakers are mounted to this monitor he is forced to endure the barely audible sounds drifting out of the master bedroom and into the study. But it's enough somehow, the faint tremors in the atmosphere that persuade the tiny bones in his inner ear to vibrate and transmit electrochemical impulses to his brain, somehow it's all enough, the crystal-clear digital video and distant analog audio, to bring Larry to orgasm again, his envy shooting upward like a geyser, sticking to the underside of the desk.

At this point, a moment of clarity stabs him: He is crouching in his boss's study, his *friend's* study, his friend, Mike McNair, who really has never done any intentional thing to hurt Larry, despite all the flawed memories to the contrary, and he realizes that he can leave now, can take his recorder and monitor and sneak out of the house and forget that any of this ever happened. He will have to direct his attention to another unsuspecting celebrity, or perhaps drop altogether the idea that he will ever lure a member of the high-profile, jet-set sorority of fame into his home, into his bed. And is such a future really so terrible? Isn't it likely that he will someday meet a nice girl who will treat him well? Does it matter if she's merely plain looking as long as she treats him with respect and loves him in spite of his flaws? Would it really be such an awful thing to let go of Jillian and Carrie and graduate to true adulthood, where real relationships are much more than hair and makeup and short skirts—

Except on the monitor now Kelly has climbed on top of Mike. She is sitting on him, grinding in a way that brings Larry immediately to attention again, the muscles in her ass almost seeming to grasp Mike like a hand, calling forth a groan from somewhere deep in his throat, there is nothing faint about *that* sound. And Larry takes himself in his hand again, knowing that he can never let go, that he has gone too far to turn back now.

A little while later he leaves them alone.

Alone except for the camera and recorder.

10

Mike and Kelly are standing in the kitchen. It's late now, maybe two in the morning, and they're taking turns eating chocolate ice cream out of the container. She feels wonderful. She feels guilty. And not just because of James.

"I'm sorry," she says.

"Sorry? About what?"

"I misled you about my beliefs on the plane. And in my first e-mail. I challenged you about science and Genesis when I don't really believe it anymore either."

"I thought I'd blown it," Mike answers. "Twice. First on the plane and then by recommending that book to you."

"The reason I. . . . Look, I wasn't always Unitarian. It's really difficult when something you believe for so long, when it stops making sense. You don't know where to turn. You have no idea what sort of foundation your life is based on, because until then it's been like someone else was looking out for you. You know? Someone was in charge, and you knew who He was, and if you follow His set of guidelines, everything will be all right. You won't be alone."

"What happened?" Mike asks her. "What changed your mind?"

"It was the intolerance. Every denomination is different, I guess. Even from one local church to the next. But more and more our congregation was speaking out on social issues like abortion and homosexuality and what have you. Our preachers said all the right things about God loving everyone but then didn't back that up with their actions or political preferences. And I would think, 'I'm here to celebrate God and love, not con-demn people different from me.' So I just stopped going. And then this girl I met in Dallas invited me to her Unitarian church one day, and it was wonderful. They loved *all* their neighbors. They didn't try to use their beliefs to influence politics, except to express their support for the separation of church and state."

Mike says, "I'm glad you found that. I can tell it means a lot to you."

"It's still hard sometimes," Kelly admits. "I challenged you because I wanted to hear the opinion of someone who had good reason not to believe, because I've already listened to enough harassment from my mom. I love her to death, but when I left our church she acted like I'd just gone off and murdered Jesus."

Mike leans forward, kneads her neck and shoulders. She leans into him.

"But see, I still believe. I believe in *some*thing. I know it's probably just an evolutionary thing, some need to belong. But even though I can see the Bible now as just a book, I still feel like there's more to this world than I can reach out and touch. It's why I was so interested in your 'collective reality' idea. I'm not so cynical anymore about spending all that money to understand the quarks and stuff. Because I sort of made fun of it on the plane, if you remember."

"I remember," Mike says. "You were pretty hard on the photons."

"But now I think it would be cool if you could understand the universe well enough to find . . . I don't know . . . something else."

"I think it would be, too."

Kelly turns around, takes Mike into her arms. His body is warm and comfortable and foreign to her. "Is that why you became interested in physics? Because you were looking for meaning?"

"I became interested when I grasped the scope and miracle of the universe for the first time. When I first realized how incredible it was that we were even here."

"But isn't that the same as—"

"Come outside with me," Mike says. He takes her by the hand and leads her toward the back door. "Let me show you something."

Mike turns off the backyard floodlight as they step onto the porch, a square of concrete before a rectangle of grass. She stands in front of him and he wraps his arms around her.

"You see all those stars?" he asks. "Look at how many of them you can see just with your naked eye. Every single one of them is a sun. Some bigger than our own, some smaller."

She loves his voice. She could stand out here all night listening to him.

"But from here the sky seems kind of two-dimensional, doesn't it? The stars look like they're all the same distance away. Imagine our planet is at the center of a gigantic, hollow bowling ball, and imagine the stars are white dots painted on the black inside of its surface. That's what they kind of look like from here."

"Okay," she says.

"But in reality they're all different distances away. And most of them are so far away that you can't see them. Our Milky Way galaxy is made up of at least a hundred billion stars, but we can only see maybe a thousand of them from here in my backyard. If this looks like a lot, imagine what it would look like if you could see, say, fifty million times more than this."

"Fifty million stars?"

"Not fifty million more. Fifty million *times* more. Try to imagine *billions* of stars."

"I guess the sky would be filled with them. How can there be so many?"

"It gets even better. You know how there are more galaxies than just our Milky Way? And that we can see them from here?"

"Sure."

"To see one of those others," Mike tells her, "you have to pick a spot where you can look all the way out of our own galaxy without encountering very many stars. Otherwise, the nearby stars will get in the way."

"Right."

"Okay, now remember that our own galaxy contains at least a hundred billion stars. Maybe more. That is an insurmountably big number. I'm thirty-two, which is about a billion seconds old. So—"

"What? How do you even know that?"

"Well, it's just math. Sixty seconds times sixty minutes times twenty-four hours times—"

"Did you do that in your head just now?"

"Well, no. I did it on a calculator once."

She smiles to herself. She's never met anyone like him. "You're such a nerd."

"A nerd?" he asks, relaxing his hold on her.

"Don't let go," she says, pulling his arms tight around her. "I mean a good kind of nerd."

He doesn't say anything for a moment. Just kisses the top of her head.

"Okay," she prompts. "So you're a billion seconds old. . . ."

"Right, and if I'd started counting the stars when I was born, one a second, I wouldn't be anywhere near done counting just the stars in our galaxy. I would have had to start counting a thousand years before Christ, and I'd still need a few hundred more years."

"Holy shit," Kelly says.

"Now think of the moon."

"The moon."

"Right. The moon looks pretty big, but it covers a pretty small patch of the overall sky. Imagine dividing the moon into fifty pieces of identical size. Imagine how much sky one of those little pieces would cover."

"Not much," Kelly says.

"Okay, now come inside. I want to show you a picture that scientists took with the Hubble space telescope."

Kelly takes his hand and lets him guide her back into the house.

"When the Hubble was built," he says, "when it enabled us to see farther into the universe than anyone had ever seen before, someone got the idea to look far outside our galaxy and see what things looked like."

In the study, Mike sits in front of his computer and starts moving the mouse, looking through folders.

"Remember how small the piece of sky was? Fifty of those pieces just to cover the moon? Astronomers pointed the Hubble telescope at a section of sky that big and came up with this picture."

He opens the image, and it is wild with color. Spots of light on a black background. Large and small, orange and yellow and white and blue, spiral shapes, spherical shapes, shapes that have no name.

"What are those?" Kelly asks.

"Galaxies. There are around ten thousand galaxies in this image alone."

"Thousands of galaxies?"

"Remember the tiny piece of the sky we're looking at. We've looked at other sections of the sky with deep field images and they all look about the same. It seems reasonable that in every tiny patch of sky where you pointed the telescope, you would see thousands of galaxies. The entire sky is almost thirteen million times bigger than this little section."

"And each one of these galaxies could have as many stars as our own galaxy? Hundreds of billions?"

"Well, some might have less. But some would surely have more."

"Holy shit. That's a lot of stars."

"And we think the matter that eventually created all those stars and galaxies—and the idea of spacetime itself—emerged from the event of the Big Bang. To understand how the universe evolved, how everything came to be, we have to understand the constituent elements and forces that emerged in those very first instants. That is basically what my job is. Knowing what all these particles are and how they act can help us understand how the whole thing got here in the first place."

"Oh," Kelly says.

"Once I began to comprehend all this, I was hooked."

Kelly reaches forward and wraps her arms around Mike's midsection. Kisses his ear. His neck. Climbs into the chair with him.

"I think I'm hooked, too," she says.

CHAPTER EIGHT

1

The receptionist beams as Steve strides into the office and announces his appointment.

"Of course, Mr. Keeley. Dr. Taylor is waiting. You can go right in."

So he does. And there is the shrink, who stands to greet him, who conveys an unmistakable sensation of Juicy Fruit and Diet Coke. Of pink sheets and stuffed animals.

"Hello, Mr. Keeley," Dr. Taylor says. "I have to say, you look much better than when I last saw you."

"Good to see you," he answers. "I feel better. I am better."

She sits in her chair and invites Steve to make himself comfortable on the sofa. But he'd rather sit in the other chair and face her this time.

"That's wonderful to hear. Did you see your physician? Or did you find something to disprove your conspiracy theory?"

"It's nothing like that," Steve says. "It's sort of the opposite. I figured out that my hallucinations haven't been hallucinations at all."

She just looks at him, as if unsure how to proceed. "Mr.

Keeley, it was very important last week when you acknowledged that the 'field' was a figment of your imagination. We both agreed the hallucinations were being caused by either the head injury, emotional trauma, or both. I'm afraid it's a big step backward to change your opinion about this."

"But that's what I wanted to talk to you about. If it turns out that I'm right, that I'm *not* hallucinating, then perhaps the entire story is real. It would make a lot more sense than trying to fabricate reasons why the nurse would lie or why records of my hospital stay would be erased."

"Steve—"

"Just listen," he tells her. "Hear me out and then maybe you'll at least try to be objective."

She starts to say something but stops herself. "Okay. Please go on."

Steve leans forward, lacing the fingers of his hands together. "Well, I was flipping channels yesterday—all I've been doing for days now is watching TV—because switching from one show to another is like self-hypnosis. It's the only way I've been able to keep the field at bay since I left here last week. And I ended up on CNN, where I end up a lot. I get addicted to watching the news sometimes. And I see this story, it's already in progress, I guess CNN picked it up from a local affiliate in Dallas. It's this interview with a physicist. I wrote down his name so I wouldn't forget it."

He pulls out the ragged piece of yellow paper, what's left of a Post-it note, pulls it out of his pants with trembling hands.

"Mike McNair. He works at that machine in Texas, the one built by the Internet tycoon? The super collider? And he goes through this entire history of physics and accelerators, how they started off small and kept getting bigger, because you need more and more power to study smaller and smaller things. The science of it was fascinating. Like when he talked about how the accelerator throws particles at other particles and then they 'see' what comes out. He said that when you look at something—say the Venus de Milo, for instance—you need light to see it, right? And light is photons, photons that are coming from the sun through windows, or from light bulbs in the Louvre, and those photons bounce off the Venus de Milo, and some of them are reflected back to your eyes, striking your retina in a certain configuration that is sent to your brain as electrochemical impulses, and that's how you see the sculpture. And if they turn down the lights, or if the sun goes down, then the amount of photons decreases, or the angle of the reflection changes, and you see *more* shadows or shadows in different places, and the Venus de Milo appears to be a somewhat different sculpture. Its reality to you is different depending on how many photons there are and in what way they are reflected back to your eyes.

"He said the super collider is like that, how what goes in—different kinds of particles—has an effect on what comes out. Because they can't actually 'see' what happens when the particles collide. But they have an idea of what should be going on, based on theory, based on previous experiments, and if they put a certain thing in and the product of those collisions matches what they expect, then they know they're on the right track. And if it doesn't, then they have to rethink the experiment or their predictions. It's a very tedious process."

"Of course," Dr. Taylor says. "Science is like that. It—"

"Right. I know that now. And this particular accelerator, this superconducting super collider, one of the main reasons it was built was to look for this particle, this Higgs thing they call the—"

"God particle. I've heard of it. I didn't realize they'd made an announcement."

"The physicist, this McNair, he made it clear that the results were preliminary, that more tests were needed, but he said they may have proven the existence of this God particle. And—get this—they think these God particles compose a field, the Higgs field, and if what they believe is true, it *permeates* everything. It's everywhere, in everything. And I couldn't help but remember what you said last week, how what I described sounded like *Star Wars,* how this field seemed to bind the universe together."

"Mr. Keeley—"

"I know it sounds crazy, but let me finish. Maybe you know all this, having gone to medical school and all, but I had no idea. I didn't give a shit about science in school. He said that everything around us, everywhere, it's all made up of tiny little particles. Not just atoms, everyone knows that, not just the sub-atomic elements like protons and electrons and that stuff, but even smaller things. Particles of matter like quarks. Messenger particles that communicate the forces that influence matter, like the strong force, which binds quarks together. Or electromagnetism, whose messenger particle is the photon, which isn't just visible light but all kinds of stuff. I mean, did you know radio waves and light are the exact same thing? Just photons? The wavelength decides if we see it or not. He said that your eyes are basically instruments designed to receive photons within a certain wavelength range, and if they had a wider range, or if we had some other sensory organ that could detect a wider or different portion of the wavelength spectrum, we could 'see' radio waves. Or the ultraviolet radiation that turns our skin brown, or whatever. I mean, I had no freakin' idea."

"If you remember, I sort of mentioned this last week."

"I know you did. I remembered *exactly* what you said, how detecting electromagnetic radiation would be a hell of a lot easier than influencing matter. Which is why I could hear Serena's thoughts but not levitate off the bed. It makes perfect sense!"

"Mr. Keeley. Forgive me for being so direct, but it's not healthy for you to think you can read minds. Or maybe pick up KROQ without a radio."

"I expected you to say that."

"No," she says. "I'm not trying to be flippant. Or alarm you. But what you're describing to me, that you truly believe you can perceive these fields, particles, so on and so forth, this is se-rious. A belief like that could seriously impair your ability to function normally in society. I'm afraid that, left untreated, you might . . . I'm afraid you might end up much worse off than you are now."

"I'm not bipolar. I'm not going on lithium, and I'm certainly not going to a mental hospital."

"I'm not suggesting—"

"Yes, you are. That's exactly what you're suggesting. And you know how I know?"

"I suppose because you can read my thoughts."

"Except the term *reading* really doesn't describe it right. It's more like glimpses, flickering visual images, combined with something less tangible than that. Some of it is simply feeling. Knowing. Like the first time I came here, when I desperately wanted to believe I was hallucinating, and yet I knew your mind was wandering while you talked to me. You were thinking about the girl. The one you've been sleeping with."

Dr. Taylor coughs. "Excuse me?"

"Does that make it more real for you? A personal example?"

"I . . . I'm afraid I'm going to have to ask you to leave."

"Dr. Taylor—"

"Please. Or I'll call the police."

"You call her your angel," he says to her. "She has pink sheets. And the taste, like bubble gum or something? You were thinking of that earlier, when I came in."

"Mr. Keeley!" the doctor says, nearly yelling now. He wonders if the receptionist will come in to see what the problem is. "I must ask you to leave at once!"

"Doesn't it interest you at all that I can do this? That I can sense it? I want to know what the hell happened to me. Wouldn't you, if you were me?"

"Mr. Keeley. Steve. I can . . . look, I can sympathize with what you're saying, because—"

pink sheets how can he know about the pink sheets?

"—but I will not accept that you can sit there and intercept electromagnetic radiation from my brain. I really must—"

"All right," he says, rising to his feet. "I'll leave. You obviously can't or don't want to help me. If you promise you won't call Dr. Dobbelfeld, I'll leave right now."

"But why don't you want me to call him? Regardless of whether or not I believe you—which I do not, I do not believe this—you do. And if it *were* true, then perhaps it happened as a result of the surgery. Intentionally or not, doesn't it make sense to contact the surgeon? He may be able to provide some insight."

"Or come after me," Keeley says. "Have you forgotten everything else? Svetlana? The nurse? The—"

"I haven't forgotten. But this is . . . these are delusions of persecution. I mean, please . . ."

But Dr. Taylor trails off, and Steve can sense that she doesn't really believe what she's saying. He can tell how much it disturbs her to not consider or objectively evaluate direct evidence.

"I guess I'll figure this out on my own," he says. Strides to the door and then stops just before it. "But I'll tell you something, Dr. Taylor. I don't know if you are qualified to be consulting patients on their emotional problems when you can't admit to your husband that you're cheating on him with another woman. I really doubt you'd recommend anyone else to take that course of action."

He leaves the office and shuts the door behind him.

2

On his way home now, directing his Infiniti through heavy traffic on the northbound 5, Steve supposes it doesn't really matter whether or not Dr. Taylor calls Dobbelfeld, because if it's true that he's under surveillance, if there is in fact something bigger going on than just his recovery from head trauma, then certainly they'll follow him wherever he goes. And if he does anything to reveal his suspicion, they'll know it. Which isn't good.

Because he's going to Texas to visit McNair.

Somehow it's important that he get close to the beam.

The challenge is to get there without being detected or followed. Unfortunately he has no idea how to do this. He can't even say with certainty that he's being followed, and even if he could, he wouldn't recognize his pursuers.

The field, thankfully, has been much more manageable since he saw the television interview. Somehow, the knowledge that it might be real has given him control over its charge against his processing power. For now he's pushed it into the background, like a computer program running behind the scenes, but Steve assumes that at some point it will rear its ugly head again whether he likes it or not.

And yet no longer can he regard the field as necessarily negative. Who wouldn't want the ability to sense the thoughts and concerns and desires of your friends, your loved ones, of a beautiful woman in a bar? But if it occurs with unpredictable frequency, or if his awareness of the field triggers mental breakdowns—even occasionally—then such a skill will do as much harm as good. Like Dr. Taylor said, there might come a time when he would be unable to function as a normal, accepted member of society. Psychiatric hospitals are surely populated with innumerable patients who possess (real or imagined) paranormal powers.

Dr. Taylor, after all, could contact his parents, his company, Dr. Dobbelfeld, and recommend to them all that he be committed. Load him up with drugs and let him wander around slobbering. Which is as good a reason as any to get out of town, to go all the way to Texas and find McNair. But he'll have to be quick about it, and careful, because until Dr. Taylor contacts Dobbelfeld, there's at least a chance he could get out of the city undetected.

Ah, shit. This is absurd. How can he, a logical, goal-oriented man, who just weeks ago had life by the balls, how can he truly believe he is the victim of an international conspiracy? A conspiracy organized, presumably, by someone in the medical community, the purpose of which is to impart to him the ability to sense particles previously undetectable by human senses? To consider his situation in such frank terms is to render it preposterous. And yet he cannot refute the evidence that has led him to this conclusion, even Dr. Taylor's unspoken admission that she has, in fact, been cheating on her husband. Look at the way she threw him out, the way she stammered and refused to listen to him. It's only logical to draw reasonable conclusions from such proof.

And yet something more instinctive than logic is pushing him toward Texas.

There is no question in Steve's mind now that he was somehow misled by Dr. Dobbelfeld, that something terrible and unjust happened to Svetlana, so his plan cannot include contact with anyone associated with his hospital stay. Another possibility is to visit his local physician, but the first thing *he'll* want to do is contact Dobbelfeld. And if Steve volunteers his conspiracy theory, here come drugs or the psychiatric hospital again. Taken together, these scenarios effectively eliminate anyone who can be reasonably expected to assist him.

He needs this physicist in Texas to help him understand. To get him close to the beam and help him understand what it means.

He needs to know what it is that he sees.

And what to do with it.

3

A little while later Steve arrives home and heads immediately to the closet in his guest room, where a black Lands' End suitcase stands waiting. He tosses in a few shirts, some pants and shorts, a pile of boxers. In the bathroom he fills his leather travel bag with a razor and shaving cream, toothbrush and toothpaste, and is on his way back to the suitcase when he senses his pursuers again. Watching from somewhere nearby.

He still can't see them, has no idea what to look for or where they might be. But this time they know Steve is on to them.

With more time, some narrow window between his decision to leave and their new intelligence, he could have fashioned a plan. Something covert, perhaps steal a neighbor's car, something. Now he'll have to simply find his way to the freeway and then hope to lose them in traffic. Steve knows the city well, surface streets as well as the controlled-access grid, and hopes that his pursuers do not. They're probably from Zurich, after all.

The field seems to emerge from nowhere as he makes his way to the garage. The walls shimmer with it, the floor almost translucent beneath his feet. He imagines the men are standing at the end of the street, and he fancies he can see them from here, through adjacent houses and those farther away. He reaches the garage and pushes the glowing red button to open the garage door, watching—seemingly in slow motion— uncountable electrons streaming from the button to a microchip in the door opener, persuading it to engage the chain drive. Atoms of hydrogen and oxygen and nitrogen flood the garage and mix with the stale air already present. He throws the suitcase into the back seat of his Infiniti, climbs behind the wheel, and backs carefully out of his garage.

It occurs to him again: Perhaps insanity is reality no one else can see.

Because the world is alive. The field is everywhere at once, everywhere he looks, although he isn't at all seeing it. It is simply *there,* in those trees and that parked car and in the grooved patterns of residential stucco.

But now he's not being attacked by it. Now he's using it.

He senses the car's energy, can feel the slight deceleration through time as he moves through space. He can detect changes in the surface of the road, in the temperature and pressure of the tires.

The men are not at the end of his street, but they must be somewhere nearby. He'll have to watch for them closely, because they will surely try to stop him from entering the freeway, where he can disappear into traffic and be lost forever.

But he does enter the freeway, accelerating onto the entrance ramp with no sign of surveillance anywhere. The field flickers inside him, all around him. It seems he is able to anticipate the maneuvers of other drivers before they make them. Traffic slows, each lane moving at speeds independent of one another, and he darts from one lane to the next, picking the fastest one at will.

He cannot, of course, simply head for LAX and purchase a flight to Dallas. Travel via mass transit will leave behind a trail too easy to follow. Instead he'll have to drive, a two-day journey across the blasted desert landscapes of California, Arizona, and New Mexico, and Steve finds himself looking forward to the raw solitude such a road trip will provide. Because sitting at home isn't solitude. Not with the sprawling multiverse of satellite-provided television at his fingertips.

Soon he reaches Interstate 10, signaling the true beginning of his long trek east. Thirteen hundred or so miles, all the way to Olney, Texas, where he hopes to—if not find answers—at least understand what questions to ask. Where he hopes to feel the beam.

In the rearview mirror he spots a gold Honda Accord. It hovers a few car lengths back in the adjacent right lane. From here he can't really see through the windshield, cannot determine if the front seat contains (two) Swiss goons. But the Accord is following him, of that he feels sure, which means he cannot permit it to pursue him through the suburbs and out of civilization. Because they could take him easily in the desert.

With no one around to witness the abduction it would be a piece of cake for a couple of Swiss thugs like these guys.

So he begins to look for creases in the traffic, gaps his car might fit through, and gradually works his way into the far right lane. The Accord edges closer, remaining in its own lane and almost pulling even with Steve's Infiniti. This is his chance. He watches the Accord, watches the highway, watches the exit for Citrus Road approaching. He's in Covina now, about halfway to San Bernardino, and he's going to take this exit, bearing down upon it as the Accord continues driving in its own lane. He's surprised at their position—because if he exits now they will lose him—but still he waits until the last possible second before jerking the wheel to the right, violating a triangle of parallel white lines and nearly broadsiding a car halfway down the off-ramp. But he uses the field to save himself, sensing the driver's reaction to him and veering out of his way. Chuckles to himself as the frightened man flips the bird at him, laughing not out of disrespect but because he has achieved success. Has escaped the interstate and deceived his pursuers. Now he can take Grand Avenue to the Pomona freeway and not get back on the 10 until he reaches Beaumont. From there he should be home free all the way to Texas, all the way to Olney.

All the way to the beam.

4

Darkness approaches from the east as he crosses the California–Arizona border at Blythe. Through the sunroof stars seem to shine down upon him, the moon blazing and white and magnified by the clarity of the desert. In L.A. the night sky is blurred by air and light pollution to an even, amber glow, and it seems to Steve that this observation is analogous to his newfound ability. The canopy of stars, like the field, is always there. Most city people just aren't in a position to see them.

Steve wonders if anyone out here is in a position to see *him*.

Headlights began to flicker in his rearview mirror as the sun descended behind him, belonging mostly to tractor trailers, but also to a number of passenger cars. Perhaps someone back there is following him, hanging back far enough to be inconspicuous, waiting to see where he'll go. But that doesn't seem very likely. Are they really going to follow him through the desert and halfway across the country? Wouldn't they have installed a GPS transmitter on his car, or be watching him from a satellite, or something more sophisticated than simply tailing him?

Logically, there isn't any way he lost those men in the Accord so quickly. A guy like him—a corporate suit whose previous goals in life included scaling the corporate ladder and finding marital bliss—did not outwit and outmaneuver a trained surveillance team. What seems more likely, in retrospect, is that the Accord was never following him at all. The surveillance—if it's there at all—is something else, something more advanced.

In any case, he doesn't sense it now. The field seems to have retreated into the periphery again, comfortably out of his way, but he wonders if he's in control enough to call it up on demand. Perhaps he could use it to drive through the night without headlights. By distinguishing between the chemical makeup of the asphalt and the adjacent desert soil, perhaps he could navigate without light.

Steve closes his eyes. After a second or two the car begins to vibrate, his tires humming stridently, because the Infiniti is veering off the road. Unperturbed, he tries again to visualize the field and its conductors, tries to imagine the way it consumed him in the days leading up to and after his non-interview, but now his gift is nowhere to be found. Which is exactly the problem, exactly why he is worried, because an intermittent ability to sense constituent particles is no gift at all. And now, still sixty miles away from Phoenix, Steve wonders what might happen if he arrives in Olney and gets close to the beam and nothing happens.

What will he do then?

The highway stretches in front of him, an infinite black ribbon disappearing into the darkness.

5

Eighteen sleepy hours and three refueling stops later, beneath a brutal noontime sun, Steve approaches Olney from the southwest on Texas S.H. 79. His ass is numb, his right arm sore from resting his weight on the Infiniti's center console, and he's so tired he could pull over to the shoulder and fall immediately asleep. But of course he cannot sleep. He must find McNair.

He was able to make it as far as El Paso without a map, but he knew nothing about Olney except that it was somewhere in the general vicinity of Dallas. The particle accelerator is a huge thing, something like fifty miles around, so it's not like he can just drive up to it. But surely there must be administrative offices, some kind of central command location, and he guesses the way to find it is simply head into town and ask someone.

The two-lane highway is wide and freshly paved, but the countryside on either side of it seems barely alive. Clusters of stunted mesquite trees stand above sparse pastures of brown grass, pastures guarded by charming oil pump jacks whose rusty, vaguely equine shapes have long been abandoned. Occasionally the landscape crystallizes into diminutive red cliffs or sinks into shallow stream valleys, but it's mostly flat all the way to the city limit, which is marked by the standard green rectangular sign:

OLNEY

POP. 15540

and a smaller sign mounted beneath that boasts:

> HOME OF THE
> ONE ARM
> DOVE HUNT

and a third, obviously much newer:

> AND THE NORTH TEXAS
> SUPERCONDUCTING
> SUPER COLLIDER!

He passes ancient corrugated steel buildings, rotting, wooden clapboard structures, the occasional squatty ranch home, and Steve wonders briefly why in the hell scientists would pick a place like this as the location of their most expensive and advanced experiment. But again it's the size of the thing— where else to put a fifty-mile-around particle accelerator except the empty, endless Texas prairie?

Finally, as he approaches the town proper, civilization emerges in the form of fast food restaurants and convenience stores and an enormous Wal-Mart. Then a fork in the road, where a clean, new sign directs NTSSC visitors a few yards farther ahead, where 79 intersects with Texas 251. And here is another new road sign, one that makes his tired eyes widen:

> NTSSC ADMINISTRATIVE OFFICE   6
> NEWCASTLE   11

Six miles. He's only six miles away.

Steve approaches the turn and is surprised as he waits for two, three, now four cars to drive by before he can merge onto the intersecting highway. This road is newly resurfaced, and suburban housing developments have gone up on both sides of the highway. He follows the drivers ahead of him, gradually accelerating to the speed limit, and watches a few more cars file in behind him. In fact, as 251 rises and falls with the gently rolling

prairie, he realizes there is a nearly unbroken line of automo-
biles occupying its southbound lane. An unbroken line that
condenses until it's bumper to bumper, and when he finally sees
the NTSSC entrance ahead, maybe two hundred yards away, he
is forced to bring his car to a complete stop. 251 southbound is
at a standstill, at least twenty-five vehicles between his own and
the entrance. News vans, passenger cars, SUVs, you name it.
And the line is barely moving. He'll be here forever.

Even worse is that not all vehicles are getting through. After
a few minutes he can see that news vans and some SUVs are
granted access, but very few passenger cars are being allowed inside the gate. He doesn't need the field to tell him that only
invited guests and members of the news media are being admitted, and it doesn't take a particle physicist to realize that Steve
himself is an uninvited guest. There isn't any way they're going
to let him in.

Besides, the beam isn't even on. It's wrong, somehow, what
he's doing. Going directly to McNair is not the answer.

Probably he should get some rest anyway, a little voluntary
sleep before he passes out and rear-ends the car in front of him.

Steve pulls out of the southbound lane, uses the Infiniti's
tight turn circle to pivot all the way back north, and drives back
to town. All the way back to the acres of anonymous parking at
the Wal-Mart, where he finds a remote spot in the grid of white
stripes. Crawls snakelike into the backseat. Curls fetally. Drifts
away.

6

He dreams of Svetlana. She joins him in the backseat, impossi-
bly, because there is barely enough room on the seat for Steve
himself, let alone a gorgeous woman curled up beside him. She
nibbles on his neck, on his earlobe, which is also impossible
since the back of his head is pressed against the leather seat.
She whispers in his ear that he should drive a little farther. Find

the reporter who helped bring the physicist's message to him. Because, unlike McNair, she will listen.

But Steve doesn't know anything about the woman, cannot remember her name, and certainly doesn't know where to find her. At least not until Svetlana reminds him of the discussion with Dr. Taylor, when he explained how CNN picked up the interview from an affiliate in Dallas. And now he does remember, remembers her name is Kelly Smith, and with a little prodding even recalls the station's call letters, WFAA. News 8.

At some point in the dream Svetlana convinces him to move on, that eventually a security guard is going to drive by and check on his car. Steve dreams that it's already six o'clock in the evening, that he's been sleeping for more than five hours, dreams that he finds the address and driving directions to WFAA on his Internet-capable GSM cell phone, he dreams that Svetlana rides shotgun with him as he finds his way out of Olney. They head east, first on Texas 114 and then on U.S. 380 toward Denton. Denton, she explains, is only forty miles from Dallas. And Dallas is where he'll find Kelly Smith.

7

It's a little after eight. Wednesday night. Kelly is reading scripts for the ten o'clock show and wondering when Frank is finally going to bring her the bad news. Jeff Pearson, after all, hasn't spoken to her since Friday, when she abandoned the execution story in Huntsville and drove to Olney. He could be avoiding her on purpose, maintaining distance so it'll be that much easier on his conscience when he fires her. Or she could be overreacting, especially considering the national exposure she's brought to the station, which will likely increase local ratings and thus advertising revenue. No GM can argue with those results.

But still, she—

Her phone rings, 212 area code. New York. It's her agent.

"Hey, Winnie," she says.

"I keep telling you, it's Winston."

This is their ongoing joke.

"Right, Winnie."

"Okay, I'll let you win this time. Especially when you hear the news I have. Are you sitting down?"

"Just reading my scripts," she says.

"ABC called. Diane Sawyer is leaving *Good Morning America*."

"Already?"

"The network wants to fly you to New York. They want you to audition with Charles Gibson next week."

She looks around the newsroom. Afraid if she says anything everyone will hear.

"Winston," she whispers. "Don't lie to me."

"I'm not lying."

"Come on, *GMA*? I've only been here for—"

"Kelly, I've been getting calls since the *People* interview. I've kept quiet because I wanted you to get some solid experience there in Dallas before we exercised the outs in your contract. But this is too big to pass up."

She sits there for a moment, waiting for an appropriate response to form on her lips.

"Are you kidding me?" she asks finally. "*Good Morning America?*"

"Are you interested?"

"Of course I am!"

"Good. I'll arrange everything with them and get back to you. But don't say anything to anyone at this point. At least no one at the station. Pearson isn't going to be happy to lose you a month after he took over."

8

The newscast is a blur, and afterward Kelly can barely remember anything she read, has no idea what banal, automatic segues came out of her mouth going into commercials or coming back from them, has no earthly clue what joke she and Ted and Troy the weatherman shared. All she can think about is *GMA* and New York.

And Mike.

Because Mike isn't in New York, and there is only one super collider, and it doesn't matter that she could make more money than either one of them could spend. What matters is that his job—his life in experimental physics—is here, and the future of her career is not.

She checks her e-mail one last time before shutting off the computer—hoping for but not finding a message from Mike—and then heads for the parking garage. She tries to convince herself that she really knows nothing about Mike, cannot say with certainty what kind of person he is, or if he'll treat her well, or if he's someone with whom she could spend a lot of time. She considers the more familiar argument, that to accept the love of another man is to admit the door to James is closed. She imagines herself falling in love, finding herself in a relationship that could truly be *the one,* and at the same time fully aware that she has been here before.

The parking garage is a haze of amber light, and her car stands alone in its assigned space. She curls her way down the spiral drive of the parking garage and then out into the Dallas night. The freeway is mostly empty, and she flies like a missile toward her home in Richardson.

GMA. What would that pay? A million dollars a year? Maybe even two or three million? These potential salaries are not real numbers to her. And forget about the money, anyway. Imagine the chance to discuss the most important events of the country and the world, imagine interviewing the president. Imagine making a daily difference in millions of lives across the country instead of delivering local news in thirty-second sound bites.

Not until her exit at McDermott do the headlights in her rearview mirror finally strike her as ominous. They've been behind her for a while, and this knowledge has been sitting patiently in the back of her mind. But for the car to come this far, to maintain a steady distance behind her and then follow her off at the same exit, this seems odd. Not necessarily a problem, but coincidental enough to worry her.

She drives on, trying not to worry. She doesn't think about the crazy e-mails she sometimes gets. Specifically she doesn't think about the most recent messages, the guy who claimed to have seen her at Target. No, she just turns up the radio and sings along with a sappy '80s song. Besides, her neighborhood is gated. And on top of that her safe room is made of concrete and sealed by a solid steel door that locks from the inside.

The car is still back there.

Up ahead she sees the comfortable and familiar entrance to her neighborhood. Unrolls her window as she approaches the gate and quickly keys in the code. The car behind her seems to increase its speed. It's a luxury sedan, German or Japanese, and she supposes this should relax her. Luxury sedans are popular in her neighborhood. But still it would be nice if the damn security gate would close more quickly. What kind of gate takes thirty seconds to close? Not a security gate. More like a vanity gate. Sure enough, the sedan makes it through.

And follows her through the neighborhood. All the way to her own street.

She opens the garage door while still several houses away, and the tires squeal as she hurries inside. The door shuts behind her. She breathes a sigh of relief.

Except that from here Kelly can't see the car at all.

She rushes into the house and to a window and looks across her front lawn.

The sedan is not there.

But it could be farther up the street, something she could see better from upstairs. So she turns and grabs the handrail, taking the stairs two at a time, and is almost to the top when the doorbell rings.

The doorbell. He's ringing the goddamn doorbell! What the

hell is she supposed to do now? Call the cops and tell them someone is ringing her doorbell? Even if she explains that a car followed her all the way from downtown, that she is a local news personality and has reason to fear stalkers, they'll want to know if the driver has threatened her in any way. They'll ask if she has looked through the peephole to see who it is.

Which, Kelly supposes, is the answer. Unless the guy has a gun trained on the door, ready to shoot as soon as she approaches, going back downstairs is not automatically dangerous. And once she's looked outside, she can run back upstairs and call the cops.

But when the doorbell rings again, Kelly wonders if she should just ignore it. Won't the person eventually give up and go away?

The bell rings a third time.

"Ms. Smith," a voice says. "I'm very sorry to bother you. If you're frightened you don't have to open the door. I only want to ask you about Mike McNair."

The door is at the bottom of the stairs. She descends to the third or fourth stair from the top—surely higher than the stalker will aim his weapon—and answers.

"Whoever you are, please leave. You're trespassing, and that's grounds for arrest. Please leave now, or I'll call the police."

"Ms. Smith," the voice pleads, "I know I'm trespassing, and I apologize. I'm only asking for a minute of your time. You don't have to open the door. I'm not here to hurt you. I just . . . I need to see McNair. Will you please help me?"

"Mike isn't here," Kelly responds. "He works at the super collider in Olney. Why did you come here?"

A long pause. And then, "I have information about the Higgs field that I think he'll find important. I went to Olney, but there was no way to get past the gate. I thought maybe you could help me contact him."

"Why me?"

"Because of the interview. Because you helped him explain the Higgs discovery."

Kelly shifts her weight and sits more comfortably. As frightened as she is, she's also a little curious to find out where he's going with this story.

She says, "What sort of information do you have about Higgs?"

Another long pause. "You're going to think I'm crazy."

"And what do you suppose I think now? Since you followed me home? Since we're having a conversation through my front door?"

"You're right," the man admits. His voice sounds lucid and clear, if it's even possible to evaluate such a thing. "Okay. My name is Steve Keeley, and I live in Los Angeles. I survived a near-fatal head injury while on a business trip in Zurich last month. Emergency brain surgery was required to save me, and since then I've experienced what I thought were hallucinations of a particle field. Or multiple particle fields. Or God. I don't know. But when I saw your interview with McNair the other day, I knew that what he described to you, the way the world worked and the theoretical role of Higgs, I knew he was describing exactly what I'm sensing. I believe I have sensed the Higgs field directly. I'm able to detect electromagnetic fields. Who knows what else. I know it sounds crazy, but I promise you I'm not."

Kelly knows that mentally ill people can appear to be rock-solid sane, but being sick and posing a threat to her are not necessarily the same thing. She descends a step closer to the floor and is about to answer when Keeley continues.

"I know what you're thinking. You're thinking that crazy people can seem as sane as regular people. But I promise you I'm telling the truth."

Kelly stares at the door. She imagines she can see him through the pressed wood, his sad form slumped against it, disheveled, and she still doesn't understand why this man is petitioning *her*.

"I never saw you before the interview, Ms. Smith. I'm not one of your admirers. I didn't even intend to come here. I drove twenty-four hours across the country to Olney, but they were only letting press inside the gate."

Kelly is impressed by his ability to guess her thought process, but that doesn't mean he's sane. "Why *me,* Mr. Keeley? Why not call the NTSSC and ask to speak to Mike? Or request an appointment with him? Why drive past Olney, all the way to Dallas, to see me?"

"Because Mike would never listen to me on his own. He'll resist what I have to say. But I thought you might . . ."

"Might what?"

"Look," he says. "There's a lot I'm not telling you, because I don't want you to immediately discount me. But my ability to perceive particle fields has predictable consequences. I'm sure you must have learned from McNair the same thing I did, how these particles of matter and energy compose the world around us, that radio waves and light are both communicated by photons."

She says nothing. This is becoming a circle, a shape with no end, and soon there will be no choice other than to call the police.

"But it isn't just the sun or radio stations that emit electromagnetic energy. Our brains do as well. And lately I've been able to sense and decode that energy. Which means . . . which means I can read minds. And also this woman, this woman I knew in Zurich who died the day after my head injury, she has been following me somehow. Helping me. I'm not religious, I don't believe in ghosts, but I've begun to believe the universe is more than what we think it is, that perhaps our life force doesn't die with us, because it's this dead woman who instructed me to come here."

Gooseflesh marbles Kelly's skin. She thinks of her discussion with Mike, about the collective reality, and then pushes the thought away. She's heard all she is willing to hear.

"Ms. Smith," he says. "I will prove it to you. When I began speaking to you, you descended to the fourth stair from the top of your staircase. And later you became more comfortable and went down another stair. That's where you are now."

Kelly hears a soft cry of surprise emerge from her lips. She's frozen where she sits.

"How could you. . . . Is there a camera in my house? Are you the one who has been sending me the e-mails? Because I am going to call the police *right now.* This is a horrible invasion of my privacy, Mr. Keeley, and—"

"And now you're wondering if the money is worth it. You're thinking that if the attention is this bad in Dallas, what's it going to be like if you get the job at *Good Morning America*? And now you're thinking of your first job in Richmond, and how far you've come, and you're wondering how you could've believed yourself so ugly when your life has come to this, crazy men following you home, beseeching you on your doorstep, and now you're wondering how I could possibly know all this, you're wondering if I've bugged your phone at work, you're wondering if I could possibly have found all this information about you on the Internet, except that you type your own name into search engines once or twice a month and have never found anything so personal as this. And now you're wondering how I could know *that,* and you're waiting for me to say something that I could not *possibly* know about unless what I'm saying is really true, and you're moving closer to the door now, and you're thinking of your senior prom, when you stayed home against your mom's appeals to the contrary, because she didn't want you to grow up successful in work but hopelessly alone, and thank goodness you're about to open the door, I promise you I am not lying, I just want someone to help me, and I think Mike McNair may be that person, because all this seems implausibly related, and—"

Kelly reaches forward and unlocks the door. She stands there a moment, almost unable to believe her hands are in fact performing these particular actions, that she is about to invite a complete stranger into her home, especially one who may or may not be crazy. And even if he *isn't* crazy, what he seems capable of frightens her even more. And still she is opening the door. And here stands Steve Keeley, not really disheveled, perhaps a little tired but otherwise a decent-looking man, and she knows that she has opened more than just her door, that allowing him inside is somehow going to change her life.

CHAPTER NINE

1

Donovan is on his way to the office, cruising through orange dawn in his black S55, when the ringing of his cell phone breaks the morning silence. He reaches down and turns on the speakerphone.

"This is Landon."

"Mr. Donovan," says Allgäuer. It's barely 7:30, he's had no coffee, and now this smug voice polluting the interior of his car.

"Hey there, Allgäuer. I guess you heard about our announcement. I'm surprised you didn't call sooner."

"I have been—how do you say it in English?—a little under the clouds?"

"Under the weather."

"Yes. 'Under the weather.' In any case, I am recovering and will soon be making the journey to Olney."

"You're coming here? When?"

"Today."

"From Switzerland?"

"I am in Geneva now. I will be departing in a few hours, and I will arrive in Wichita Falls no later than five o'clock your time. I would like you to be there when I arrive."

"Five o'clock? It's eleven hours from Zurich to Dallas alone. By the time you make your connecting—"

"Mr. Lange has been kind enough to make special arrangements for us. My doctor and I will be traveling by Concorde. We will arrive at Sheppard Air Force Base in Wichita Falls. Please be there by four in case we arrive early."

"Concorde? I thought those were retired."

"Only the commercial models. This is a special plane built for Mr. Lange."

Special plane? "I don't understand. Why are you coming here now?"

"Circumstances I did not foresee have changed my plans. Thanks to your impulsive announcement, we must prepare for an encounter I did not expect to occur for several weeks. You should have contacted me first, Landon."

Donovan's hands squeeze the steering wheel hard enough to press indentations into the leather. "I've done exactly what you asked me to do. You never said to contact you if we made a discovery here. Lange never said anything about it, either."

"The security attendant will be instructed to grant you access to the base. You will be further briefed when I arrive. Do not tell anyone I am coming, including Samantha. Do you understand?"

Through clenched teeth, Donovan says, "Yes, I understand."

"Thank you, Landon. I look forward to finally meeting you in person."

The phone disconnects, and a few moments later he turns into the NTSSC gate. Waves at the attendant, Louis. Tries to comprehend the significance of Lange arranging a Concorde flight for Allgäuer, a flight that is going to arrive at a United States Air Force base. The construction of the NTSSC demonstrated that Lange is connected in ways that he is not, but to send Allgäuer over the ocean in your personal Concorde, to land that plane at a military facility in a post–9/11 world, these things speak of a power network that Donovan can only begin to appreciate.

He's familiar with the stories surrounding the Trilateral Commission, the Council on Foreign Relations, even the Illuminati. Conspiracy freaks clog Internet servers around the globe with websites devoted to "exposing the true leaders of the world," to the grand plan of the oldest and richest families to create a new world order that steals liberty from the common man. The idea apparently stems in part from Christian fundamentalists and their fear about the Book of Revelations, where the Antichrist rises to power and unites the nations of the world, and anyone can see these people are stretching and confusing the truth to force current events into their mythology. But as crazy as it seems, Donovan can't help but wonder if a kernel of truth exists somewhere in the chaos of their ideas. Look at Lange's apparently boundless influence, his relationship with Allgäuer and that effect on the private super collider. It's not the first time Donovan has wondered about who might be pulling the strings from behind the curtain.

He wonders how close he is to some answers.

2

After three days of print and television interviews, after hours of answering questions and fielding phone calls, Mike refused to schedule any interviews for Thursday and Friday. This morning he relishes the thought of just sitting in his office, staring at his computer monitor, sifting through his overflowing in-box and maybe browsing around the Internet. It's crazy the way a life can change in the span of a few days. Crazy how Larry's revelation became Donovan's mandated press release, which brought Kelly closer to him, the local interview that went national and renewed interest in the field of particle physics. And to think it all started when Donovan brought in Samantha. It was she, after all, who found inconsistency in the detection software, her blackmail that brought Larry to Mike.

And since Samantha hasn't been to the office in a week—not since he told Donovan about the possible Higgs events—Mike hasn't been forced to confront her about it. He doesn't know what he would say anyway. She tried to take his job, to steal all his work and claim Higgs for herself. But who knows when he would have caught on to Larry without her?

Of course Higgs isn't a complete certainty at this point anyway, considering there hasn't been much chance to confirm the events Larry previously discarded. But tonight they'll begin their first beam run since the announcement, and it's exciting, and—

The phone rings. Mike looks over at it, determined not to answer unless he recognizes the number. He does. It's Kelly.

"Hi there," Mike says. "What are you doing up? I thought you stayed in bed until ten o'clock."

"I need to see you."

"Is everything okay?"

"I'm fine. Don't worry about me. But I met someone last night who needs to talk to you. We both do. It's . . . it's very strange, Mike."

"Kelly," Mike says. "Are you sure you're okay?"

"I'm fine. I promise. But what I have to tell you. . . . Look, I don't want to say any more on the phone. I already called in sick to work. I'm going to drive over later. Probably this afternoon. What time are you leaving the office today?"

"Maybe four or four thirty. You're going to drive all the way to Olney?"

"What, you're already tired of me?"

"Not hardly," Mike says. "Just concerned."

"Don't worry, Mike. I'll be there this afternoon."

"Can you at least tell me who this other person is?"

"Let's just wait until I get there. I'll see you around five, okay?"

Mike sits there for a moment, wondering what could be wrong, and then goes back to the never-ending list in his in-box.

3

Larry is still asleep when the doorbell rings.

He's dreaming of Kelly Smith, the lovely way she likes to lie on her side while (Larry) curls up beside her.

The doorbell. Again.

He crawls out of bed, wondering who in the hell could be bugging him at *this* hour of the morning. And it better not be some fuckface door-to-door salesman, by God.

The doorbell rings again, and he's pulling on a pair of shorts now, and a T-shirt, and in the back of his mind he thinks something is wrong with the light coming through the windows. Wonders if maybe he overslept a little. Turns a corner and looks out the peephole and there is Samantha, standing on his front porch.

He pulls open the door, squinting at the sunlight. At the humid heat. Man, it's going to be a scorcher today.

"Larry?" she asks. "I'm sorry. Were you asleep? Are you sick?"

"What are you doing here?" His tongue is thick and dry. Someone may or may not be pounding a wooden stake into his temple. There is a chance he may have consumed some alcohol last night. He may have served himself a cocktail or ten with dinner.

Samantha seems agitated. Looks upset.

"Can I come in?"

"I don't think so," Larry tells her. His house, if he remembers correctly from sixty seconds ago when he stumbled here from his bedroom, is not exactly in what some might call "tip-top shape."

"Look," she says. "I was sent here—to Olney—for more than just luminosity improvements. Landon was instructed to give me full access to the facility, but not for the reason you think. It wasn't just to take the Higgs discovery for myself. There was more."

"Why did you come so early in the morning to tell me this?" he asks her.

"Larry, it's nearly six o'clock in the evening."

"What?"

"Please let me come in."

He finally does, mainly because he wants to look at a clock and prove her wrong. There's no way it's nearly six o'clock. No way he slept an entire day away.

Samantha picks her way through the living room, past empty pizza boxes and purple Crown drawstring bags, and finds a place on his sofa to sit.

"See," he says, pointing at the big digital numbers on the cable box. "See, it's only . . ."

The clock reads 5:51.

"Larry," she says. "You've been drinking."

He stands there for a moment, then thinks better of it. Sits down on the floor and looks across the cocktail table at her.

"I've had a rough couple of days," he admits.

"Well, please pull yourself together, because I need some help. Will you help me?"

"Why should I help you?"

"Because this situation has gone bad for both of us. I may have put the thing in motion, but you sure didn't help by going to Mike."

Still staring at her.

"I think we both could squeeze something out of this," she tells him, "and I don't want to go to the office by myself. I think something is going to happen soon."

"Where have *you* been, Sam? Everything already happened."

"I'm not talking about Higgs. I'm talking about a bigger project. The one I've been helping Karsten with for years."

"Who's Karsten?"

"He's German, but he lives in Switzerland now. Look, I don't have time to go into details. He was a military scientist during the '30s and '40s. About fifteen years ago he came to CERN and brought this boy with him. The kid couldn't have been more than eighteen. He was autistic. And—you're not going to believe this—but when we turned on the beam, this kid would go crazy. I could barely believe it myself, even when I saw it. We would be in the counting house, or in the office, and even once we were in town, maybe five kilometers outside the ring. He knew when the beam was on, and he didn't like it."

Larry sits there, listening to this, wondering if he's still asleep, wondering if he is perhaps in an alcohol-induced coma.

"I am not making this up," she tells him.

"You've lost your mind," Larry says. "Or you're trying to fuck me over somehow. One of the two."

"Larry, I'm not. I'm not trying—"

He raises his hands. Becoming a little more coherent now. "Okay, fine. Let's say, for the sake of argument, that you're telling me the truth. Why? Why are you coming to me now?"

"Because there is another experiment," she says. "A man here in the United States. I was supposed to be on the inside, just in case there was any problem getting this guy near the detector. Now Karsten is coming here to the super collider, and I want to be there if he brings the test subject."

"Why now? What's the rush? Why not wait until the Higgs thing dies down?"

"Because Karsten is old. He's dying. And I think he's going to try something crazy. I don't know what it is, but I want to be there when it happens."

"I still don't understand why you've come to me. You're Karsten's contact here. Why didn't he arrange this with you?"

"I don't know. He's trying to shut me out for some reason. But I have plenty of friends in Switzerland, I know he left for the U.S. today, and as far as I'm concerned, that means he's coming here."

Larry considers this. Samantha is surely stuffing him full of bullshit, although he can't really think of a good reason why. She could just drive to the super collider if she wanted. She still works there, after all.

"And you want me to go with you?"

"I'm not sure what's going on. I don't want to go by myself."

"I guess I don't have anything else better to do," he says finally. "Should we go now?"

"Soon," she answers. "He'll wait until most of the normal staff is gone, for the overnight shift. He wants to be there when the beam reaches full energy."

4

"Hi," Kelly says as Mike opens the door. She steps through the doorway, into his arms, and the breezy smell of her perfume, her toned and yet somehow inconsequential frame against his, her newfound dependence on him—the entirety of this is something he is hesitant to examine, in case the reality of it is found to be completely without merit. In case he turns out to be dreaming.

"Hi," Mike says.

"And this," Kelly announces, "is Steve Keeley. Steve, meet Mike McNair."

Steve is tall and solid, rugged and tanned in the face, a man you might regard with distrust. Distrust because the average woman is prone to falling for guys like this. Because your own girlfriend has just driven him here from Dallas. And yet there seems to be a kind of desperation in his eyes, so Mike tells himself not to get carried away.

Steve steps forward and shakes his hand heartily. "Very pleased to meet you, Mike."

Mike leads them out of the entryway and into the kitchen, where he pours three glasses of iced tea. Steve stands there looking at them, then looks away, and no one seems to know how to start.

"So what's this all about?" Mike finally asks. "Kelly seemed pretty upset. So upset that she drove here with you instead of going to work."

"Where do I begin?" Steve asks.

"Maybe with the beginning."

"The beginning. Okay. I sustained a head injury in Zurich several weeks ago. A brain surgeon there saved my life. Afterwards I began suffering hallucinations, or at least that's what I thought they were until I saw your interview on CNN."

"What does my interview have to do with your hallucinations?"

"Before that I didn't know anything about particle physics. I still don't, obviously, but what little I did learn shed light on my experiences."

"Okay."

"Look," Steve says. "You're going to want to dismiss me immediately. I understand this. All I ask is that you listen to everything I have to say with an open mind, just like any other phenomenon you might observe in a laboratory, all right?"

"Okay," Mike says again.

"I don't *see* any of this. I think my mind wants to translate the sensations into visual images because that's the only way I can relate to them."

"You don't see what?"

"The Higgs field. Electromagnetic radiation. Particles of matter."

"Excuse me?"

"Before I ever heard of Higgs, before your interview, I began to sense what I thought of as a field, what seemed like an all-encompassing universe of points, waves, something—I couldn't really determine its nature exactly, but I understood it in a fundamental way. How the relationships between the constituent particles of this field and the matter within it determined something important. Like weight or mass or something. It's hard to describe. As if the density of the field varied according to the different types of matter particles."

"That's certainly a workable description of the Higgs field," Mike admits. "But . . . I mean, are you sure you'd never read or heard that before? Our search has been in the news quite a bit since the super collider came online."

"Just show him," Kelly blurts. "Just do the same thing with him that you did with me."

"Do what?" Mike asks.

"Just a minute," Steve says. "I want him to understand everything first. I want to tell him how I came to be here, the bigger picture of it all."

"You're burying the lead," Kelly groans.

"What?"

"That means you won't get to the point," Mike says. "News speak. I learned that one the hard way."

"Okay," Steve says. "Let me spell it out, at least the way I see it. This doctor in Zurich, I believe he did something to my brain. Intentionally. To enable me to sense the constituent elements of matter and energy. And I think he may be working with others, because someone has been tracking me since I got back to the States."

Mike frowns and subtly pulls Kelly closer to him. "Have you talked to anyone else about this?"

"I have. I explained all this to my psychiatrist."

"And?"

"And later I decided she couldn't help me."

"If you'd just *do* it," Kelly pleads.

"I visited a prostitute in Zurich. I fell out a window. When I came to I thought I could float off my goddamn bed. It seemed like if I could just influence this field somehow, then I could levitate, and my legs—which hurt like hell—if I could levitate then I wouldn't have to put any weight on them, you know? And why would I think I could do that when I had never heard of Higgs before?"

"Well, for one thing it doesn't necessarily work like you think," Mike points out. "Just because the influence of Higgs assigns mass to particles of matter, that doesn't mean you can simply—"

"He read my mind!" Kelly says.

"What?"

"After I got out of the hospital," Steve says, "I went back to Cabaret, the place where the prostitute worked. Her name was Svetlana. When I got there the place was closed. And Svetlana was dead."

"Dead?" Mike asks.

"The police say she fell to her death, fell just like I did. And they couldn't find the owner for questioning. They couldn't find the man I struggled with before I went out the window."

"And you think the coincidental nature of this woman's death means there is some sort of conspiracy. To eliminate witnesses. Only why would they care who saw you at the Cabaret? Your being there doesn't implicate anyone who chose to perform experimental surgery on you."

"No," Steve says. "It doesn't. Her death could be entirely unrelated, as you say. But I left a very expensive piece of jewelry in my clothes there. A diamond engagement ring. When I awoke from my coma, the nurse explained how the prostitute had returned the ring to me a few days after my arrival in the hospital. But the Zurich police later told me that Svetlana died the morning I was admitted. So there isn't any way she could have brought it later."

"Maybe one of the other women brought it," Mike offers. "Did you ever think of that?"

"Svetlana was Russian. The nurse said it was a Russian woman."

"Was she the only Russian working there?"

"Well," Steve says. "I don't know. I never thought of that. But . . . I'm not sure a woman who didn't know me would return a twenty-thousand-dollar piece of jewelry."

"I'll grant you that," Mike says. "But it's at least possible, isn't it? And what is more believable? That an honest prostitute returned your ring, or that you are at the center of an international conspiracy, the purpose of which is to grant you mystical powers, return you to your normal life, and then see what happens?"

"This is ridiculous!" Kelly cries and pulls away from Mike. "It sounds preposterous, what he's saying, I know. Who knows if there is a conspiracy or not? But he *told* me things, Mike. He stood outside my door and knew every time I moved on the staircase, he knew about my senior prom, he knew things no one else could have known."

"Your senior prom?"

"Just do it," Kelly says. "Come on, Steve. Just do it. Do it. Read his mind. Show him what you showed me so we can stop talking about *if* it's possible and start figuring out *how* it's possible."

"I'm trying," Steve says. "I've been trying. But I can't . . . it doesn't always happen when I want it to. It's not something I have access to on demand."

"You did with me."

"It was quiet. Maybe it's easier at night. I don't know."

"It's after seven now," Kelly says. "Do it, Steve. Just do it."

"I can't!"

Mike steps closer to Kelly again, who pretends to push him away, but he pulls her toward his body anyway. Something is not right with this man in his kitchen. He is almost certainly mentally ill. Yes, Mike promised to be open to any possibility, but obviously there is no way he can—

"He's turning red," Kelly says.

"Mr. Keeley?" Mike says. "Steve? Are you all right?"

"My head. God, my head hurts."

"Look, Mike. I swear to you, he did what I said. He could not have known . . . I mean, there's no way he could have known about the prom, about *GMA*, there's—"

"My head. Oh, God."

Mike's thoughts are in disarray, wondering what the hell is

going on here, how Kelly got herself (and now him) into this mess, when the glass in his hand begins to . . . to. . . . Something isn't right. It's vibrating. Or humming. Or *squirming* in his hand somehow. It feels as if a trillion tiny insects are crawling over the surface of the glass—

". . . holy fucking shit this hurts . . ."

—and he is about to put the glass down so he can attend to Steve—who has collapsed to his knees, clutching his head—when the glass shatters in his hand, shatters and nearly liquefies, leaving him with a clear paste of glass shards and dripping tea and what looks, unbelievably, like sand.

5

Donovan sits in his car, watching from a small parking lot as the Concorde touches down, twin clouds of smoke curling around the rear tires. It's a funny-looking plane, coming down at a weird angle with its nose pointing down. It reminds him somehow of a goose. The neck and the beak. Something.

A few minutes later two men approach his car with a military police escort. One short, with bushy black hair, and the other taller, bigger, and silver-haired.

"Mr. Donovan," the taller fellow says. He offers his hand, and Donovan shakes with him. "I am Karsten Allgäuer. Very nice to meet you in person. This is my colleague, Markus Dobbelfeld."

"Hello, Markus," Donovan says. Then to Allgäuer, who looks much older than he sounded on the phone: "Will you tell me what's going on?"

"We are very late. It is after seven o'clock. You are ramping up the beam for tonight's run, yes?"

"Soon, but—"

"We should get into the car," Allgäuer says. "I will explain on the way to Olney."

For some reason Allgäuer doesn't feel comfortable speaking

freely until they are off the base and speeding down the high-way. Donovan is pissed that they both chose to sit in the back-seat. This isn't a limousine. He's not their fucking driver.

"This is a very exciting time, Landon. A project many years in the making is finally about to pay rich dividends."

"What sort of project?"

"Do you remember when I spoke to you about the rapid advancement in technology? How we would eventually claim the ability to control time and space?"

"How could I forget?"

"The journey to this final result will no doubt be an inter-esting one, paved with startling successes and disappointing failures. There will be many milestones, and tonight you may witness one of them."

"Really."

"The human brain has long been, by a wide margin, the most capable computer in man's known universe. Our lightning-fast, binary microchips have proven no match for its complex as-sociative ability. And while scientists believe our pattern recog-nition capability emerges from the interaction of billions of neurons, there is also strong evidence that the rule sets used by the brain are not particularly complex. Simple rules, billions of connections, a tremendous amount of storage, and eventually you have intelligence—and ultimately consciousness."

Allgäuer pauses, as if he's waiting for Donovan to say some-thing. But Donovan just keeps driving.

"Obviously," Allgäuer continues, "the brain cannot compete with modern computers when it comes to processing speed. Transistors fire many, many times faster than neurons. But with the brain's massive parallelism, the overall number of calcula-tions still outnumbers most computers. Your Texas Grid, how-ever, considering its enormous number of processors and high network speed—with the right instructions, it might be possi-ble to simulate the operation of the human mind within its architecture."

"If you say so," Donovan says. "But isn't the structure and software of the brain, the connections and the rule sets, aren't those the hardest to replicate? Doesn't the brain grow new connections in response to things it learns? That's why studying and practice improve your ability."

"You are correct. What we need is a way to scan or monitor the brain to understand how it works on a fundamental level, and how it changes with regard to new stimuli. We would never try to replicate this exactly in a transistor-based computer—you must design something unique to make the most of the hardware architecture and its strengths—but using the lessons learned by nature is a good place to start, don't you think?"

"Let me get this straight. You think you can turn our Grid—much of which already operates as a neural network, anyway—you think you can turn it into a learning computer as powerful as the human brain?"

"Landon," Allgäuer says. "That is only the beginning."

6

Steve awakens in an unfamiliar bed. Kelly is sitting beside him, and Mike stands a few feet away. Steve's head throbs as if it's full of boiling water.

"How long was I out?"

"Not long," Kelly tells him. "It's only been a few minutes since we carried you in here from the kitchen."

"And the glass?"

"I don't know how to describe it exactly," Mike says. "Some sort of disintegration. Some kind of chemical or molecular change."

Steve closes his eyes, pleased.

"You did that?"

"I arranged it. I manipulated the energy around the glass, in the glass, I don't know. It's not like it came from me. I just organized and focused energy that was already there. There is a lot of it, all around us, everywhere. The best way I can describe it is as a little chain reaction. Push one domino and others fall."

Mike grunts. "Have you ever done anything like this before?"

"No. Until now I could only sense fields. I couldn't influence them. And however I managed it this time, it hurt me. Badly."

"If I hadn't seen with my own eyes," Mike says, "I wouldn't believe it."

"Me, either," Steve agrees.

Mike sits down next to Kelly and puts his hand on hers. "So can you explain it better?" he asks Steve.

"I'll try, but it's so intangible. When I first became aware of myself in the Zurich hospital, while I was still in the coma, I thought of the pain as a field, a wide, defined area of discomfort, with clusters that were localized and excruciating. And then there was this feeling of emptiness, of whiteness, that came over me, which was also a field of some kind, but much, much greater in scope. I think I was convulsing. I think I was dying. I got the distinct impression that the white field was death, that if I hadn't lived I would have been absorbed into it somehow."

"Are you religious at all?"

"No."

"Well, I've read about near-death experiences similar to what you describe. Sometimes there is a tunnel—"

"Yes! Later there was a tunnel through which I could see the field of white, I think, and within it I felt this great, unseen presence, infinitely vast, infinite energy, infinity, period. And if I passed through the tunnel I would be able to see everything and know everything."

Kelly looks at Mike, her eyes open wide.

"Hold on," Mike says. He stands up, walks over to the window. Looks out on the orange dusk of the backyard. "It could've just been a hallucination. Like I said, there are thousands of documented cases of near-death experiences, and several theories have been suggested to explain the phenomenon. Most re-volve around the idea that the brain, in an effort to diminish the emotional pain of impending death, soothes itself with anesthe-sia. Sort of how painkilling endorphins flood the bloodstream when you break your leg.

"The human brain's greatest ability—pattern recognition—is both an asset and a liability. We easily make associations that for a computer are enormously complex, but we also tend to see patterns that aren't there. Like when people experience life-threatening trauma, the brain often assigns religious em-phasis to ordinary events, because we've been conditioned to believe it."

"That's a very clinical way to look at something that might be much larger than us," Kelly says. "That might not be measur-able in a laboratory."

"I know it is. But I'm a physicist, remember? Science may not be romantic, it might not make it easier to sleep at night, but it gets things done. We're able to fly around the world and send e-mail and cure disease because of science. Maybe there is something else, some kind of transcendental reality, collective, whatever. But how do we know if we can't measure it some-how?"

"So you think his ability to read thoughts, to dissolve that glass, can be explained purely with science."

"Of course," Mike says. "Any physical phenomenon can be explained with logic if you can gather enough information."

Steve opens his mouth to say something, but Kelly is quicker.

"He came all the way across the country to see you, Mike. And when he couldn't get to you, he came to my house, con-vinced me to bring him here. Isn't it possible there is something larger at work?"

"Not necessarily. He saw us on television. The Higgs discov-ery struck a chord with him, so he found us."

"Struck a chord? It happened within weeks of his head injury! It's at least possible that he was brought here. I mean, if you ever wanted a case for that collective reality—"

"Kelly."

"I'm just saying that it doesn't seem very scientific to take one of the possible explanations for his ability and dismiss it. I thought scientists were supposed to consider everything, regardless of whether it fit into your expected outcome."

"But I can't consider this collective reality if I can't measure its effect. Yes, maybe that's the reason, but I have to operate as if it isn't, because otherwise I have to throw out the entire experiment."

"He's not an experiment!"

"Hey," Steve says. "Do you guys want to hear what *I* have to say about it?"

Mike and Kelly look at him, then at each other.

"Of course," Kelly says. "Sorry."

Steve thinks of the first day, when he woke up, and tries to find that uniquely skewed perspective again. "I can tell you this much: the field, or fields, these things I experience, that my brain tries to 'see,' that is one thing. And it's local. It's like looking at the world in a different way. I think of it like a soup of particles, mass and energy all interacting. Everything is connected. Bound together. Like everything that happens influences something else."

"Isn't that sort of like chaos theory?" Kelly asks. "The butterfly effect? Tiny changes have a ripple effect and eventually add up to large, unpredictable events at a great distance?"

"Maybe," Steve says. "But maybe the effects aren't unpredictable. Maybe they are measurable with the right perspective."

"Chaos theory renders the effects unpredictable because it's impossible to measure any complex system with infinite accuracy," Mike says. "You can't begin with perfectly knowable conditions, so determinism—the idea of absolute cause and effect—is basically made irrelevant. Even the smallest difference in initial conditions produces dramatically different results."

"Okay, so maybe they are predictable in the short term," Steve suggests. "Or maybe it's possible to read patterns in the chaos."

"You may be right on that note," Mike says. "Part of the theory postulates that chaos on a microscopic scale could be necessary for larger-scale patterns to arise."

"But the particles," Steve says, "they're only part of it. The presence is something else. Well, that's not exactly right. It's like . . . it's like the presence is the same stuff as the particles, but also more. In the business world we call it synergy, where something as a whole is more than the sum of its parts. Like a photograph is more than just the grains of color that comprise it."

Mike opens his mouth to say something, but Steve stops him.

"Svetlana, the prostitute? When she came to me in dreams, you know what it felt like? It felt like *she* was the presence. Like she had . . . I don't know . . . condensed from it."

"That's interesting," Mike says. "I may have heard of a theory that could support an idea like that."

"What?" Kelly and Steve ask at the same time.

"It's the idea of the universe itself being a living entity. Alive. Evolving."

Steve says, "I don't—"

"Well, if you consider that the Big Bang spawned the universe, that all matter and energy, that even space and time are its consequence, then even we, humans, are basically an extension of that universe. I mean, you look into the night sky, at pictures of galaxies, and you say, 'Hey, that's the universe.' Well, people are also the universe. We are, literally, stardust. And since we are also sentient, since we've evolved enough to ponder our own existence, then by definition so has the universe. The universe itself could be considered alive, to have evolved over time, and now, through the use of a small, sentient device in its metaphorical brain—us—it's able to ponder its own existence."

"But how does that relate to his 'presence'?" Kelly asks.

"Think of that collective reality idea, where consciousness itself may not belong to us. I mean, I don't believe this, there is nothing in science to support it, but it would be like all the particles of the world make up a sort of relational database. In the computer world a relational database is a set of tables that allows the user to manipulate data in many and complex ways based on the data's structure and a set of rules. So in this case, for the sake of analogy, you'd be talking about a sort of universal relational database. And I suppose if you know the rules, how the relations are made, if you have access to the data—which in this example might be the collective, perceived reality of all matter and energy in our universe—then you can know almost anything, even make predictions based on the data. Perhaps you could tell the future. Or with enough energy at your disposal, make dramatic physical changes to the world."

"Changes to the world?" Kelly asks. "What do you mean? And where would this energy come from?"

Mike looks at Kelly and then at Steve, who has obviously made the same connection.

"From something like the super collider," Mike says. "A machine powerful enough to create small-scale collisions at energy levels similar to the Big Bang."

From the beam, Steve thinks.

"Do you want to go there?" Mike asks him. "I can hardly believe I'm asking you this, but I saw what happened to the glass with my own eyes. Do you want to visit the super collider while the beam is on and see what happens?"

Steve nods.

7

By now Larry's hangover has grown huge, woolen legs, legs that are stomping around inside his mouth, rattling the throbbing cage of his skull. He's eaten a handful of Advil over the past three hours and has forced down a gallon of water. They're speeding down 251, nearing the entrance to the NTSSC administrative complex, and Larry is fairly sure he's going to throw up any minute.

"How can you possibly know if he's coming here tonight?" he asks Samantha.

"He'll be here," she says. "What I don't know is where. I don't know if he'll go to the administrative offices or over to the GEM building. We never really could tell if proximity to the collisions made a difference."

Larry watches her speak these words with complete sincerity. Proximity to the collisions. Insanity. It's his proximity to *her* that's the problem. Sucking him further into madness than he already was.

"You really think he'll be here tonight. Not tomorrow? Not next week? We run the beam all the time."

"I was told he's coming tonight. Besides, if he doesn't, then no harm done, right?"

Larry grins. Says nothing.

"Let's try the administrative offices first," Samantha says.

CHAPTER TEN

1

For a while Donovan drives alone with his thoughts as Allgäuer and Dobbelfeld sit in the backseat and speak to each other in German. He hates it when people do that, converse in a foreign language in his presence, fully aware that he can't understand them. On the other hand, a man of his intelligence and stature ought to speak multiple languages, something he cannot do, something that is a constant source of embarrassment to him.

Finally, as they near Olney, Allgäuer switches to English and says, "Donovan, are you familiar with the Swiss scientist Albert Hoffman?"

"No. Should I be?"

"My experiments with derivatives of certain hallucinogenic drugs were inspired by his work. I was very interested in the altered mental state produced by these drugs, in how that state might be connected to possible extrasensory ability, and in 1941, after studying with Hoffman for several months, I administered a derivative of ergot alkaloids to an eighteen-year-old male whose reaction was dramatic and remarkable. He was given the drug while asleep, but within ten minutes he awoke and began scrambling around the laboratory, screaming about monsters and ghosts and such. This patient expired before he could be subdued—cardiac arrest was the apparent cause of death—and we would have assumed his experiences to be hallucination if the lights and several sensitive electronic instruments in our laboratory had not been mysteriously (and indirectly) damaged during his struggle. This proved nothing by itself, of course, but when a similar incident occurred with another patient two years later, I began to really wonder if these patients were somehow affecting their environment by indirect means. The Allied victory in World War II ended my research for a while, but later I began it again in the United States. Very near here, as a matter of fact."

"You still haven't told me what you're doing here now," Donovan says.

"I experienced sporadic success for many years, mainly due to a lack of available test subjects. Without a properly controlled scientific environment, it was difficult to separate success from coincidence, and since this drug was similar to but chemically distinct from LSD-25, some of my colleagues were inclined to believe the phenomena were somehow acute hallucinations. Still, we continued our experiments, eventually acquiring patients suffering from mental illness—especially schizophrenia—and in 1964 and 1979 there were dramatic demonstrations of possible telekinesis and even environmental control on a large scale. But still we could not be sure, and besides, the patients always died soon after the compound was administered. Success is irrelevant if no practical application emerges from it. Eventually I returned to Europe, settling in Switzerland, and it was there that I experienced my most promising success yet."

They pass through Olney and now approach the super collider on 251. Donovan can hardly believe what he is hearing, All-gäuer's claims of fatal ESP experiments on human subjects. It's nothing at all like what he expected to hear. Or wanted to hear. Because as much as he longs to understand the invisible power structure from which he has been so conspicuously barred, Donovan doesn't want to hurt anyone, regardless of what abilities might emerge from the research.

"It happened that I was fortunate enough to procure a high-functioning autistic who also exhibited savantlike abilities. He could perform lightning-fast numerical calculation and could perfectly perceive the passage of time without a clock. Those things by themselves may sound extraordinary, but most extraordinary to me was his unique ability to somehow tolerate the psychological effects of the compound. His observations, Landon, were startling. He described what I concluded must be an interpretation of numerous vector fields in the laboratory. Electromagnetic fields, the fluid movement of air molecules, even what I believed at the time to be the gravitational field. It was remarkable. For many weeks I conducted a battery of tests, but the conclusive evidence emerged—as it often does—accidentally. Over time the subject noticed that the vector fields were altered occasionally, that these changes followed a pattern, and we eventually traced this pattern to the schedule of beam runs at the nearby CERN high-energy physics laboratory."

"What?" Donovan asks. "He could tell when the beam was turned on?"

"There is more. When I finally arranged a visit to CERN during a beam run, the patient became quite agitated. He claimed to have experienced an intense sensation of being watched. By multiple observers. And when I asked him who these observers were, and how many, this man—who, remember, could carry out astonishing numerical calculation—this man informed me the number was 'too many to count.'

"I asked if there was a problem seeing all of the observers, or something else that prohibited him from counting them, but his remarkable answer was—I repeat this verbatim—'the number is simply too large.' And when I asked if he could calculate this number, given enough time, or if a fast computer could calculate the number, he answered 'there is not enough time.' "

They pass through the NTSSC gate and Donovan drives them toward the administrative offices, per Allgäuer's instructions. He asks, "What do you think it meant, Karsten? All these observers, too many to count, what did you take from that? You must have done additional research, or else we wouldn't be here now."

"It is a miracle," Allgäuer says. "The universe."

"The universe."

"It's a miracle, and it's there for the taking, for whoever develops the ability to harness it. Like horses to ride, like oxen to plow. Like dogs to hunt."

"What do you mean?"

"It's alive, Landon. The universe is alive."

2

The three of them speed through the night in Mike's VW Passat, bearing down on the super collider. Mike's mind is racing, the spinning flywheel of a redlined automobile engine, as he revisits the improbable sensation of a glass ceasing to exist in his hand, as he struggles to comprehend a human being who can influence his environment in unbelievable ways. He feels like a man who is convinced beyond any doubt that he has been abducted by aliens. He sees in his future the desperate attempt to explain to his colleagues what he saw with his own eyes, what he felt with his own hands, as those cold and reasoned men and women regard him with pity. And yet Mike cannot ignore the implications of Steve's ability, which are staggering, which are almost beyond comprehension.

If he can sense these fields, if he can detect particle interactions at the super collider, what else could he possibly know? Could he shed light on the biggest problem in modern physics, the apparent incompatibility between Einstein's relativity and quantum physics? Could he answer basic questions for cosmologists about the origin of the universe, about the void from which time and space emerged fourteen billion years ago?

Could he give meaning to it all?

Because, let's be honest, understanding how everything works is only a partial solution. If Mike were given a key to the city, if someone handed him a blueprint to the functional universe, would that really be the answer? Did he really think he would ever truly understand the nature of existence? Or has his life in physics simply been delaying the eventual fugue state of existential despair, a man with nothing left to research, no more questions to ask, no reason to get up in the morning and maintain relationships with the same group of unknowingly doomed people?

"I think there is a device inside my head," Steve blurts.

"What?" asks Kelly.

"A device?" Mike says. "What makes you say that?"

"I think that's how they're tracking me. That's why there was never any physical surveillance. It was always this device in my head."

"Why do you think you have an implanted device?" Mike asks again.

"I don't know. I just know it's there. Somehow it allows me to decode the extrasensory input, I think. And it's also a communication device. Except that. . . ."

"Except what?" Mike asks him.

"It doesn't seem to be in any one place. It seems to be everywhere, inside my entire brain."

"And you can sense this?" Kelly asks. "You've identified the very device that allows you to do the identifying?"

Mike pulls off the highway and guides his car toward the NTSSC gate. He smiles as Louis, the guard, waves him inside.

"There is a device called a neuron transistor," Mike says. "An electronic device implanted in the brain that can cause a neuron to fire or suppress it from firing. Maybe something like that was implanted during your brain surgery."

"But if I'm the subject of some kind of experiment, why allow me to leave the hospital? Why not keep me there to study?"

Mike pulls the VW into his parking space at the administrative office and kills the engine. He gets out of the car, Kelly and Steve do the same, and together they walk toward the administrative building. The only other car in this front parking lot is the security guard's Olds Cutlass.

"That's a good point," Mike says. "But I have an even more fundamental question."

"What's that?" asks Steve.

"How were you selected for this? When were you identified as a candidate?"

"What do you mean?"

"Did someone at the hospital pull you into a special room and say, 'Let's experiment on this guy'?"

Steve doesn't answer right away.

"Because waiting for head trauma victims would be a poor way to find subjects, if you ask me. And brain injuries might ruin their experiments."

"I've never really thought about how I was selected."

"What about this guy you struggled with at the Cabaret? Before you went out the window? What was that about?"

"The bouncer?"

"How do you know he was really a bouncer?"

"Well, I—"

"Maybe the guy wasn't trying to kick you out. Maybe he was going to make you stay. If someone there was on the lookout for possible candidates, it might explain why they shut the place down, why everyone was gone. So you couldn't go back and draw attention to them."

Mike uses his keycard to unlock the glass doors, and the three of them walk through the foyer, past the reception desk, which should be manned by a security guard and isn't. A newspaper is draped over the chair, and a half-eaten Snickers bar sits inside its wrapper on the desk. This is no good. Even though there is probably no one in the building right now—anyone working this late will be over at the detector—the security guard shouldn't leave the reception desk.

"Right now," Kelly says, looking at Steve, "I'm not sure it matters why you were selected. Aren't you more concerned about what they plan to do with you?"

"They've been monitoring me," Steve agrees. "There must be some kind of plan."

"The most obvious thing would be military use," Mike suggests. "If there really is a device in your head, and if it functions the way you've described, maybe you can achieve two-way communication between the electronic and neural worlds. That would open up all kinds of possibilities. Perhaps you could communicate with other people who had these enhanced brains, or even synch to your computer like a Palm Pilot."

"Synch to your computer?" Kelly asks. "Download your brain into a computer?"

Mike considers looking for the guard—he's probably in the bathroom—when he notices light under his office door.

"That's one thing," he says. "I guess if you could do that, assuming there was a powerful enough computer, it could be like a sort of immortality. Even if your body died, at least you could still be self-aware."

Steve looks at Mike and then back at the door, as he stops, as they gather in front of it.

"We should leave," Steve says. "It was a mistake to come here."

"The guard—" Mike begins.

"Disposed of."

"What?" Kelly asks.

"He's in there," Steve says. "I can sense him."

Kelly looks at Mike, then at Steve. "Who? The guard?"

Mike's office door opens, revealing a tall, silver-haired man that he doesn't recognize. Behind him lurk Donovan and another unfamiliar man.

"Mr. McNair," the old man says. He's pointing a small handgun at them. "I'm Karsten Allgäuer. I've come to use your machine."

3

Allgäuer waves the three of them through the door and herds them into a corner beside Mike's desk. Steve walks as instructed but never takes his eyes off Dobbelfeld, the doctor who he thought saved his life but who apparently only loaned it to him for a while.

"Mr. Keeley," Dobbelfeld says through the doorway. He's holding an electronic device of some kind, like a PDA but larger. "I trust you are okay? You haven't been injured?"

"Not since you left something in my head during surgery."

Allgäuer laughs heartily.

"At least you still have a sense of humor," he says, and then turns briefly toward the man Steve recognizes as Landon Donovan. "It's almost startling, the difference between my drug therapy and this technology of Dobbelfeld's."

"Drug therapy?" Steve asks. "What are you talking about?"

"You may believe that yours is a singular ability, Mr. Keeley, but you are actually the latest in a long line of test subjects. The end result in a project that has spanned more than fifty years."

Steve looks at Mike, who has pushed Kelly behind him, blocking her from the barrel of Allgäuer's gun. "I'm sorry," he says to them. "I'm sorry for dragging you guys into this."

"But what do you want with him now?" Kelly asks Allgäuer. "Why are you here with a gun?"

"You installed neuron transistors in his brain," Mike says. "And now you're here to see if Steve and the super collider can be used as some kind of weapon. Right?"

Allgäuer laughs.

"It's not neuron transistors," Steve says.

And he can feel them, can detect their interaction with his own mind, with neurons and glial cells, can sense their emerging sentience. He realizes for the first time that his episodes of detached reality, his newfound extrasensory perception, have been caused by a cascade release of neurotransmitters, the chemicals that facilitate communication between nerve cells. His brain's biological structure has been compromised by microscopic machines. Hijacked by them.

"They're nanomachines," he declares.

"Nanomachines?" Mike asks.

"Mother of God," Dobbelfeld says in German, awestruck. "He can sense them. Karsten, I do not think it wise to—"

"Shut up," Allgäuer snaps.

"Karsten," Donovan says. "What's going on?"

"It's like the neuron transistor," Steve says to Mike. "But much smaller. There are millions of them. They've . . . they interact with my brain cells. Introduce new configurations into the neural network. It's how I've seen these fields. It's like I'm unlearning patterns, redefining consciousness to accommodate the larger scope of—"

"That is enough," Allgäuer says. "We have not come all the way from Switzerland to listen to this navel gazing. Donovan, the beam should be reaching full energy by now, yes?"

And even as he listens to Allgäuer's orders, Steve can see behind them, can tune into the man as if he were a radio station. He knows now that Svetlana and the bouncer were paid to watch for lonely guys like him. Knows that Svetlana changed her mind after it was too late, and that she and the bouncer were murdered when their attempt to abduct Steve failed. He knows that Allgäuer pays contacts like them all over Switzerland. He sees how desperately the man wants this experiment to work, and he understands why, because he can sense the memory of Jonas Kornherr, the autistic teen who Allgäuer believes felt the intelligence of the universe.

"The beam is already at full energy," Steve says. "But it doesn't matter. You're mistaken, Karsten. It's not alive."

"You have no idea what you're talking about." Allgäuer turns to Dobbelfeld, speaks lower, in German again. "This is amazing, these things he knows. Do you have contact with the machines?"

Dobbelfeld nods. "As far as I can tell, all the machines are functioning properly. He must be decoding electromagnetic signals from your brain. These are dramatically better results than I anticipated."

Steve looks at Mike and Kelly. "He's been experimenting on innocent people for years. He stumbled across a variant of LSD that altered perception enough for people to sense vector fields. But the drug killed every test subject. Every one of them. Including the autistic boy," he accuses Allgäuer. "After you pumped him full of it for almost two years."

And now Steve sees a terrible truth, something he wants to turn away from, but where is there to go?

"I'm not the only one?" he cries. "You've injected these machines into three other people? Who all died because of them?"

Allgäuer's face reddens. The hand holding the gun quivers. "If the machines are working so well, why is he standing there like nothing is happening?" he yells at Dobbelfeld.

But something *is* happening. Steve can sense the beam, the billions of protons circling the main ring at nearly the speed of light, can sense the occasional collisions that occur when these bunches of protons cross paths. Even from here he sees them shattering into their constituent pieces, sees the shrapnel from the collisions being deflected in every direction, sees them lodge in the detector. He sees these things because they disturb nearby fields of matter and energy, because every particle interaction in the universe disturbs every other in some small way, and the closer you are to those interactions or the more powerful they are, the more easily the effects are detected.

What he doesn't see is the universe reacting with purpose. It seems to be a machine with no intelligence. And so he thinks the presence must have been an illusion. That since his pattern-loving mind was not powerful or experienced enough to handle the new stimuli, it was forced to translate them into apparitions like Svetlana.

But he does see how the universe could be *made* to be smart. How particles could be made to convey information. He sees a future where man becomes more and more adept at manipulating his environment, at sharing information, he sees a Grid like the one here at the NTSSC becoming a global network, more and more processing power generating better and better technology, until man is capable of anything. Perfectly repairing his own body. Stopping the aging process. Combining his biological brain with man-made processors to become a truly ascendant being. The ultimate creation of a collective intelligence that might truly turn out to be a new type of existence, one of pure thought and exploration, man no longer restrained by the ancient need to satisfy his bodily instincts. A collective entity like this might be considered a kind of god, a god unburdened by guilt and pain and religious dogma.

He sees all of this in a moment of vision, the pure transcendent magic of it, and in the same moment he sees what Allgäuer means to do with the super collider, what destruction he might cause in a desperate bid to derive meaning from the universe.

In his predictable bid for immortality.

4

Mike reels at the unreality of a gun being pointed at him. An actual handgun.

The unreality of this entire evening, in fact, first the glass dissolving in his hand and now this implausible exchange between Allgäuer and Steve. Donovan just standing there with Allgäuer, silent, the billionaire brazenness stripped away somehow.

Mike tries to make logical deductions from these preposterous events, determined to find a reasonable way out of this quandary. Because nothing good can come from these German-speaking men and their experiment on Steve. Nothing good can come from the gun. Mike must protect Kelly, find a way to get her out of this room alive, and hopefully defuse the situation enough to keep Steve and Landon and all of them out of harm's way.

But how to do this, exactly?

And still, the idea of nanomachines in Steve's head, altering his brain chemistry in a way that has somehow affected his sensory perception, this is something he almost cannot comprehend. Yes, the technology to do such a thing has been in development for years, and yes, he has seen the truth of Steve's ability with his own eyes, but how can there be technology so much farther advanced than anything he has ever read or heard about?

"Mr. Allgäuer," he says. "This is out of control. There is no reason for Kelly to be here. We can work this out without her."

"I'm not going anywhere!" Kelly hisses from behind him. "I'm not leaving Steve behind when I'm the one who brought him here."

"No one is leaving," Allgäuer says. "Until Keeley and I complete our transaction."

"It won't work," Steve says.

"What transaction?" Mike and Donovan both ask.

"He thinks the universe is alive," Steve continues. "He thinks that someone with my ability should be able to communicate with it somehow. That being in close proximity to the collisions at a high-energy physics laboratory will open some kind of communication channel between our world and his world of particle intelligence."

"But if that were right," Mike says, "it would be a miracle beyond words. Why force the issue with a gun?"

Allgäuer says nothing.

"It doesn't matter," Steve says. "There is no intelligence. There—"

Allgäuer nods, and Dobbelfeld enters a command into his electronic device, and Steve falls to the floor.

"Steve!" Kelly says, and rushes to him. "Steve, what's wrong?"

"They may be inside his head," Allgäuer says, "but the machines are under my control."

"What are you doing to him?" Donovan asks.

"What did you do?" Kelly screams as she leans near Steve's face, apparently to check his breathing.

"He's just unconscious," Dobbelfeld says. "A kind of artificial coma."

Allgäuer watches the doctor as he continues to work on the electronic device. "I was curious," he says, "to find out if Keeley could sense the intelligence as Kornherr did. He cannot. But that does not mean we cannot harness his brain to do it for us. The machines in his mind receive and transmit information via high-frequency radio signals. We will connect him to the Grid, and we will instruct the machines to send a signal into the heart of the detector, and we will wait for a response."

But this is no good, Mike thinks. Just a nudge to some physical constant, such as the speed of light or charge to mass ratio on an electron, and there could be a lot of rearrangements on a subnuclear level that would have dramatic consequences on a macroscopic scale. Like a runaway chain reaction, for instance, that could destroy the entire universe.

"Stop," he says to Allgäuer. "You have to stop this."

"How much longer?" Allgäuer asks Dobbelfeld, staring at Mike, still pointing the gun.

"I need a minute, maybe two." But the doctor's hands are shaking, and his fingers aren't rushing to enter instructions into his PDA-like device.

"Dobbelfeld," Mike says. "Steve can do things I wouldn't have believed possible. Tonight I saw him rearrange the molecular composition of a drinking glass. If you enter this ability into a high-energy particle collision, the effects could be unpredictable. You could kill us all."

Dobbelfeld looks up.

"Do not stop!" Allgäuer says.

"Dobbelfeld," Mike pleads. "This is lunacy."

"Shut up!" Allgäuer yells. "Or I will shoot you. And then I will shoot your girlfriend."

Mike weighs his options. There is no way to know what will happen if they tune Steve into the detector. Probably nothing. Should he risk his own life on a hunch?

He makes eye contact with Donovan, trying to convince him without saying so to grab the gun. Donovan ignores him.

But even if nothing happens during their experiment with Steve, what about afterward? At the very least Allgäuer will take his test subject back to Switzerland with him. Can Mike stand by and just let that happen? He doesn't understand how Donovan can just stand there himself, when he is just feet away from Allgäuer. He could reach over there and grab the gun. He could do something.

"Hurry," Allgäuer says.

Mike doesn't understand what the rush is. The beam run will go on for hours. But perhaps he *does* understand, perhaps he can even comprehend why Donovan is standing there, doing nothing.

Because they want answers. They want to be led out of the darkness. They want a drug to wipe out their existential despair.

Mike understands this.

The instinct to survive is not original to humans, but the knowledge of eventual death might be.

Even if death could be delayed or avoided, even if man eventually commands his entire universe, does it really matter? Because what comes next?

This is why Allgäuer risks unimaginable destruction looking for something else. Why humans cling desperately to routine and tradition and custom. To hide the essential truth of life. To hide the doom.

Because the genetic survival instinct is incompatible with high intelligence.

Mike's reptilian brain says *stay* while his human mind says *go*. An inner battle: *live another moment at all costs* versus *risk death to secure a life worth living.*

Mike ignores his trembling hands. He looks down at Kelly, still with Steve.

He rushes Allgäuer.

5

In less than five seconds, these thoughts of Kelly's, skipping through her mind as if across the glacial surface of a frozen pond:

Surprise as she sees Mike's blurry form rush past her.

The reality of her own cowardice. The selfish, arctic terror of her own impending death. She should be helping him.

A gunshot. Mike stumbling, collapsing into Allgäuer. Another gunshot. Ceiling tiles raining dust.

Steve moving.

"Dobbelfeld!" screams Allgäuer as he struggles with Mike on the floor.

She must help Mike. Scrambles to her feet.

A groan from Steve. She looks back.

"Run," he says.

She scrambles to Mike, screaming.

Donovan runs past them, out the door. Dobbelfeld follows.

Another gunshot. Allgäuer rolls off Mike, a starburst of blood spreading across Mike's white shirt.

Run, Steve says again. Except she is not hearing it. It comes from everywhere and nowhere, this command, assaulting her senses as if broadcast by a million-watt loudspeaker.

Run!

"Get up, Mike," she cries. "I know you're hurt, but I can't carry you. You've got to get up."

"Run," he answers. His voice is liquid, gurgling. "Kelly, go."

"No!"

Memories flash rapidly: Mike's cologne as he shuffled past her on the plane, the e-mails, chocolate martini on his shirt.

She looks back at Steve, hoping he has somehow risen, hoping he can help her carry Mike. But something is not right with him. His wide eyes point straight at her, but they aren't seeing, they're crawling with electricity, alive with yellow vessels of energy.

Steve can't help her. He's going nowhere. He is, in fact, the source of the distress.

An escalating hum, energy building, swelling around him. He's glowing. Blue and yellow and somehow translucent, and the colors are crawling toward her, and—

6

Larry stands outside the door, looking in. It's the story of his life. He and Samantha have watched most of this exchange, hesitant to enter the room with a gun present, and now even she is gone, having followed Dobbelfeld when he fled, demanding to know what happened.

Kelly kneels over Mike, crying, begging for help.

Larry stands there, watching Mike die.

He knows something else is happening here. He can feel something wrong, the hum, in his bones and in his mind.

He could just let go. Let it all go.

But he also imagines the look on Kelly's face when he appears in the room. An unexpected savior.

He opens the door and steps inside.

7

He's awake now, his mind somehow free.

Steve does not want to destroy the super collider, but he sees no alternative.

In a perfect world, the benefits of a machine would far outweigh the costs, but this situation is far from perfect. A man desperately searching for meaning is a dangerous man, and Steve cannot allow him access to the machine, can allow no one access to it until mankind has truly accepted the concepts of logic and reason and the value of all life. And so he concentrates on the particles as they circle around the ring millions of times per second, concentrates so that he can direct them elsewhere, focus them through field, and the energy begins to run farther away from him, it whips around the room like a live wire, vaporizing everything in its path, he must get it under control, must focus it where he can do some kind of good, and he no longer possesses the strength to open his mouth, but he must make them understand, he can send them this, transmit this to them, and—

8

You have to run! Now!

Run!

Kelly hears footsteps behind her, and there is Larry, and she cries her thanks even as he threads his arms under Mike's. Kelly grabs Mike's feet and together they lurch out of the room, reaching the main hallway just as the lights go out. She sees Steve lying on the ground and she doesn't want to leave him, either, but of course they cannot stay. They reach the glass exit doors almost running, and she guides Larry toward Mike's car, fully aware that something is terribly out of control.

Donovan and Dobbelfeld have vanished.

They load Mike into the backseat, where Larry fishes the

car key out of his pocket and then climbs into the driver's seat. Kelly opens the door on the other side just as the car starts.

Larry backs out of the parking spot and points them away from the administrative building, accelerating.

They speed through the night, toward the exit. But will it be enough? The ring surrounds the town. Its circumference is fifty-four miles. They'll never get away in time.

9

Mike hears it now, an alternating, whipping sound pitching high and low, like an enormous jump rope orbiting around a giant, phantom girl.

Like the metallic resonance of a long, flexible handsaw being flayed back and forth.

Like the subsonic rumble of a tornado.

And he watches the sky through the rear window as they drive away, half expecting it to light up with explosion, cringing as he waits for the shock wave to push his car off the road. It's unimaginable that his brief contact with Steve Keeley has come to this. That the miracle of his fantastic perception should be so rudely and abruptly ended by selfishness and violence. Anger pushes through the shock and pain of his bullet wound and he doesn't know where to direct it. Who should be responsible for destroying man's extraordinary chance to find stunning break-throughs in physics, in the search for human truth?

The men who created Steve, after all, are his destroyers.

10

Kelly's breath hitches as they reach the highway and turn right. She glances behind them, from where they came, looking for fire or smoke, but instead she sees more of that bluish-yellow light, whipping about like an unmanned garden hose shooting a jet of water everywhere. Tearing holes in the administrative building, vaporizing asphalt and grass and trees, even disappearing into the night sky. But gradually the jet seems to focus, the unorganized beam tightening, and then it disappears, perhaps underground.

And Kelly somehow knows that when the sun rises on this place in the morning, the fifty-four-mile ring will be gone.

1

From the front page of the *Dallas Morning News*, two days later:

TRAGEDY, MAYHEM AT NTSSC IN OLNEY
Physics campus in lockdown after mysterious accident

Staff and Wire Reports

OLNEY, TX—Officials at the North Texas Superconducting Super Collider have shut down the $12 billion facility as the FBI investigates a mysterious explosion at the administrative office complex near the southernmost point of the 54-mile ring. Early reports from state and local authorities indicated a possible security breach, and foul play is suspected in the baffling destruction of the NTSSC 90,000-square-foot nerve center, which is located six miles south of Olney. Word also spread of possible damage to the ring, a collection of nearly 9,000 dipole magnets located in an elliptical tunnel 200 feet underground. The type of damage and how it may have occurred is not known at this time, but one government official, who chose to remain anonymous, spoke of a "power surge" at the facility so large that the bloom was detected by an orbiting NASA satellite. The cause of the possible surge is unknown at this time.

Just last week the NTSSC announced a possible breakthrough in the search for the Higgs boson, an elusive particle referred to by some as the God particle . . .

2

From the *L.A. Times,* another day later:

VALENCIA MAN MISSING
By Chera Lopez, *Times* Staff Writer

LOS ANGELES—Steve Keeley, 34, of Valencia, is missing after apparently driving away from his home earlier this week. Keeley was last seen by a neighbor who claimed Keeley backed quickly out of his home and sped away, leaving his garage door open.

According to his mother, Betty, of Grand Island, Nebraska, Keeley suffered severe head trauma last month while on a business trip in Zurich. Keeley was employed until recently by Automotive Excellence, a Swiss-based auto parts manufacturer. A representative from AE would not comment on Keeley's sudden departure from the company two weeks ago, and strangely, no record of Keeley's hospital stay in Zurich could be found. Keeley also never visited his physician regarding the reported head injury, although a local psychiatrist, Dr. Shelly Taylor, admitted to seeing him twice over the past two weeks. Dr. Taylor has been contacted by Valencia police and possibly the FBI about

Keeley's disappearance, but when asked to comment by the *Times,* she declined.

3

From *swissinfo* (English version) twelve more days later:

Pharmaceutical Researcher Missing

swissinfo October 28, 2005 7:58 AM

Prominent Geneva scientist Karsten Allgäuer, also a board member for pharmaceutical giant Rubisco, has been reported missing by his brother, Daniel. Sources close to Mr. Allgäuer indicate that he made a trip to the United States on 29 September. There is no information at this time regarding the nature of Allgäuer's trip to the USA or when he planned to return.

4

In Dallas, Abraham Lange reads these stories and curses himself for underestimating the seriousness of Allgäuer's work. After nearly sixty years of fits and starts, enduring failure upon failure, after watching intelligent and reasoned men go to such lengths in their desperate pursuit of the secret, of the truth, he had nearly given up on the research. Allgäuer in later years had grown increasingly erratic. Willis marched his followers into the south Texas prairie and vanished with them. But still, the resolve of these two men, these old friends, had been strong, and their sporadic successes had been tantalizing.

Then Lange arrives in Olney.

He can scarcely credit what he discovers there.

He must locate Allgäuer and Dobbelfeld. They must find a way to continue this research. Not here, not considering what's left of the facility, but the Large Hadron Collider is coming online at CERN in 2007, and this means another chance for breakthrough.

Another chance to finally seize the truth.

5

At United Regional in Wichita Falls, Kelly sits in an uncomfortable hospital chair, sea-green vinyl mounted to a skeleton of aluminum, waiting for Mike to wake up.

His surgery stretched several hours, and afterward the doctor, a young, overweight man from Pakistan, declared the procedure "very much successful."

And so she waits, her mind reliving the implausibility of the previous twelve hours, an extraordinary sequence of events she can hardly believe really happened to her.

They turned north after leaving the NTSSC campus, speeding toward and through Olney, reaching over 130 miles an hour as they rushed toward Wichita Falls. Larry squealed through town and somehow found United Regional, where he dropped them off at the emergency entrance and then left to park the car. He promised Kelly he would be back shortly to sit with her, to keep her company as they waited for the ER staff to evaluate Mike, but he never returned. Later, while Mike was in surgery, she explored the parking lot until she found Mike's car, unlocked, with the keys still in the ignition. She has no idea why Larry would do such a thing.

Kelly hears a noise from the bed and looks up to find Mike blinking, his eyes surely struggling to focus, his mind working to understand where he is and why.

"So I'm not dead yet," he says to her. His voice is broken like a poor mobile phone connection.

"Not yet," she says, rising to greet him.

He smiles. She leans down and kisses his dry lips.

"That's a good reason to wake up," he says. "During surgery I kept trying to decide whether or not to go through that tunnel.

Toward the light. If I'd known you were going to be here, it would have been a much easier choice."

"There was a tunnel?" she asks.

"Just kidding."

"Right. Ha fucking ha."

"So what happened to Larry? I know he ended up at the super collider somehow. Was he in the car with us when we left?"

"He helped me carry you to the car and drove us to the hospital. I tried asking him why he was at the office that time of night, but he wouldn't answer. And then, after he dropped us off at the emergency entrance, he just disappeared."

"Larry has been having problems, Kelly. Emotional problems."

"What kind of emotional problems? For how long?"

"For as long as I've known him," Mike says. "Let's just leave it at that."

"Do you think he'll be all right? Where will he go?"

"I have no idea."

Later, after the doctor drops by to check on him, after Kelly returns from the hospital cafeteria with some substandard rotisserie chicken, she asks him about the night before.

"What the hell happened back there, Mike?"

"I don't know."

"That light. That blue light. Do you know what it was?"

"I don't know. Steve tapped into the energy of the super collider somehow."

"But the detector isn't beneath your office, right? It has to be on the ring somewhere."

"The GEM isn't below the office, no, but it's not far away, either. We built the administrative offices nearby since it's the primary detector."

"So what did he do?"

"I don't know. The implications of matter and energy fields, the interaction between them, are something we obviously don't understand very well. What happened doesn't seem possible to me, but the thing with the drinking glass didn't seem possible, either."

"I felt him talking to me," Kelly says. "He kept telling me to run."

"I felt it, too. I'm sure . . . I mean, there has to be a scientific explanation for what he could do, for what happened there. There is so much research to do, so much we have to learn. Our understanding of the universe is constrained by what we can see and what we can deduce with current knowledge. Mathematics, relativity, quantum physics . . . these things expand human understanding, because many of their outcomes don't jibe with reality as we perceive it. You don't see the world as an infinite dance of particles, but that's what it is . . . at least as far as we know. Who knows what forces, what structures exist that our current math and physics can't resolve? If you brought a person from the days of Ben Franklin and showed him the world today, he would think we live in a world full of magic. The sound of Mozart from tiny, hidden speakers in someone's living room? What about television? Airplanes? Microwave ovens? They would seem like witchcraft, like miracles. And these are inventions of the twentieth century. Imagine what life will be like in twenty years. In fifty."

Kelly shakes her head. "I still don't understand about your building, though. I don't understand what he did with the super collider, with the particles."

"I don't either," Mike says. "I'd like to find out what's left out there."

But when Mike tries to get Donovan on the phone, he can't. And several days later, when the Pakistani doctor reluctantly releases him from the hospital, NTSSC security will not allow them inside the gates.

6

Later that day Mike's cell phone rings, and he answers, hoping it will be Donovan.

"Mr. McNair, my name is Abraham Lange. Do you know who I am?"

"No. Should I?"

"I'm responsible for the construction of your facility. Landon Donovan did not possess the resources to do it on his own, so I stepped in and helped him."

Mike remembers his conversation with Donovan about the investors that pulled out, how he spent all his money on the project and it still wasn't enough.

"What do you want?" he asks Lange.

"I would like to understand what happened at my facility. I want to know if you can shed some light on what happened."

"I don't know how I could do that," Mike says. "I can't even get on campus."

"There's no reason to come here. Everything is gone."

"It can't *all* be gone," Mike says. "There must be debris, remains of the buildings, something."

"The detectors still exist. The buildings where these people work are mostly intact. All scientists and technicians are still alive. But the ring is gone, and there are bizarre abnormalities on the grounds."

"So there *is* something to see."

"There are stripes of brown weeds through our lawns of manicured grass. Trees that look to have been shorn in half, yet the ground beneath them is not damaged—just different. Some of the campus roads are . . . This is difficult for me to believe, but there are places where the asphalt is gone and there is just . . . red dirt. All the roads out here were red dirt and gravel before we paved them."

"What are you saying?" Mike asks.

"There is an old yellow house here, Mr. McNair. Where the

main administrative building was, there is an old house. And a corrugated steel barn of some kind. Some old cars."

"What? That doesn't . . . you're not—"

"We found a newspaper on the porch. Fresh and bound with a rubber band like it was delivered yesterday. The date was April 10, 1979."

"I don't think I believe that," Mike remarks. "Can't I come out there and—"

"Your girlfriend is a news reporter. I don't think so."

"I won't . . . I mean, we won't—"

"Do you know what happened in this region on April 10, 1979?"

"No."

"There was a series of devastating tornadoes. One of the worst outbreaks in U.S. history. The tornado that ravaged Wichita Falls was arguably the worst ever to hit a populated area."

"So someone is playing a joke, then," Mike says. "Leaving that paper." But he doesn't believe what he's saying even as the words come out of his mouth. A yellow house? A barn? A newspaper from the past?

"Did you know that Karsten Allgäuer lived in Wichita Falls in 1979? And that he performed secret research at Sheppard Air Force Base? Did you know there was an F5 tornado that hit the base in 1964?"

"What does that have to do with the super collider? What was your relationship with Allgäuer? Didn't you know what he was up to?"

"I fund many projects, Mr. McNair. I cannot personally oversee every one of them."

"Mr. Lange, why are you—"

"I can hardly believe what happened here," Lange says. "These time anomalies. The implications are staggering."

"Then let me come out there and inspect the grounds myself," Mike says.

"No. And do not tell anyone what I have revealed to you today. If you do, I will find out, and you will be sorry. Do not underestimate my ability to monitor you, or my resolve. Good day, Mr. McNair."

7

Mike's anger, his sense of loss for the scientific community and the world, is not quick to dissipate. He imagines his life so far as a winding marathon route, a road through stretches bright and dark, marked by occasional checkpoints, on the way to eventual demise—the same doomed existence endured by every human ever to walk the earth. But then suddenly, in a flash of insight, he had been shown a shortcut, a secret door through which he might have seen the grand finish line in resplendent glory. And just as suddenly someone had slammed that door shut, shut tight, and now he must try to figure out how to open it again.

There are secrets out there, and he will likely spend his life searching for them.

But he also comes to realize that while the loss is devastating for the advancement of science and human understanding, for his own doomed existence in the universe, he has a duty to recognize what happened to the people that night at the super collider. The questions he asks about the universe may be important to him, but there is something just as important—if smaller in scope—to consider. To mourn.

The loss of a life.

At work, Kelly is able to access law enforcement–style investigative software and easily produces the names and phone number of Steve's parents. The next morning Mike places a phone call to Grand Island, Nebraska. A woman answers the phone.

"Is this Betty Keeley?"

"Yes, it is. Who is this?"

"Mrs. Keeley, my name is Mike McNair. I was the head physicist at the super collider in Olney, Texas. Are you familiar with that facility?"

Betty does not answer for a moment. And then, very quietly, "Yes."

"I'm calling to tell you about your son," Mike says. "He was an extraordinary man."

8

Larry on a Greyhound bus, staring out the window, at the Martian landscape of southern Arizona. Drawn west not only by the torque of a gasoline engine, but also by the inexorable pull of female attraction. Led there by their navigational starlight.

His destination: Hollywood, California.

9

Kelly is spellbound as usual by Conan, and Mike, too tired to wait out the show, gives up on sex for the evening.

She invited him to stay in Richardson while he recovered from the gunshot wound, from the depressing reality of his post–NTSSC career, and one month led to two, and now they've settled into a rhythm that Mike finds mostly agreeable. If there's any problem, it's that he sometimes wants to reject it, the whole idea of a relationship with Kelly, because one cannot look at the sequence of events surrounding them and conclude that it was all pure coincidence. That he sat next to a Dallas news anchor on an airplane, that their local interview was picked up and broadcast nationally, thereby allowing Steve to find him, leading Steve to the super collider where he could confront his demons—these events seem to line up so well, in such organized fashion, that even a physicist like himself has trouble ignoring the preordained nature of it all. The inherent fate of it all. And still those words uttered by Steve, the words that confirm his core beliefs and at the same time frighten him like nothing else could: *There is no intelligence.*

No intelligence, but perhaps the eventual outcome of incalculable particle interactions over time? A universe of perfect determinism?

He has considered leaving Kelly in protest, as a demonstration of his free will, but of course the deterministic view would mean even *that* event was preordained.

And now Kelly will be leaving for New York soon, beginning the network news chapter of her shooting-star life, and Mike will have to decide if he wants to follow her there. More fundamentally, he'll have to decide how to proceed with life itself. Until now his existence has been defined by a painstaking particle-by-particle search for truth, but now there is something more interesting (and likely more elusive) to search for. The shortcut. The porthole that looks upon a new perception of reality.

He drifts, away from the nasal trumpet of Conan, away from her hand absently stroking his head, into the gloaming of near sleep. And flashing images: the near miss with a GMC truck on 75 today, the apple he ate for breakfast, the impossible memory of a towering blue roller coaster behind the NTSSC administrative office. And then deeper he goes, beyond the faux reality of dreams, consciousness fading, REM slowing, a flickering image of Steve Keeley's smiling face, a brown-haired girl in a red dress, a building with CABARET spelled in blue letters. These images float past, tethered to his consciousness for mere seconds before pulling away. He will not remember them in the morning. But he will wake up with a little extra skip in his step, on the right side of the bed (so to speak), and he won't know why, and maybe the slight adjustment in his brain's network of neurons and chemical transmitters and memory configuration will induce him to visit the jewelry store, and perhaps afterward he'll be in possession of a ring, and maybe later he'll get down on his knee and ask a certain question, and it will be a while before he makes the connection between the ring purchase and these images, before he is granted access to the data, before the rules are presented in their miraculous elegance.

This novel was inspired by a nonfiction work written by Nobel Laureate Leon Lederman with Dick Teresi. *The God Particle: If the Universe Is the Answer, What Is the Question?* is a book that weaves humor with lessons about physics and helped me understand the history and purpose of particle accelerators. It was published in 1993, just before the Superconducting Super Collider project in Waxahachie, Texas, was killed by Congress. The cancellation of this massive and important project was a brutal blow to thousands of high-energy physicists in the United States and abroad. In 2007, the Large Hadron Collider at CERN in Europe is scheduled to go online, and scientists there hope to learn more about the structure of our universe, including the possible existence of the Higgs boson, which Lederman called the "God particle."

Other sources of inspiration and research for this book include Brian Greene's *The Fabric of the Cosmos: Space, Time, and the Texture of Reality,* Edward O. Wilson's *Consilience: The Unity of Knowledge,* Ray Kurzweil's *The Age of Spiritual Machines: When Computers Exceed Human Intelligence,* Diane Ackerman's

An Alchemy of Mind, and the Web site for the American Museum of Natural History in New York City, www.amnh.org. I would also like to acknowledge the novel *Einstein's Bridge* by John Cramer, which I thoroughly enjoyed and which helped me understand what life might have been like at the real SSC. Mike's notion of a runaway chain reaction on page 284 was suggested to me by author and friend Matt Reiten. Larry's ranting e-mails were inspired, in part, by music composed by the electronic band Juno Reactor. And finally, the line quoted by Karsten Allgäuer on page 153 was taken from *The Corrections*, by Jonathan Franzen.

Somewhat more than my first novel, *The God Particle* was largely fashioned from accepted theories in physics and other scientific disciplines. While much of what happens in the story is obviously speculative, research for this book opened my eyes to the amazing and sometimes bizarre realities of our everyday world. Useful links and information regarding experimental and theoretical physics, brain research, and other subjects mentioned in the book can be found on my personal Web site, www.richardcox.net.

August 5, 2002–October 6, 2004
Richard Cox
Tulsa, OK

PHOTO: © CHERA KIMIKO

RICHARD Cox is the author of *Rift*. He grew up in Texas and currently lives in Tulsa, Oklahoma, where he is at work on his next novel. Visit the author's website at www.richardcox.net.

ABOUT THE TYPE

This book was set in Minion, a 1990 Adobe
Originals typeface by Robert Slimbach.
Minion is inspired by classical, old-style
typefaces of the late Renaissance, a period
of elegant, beautiful, and highly readable
type designs. Created primarily for text
settings, Minion combines the aesthetic
and functional qualities that make text
type highly readable with the versatility of
digital technology.